Unavoidable Fates

The Rise Chronicles

Trevor F. Coelho

ISBN: 9781089699705

DEDICATION

To my wonderful support crew, you're amazing.

CONTENTS

THE WALLS OF WINTER

5yrs A.E. N. Dakota Abandoned State

Matthew knew it was all a dream, it had to be with the sun rising in two places. His throat was tight as he tried to speak but he lacked the air to form any words.

Standing on a beach of snow-white sands, looking down he could just see something, faintly glowing at his feet. Four strange objects floating in the black waters lapping at his toes, the inky waters slowly swirling around his ankles.

Four of them in all, they bobbed back and forth before him, each time the waves carrying them a little further away, just able to make them out in the surf.

The first, a perfectly round ammonite shell, the striking green glinting in the sun.

The second was a sharply edged triangular cut white crystal that sparked faintly as it clicked against the others.

The third was alluring most of all, it's roughly hewn shape, a teardrop made of red coral.

Lastly, was a perfect cube made of weathered deep blue wood, and floated out the furthest from his reach.

Such strange shapes floating there, he knew, as soon as he took one the others would be swept away, not gone forever, only for now.

Matthew scooped into the water and found the coral tear in his hand as he curled his fingers. It had dug into his palm but didn't hurt, it felt right like it had always been a part of him.

He watched as the tear faded and he stood marked with the curled fang of red staring at him from the back of his arm.

As Matthew stood there looking up at his arm a flash of light called his eyes skyward.

A storm was coming, the waters around him rising as the tide came in fiercely, he looked up at the clouds and saw the storm rising in from four different fronts.

Raging sands dashed the land apart to the north, in the east funnel clouds black as pitch blotted out all light, in the west torrential rains washed away everything. But to the south he felt a call, steel grey clouds shrouded the sky as flashes of lightning exploded in showers of fiery rage.

The red tear mark hummed softly, its deep song gilding his soul, and drew Matthew out onto the waters of the lake a direct path built up strong beneath him made of stones that seemed to only be there as he jumped from one to the next.

Even as the world shudders under every blow he stood strong, the storm threatening him with death from every fiery bolt of plasma tearing reality asunder. But not one came close, instead, they seemed to welcome him, heralding his arrival and enveloping him in a loving embrace.

He felt charged, powerful, warm, and passionate.

The relic in his arm hummed deeply, the subtle glow of red lines forming little teardrop cracks that pulsed with heat. He held his hand up and split the storm with a wave, the sky clearing, and the lake waters becoming as calm as glass.

The water here was crystal blue, with little trees like charred skeletal hands reaching up into the sky.

A misty veil parted in the distance, a pair of pillars jutting up from the calm waters.

One of smooth white marble struck through by golden veins, the other, square-edged and pitted of blackest obsidian.

At the top of the marble pillar sat a spear of gold, and on the obsidian pillar a shield of purple crystal, both held in place by thorny black vines.

Matthew walked closer till he could touch the stone pillars, the vines shying away from his touch to reveal words carved into them glowing from within. On the spear pillar ***Nequit Vis***, and under the shield, just one, ***Indissolubilis***. He could almost reach them but even as he tried the vines tightened and he knew that whichever he grabbed the other would be lost as the pillar crumbled into the lake.

He had no idea which to choose, to be a shield that cannot be broken, or the spear that cannot be stopped.

He couldn't resist the urge to try though, he knew neither alone could win the fight that was coming, but as he tried to reach for both the vines shrieked at him. The pillars crumbling backward, the vines took both spear and shield into the crystalline depths and left Matthew on his knees with a great feeling of loss.

Just as the storms began to close in though hope bubbled, up ahead he saw a light that had not been there before, it pierced the sky casting black shadows and eerie figures all around him.

Getting to his feet he fought back at the screaming winds and shrieking voices that battered him from the storm. Step by step getting closer till he could see it.

Made of two slates of metal, black steel etched with gold and bound with rings of silver.

A book...?

Matthew reached down and closed the book picking it up and the world around faded away like a heat shimmer.

The path was gone, the trees gone, and the storm too, all that was left was Matthew. He stood on the water now, tiny ripples forming as he walked along. He knelt and touched it, finding it solid to the touch, his reflection beneath him replaced by the stretching branches of a leafless tree.

He had seen this before, knew it so well, his connection to the pattern of fate like this very tree, endless, vast; so long as he did things right.

"Wow," he jumped at the sound of his own voice. "I-I, I can talk?"

"*Cough*!"

Matthew turned to see a man behind him; or rather, most of a man. His eyes were all Matthew could see but he was certain he was sitting there.

"Hi, ah-"

The man waved his hand, and Matthew fell mute again.

"In the absence of light, darkness shrouds the most reasonable mind. Yet in the absence of darkness, the light blinds even the most righteous soul. We are the balance makers, and the book is the greatest weapon one can hold. It is a shield and spear, knowledge an edge that cannot be stopped, and a truth that cannot be broken. Whether we are wrong or right, the pursuit of knowledge brings balance with facts… It's interesting to see someone try to be both shield and spear…" The eyes grew brighter as if the man was laughing. "So, is this really what you want?"

Matthew nodded and felt a pop, his voice suddenly back, so he cleared his throat and voiced how he felt. "To have one but not the other can be disastrous. A spear that only ever strikes never pauses to consider if it should. But a shield that can only defend remains immobile, never moving forward."

The blue-eyed man stood up to tower over Matthew. "Within the knowledge to apply both lies wisdom. Wisdom to even question if either should be used at all."

"This knowledge, if this book is what you say it is, then it would be better to keep it, rather than only be one half of something incomplete." Behind him, a shield appeared to his left, and a spear to his right, the book still clutched in his hand.

"The choice is yours."

Matthew barely glanced at either before going back to

the cover of the book.

"Darkness or Light, they live inside us... inside you. Find the balance, or make it. We will see how you do this time."

"So what, has this happened before?" Matthew asked, looking up at the man.

"Yes, and no," he said with a shrug, "This has both happened countless times, and at the same time is the first time it has ever happened." The man laughed heartily suddenly, "Multi-dimensionalisim is weird like that. But learn to quiet your mind and listen to your instincts like you did here, and you will go far."

"Well, that's fortune cookieish. Wraps it all up so I have nothing else I can ask without being told something like; Follow your destiny; pretty convenient for you."

"Oh boy, is it ever."

"I know you, right? Azure?"

He nodded.

"There are three of you, but-"

"But that's not enough; right."

"So what now?"

"We watch, we wait, and we gather our forces, people like you who will make a difference."

"So the war is coming?"

"The war is here. The Wytch-Hazel has risen, and we're running out of time."

"I can help, find the others," Matthew felt suddenly sick knowing now this was no mere dream.

"Both sides are pretty even," Azure said.

"So when do you step in?" Matthew asked cautiously.

Azure looked up, his swirling blue eyes cast in a dark light, "When there are no sides left."

He faded away, the small seat he had sat on suddenly coming to Matthew. It was like the ground slid by under his feet and Matthew had to throw his arms up to keep his footing as the white stone wall rushed to meet him.

When he stopped he was standing in front of a wall

made of metal and stone, huge towers topped in snow and dripping ice. It loomed over him ominously, darkness clawing at the base of the wall, holes blasted in it revealing slabs of steel that looked like old shipping containers that had once been in the heart of the wall.

ding ding ding

Matthew looked behind him at the sudden chiming.

"**Order up!**" Called a man at the counter.

Still in the dream world he found himself now in, he was in a busy diner full of customers, tables being bussed by shadows that whisked between the patrons.

The wall was gone, the frozen wastes vanished, instead he stood in amidst the smells of delicious food, and noisy people.

Azure looked up at Matthew from his seat next to two other shadowy beings, one all red, the other a hazy green shot through with yellow sparks

"*Come find me when you're ready Matthew.*"

"How do I know when I'm ready?"

"*You'll know.*"

Matthew woke up, shooting forward from the shock. He was still where he had Fallen asleep next to his friends, all of them huddled together. It was the warehouse they called home since the city had Fallen to the seed, boards on every window, and heavy barricades at the door. He shook off his blankets and rolled to a sitting position, another refugee coughing in the back making him look around.

"Oh look," came a whisper from the far side of the room.

Matt looked up to see a shadowy being in the window sitting on the ledge there.

"It's snowing…," it turned to him with eyes swirling brown and gold. "And it may never stop."

He got up and shuffled closer, "What?" Snow wasn't odd here in Dakota, but never stopping?

The shadow put a finger to their lips and hushed him before looking back out between the boards across the window.

"A cold and long winter is coming, one only the strongest will survive." It turned to him with a wicked grin of scarlet light splitting its face as its head tilted at an unnatural angle. "I wonder how strong you are Matty?"

Matthew looked down at his arm and felt it, a deep hum in his bones that shook till sparks danced between his fingers.

The shadow seemed to frown.

Matthew just smiled, "Guess I won't have to wait long to find out."

FALL NO FURTHER

9yrs A.E. Eastern Canada

The frozen snow crunched with a wizening glassy chime that echoed through the frosty air around Nancy as she marched through waist-deep drifts of heavy snow. The uneven ground of the field had not seen travelers in some time which made it hard to stand let alone walk and made her wary of where she put her weight with every step. The snow had been coming down harder since she had crossed out of Ontario, and the farther she went the colder it was getting too.

It was just as Master Luse had said would happen, but not one of them knew how to stop it.

Or at least they weren't telling anyone.

Nancy hardly cared, she had to go on.

It had been almost two weeks now, trudging through the snow, looking for the source of the voice inside her, the one who told her to keep going, that little voice that whispered to her. Only it knew why she was broken, so it said.

She had trained like everyone else, more than anyone else. Mastering her skills over the mind. She had learned to manifest electricity from nothing, a task even the other Teachers said was rare. She pushed herself hard, harder than anyone else in her class, pushed beyond what any of the teachers said was even possible, made her daughters look weak by comparison. She pushed her mind into the depths of the world and felt its breath beneath her. What she found there was like nothing she had ever felt, a wellspring of energy filling her from within, but, just like they had told her, that much power was never meant to be hers.

Her hubris cost her everything, stripped of rank and cast out, her head hurt thinking about it. Her punishment was to be left with no memories beyond the mistakes she made.

Nancy fell to her knees as another headache wracked her, her chest getting tighter as her head felt like it was shrinking around her brain, breathing hard so her breath came in ragged gasps. The cold snow blew over her in a heavy gust from the east, the drifts moving so quickly that they began to cover her as she lay there. She pushed herself to her feet - a struggle made harder by her numb frozen body - and pulled herself over the ridge.

She lay there only a moment, looking down into the snow-laden valley that was now the city of Montreal. Though it was hard to tell, having been buried in snow. The entire place had been choked violently of all life, well, all life except whatever was calling her making her vision swim from the pain that continued to strike her between the eyes. But she knew she had nowhere else to go, so she pulled her coat tighter still and continued down to the city.

She couldn't say how long it took after her car had died and she was forced to walk, but she was finally here. She wasn't startled by it all really. The city had been overgrown thanks to the Seed that had been pushed across the north from the states during the summer, but then it had started to snow, and now it seemed it would be the harshest winter since twenty twenty-one. It was a surprise all the same though, she had no idea the seed had made it this far before the winter had set in. The growth of vines, and the flowers still blooming…

"Bloom…," Nancy hissed, looking around, but no one was there to need her warning. Only Nancy was there, and she wasn't afraid. She knew deep down she would be, but couldn't bring herself to walk away. Instead, she went right up to the flowers without pause. It was larger than any she had seen back near Winnipeg its fleshy red petals pulsing ominously, the body it had sprouted from still nourishing its roots. She brushed back the snow to look at the frozen face, a young woman, she was still so beautiful, even with her face frozen in fear. Roots burst from her mouth and chest where the deathbloom had pushed through her ribcage, yet no decay had set in. She looked as youthful as she would have when alive, a side effect as the cold preserved her and the bloom kept her mind alive.

As she saw Nancy her eyes went wild suddenly and the Bloom began to slowly turn. Nancy was careful not to touch the roots or the flower itself, her presence alone enough to make it turn to her. She knew that the slightest hint of heat from her body and the flower would shriek and belch its poison. But she felt safe despite how it had begun to slowly lean towards her, the short gold needle-like fangs reaching out tasting the air for her.

She shivered and stepped away from it, it was good that she had little warmth left, she was freezing.

Nancy was quick and picked her way through the streets, the main road was a hazard though so she was careful. Four and a half years of snow sweeping the streets had covered everything, the ground beneath her creaking and groaning with metal screeching as she tread slowly across buried cars. Here and there the roofs of trucks and vans poked up, but it was safer than the sidewalks. Along both sides of the once-busy streets, it looked like a garden. Trees that had once been Seed drones clawed up at the buildings where they had taken root to spread their pollen, the deathbloom's turning towards her fangs reaching out for Nancy.

It started to hum, a soft purr that made her lean in as her mind sought any kind of comfort, but as she did it felt like claws grabbed at her heart. Her heart ached, her head screaming that the broken don’t deserve rest.

She tripped sideways grabbing only air and her foot came down on something hard under the snow. It cracked and she knew she was on some car and not a snow bank, standing on its sunroof. It cracked under her heel and her leg plunged into the car, slashed open by the shattered glass, but the cut was not what scared her. Her foot stepped on something soft. She looked down, eyes widening in horror as the bloom in the driver's seat began to move.

The body lifted with some force, and she was tossed aside as the bloom rose through the roof dragging itself from inside its improvised tomb. It reared back, its throat bulging, stomach deflating as the parasite within pushed up from its cracked torn throat. It burst out, bones snapping under the force with a sickening crack. It opened wide, the blossom more like a blood-coloured angel's trumpet, and began to scream. The shrill cry split the air and was returned a thousand-fold, even the deathbloom's joining in.

The bloom was thankfully slow, trapped in that car it had grown but had no energy being out of the light. It shambled slowly forward, clawing the air with blackened fingers. This bloom was huge too, its corpse puppet staggering under the weight.

Nancy scrambled up, and called energy to her, finding focus in her mind to remember the main weapon of any kinetic, psire as they called it, psychic powered fires burning in her heart.

Nancy raised her hand and felt the energy pool in her fingers, but nothing happened. Try as she might, a flame wouldn't form, the energy was there, but the control was gone, her hand just felt numb.

She shied back and was tripped – another bloom, this one right under the snow – she fell but pulled free leaving her boot behind. This bloom pushed itself up out of the snow and fell over, wiggling along the ground like a snake slithering towards her dragged along behind its winding bloom. She looked at her missing boot clutched in its jaws.

“Fuck it,” she could get another. She did however give praise that her healing ability had not abandoned her too.

She got up, adrenaline pushing her on, and ran as fast as she could. She ran, and ran, and ran. For as long as she could. She turned down alleys filled with screaming flowers and passed through streets of rising bloom. She ran till she could almost run no more. Ran so far and so fast, that she didn't see the bloom that tackled her.

Open roads and a Nun

12yrs A.E. Colorado, Abandoned States

Straight highways floated off into the endless horizons, painted in hues of early morning dusky blue as first dawn began creeping up on Chris' shoulder. The only sound in the world was the motor roaring between his knees, his hands gripping lightly on the controls of his old bike as she sped on chasing the dark into the southwest.

Chris had been riding for a few hours already, and again it seemed he would see not another soul on the empty roads, or at least, he hoped after the last encounter he had had.

The world had changed greatly after the Event nine years ago, it was a harsher world now, a place where the strong or stupid alike knew it was no place to be alone. Which meant certainly avoiding a person who was, usually.

The world had been sick before the seed and their pod's had landed and started to terraform everything. Certainly not the cure Amanda Pope had told the American people it would be in her resignation declaration. It was just a fact; all the gun-toting rednecks in America couldn't have made a dent against a species that breeds like the virus the seed used. Even in death, they were still releasing spores into the air to choke out the native life. Animals mutating, and people mutating worse. Most of the states had already Fallen, with only the colder northern states avoided by the seed, and even then, only during the winter months.

Nothing stopped their virus from spreading.

Those who weren't immune to the virus or allergic to the spores that carried it got it the worst, they became the bloom

- the reason Chris was heading south - a parasite that infected the body and mind, turning people into puppets. The only saving grace was that they were bound to the cold. Their bodies burned so hot they needed the cold to keep them alive, some sick way the bloom used to keep its host alive by supercharging their mitochondria.

Even the so-called Immortals Azure, Rojas, and Luse, with their seemingly infinite power, couldn't figure out a way to turn people back without killing them. The bloom dug in and completely replaced all of their host's organs and blood vessels. But it wasn't over there, then they started to twist their host's mind, whispering to them, taking control quickly using their host's veins like creeper vines to control the whole body.

Though many had argued to keep trying, Chris had been inclined to agree with those who sided with the immortals. Chris, having been present for some of their experiments to find a cure - regrettably so - now felt it was kinder to kill the things once they turned, but after that realization hit, he realized the slippery slope that led too. So Chris had set his foot down, and he left Winnipeg. He didn't want to be a party to any of this, he wasn't a soldier, and wasn't going to play at it either.

Azure had said Chris would understand one day, that it would all make sense, and that even leaving was a part of the bigger plan.

The motion of fates was unavoidable, he had said to Chris, and to that Chris had said, *watch me try*, and rode off.

Hitting the road though had meant change, and nothing had changed like the weather. The heavy air was a real difference from Canada by a huge stretch. While the north seemed a permanently frozen waste, past South Dakota it was hot, sticky sweat already trickling down his neck into his leathers. Here the influence of the bloom was something you saw everywhere, their massive alien plants stretched up into the sky like giant aloe but were anything like them. The spiny blades towered above most buildings, their creeping roots devouring the once human terrain until they became the towering trees he was passing now. Buildings hit by the seed barely stood, collapsing in on themselves wherever he looked. To the skyline west of him, he could just barely see broken spearheads of steel and glass reflecting the rising sun from the east. The rusted ruins were home to nothing but mutants and wild seed making more mutants, a desolate place to avoid as seed always sought out cities to convert first.

Crossing the arid landscape south of what had once been Denver more of these mutated monster cacti rooted in the road blocking his path. Finally forcing him to slow a little to look for a place to pull through, the narrow route taking him a bit too close for comfort back if he didn't muddle through. He knew he could just flatten the things with his powers, but a feeling of discomfort made him pause and he instead hugged the gravel side tight and drove past the reaching creepers instead.

He wasn't about to let some plants stop him, but what did stop him he would have never expected.

Coming around the plants he pulled off the road and onto the dirt track, he leaned back in the saddle driving slowly while looking at a woman standing on the side of the road.

Her leg up on an old letterman's bag showing more than a little thigh she clearly had no shame flashing her neon green and black stockings and garters. Tall and rail thin except for her hips which showed off her only curves in the long dusty black dress she wore, she looked worlds removed. She had short blonde hair, and a mix of bones and letters tattooed on the backs of her hands, she was quite the sight. But it wasn't her looks that made Chris stare, no, it was that topping it off was the massive joint she held in her teeth. Practically a cigar, the smell almost overwhelmed him even with his helmet on, and yet she seemed almost sober, her eyes were a clear pale green not red in the least.

She smiled around her smoke, and brought her hand up thumb high, "Going south?" She asked in a sweet tone.

Chris opened his visor and looked her over, "Yeah, but-"

"Great," she bent down and grabbed her bag then jogged over to him.

Chris had not seen another human in days, not able to count the ones he saw the night before last which had been a very angry group of people he met as he had tried crossing into the Denver city proper. Most of them had been coughing and hacking from the bloom plague, and screaming he was unclean, so they were too far gone, but this woman was different, coughing only after she took a long pull on her joint. She passed it towards him - which he declined - before tamping it out on the heel of her heavy-looking boot. She then tilted her head and exhaled slowly with another little cough, the smoke seeming to flicker a heavy blue-green as it flowed away from Chris unnaturally, sending a shiver down his spine.

Now it made sense, "You're a kinetic."

"Of course I am," she said, looking confused, "So are you. I sensed you coming so I set up here to ask you for a ride."

He felt a cold pit well up in his gut, the tweaks of the strings pulling on him. Azure and his little crows throwing words like freedom, and that you can go where you want, all the while in the back pulling at the strings they laid to tug everyone where they wanted them.

The urge to drive off right there was strong, but she was already at his side.

"I can control fire and anything kind of hot. What a gift of god you are though, I've been walking for days since my car ran out of gas."

He was about to make a crack about how a pyro could run out of fuel when she pulled a length of black and white fabric out from behind her bag and crammed it on her head to complete her outfit, again stunning him.

Chris's jaw dropped, "You're a... you're a nun?" He stammered seeing her in her full habit.

She nodded and turned to him, taking his hand and shaking it vigorously. "Sister Kendra Shade, of the chattering order of the Ladies of the Valleys Devotion. Now also," She paused and leaned back, waving her hand so her name appeared in the air backwards, "Kendra, pyrokinetic of gods blessed." She stopped and squinted then waved her hand again so the letters spun which just made it worse. She shrugged though, and went on, "I mean we never did get our full backing of the church, but-"

"Wait, what?" She was going too fast, and it made his head spin, "Since when do kinetics have a church?"

She snorted, "Fuck no, I mean Valleys Devotion. Stuffy shirt Vatican men didn't like women smoking pot, even if they're praising God. But whoever needed the man to tell them they could praise god and all his - or her - bounty?"

Chris closed his mouth with a snap, she wasn't wrong.

He shook his head, "Well, that's a bit easier to mentally chew on. You said your name was Kendra? Shade was it? Well, I'm Chris, Chris Doyle."

"Nice to meet you Chris, always loved that name, short for Christian. And yup, I'm Kendra Shade, and before you say it; I know it sounds like some pornstar name, but no, I'm not, nor ever was. I only ever got down on my knees to pray to the lord above. Actually tried to change my name once but Sister Marguerite at the convent told me it was a waste of time and money, and to just own it like a boss."

"But, you're a kinetic?" He stated, "And a nun," feeling a bit bemused he leaned forward in his seat.

Kendra nodded, "And you're a biker. This'd make a great joke right? A nun and a biker are riding through the wasteland, somethin, somethin."

This whole thing felt like a setup, "And how did you know I was here?"

"Oh, that, well see I sensed you using your power. I guess that's how you move that thing without gas? Just a controlled flame in the motor? That's a neat trick."

"And no one sent you here for me?"

She cocked her head looking at him sideways, a small spark at her fingers casting a green glow behind her.

"Should someone have?" She asked, looking suddenly wary.

"Just wondering," he added with a shrug, still not convinced she was so innocent.

"Hey if you're on the run I'm cool, I've been on my share of the rough side of the tracks. Snitches get stitches, I get that. And besides, you couldn't be a bad guy, a bad guy wouldn't have stopped to help me."

"Guess that checks out," he replied sarcastically, rolling his eyes.

She nodded, "Besides, if you creep me out I'll send you packing, biblically." Her whole hand burst into green flames now, the heat scorching in intensity, but her smile was still so sweetly innocent.

He couldn't help but laugh, as annoying as she was he could use the company.

"Hop on. I can't promise how far I'll take you, but the least I can do is give you a lift for now. I'm heading west as soon as I find a good route," he then reached into his side box, fishing out his spare helmet and handing it to her.

"I'm good dude," she replied, hiking up her dress again and hopping up to straddle the back of the bike.

"My wheels, my way," he growled, trying his best to ignore her lewdness.

She shrugged and grabbed it, shoving it on her head "Perfect fit," she mumbled happily. Now home to Belair," she stood in the stirrups pointing off, "No? Not a fan of the prince?"

Chris just rolled his eyes. He had always assumed that nuns would be all pious and holy, but this woman was getting on his nerves already. Kendra had the mouth of a sailor and smoked pot like a chimney; flipping up the visor to light up another tinier joint as they stood there.

He started up the bike, "Aren't you setting a bad example, smoking that?"

She smiled and pet his helmet, "Awe, with that handlebar mustache I didn't know you were under the age of twenty-five?"

"Hardly," he scoffed.

"Then what's your problem? As with all things in life moderation is key," she smiled and puffed at her joint.

"Moderation; right."

"Don't judge dude. This herb is of gods creations, it brings clarity to me, and brings me closer to his… umm… you know, I'm trying to remember how sister Marguerite put it, but I really can't."

"Is it because you're too baked?"

"At that time maybe. This stuff doesn't work on me for more than a few seconds now. Kind of a drag really, but my body clears away intoxication as fast as a paper cut."

"Yeah, heard that from a guy who was trying to get drunk. All it did was make him have to pee a ton."

She grimaced and coughed loudly as she laughed, "Dude, T.M. F'n I."

The rest of the day was much the same, she had snuck earbuds into her ears under her helmet and loudly sang while he drove. She played loads of different music, none of it bad, but so off key, he considered more than once to sharply turn and eject the daffy bird. Thankfully his better side won the argument, and so she remained seated until they slowed and coasted into the dusty gravel parking lot he had been led to by signs along the highway.

The old faded red building was not large, its barn-like aesthetic giving it a rustic look. The side of the building facing north had taken the worst of the weathering it seemed, humidity peeling the paint on the side of the wall, obviously once a giant mural. He pulled off his gloves and closed his eyes, reaching out with his power. He could feel the tiny flecks of faded paint, once a beautiful painting he saw the flow of time that had degraded it, their tiny molecules clinging to their legacy. He reached out with grasping threads of energy and found it wasn't all gone too. The heart of the art baked into the image, it was like feeling a fading soul that begged for rebirth.

When he opened his eyes he looked not with his own sight, but with his power. He saw what it had looked like, the subatomic particles that had been the colours were still there he just had to rearrange them. He let the work flow back to rights, the white wall with their bright golden-eyed owls, and feathers all beautifully detailed. But he knew it would never last, so he twisted the molecules and layered them heavily with weaves of stone and heavier elements pressing them tightly together and when he was done stepped back to marvel at his work, his fingers tracing the lines of the artist's name.

"Well, Ray Shaw, a bit of you will survive the tests of time."

"That was impressive," Kendra said, "But, how'd you do that?"

Chris spread his hands wide and let the energy dance between his fingers. "I just replaced the molecules with carbon particles and pigmented them with heavier elements."

"So it's diamond now?"

"I, ah… No. It's more like carbon fibre," he said, running his hand over the rigid surface, "I never figured out how the immortals like Azure could just make diamonds. But I can make solid things harder."

"Phrasing," she said with a wink and a snort of laughter. She took off the helmet and her coronette, running her free hand through her short-cropped dirty-blond hair. "So, are you going in?" She asked.

He nodded, "Yeah, I needed a break, been riding all night till I saw you." Chris was tired and started to take off his coat but as he did he remembered his tattoos and stopped. It wasn't that he was shy, he loved his ink, and clearly, from the tattoos on her hands, Kendra had many too.

But one of the last tattoos he had gotten, well, it stood out.

The visage of the scantily clad nun with pink hair sporting a knight's sword and grenades was a classically done pinup, sitting astride a giant bomb with her habit blowing in the wind. It was all in all, a striking and colourful beauty, and he loved the picture, but now as he stood next to a self-proclaimed nun he felt awkward. Even with the crass woman literally in the process of hiking her dress up to fix a garter with no regard to him standing there.

As she slid her delicate fingers into the top of her stocking and fiddled with the clip he felt a deep heat creep up his neck into his cheeks so he turned to instead fiddle with his saddlebags.

He peeked back over his right to see if she was done, "Not to pry Kendra, but-"

"You know," she said, suddenly on his left, "That's what everyone says before they pry."

"It's just, I uh, well. You're travelling alone, but I thought Azure told you to find your sisters?"

She shook her head, "I'm not alone, God is alwa-"

"I mean other people," he cut in.

She smiled, "Gotcha, yeah no, see, I did find my sisters. But then I-" She trailed off, as if not sure what to say. "Let's just say, I've had a… change in my life."

He kept his guard up high, he had never met a kinetic who wasn't working an angle.

"And you say you're from California?" He asked as he pushed the door open.

"I was, or am, no, was. Look, I got stuck in Canada during the Event, a layover in Winnipeg before I headed back south, and when I woke up ta-daa! I was surrounded by green flames with God in my head telling me I needed to gather my sisters."

Chris couldn't contain a snort.

Kendra looked at him, "What, let me guess, just because you don't believe everyone else is wrong?"

Chris immediately felt the heat rise again, her words striking him as she passed judgment. "I just. Well, I hate to burst your bubble, but that wasn't God you spoke to."

"You're like me," She paused in her search of the front counter, "Surely you felt it, the one with the blue eyes, that voice was like a choir of the saints. How could it have been anything else?"

"I did, but I also met the one who spoke to me, also, there's three of them. You're saying god is multiple people?"

She looked confused sitting back on a desk chair. "No, but he, or she, they work in mysterious ways."

Chris sighed, "The ones who woke us up, they're immortals and yeah they can do some crazy things, but they're not gods, let alone the God."

"Ah," she pulled another joint out and lit it, taking a long pull on it, "So, you're an atheist."

He threw his hands up, "What are you doing here? Why are you bothering me? Or are you going to say God sent you, 'cause that I may believe."

"Dude, I was just heading south."

"Why?!"

She looked a little angry, a flash of green coming to the depths of her eyes as he started her down. "I'm trying to find some people."

Chris snorted. "Well if you're looking for gods you'll find them sitting in a bar back in Winnipeg."

Her face scrunched up as she hacked a smoky cough, "Buddy you are mean. No, Go-" She caught Chris's eye and bit off what she was going to say, then said, "I'm looking for some kids."

"What're you talking about?" Chris kept her gaze, the serious look in her pale green eyes like steel.

Kendra tapped out her ashes into a tray on the desk, "Yeah. I had a vision, and let's just say that was the last straw for the other sisters. These flames, visions, all of it. To them, I look a lot more like a demon than a messenger of god."

"What was the vision of, Kendra?"

"A group of kids led to a gallows before a swarm of hooded men and women." She tapped the counter, waving the lit tip of her joint in the air so that the smoke and ember made the scene come to life. "They're like scarecrows, standing in a field of grass, and as the kicking bodies don't end the scarecrows hobble forward and scream, belching blue fires. Betrayed by monsters, demons hiding among them, whispering lies. I don't know how, but I know I have to save them."

He had not been one to put stock in these visions that some kinetic people said they had. But it didn't sit well either. He had never had so much as a bad dream since the event nine years ago, or if he had he had never remembered it.

"The bloom are cold bound, they can't leave the north for more than a few days. And even then, they scurry back quick as their instincts send them looking for a snowbank to bury themselves in."

"Yeah, I know, but-"

"No, what you are showing me here is something else. It's clearly a bloom," he pointed at the smoky image, "But that can't be."

Kendra shrugged, getting up, "Whatever. Thanks for the lift here anyways."

As she turned her dress caught some of the leaves on the ground, leaves he noticed that looked oddly out of place. There were no open windows here, and barely more than a shrub around on the property. He stooped and picked one up to find it was made of paper, and what stranger still lay hidden under those leaves.

"Well, regardless, it appears you're on the right track of your hunt."

He pointed and she looked down, her eyes going wide as she saw now what it was he found.

She waved her hand, a crackle leaping through the air catching the paper leaves aflame in a flash, the burning embers wafting up through the air lighting the scene from above. Dozens of names were scrawled in charcoal or scratched into the floor by any means.

"What do you make of this? A bunch of them are saying, Loves, Loves, almost all of them. Loves, you think that's where they're taking them?" She suddenly whipped around, her eyes lighting up with green fire. "Loves, the diner! It's just south of here near this big dispensary."

"Kendra I-"

"I know, it's not your fight, but please, I need to get there. You have powers too, you have heard the voices calling us to duty." She pointed her finger at him like a knife, "It is our responsibility to use our gifts to prote-"

"Stop it! I left Canada because I was sick of hearing that crap. I didn't ask for it, I just wanted to live a normal life, collect comic books, write poetry, and ride my bike across the country. But I also know these kids didn't have a choice either. So quit trying to convince me, and get on my bike, we have a long ride."

"Dude, reading comic books and riding motorbikes don't make you a hero," she shouted, "It's the will to do something about injustice."

"I never said I was out," he didn't even turn, just shook out his coat behind him as he turned and pushed the door open with a burst of power.

He let his power cascade, the building tearing apart from the force twisting at his command like clay in a sculpture's hands. The image of every animal beginning to rip free from their two-dimensional prisons set free as he brought each image to life soaring into the sky into a tower a hundred feet tall. Roaring pumas, screeching eagles, flocks of crows, the natural world of this artist became a statue of predators and prey made of canvas harder than steel but thinner than paper.

When the storm of art came to a rest the daylight blazed across it casting the work in a structure that would test the flow of time.

He got on his bike and looked at Kendra who still stood in the heart of it all looking up.

"You coming?"

She looked at it, then at him, gave a little nod and walked over. She reached back and flicked her smoke over her shoulder, the burning end lighting up in a quick burst to fade to ash on the breeze, but the effect didn't end there. He could feel her energy at work as sparks flicked through the air. The tower erupted with fire that defied physics, a whirling tornado of green that shot out of the top into the sky.

"That was dope dude," she chuckled, "But if you want to put the fear of god into a bastard's heart, you have to make sure they know you're coming." Kendra took out her big stogie and lit it, and had a long pull. "This ain't gonna bug you?" She gestured at herself.

Chris shrugged, "I've been told I tend to lead the argument. And you do certainly get on my last nerve-"

"But you like me! You really like me!"

"Hardly. I'd just never let a kid be hurt if I could stop it."

She nodded to that and hopped on the back again as he poured energy into the motor and the bike roared to life.

She poked him in the ribs, leaning close to shout at him, "Maybe you've got a little comic book hero in you! He must be reeeeal tiny though!"

"Short jokes," he laughed, "You're just, wow, classy. You know I know a few jokes too, and they-"

"Could make a nun blush?"

Cutting him off as she did he was suddenly hyper-aware of how she clung to his back.

He shivered slightly and flipped his visor down, "Just hang on."

The sun was near to setting when something set Kendra off and she thrashed on his back. Not sure what was going on Chris pulled over and off the road.

"Shit, shit, shit!" She shouted practically flopping off as he pulled to a halt.

"What is it? What's wrong?" He tugged off his helmet setting it on his handlebars.

She stomped and flailed her arms cursing loudly but rounded on him suddenly.

"They know, they know we're coming!"

Chris felt confused, "How could anyone know we are here?"

"It's, well. Ugh," she pointed at his bike. "You, you're using your powers to run the motor. Dammit! Oh, Lord forgive me. That's why my vision changed the other day! Dammit! Lord forgive me."

"Hold on, how could anyone other than a kinetic know, no, none of this makes sense-"

"Dude, I showed you, they're the bloom. Only these ones, they're like us too."

"That's not possible, any-" he was going to lecture her about what that meant but decided against it. She seemed flustered and stomped about cursing, she seemed to believe it, even if he didn't, and Chris couldn't help himself.

"Well then, if they're expecting a kinetic coming down the road. I better not disappoint them." He grabbed his helmet and slipped it back on, and before Kendra could stop him he revved up. "Make sure you aren't late!" He couldn't believe what he was doing, his head was spinning, the feeling he was being pulled, like tiny hooks tugging his limbs into action.

Bloom, in this desert, it couldn't be possible, they could never have lived long enough to make it even to get this far, and the heat would have killed their host. They needed hosts to spread, and the only people he had seen were allergic to the alien virus, nothing more than carriers with a cough.

Chris was so wrapped up, deadlock focused on his thoughts, that he wasn't looking where he went through. The glint of silver reflected in his headlight in the instant before he was suddenly launched forward. Shooting ass end forward over his head his bike and him flew into the air rolling into the pavement with a crunch that threw him into darkness, finally alone, no thoughts left.

As he came too he could hear the mumbling of many voices. Some of them were singing shrilly, but he couldn't see, speak, or even move. The smell of stale hay and horse filled him with every breath, a heavy canvas bag tied tight over his head.

"See, it's a demon, it's already healing."

"Take its head off, it always kills them."

"We tried that, his skin is like iron."

"Yet further sign he is an unholy thing, bring him to the Preacher."

Chris did his best to stay limp, trying as best he could to play dead and hold out long enough for Kendra to sneak up. They dragged him by his ankles a fair distance away, the smell of burning oil replaced by heavy woodsmoke. He was more than ever thankful for wearing his leather jacket as he barely felt anything more than the occasional bump.

More than wood smoke filled the air, and the sound of many people muttering was like a buzz under the coughs of the sick. But there was something else drifting on the wind.

At first, he felt it like an itch between his eyes, a niggling twitch pervading his mind. But as his head cleared and his body healed he could tell what it was. He had felt it before, back during his training under Azure; it was the touch of a kinetic trying to break through his mental defences. On instinct, he pushed back and was immediately kicked hard in the head making his teeth rattle.

"None of that now," someone whispered in his ear. That voice made Chris cringe and lay still, an oily sound if sound could ever be, it felt as if it coated his ear in filth that sought to roll into his brain. "It's awake, Preacher!" The same person then shouted over him.

"Why has it not been beheaded?!" Came back a gravelly growl.

There was a scramble as several people fought to yell louder than the other but in the end, they all fell silent as the man who had whispered to him now spoke.

"It is a physically strong demon, not mentally, but its body is tough. The metal wires it hit should have cut it to ribbons but they didn't even cut its jacket." With that same raspy voice, Chris tried to think where he had heard them before.

"Hmm, very well," when the man hummed it sounded like a bumblebee the size of a bus, a strange vibration that made Chris' bones quiver. "Tie it up and let the demon bear witness as we cleanse these children!"

There was a roar of cheers mixed with a chorus of painful-sounding coughs and Chris was again dragged around. He was pulled to his feet by strong hands, his feet trying to find the ground only kicking about aimlessly. He was then slammed up against a square pillar of wood, his arms yanked back painfully and tied up securely. The sound of heavy footsteps drew close as someone came up to Chris and yanked off the hood.

The light of torches glinted off the metal of scythes and other sharpened implements, few if any carried guns that stood within eyesight which meant they knew at least how useful those were in this age of monsters they lived in. A few who stood up on the stage he found himself on even carried long swords and a long curved knife dangling from their belts.

Chris could hear their jeers, cries for his head, and pleas to hurry and cure their child, but it all felt muffled. His head felt stuffed with cotton, a rustle in his ears crackling like tin foil.

"BROTHER'S AND SISTER'S," shouted one of the swordsmen, "BE QUIET!". He raised his hands, shushing them till the only sound left was the snaps of the torches and the whispering rumble that buzzed through the air. "The Preacher has gathered you, his flock! To share his words, and to save these children!"

Another wave of cheers shook the air, and again he raised his arms for silence.

"The good Preacher, he fights the darkness," he stepped aside, turning to face Chris then. "This, this DEMON! They tempt our children! They steal our loved ones! They have destroyed our world! But! Worry not-"

He raised his hands high again, the mob in rapt silence watching him in awe. He looked down at Chris, his face in shadows, eyes glowing in the darkness like some feral beast.

"Their days, are, NUMBERED! Can we get an AAAA-men?!"

"A-MEN!"

The single word rang the night like a funeral bell, and every face in the crowd turned to the stage in reverence. Eyes hot with the glow of fervent devotion they starred with piercing gazes that made Chris want to be sick. These were not people, they were blindly devoted and not to the god they claimed to be.

Heavy slow clapping started up making Chris turn his attention as the other swordsmen raised their hands high and a tall thin woman stepped out between them.

Her hair was white at her temples but flowed down her shoulders in a cascade of black locks tied in the middle of her back with a simple wooden bangle. Her clothes too were unremarkable, a simple black dress not too unlike the nun's habit Kendra wore. She stood tall and proud coming around to the front of the pulpit.

"Sweet children, we have come here to seek a way to free these sweetling babes who have been led astray." She waved her hand back and Chris let his eyes follow, regretting what it was he saw. Hanging by their necks over a dozen small bodies kicked and thrashed hanging by their necks from a massive gallows rig. Each one still moved though a few ropes hung empty too.

She saw Chris staring and smiled at him fondly.

"See how he shows no remorse for what he has done!" She lunged with the speed of a viper, blade skittering across his face and snapping his head sideways with a crack. She grabbed his head and dug the blade into his neck pushing hard, "See how they don't bleed, see!"

Cries rose for them to kill him, to cut off his head, to burn him, and countless more torturous ways to do the sickening deed. But still, this Preacher smiled like a clown on stage.

"No, no, no, death is too sweet a release! Did we die when the monsters fell from the sky?"

"NO!"

"Did we run and hide when the armies fled and left us to cough and die in the spreading plague?"

NOO!"

"And will we let the demons from the north poison our children?"

NOOO!"

"The nays have it, kinetic," she whispered in his face.

She stood up and walked back to the head of the platform before turning back to Chris. He was so focused on the swaying bodies of the still-living children.

"Yo-you, you-"

A heavy hand struck him hard, cutting off what Chris was trying to say.

Chris looked up into the face of the man who had hit him. His eyes were not like the one swordsmen, or like the Preacher's. Chris scanned the crowd, the same eyes stared back at him from many more, dark eyes that seemed to glow in the dim light. A predator's gaze.

The man over him suddenly coughed and slid his sword back into his crude sheath, seemingly satisfied with Chris' silence.

"Well then," the Preacher called, "Shall we heal these children?"

The crowd again burst with gleeful manic cheers, but the Preacher and so many more just smiled.

She walked to the first of the swinging children and held out her hand, one of her swordsmen coming forward with a heavy bible.

"Saint Michael, oh ye greatest of the Archangel, defend us in battle." She suddenly slashed her knife across the child's chest. "Be our protection against those so wicked, and the snares of these devils." She struck again, this time downward, a deep gash that made the child swing wildly. "May God rebuke him," she struck again crosswise, making the wound deeper still. Chris could hear the child now, their cries of pain, but already they were beginning to heal. "So we humbly pray," she raised her hand and cut her palm so blood flowed, "And to thou, O Prince of the heavenly host." She pressed her palm to the child's unbleeding wound. "We pray, by the power of God." The child began to jerk and buck but could not shake her grip, a deep howl growing under the hood. "Thrust into hell Satan." Her smile was a twisted sneer only those on stage could see. "And all the evil spirits who prowl about the world seeking the ruin of souls." The child had begun to slow now, their body no longer twitching. Two of the men came forward to pick them up and carefully remove the rope. They held up the child and pulled off their hood to reveal the happy smiling face beneath. The Preacher turned back to her adoring flock raising her hands high, "Amen."

Cries of amen, and other blessings filled the torch lit night. Crazed shouts to go on, to save the rest, but she heaved suddenly sideways reaching up black sludge and a man caught the Preacher before she could collapse to the ground. Whatever charlatan act she was pulling must have been actually taxing, or she was a great actor.

"Please, please, everyone, give us but a moment and we-" The man holding her up, held her with great care but she squeezed his arm and stepped away, going to the young boy who stood smiling and waiting. He winced a little as she took his hand and held it up.

"Show the demon, there is a cure Charlie."

The boy walked over to Chris, that innocent smile twisting as he saw him. He walked over tearing at his tattered shirt showing off his bleeding wound.

"See mister, we don't hurt anymore, we are so happy," the boys back to the crowd none but him could see as the boy's skin wriggled and moved, the corners peeling open as he laughed to reveal the wriggling bloom in the gaping cavity where his heart and lungs should be, a strange glowing orange mass just below in his gut Chris had never seen in a bloom before. Never known that a transformation could happen so fast.

Chris still could barely move, but he lunged and spat, heaving at his bindings.

One of the swordsmen came around and the boy's chest closed quickly. He wrapped the boy in a blanket and held him up high on his shoulder. "SEE! See how the demon does not rejoice at gods hand! See how the Preacher, has saved our son!"

The crowd was livid now, they shook their steel, screamed and revelled in their perceived miracle.

The Preacher stepped up and squeezed the swordsman's arm lovingly, "A days rest and we shall heal even more of these yet innocent lost lambs, healing our son took more than we thought. But heal them we shall," she grabbed a torch then, raising it high to reveal the dangling boots of more men women and children who struggled in the trees above, hanging like grapes on the vine waiting to be plucked. "We will heal them all, and grow our ranks, and we will raise an army of wolves! And we will drive ourselves like a spear through the heart of the demons of the north!" The Preacher's words were like acid in Chris' ears, burning at him, and he felt as he began to slip, the rustling in his head growing to a point where he could hear it clearly, hear the whispers.

Hate them, fear them, kill them, feel weak, hate, hate and fear, fear them, weakness, sickness, be sick, hate them, kill, bludgeon, maim and murder, sick and fearful…

The string of evil drove like needles into him, his eyes closed he could see them, threads connecting to him from over ten different places out in the swollen mass that surrounded him. One even came from the swordsmen on stage who had spoken first. The threads pulled on his defences, probing for any weakness, all while filling the air with their hatred driving the poor fools who were just sick and scared to madness. He could feel himself slipping, the whispers growing as the light faded.

"Is this a private party?!" A bright flash of green flame sliced through the air and set the ground on fire forming a gap between the mob and the platform.

Kendra was a sight for sore eyes as she stepped out of the shadows.

"I heard you preaching and thought I may weigh in as a servant of God myself." She held her head up high and stomped up the steps with her heavy clunking boots drawing the eye of every one of the swordsmen, and the Preacher herself.

The Preacher hissed, "Unclean thing! Demon! You would do well to learn your place!"

Shink

The sound of steel rattling from leather rang out, and like a bubble popping Chris was suddenly released.

He took a deep breath and looked around, he could feel the power from Kendra, floating candles lit with green flames all around them. Whatever she had done blocked the whispers out, and protected them from the mob, but it wasn't enough. He could see it on her face, she was holding back the fires with all she had, she was creative, but not powerful. Her little candle trick wouldn't work forever.

He caught the eye of the Preacher. "Give it up Bloom! We have you now, answer me an-"

"FILTH! You don't frighten us!" She spat the words, pointing out into the crowd. "Take them! God will protect you!"

Chris looked out into the ranks and saw them now, the bloom in the midst where the torches had stood. Their illusions gone, he now saw the glowing blue trumpets sticking up above the mob. Their bright blue light stood out brightly and cast an eerie hue over the people around them. Their ability to winnow into the minds of people was strong, the illusion so real he had truly believed it all too.

Chris looked up to see the same blue flower sprouting up from the throat of the torch-bearing swordsmen, the other three men vacant-eyed scrambled for the rusty machetes at their belts, tattered clothes and cobbled armour a far cry from the lavish clothes they had been wearing a moment ago.

They were all trapped, trapped in their own heads, fed hate, and fear, and rage, so much so they were blind to the truth.

"You really are sick," Chris calmly said, finally slipping free from his bindings. He turned to look at Kendra, then out at the surging mob rushing towards the stage. Faces twisted in rage, weapons held at the ready, they were ready to commit murder in the name of fear.

But Chris was not like them, he could see it on Kendra's face too. Even if these people had been willing to go along with this murderous cult it wasn't their choice. Their minds were poisoned, he couldn't kill them even in self-defence, even as they threatened his life, and that sickening smile on the Preacher's face said she knew it too. The people were misguided, led astray by this creature that called them her children.

Luckily though, Chris had always known he couldn't use his powers to hurt someone.

"Hey Kendra, do you know what they called me back in Winnipeg after the Event? After I got my powers?"

She shook her head, still standing between the crowd and him, brandishing flames he knew she would never use against an innocent - if foolish - mundane person.

"They called me, the Basilisk."

With that, he embraced the energy inside himself and let loose. His ability to control density and make solid objects harder catalyzed the muddy and dust-covered people, fine particles of grit growing like a shell harder than steel, freezing them solid.

Kendra looked at the petrified people, then at him.

"They're not-"

"No, they're alive, but they're not going anywhere till I say otherwise." Chris rounded on the Preacher, "And you're next."

The bloom backed up, seeing the others frozen, the Preacher however was not as daunted.

"I call your bluff kinetic," she sneered and came around her puppets, "You're expending a lot of focus. Would have been better had you simply killed them, not wasted your energy to hold them."

He pulled his coat off now, the coloured bands on his arm blazing with light as he held his power. "What are those things, what are you for that matter, how is it that the heat hasn't killed you?"

She smiled, "Did you think all bloom are the same? No, we are evolving, others have Fallen already too, brothers and sisters who longed to spread the good word."

He stuck his thumb at Kendra, "I've got enough godly people right here."

"Oh, oh no, I pray not to god, no, I pray to the true queen of the bloom, our mother, the first of the Fallen, may the Wytch-hazel guide my hand," she raised her palms up, her robe billowing oddly as a long shoot sprouted out her sleeve. Thin, long, and bright red it was like a serpent from the garden, covered from tip to end in silver thorns. It glowed ominously casting a flickering orange-pink light from within its sealed bulb.

"With the gift she gave me," she shouted at the sky, "We gained a means to leave the cold, care to witness how."

"You can shov-"

The Preacher lunged in, her bloom opening like a firecracker into a starburst of sparks, metallic thorns along the tightly closed blossom slashing at Chris like a whip. He was lucky by a hair, Kendra pulling him back just in time as the spear-length bloom slashed through the planks splattering orange fluid everywhere.

Both Kendra and him backed away, the boards turning black as creepers of steam rose all around where she had struck, hoarfrost creeping rapidly around the damage.

Chris could feel it in his chest, breathing in heavily as he regained his footing, the air was colder, and not just a little. The people closest breathing still inside their stone shells even began to give off mist.

"So, that's how," he chuckled, cracking his knuckles.

"Indeed," she hummed, still with that wicked grin, her voice carrying up from inside the flowering tip of her bloom. It opened up slowly, unfurling like a corkscrew till it was almost double its length. It was a deep red, tiny bulbs lining the inside of its length, the whole thing glistening with moisture, dripping orange specks that froze all it touched. "We carry the north in our heart, and our ladies will into the south." the blossoming buds quivered as she spoke, her mouth never opening the whole time.

He sighed and shrugged gently out of Kendra's white-knuckled grip. "I knew that some bloom were smart, but I figured a kinetic would have had more sense than to let themselves be twisted into a monster."

Chris leaned back examining the bloom, its long thin body in blossom looked frighteningly beautiful.

The blue one beside her had not moved the whole time, it just stood there, pushed out through the man's distended throat. Opening up like a fancy vase it looked like it was made of glass, except as it breathed and its long thin fangs slid out into the air. The others in the crowd were much the same, shining blue, denizens of this living nightmare. The steady stream of whispering coming from the one on stage told Chris all he needed to know, that was the one creating the illusions.

"This is over bloom. You can't beat us alone," Chris flexed his hold on the people making the blue ones grow quieter.

"We are called Preacher Satin," she said, still smiling like a broken puppet.

"Oh, I assure you, I don't care," he responded with a chuckle.

Her demeanour changed, her shoulders back, head held high, "This one is infected," she pet the cheek of the young boy she had called her son. "And this one, well, his inferior genes saw him as a mere carrier." She grabbed the back of the head of the man who had called the boy his son. "Both of them are useless, no better than weeds, the child will maybe become one of the yellow if we are lucky, it's the inferior father to blame. Not us, no, We, are, perfect."

Chris snorted, "Hardly."

She shot him a glance.

"I'm just saying, if I can beat you, you're hardly perfect."

"This poultry few meant nothing you see, as long as we live," her Bloom opened up fully a heavy mist flowing around her as the air super-cooled. Her bloom then seemed to shrink, the flower spinning as it coiled up closing tighter, the long thorns folding down and retracting. Then it slowly slipped back inside her sleeve, a sick wet sucking sound resonating as it returned inside her. She turned to look at Chris, her acrid words now coming from her own mouth, "We can always grow another garden."

It hit him then, what the Preacher had been doing, but it was too late.

Before he could react she shrieked, with all of the other bloom around them joining her. The whispering went from a low hum to an ear-splitting wailing siren; he slipped and fell backwards, not enough to break his concentration, but enough that it shattered his eardrum.

But the damage was done, by the time they had healed enough to stand the Preacher was gone. The blue bloom he had held were all dead before the moon was above them, drying up like lilies in the sun even in the cold desert night. It seemed whatever the Preacher had done to them was undone just as quick, or some other hand was at play here.

The rest of the people were not much better, half-starved, and paranoid; most he just kept frozen rather than risk them causing problems. It took quite a while to get the still living people down from the trees, each one a kinetic, many if not most children and teens. Their healing kicked in and most were at least physically fine, but their minds were fractured. Many could barely do more than look straight without crying, and any who saw the frozen faces of those who had captured and tortured then broke down. No one could have blamed them for it, some of these kids had hung here for a week or more.

Chris felt the rage inside him building; he had defended himself during the Event, he knew fear, but these were kids - kids with powers, sure - but kids all the same.

The moon was setting before they finished the last child crying in Kendra's arms as she tried to tell him the monsters were gone. One kid had been sitting on the edge of the stage a long time, most of the rest off behind the stage making use of the camp the mob had been using. A young girl, maybe six or seven he couldn't read her. She had been sitting there since she had pushed away Kendra. Just sitting there, staring at the mob of adults.

"They can't hurt you," he said quietly sitting down next to her.

Her eyes never left them, but she smiled. "I know that," it was sudden and quick and he acted mostly on instinct as he felt her lash out. The person in the crowd, her target, was nearly hit by a bullet of air.

Chris hardened the woman's shell prison, noticing the other marks on its face; it wasn't the first pot shot the girl had taken, but it had been the strongest that he had felt it.

"Why did you do that?"

She shrugged, "Because, that's my aunt."

Chris looked at the face of the woman, twisted in rage he could almost hear her raging scream. "Did she-"

"She gave me to the Preacher. Said I was a monster," her voice was so clear, so calm. It was harder still to get a read on her.

"She didn't mean to, the bloo-"

"No, she did, she killed my daddy weeks before this place. She said it was an accident, but I knew she pushed him down that hole with the monsters. Now I feel stronger, I can hear her thoughts. She was always like this."

Chris sighed, he had seen this back home, kids so powerful they could hear thoughts. He wasn't any good at it, but he could understand.

He pet her head, "She can't hurt you now, we won't let them."

"But I don't get it, why don't you hurt them? Why can they do it and it's okay?"

Chris shook his head, "It's not fair, but no one deserves it. But you can't let how people treat you, make you like them. You have to be better than them."

"I am better," she worked up another bullet of air and shot it at her aunt, but it again did little.

"Having power doesn't make you better, uh-'

"Mary," she cut in.

"Did you, wait, are you reading my thoughts?"

She nodded.

"That's lesson one. Power doesn't make right," he flicked her ear.

"Hey!" She squealed, turning to him.

He just smiled, "Sorry, but I never had kids, but growing up that always got my attention." He stood up and turned to Kendra who was sitting with the group of kids around the fire in camp. "You may not get it now, but as long as you try, you'll learn. Come on, you need to get away from these people, find your real place, your real family. Kendra's going to take you all to a place you can call home."

He felt a tug at his side and looked back to find Mary there, her hand held up to him.

He took her by the hand and they walked back to the fire together.

Kendra looked up at him, then smiled at Mary seeing them. She then teasingly jabbed him in the ribs, "Getting soft on me, Basilisk?"

He shook his head, but chuckled mirthlessly, "No, not yet," he looked down at Mary, and at the other kids, "You look like you could use a hand though."

She nodded, "Kinda puts a kink in your road trip, doesn't it?"

"I left too soon," he said, the words catching in his throat. "There's a lot of people I would have liked to say goodbye to, but I'll never get that chance. I'm not going to walk away this time, not yet."

Kendra smiled and stood up, "Thanks, Chris."

"Pfft, don't thank me yet. You're all stuck with me now."

Mary suddenly squeezed his hand.

"What's up kiddo?"

She fidgeted shyly and looked at the others. "I can still hear them."

Chris nodded, "When we get far enough they'll get quieter, and we can help you learn to quiet them."

She shook her head, "Not them." She tugged Chris so he had to lean over to hear her whisper. "I can hear the monsters."

Chris looked around, whispering too, so no one could hear them. "Are they close?"

She shook her head.

"Okay, well, what are they saying?"

Her eyes met his, a spinning swirl of purple and red, the true sign of mentalist kinetic, and powerful from how he felt it radiating from her.

She squeezed his arm tight, pulling him close to hiss quietly in his ear.

"*War is coming kinetic's…*"

COFFEE FOR TWO

9yrs A.E. Eastern Canada

Nancy came awake with a start looking around the room flopping about and fell almost out of bed. She was home? Had she left? Her head felt like it was splitting. Her mind flashed and she froze, the light in the window outside reflecting off the tower in the distance. The school.

She fell back against her pillows and smacked the back of her head hard against the headboard.

She cursed, but the pain was gone just as quickly as it struck.

She heard the shuffle of feet on the carpet, the door creaking open as the pleasant smell of strong fresh coffee filled the room. She sat back into the covers.

Her husband Ben came through the door and smiled at her. "Three milk, one sugar?" He piped up as he sat down on the bed next to her.

She nodded and sat up, reaching out and taking the cup from him, but grabbed his collar and pulled him close.

"How about we make it extra today," she purred, "And you give me some sugar," she kissed him slowly, his warm hands running up her back gently massaging her as he hugged her close.

She pulled back reluctantly and she reached up and tapped his nose.

"Reset button," she chuckled.

He laughed and held out the mug in his hands.

Her head suddenly twinged and Nancy's vision swam, and she grabbed her head where she had hit it.

"Nance," he looked at her worriedly, "You okay?"

She nodded as her vision steadied, "Yeah, just had a bad dream, then I hit my head."

He nodded, "The bloom dream again?"

She nodded back, "It was worse than I remember Benjie, so much worse, I think I…"

He kissed her suddenly, big brown eyes looking at her, "Good thing the bloom all died off in the heat."

She just sat there a moment, head still fuzzy, "Yeah."

"Drink up love," he said quickly, "You'll feel better with some caffeine in you." He had been up early, like that every day she could remember since they met. There with a hot beverage in hand to encourage her to greet the morning - before it was noon. She wiggled over to him, coming to sit in his lap and leaned back against his chest taking a long sip of her drink. The hot warm brew graced her lips with a rich flavour, caramel, and cream, with a hint of sea salt that added so much to the flavour. He sat back with her giving a happy sigh and pulled her close, Nancy nestled into his arms and enjoyed her drink as he playfully caressed her.

"I have to go get some potting soil from the green thumbs at the school for my wych-hazel, wanna come with?" His hands slid slowly up under the front of her nightshirt, she couldn't help a giggle as he squeezed and played with her.

She swatted at his hands, "Are you going to behave? Or are you going to be a pervert?" She asked, feigning a stern voice.

"Haven't decided yet," he shrugged and gave her another squeeze. He kissed her cheek and inhaled deeply his eyes on his coffee just out of reach. He looked at her, then the cup, then back at her, then his coffee, desire of a different kind in his gaze.

"Ooooh, ho, no… you get your own coffee," she teased

"But my hands are warm…" he flexed his fingers making her squeak.

She pulled reluctantly out of his grip and scooted off his lap grabbing his mug off the nightstand. Then just to be a brat sat there taking a long sip from his coffee, smacking her lips loudly.

"Mmmm… so tasty."

He chuckled, and though she mildly regretted it, she sat back in bed. She still felt shaken from her dream, and his warm embrace made her feel better.

She set her coffee down. "Can we, just cuddle a bit?"

"You okay?" He asked, a hint of concern in his tone.

Nancy nodded.

And so, they lingered a while, enjoying the moment till her lovely husband finally got up. Kissing her again as he did.

"Got to go mow the lawn, Hon. When you're ready we can walk to the Co-op."

She blinked. "I don't wanna get up." He just laughed and grabbed a shirt from the closet and tossed a pair of PJ bottoms at her.

She caught the silky pants and rolled over and grumbled over having to get going too. She tugged on the pants and grabbed up the hoodie he had been wearing before changing pulling it on, it smelt like him.

If he was up, she might as well be too.

Nancy pulled her hair back into a bun with an elastic. She shook out her nightshirt and folded it over the couch in the corner. She piled up the pillows and smoothed out the covers on the bed. Nancy wasn't a clean freak but…

She stood up, mind blank.

Her husband… What was his name? Benjie… no, Benjamin…? Ben?

A mild panic flooded her mind as she tried to recall, Ben? How had they met again? They had been married for years…

How long was that though?

Another blank.

Worry gripped her heart. What was happening? Were they even married? She looked at a framed image of them on the nightstand. It was them, wasn't it – a beautiful photo of them in Florida – but their faces, his face, who was that? They had gone to that sunny locale for their anniversary… How long ago was that?

She didn't know what to do. Her mind was racing. She looked up at the mirror on their dresser and the room around her was gone.

The mirror hung in the air, suspended in a wall of ice, a frigid wind blowing across her. Her face was gone, the polished surface reflecting a flower where her face should have been. Fleshy red petals pulsed away as they gnashed teeth in a gaping maw as she let out a scream.

She blinked, and when she opened her eyes, things were not any better.

She was standing in a field of snow, with deep drifts swirling up her waist as if she had been standing there for a long time. She swayed where she stood, unable to move her body, jerking against invisible bindings her body not in her control.

No, not bindings, against her own body.

She tried to scream, but no sound emerged. She wasn't in control.

This is a nightmare

The thought flooded Nancy's mind. She blinked rapidly to clear her vision, but still, nothing changed. Only able to move her eyes, she could see other people frozen in the snow. Like a crop left to the frost, humans stood swaying in the gale-force winds.

This has to be a nightmare, why am I not cold? She asked herself. The snow and wind blew fiercely at her rippling across the frosty field, but there was no sensation in her skin, unable to move like she'd been caught up tight in iron-strong threads of spider silk. But none of the others around her were restrained, they just stood there jerking a bit now and then.

It's just a dream, this is a dream, I'm dreaming

She tried over and over and over to convince herself, closed her eyes and tried hard to drown out the sound of the wind. But as she screamed in her head she began to feel so tired. Her eyes wouldn't open anymore. And in no time at all, the darkness claimed her.

Will and Not

16yrs. A.E. New Winnipeg, CA

The air in the hall was charged today, everyone talking as they watched the two Teachers getting ready. Emily sat up in the back of the auditorium at the top row, far from the others. She pushed up the glasses on her nose with her middle finger and looked around. She could see the whole floor from her perch, and the others in her class, minding their behaviour. As head of her class, she wanted to make sure all twenty-six of her classmates were at their best; which they rarely were.

They were all over the hall though with this mixed class, the massive hall so packed that people stood in between seats or sat on the railings between the levels of the bleacher-like rows that encircled the room. Even the stairs down to the massive nine-foot-wide training circles in the center of the hall sat handfuls of students and teachers alike.

After all, it wasn't every day one of the masters was going to teach a class.

The hall was designed for training combat kinetics and as such had all number of random things around the hall floor. Anything that they could make was provided. The only thing missing was the training puppets that they usually had standing at the edge of the training floor. The master had packed them all away, and Emily had heard that today was a live training class. The masters had been on edge the last few months since a handful of people had gone missing without a trace. Their disappearance had been so startling to the masters that this class had been set up. A class on how to break mind-works. As the class rep, she had signed up their class right away, just in hopes, this might bring up their class scores.

Try as she might, they were seen as one of the lowest-ranked classes in the whole school because of their grades. Emily hoped this could change that though because for once their weak link was their ace.

She looked over at Wally two rows from the ring, as close as he could be as always, and focused like a laser. She knew he wasn't watching her, but she knew Wally. He was always aware, his kinetic powers weren't strong, but he was sharper than anyone. So when she lingered on the back of his head she wasn't surprised when he held up his notebook with the words, *Bush League*, scrawled on it. He was always so focused, constantly striving to get stronger, but it was never enough. Wally didn't have much power, to begin with, and of everyone in their class, if not everyone gathered here, he had never found his center. Yet that never stopped him from trying, and she respected him for it. She shook her head and flicked a marble at him with a bit of power. It bounced off his book and he ducked down to catch it up. Still, he never let his eyes leave the scene in the ring.

A shudder ran through the air and Emily turned to watch as the Teachers squared off again. She had seen this more than once, the training bouts between Master candidates were always open for anyone to watch. Both Teacher Derek and Teacher Susan were powerful dual element wielders, soon-to-be masters candidates, and very powerful.

Today though they were here to help the master in his lessons. A lesson on how to fight another kinetic, in melee combat.

The class sat in silence as the air in the huge hall seemed to crackle and flicker like a heat shimmer. Both Teachers putting out a massive amount of power stood on either side of one of the circle's wooden training swords held in whatever preferred stance they used. They hadn't moved an inch closer together since they had started, only circled each other, but the room crackled with latent power.

The room suddenly shifted a little, making every student take a deep breath at the same time as master Adam stepped between the two Teachers.

They said he was nearly immortal, he certainly looked like a child, having not aged since the event nine years ago. He was also one of the highest-ranked masters and was rarely at the school, the rumours said he was a diplomat to the aliens, and that his wife was even one of the ones who had made the Seed. He was first and foremost a master though and above many of even the most suited to teach this class with his skills.

When Emily looked into his eyes she threw away the notion that she was looking at a child, his haunting gaze drawing her in, even from this far back. His irises were like most masters, changing as he embraced his center. Emily could see the way they were fragmenting and snapping back inside the confines of his ocean-blue eyes. The sign he was a true pyrokinetic.

She didn't need to see his black hooded duster to know he was one of Azure's crows, a man of the High Order. Yet she hoped the rumours about Azure's chosen were just rumors.

Master Adam smiled kindly, a smile that showed in his eyes by how the fractals danced so gaily. But when he spoke Emily felt bad, as she ended up wishing he hadn't.

"**Reaching inside yourself is easy**," he started, the vibrations running through Emily again as his voice carried out to the hall sending most around her into a cringing murmur. His voice sounded like it was made of many voices smashed together, young and old male and female, it was quite the mind-warping sound. He must have noticed all the people wince though because Emily again felt a shift in the aether and when he spoke this time it was not as harsh. His more child-like voice came out clearer, "With the aether inside us, anyone can learn to affect the world and those around them. This is channelling, you are all aware of this." He raised his hand and a skeletal form made of electricity stepped up out of his body - one of his effigies they called it - it turned and stepped over beside Teacher Derek. "But there is more to our powers. That which lay outside of our mental reach," a second effigy stepped out of his body and walked over to where Teacher Susan stood. "This is the flow..." A flare grew inside both of the effigies till it touched the two Teachers, tendrils of light and electrical discharge connecting the Teachers to the strange crystalline blue constructs. But as the link formed the colour changed. At first blue, they were now pulsing through with other colours. Shades of green and gold flashed through the one behind Teacher Derek, and sharp squarish pulses in green and white in the one behind Teacher Susan.

It reminded Emily of their eyes, and it dawned on her that what she was seeing was a reflection of the human nervous system made clear. She was amazed and looked at her hands in wonder; this same flow was in her too.

Master Adam looked at them both and nodded in satisfaction, "Now that's ready. So this is the energy within, see how the energy shifts as they focus." Sure enough, as the two Teachers opened and closed their hands and began basic stances, so too did their effigies. The energy swirled and moved, growing stronger from one hand to the other as they formed little fireballs of psire in one hand and switched to a one-handed sword stance.

Emily had seen this done with the glass puppets in class, but never in real time. Working with puppets was always a delay as you had to move the energy through it. Here she could tell how much easier it was as the effigy just reflected the way they were working the flows of aether inside themselves. She could see it clearly, and it was amazing to imagine that's what was happening when she did this too.

Master Adam tapped his heel on the boards loudly and both Teachers stopped, "As I said though, this energy is not alone. So much more exists beyond our senses." He raised his hand and the air suddenly began to crackle, the feeling when he had first stepped in coming back. "That energy is just as important to know."

He tapped his heel and the Teachers both changed to a form she had never seen – at least not in training – it was like some kind of crazy martial arts stance from the movies. Standing sideways feet planted their arms out to the sides she watched as the effigies mirrored their doubles. As soon as they did, an aura began to grow around them. It was like the northern lights, deep swirls of yellow and blue and red all jumbled in ribbons that surrounded them.

Master Adam reached out and the swirls twisted towards him and retreated, "And this is that energy. It connects us all, binds our forms together, and gives life to everything all around us. But, though it gives us power and life, it can be used against us too."

Both Teachers again seemed to inhale, the energy visible to everyone there now making it clearer what they could not see before.

Both Teachers took a normal stance again, standing idly like they had when class began. Anyone with aether sense could have easily told otherwise, Emily was not one though so all she saw was her teachers. Even without aether sense though she could feel the air as it hummed, and looking at the crackling energy forms of Master Adam's effigies now Emily could see why.

The tendrils of aether from both Teacher Derek and Susan had wound together as if fighting to get closer. They strained and pushed, tugged and shoved, but they seemed equally matched. They didn't look to be fighting, they just looked like they were glaring at one another. But from how the aether roiled around them it was clear so much more was happening.

Master Adam stepped to the edge of the ring again, "When we use mind-works on a mundane we rarely encounter this." This was like a wrestling match, with one kinetic trying to overshadow their opponent, "This technique is used to drag them into the mind of the other where the real power is. It is easy to detect. Easy to mimic. Yet difficult to handle if untrained." He turned to the Teachers and nodded.

The struggle went back and forth, both of them trying to gain the advantage. They even started to do things to throw off each other. Trying to break the concentration of the other by slightly shifting energy to throw feints at the other. Then it got interesting. They suddenly rushed in now striking at one another, giving up almost all altogether using aether to attack but simply trying to overpower the other with their swords. But it was hard to expend that much concentration when you were locked in against someone who was trying to force their way into your head. Emily knew how to get inside a willing mind, but an unwilling one… she had never even thought about it.

Emily could barely look away, but out of the corner of her eye, she noticed Wally.

Usually one of the quiet kids in the class, he seemed a bit angry. She appreciated him for how calm he usually was and with his long blonde hair he looked dashing, most girls thought so. That however made him less than welcome by the other boys in their class.

She turned in her seat to look down at him, pushing up her glasses again, and gasped as she watched his hand twitch and twist suddenly hard up behind his back. He didn't flinch, didn't look away, just grit his teeth a moment. He just stared off at the other side of the hall, where a group of tough-looking boys stood around one who sat in the bleachers there like a king on his throne.

Ralph Smith and his cronies, a bunch of high-class students, were all well-known for being bullies, and Smith was a personal tormentor of Wally's. All of them were grinning like devils, and the air was so full of aether she couldn't sense what he was doing but it was clear he was twisting Wally about trying to make him make a scene.

Wally however was practically a stone; it was part of why Smith liked to pick on him. Wally never let anyone get a rise out of him, and Smith took that as a challenge.

Smith was short and broadly built and excelled at their physical skills classes. Few could beat him in power too, his abilities rivalling many of the first-tier Teachers. But what he had in power he lacked in control, at least usually. It seemed he had been practicing, and Wally was his test dummy today.

Emily stood and excused herself as she bumped past people trying to watch. She fumbled her way down the rows to the row just behind where Wally was standing. He was trying hard to resist, but he had not used his powers. He refused and she knew it even without her senses. Wally would never do anything to make a scene.

Emily however was not above it.

She reached out with a needle of energy and drew a marble out of her pocket. She aimed at Smith and charged the little glass ball with kinetic energy. It wasn't enough to do more than stun the rotten punk, but he was going to remember it. She loosed the bead with perfect aim.

Unfortunately, someone else was faster.

A sparkling hand of crackling plasma extended out from master Adam's body, effigy upon effigy like a human hydra of lightning reaching out and catching the marble before it took Emily's mark. The Master's eyes focused now on her, and Emily felt the weight of that gaze as his voice turned stern.

"**Are we boring you, Miss Emily?**" He asked with countless tones of disapproval.

The entire class had stopped now, even the other Teachers were focused on her and Master Adam.

She shook as she felt his power turn on her, "I-I, I'm sorry Master Adam… I was-"

"I know what you were doing, but do you?" He didn't seem angry, but Emily still felt scared. His effigy reached out to her, moving from where it was to her in a snap like lightning, returning her marble. "Teacher Derek, Teacher

Susan," he said softly. "It appears we have volunteers for the student demonstration."

Emily hung her head; she knew she was no match for anyone here. Sure, she was the best in their class, but that was like being the shiniest lump of coal. She walked around a teacher near her and down to the front.

Master Adam however raised his hand, "Not you miss Emily." He pointed to Smith with one hand, and one of his effigies rose and pointed at Wally.

She froze. What was going on?

Master Adam looked at her shocked face, "Did you think I was so blind that I did not see what was happening here? I was curious to see what was going to happen. Now misters Ralph Smith, and Walter Black, to the circle. We all wish to see what you have learned today."

Emily looked at Wally, she mouthed the word.

Sorry.

But Wally just shrugged and rubbed his joints. His arm and hand were red, but his healing had already faded the bruising from Smith's torture to nothing more than a faint splotch. As Wally passed her he gave her arm a quick squeeze, she knew his easy smile was meant to be reassuring, yet somehow it made her feel worse.

Once both boys were in the ring, the teachers stepped out to the edge. Then, master Adam recalled his effigies and summoned two new ones.

They stepped over to where Wally and Smith stood and as before became entangled with their energy. The one behind Smith looked like it was ablaze, black flecks of light mixed with purple and yellow swirling inside it, the energy barely contained. It flexed and moved as he did though it stood much taller than the person it mimicked, ripples of light peeling away. The one that attached itself to Wally however was strange, the light inside it was faint, almost clear as if made of glass like the training dummies. It wasn't until you looked closer that you could see gossamer threads like spider silk floating up from the effigy, a faint pulse slow and steady that radiated down from his head through his body and touched everything around him.

Far less impressive than the show Smith made, it was a different kind of impressive.

Smith looked at their effigies and smiled, “Wow. Thank you, master Adam, this is an honour, and thank you for saving me from Ms. Hartman’s little prank. Wally ol'buddy, are you ready to spar?”

Wally just shrugged, “I guess Ralph…” Many around the room giggled at that. Smith hated being called by his first name, and it showed.

The look of hate on his face was plain as day, though it flashed only a moment.

"I must ask though Master Adam, why are we learning to fight like this? Aren't our powers better than a sword?"

Master Adam nodded, "At times that is true Mr. Smith, but what happens when you face another kinetic? A more powerful one than yourself at that?"

He sneered at Wally, "Oh, but why would we fight each other?"

"Kinetics come from all over, and not all share the same loyalties and beliefs as those who follow the Immortals." He signed heavily as if this was common knowledge. "For that reason, you all must know how to defend yourselves. To make sure if you do come against another who can match your power, that you stand a chance."

"Well, no other kinetic will see my unique style coming," the pompous lout crowed.

"Oh...? And why's that?"

"Guess no one told you, Master, you aren't around the school much. But in this school, I'm the strongest here. Master Samuel showed us how to gauge our strength, and I'm more powerful than everyone here, even more than Teacher Susan and Teacher Derek."

Master Adam's smile only grew at that, "And what happens when you're not?"

"But I-"

"Mister Walter! Square off!"

Wally bowed, "Yes Master Adam."

Smith made a rude noise as Wally entered the circle and took up a wooden sword.

"Wally, he's one of the weakest of us here."

"Is he," Master Adam smirked, "I wasn't aware of that...? If I remember though, your father says you're rather clever, let's see what you can do boy."

Smith looked livid, his power called into question.

"Just don't go crying to that librarian when I spank you in front of everyone here Weenie, I mean, Wally," he turned to Wally, taking the blade from his grip easily.

The blade however did not stay in Smith's grip, a crackling effigy reaching around him and plucking the wooden sword from Smith's grip.

"Demonstrate what you can do, without being armed. This is a lesson, I wish you to learn something," Adam chided.

"That's right, I can beat him," he flexed his muscles and the power inside his effigy seemed to swell and bulge like a balloon animal stressed in the wrong ways. "So, let's not keep master Adam waiting!" He stepped sideways and widened his stance bringing his arms out wide, copying the stance the Teachers had demonstrated.

Wally just stared at him with those dark eyes, he didn't take the stance either. He stood there, seemingly aloof, but there was a determination to him. There was always that quiet to him, like a caged animal watching the free.

Emily didn't know what she had been expecting anyways as Emily had never seen anything like this, but it was common knowledge Wally had yet to find his center. So it was, and so she guessed this was what that looked like. After a moment though he looked at Master Adam, then took up another blade, and took a different stance altogether as the faint shimmering light inside him fluttered. His aura faintly glowing was set through with jolts of blue static kissing the air just around his effigy.

Smith smiled, and even laughed, “That’s it?! Master Adam, is this even fair?” He stood up and his aura swelled again, the purple effigy glowing behind him as it reflected his control over his own aether.

“Don't boast Mr. Smith. Please, proceed," his words seemed direct, but his focus was not on Smith at all. And with a nod from Master Adam, it began.

Wally, as was Wally, bowed to his opponent; but Smith was not so courteous, he just sneered and attacked. The same tendrils as the Teachers had used made it to Wally, surrounding him like a fog. But what happened next was not what someone may have expected. While the two teachers had gone back and forth, and the fight seemed even, there looked to be no competition here.

Wally just stood there, his effigy seeming just as unfazed.

Wally stood up straight and seemed to be completely at ease, just giving a quick swing of his oak blade as if waiting for Smith.

Emily had seen this with him before Wally had been raised by one of the caretakers in the school, he had grown up with the notion he had to follow the rules to a T, with no exceptions. So even when others used their powers on him, Wally wouldn’t. Now Wally was permitted to do just that, and in something, she already knew he was good at, but still, he saw this as an unfair fight.

Wally and she had spent many days training, trying to find his center; what they had found instead was he was good at directing power from others. It was like watching a stone in a river as he forced Smith's power to divert around him. The purple ribbons of light swirling and snapping at him could have been his aura from how little it fazed him. His aura just pulsed dully, little sparks now and then snapping about.

Smith’s smile slipped a moment.

“Hey, janitor's boy," he sneered, "If you’re not careful I’m gonna make such a mess here your dad’s never gonna get this place clean!”

Wally smirked at Smith, and with a little effort stepped closer. The pressure he must have been under was incredible, Emily was able to see it, it was like they were more than one person's. Even Teacher Susan was having a fit on the sidelines, Teacher Dean's jaw dropping as Wally made another step. That much aether bearing down on a person should have had him locked down, but not Wally.

The air was electric, almost as much as when the Teachers had been facing off. Wally's wrist suddenly turned up and she watched as that same clear shimmering sparkle from inside his effigy creeped out along Smith's torrent of aether. It sparkled and danced, avoiding every attempt to be cut off. Pulling the lines of aether in, holding them, and catching more as others formed and tried to attack.

Somehow Wally was winning.

Smith was looking worried, with all his power, he still couldn't stop Wally from advancing. But he looked more angry than worried and smiled a wicked grin still. His assault let up a little and a tendril of energy whipped out to touch one of the medicine balls that lay at the side of the room on a rack. He stopped and looked at master Adam, but their instructor didn't even blink. With that Smith hurled the ball right at Wally's head.

Wally had seen it coming and shifted to the left ever so slightly his blade connecting with the ball, sending it sailing high across the room and through a window.

"**Any distraction can mean defeat in a fight between two kinetics**," master Adam said suddenly. Speaking up over the dead silence and oppressive pressure, his voice made many jump at the sound of his personal chorus.

But Smith didn't stop at one ball despite how little effect it had. Item after item, he flung anything not nailed down at Wally trying to break his concentration.

Wally would only stop for a moment though, long enough to block or dodge, before walking towards Smith again.

And as he drew closer Smith began losing his cool even more.

Emily walked down to the edge of the stairs, people in the bleachers now standing in awe making it hard to see from where she had been. Most everyone was standing with jaws hanging open now, even the teachers looked amazed. To see someone as naturally powerful as Smith go up against someone as obviously weak; and yet Wally could not be stopped. Or at least that's what she thought.

"Wally…," Smith said quietly, "You're not bad, but you're not as unflappable as you think." Wally was only a few feet away from Smith now his wooden sword held up defensively, the things Smith threw going wide around the room. A small ball suddenly whipped past Emily and struck a teacher who doubled over in a coughing fit. It had missed Emily by only inches, but dodging the one had only put her in the path of a second bit of rubble that hit her arm.

She cried out as it stung her, and Wally stopped. Turning he looked over his shoulder, and Smith smiled cruelly.

He attacked with malicious fervour, tendrils of his aether piercing into Wally at last. It caught him in his middle and twisted up and down Wally's legs like a creeper. His effigy wound up in purple vines with yellow thorns wrapping around its legs.

Wally didn't show it, but Emily could tell from how it looked how much pain he must have been in. Still, though Smith wasn't pleased, Wally never flinched, never moved back, and that made Smith all the angrier.

Master Adam raised a hand and stepped forward, "That's it, end this, you can't win boy."

"Yeah…," Smith yelled too, "Give up!"

Wally just stared forward, not saying a word, and took another step forward, blade still outstretched.

She saw it then, flows of aether wrapping the blade, cutting through the storm like an icebreaker on a ship.

Master Adam's voice grew louder, "I said stop this before someone gets hurt!"

But despite his demands, Smith kept raging, and Wally kept going, and at last, in range, Wally was on Smith.

He raised the wooden sword, and brought it down, slow as molasses, it came down undeterred. Smith whipped blasts of energy out at Wally trying to stop the blade from coming down, but it was no use, and the edge bopped him once.

The scream that tore through the room was like nothing Emily had ever heard before, bestial and crazed, Smith stood frozen in place, face twisted in a rictus snarl of rage, eyes empty of light in a swirling white shimmer.

Master Adam raised two more of his skeletal electric effigies and tried to force the two boys apart. But as soon as they touched them, they instantly began to fade away as if sucked into some invisible wind. Master Adam looked all around the class and waved his hand sending a shimmer of sparks through the air. It was as if something were there, invisible but everywhere. He turned to the class and shouted; all semblance of composure gone. "Everyone get out of here… **NOW!**" The word now came as a bellow, a hurricane of otherworldly voices that sent everyone running for the doors.

Emily couldn't run though, she was fixed, staring at poor Wally instead. She tried to go to him, but two steps were as far as she got when she was struck by something in the air, a swirling mass of energy from Smith sweeping past her, slamming her against the wall.

She looked up from the floor to see a dark aether swelling up out of Smith's eyes and mouth. Bubbling up like tears of tar it coated him to the floor in an oozing pool that crackled with plasma. It was clear he was in terrible pain, his body twisting and contorting. Emily couldn't see Wally from where she'd been thrown, but she could hear his voice. He screamed, just barely heard over the sound of crackling energy, his shadow thrown across the wall as bursts of light flashed over and over.

Master Adam was still there too, he stood over her, a mass of his effigies surrounding them like a cage. He looked like he was focusing hard, the energy in the room tearing everything apart.

There were others too, all around the rows of seats in the hall she could see. A dozen or more, all wearing black hooded dusters like his, their faces shrouded. They seemed to be doing something, but her head was still swimming and she couldn't tell with her senses so flooded.

She grabbed master Adam's coat hem making him turn around, his eyes aglow were filled with worry as he spoke too. "Emily, I need you to run!"

She tried to stand, but she was too weak, "I… can't stand…," she pulled herself forward.

He turned back to the hall, and more of his effigies rose around him. Their bodies changed and shifted till their energy formed a second layer to his barrier.

A cracking sound tore through the air as the seats and stands all around began to crack, raging winds beginning to tug on her clothes, and she looked up to see a speck of darkness hovering above the room. It twisted the air, distorting everything around it, a horrifying realization coming to her as she tried to back up.

A black hole.

It was forming, barely contained by the kinetics in black as it grew.

Emily had never seen anything like this, but she had heard it was possible, the power of a kinetic growing to such a level that they could even control gravity. Smith was going to burn himself out, but it looked like they were being dragged with him.

She watched the air as it shimmered, the combined force of so many kinetics warping reality.

So many glowing eyes lit beneath black cowls, so focused. The chairs All around the room were gone, everything in the room that was not tied down, even some of the room that had been was just gone. It had formed a wall of shattered debris that orbited the growing speck of darkness.

Emily's healing wasn't working fast, and she could barely move, as much as she tried. Every inch she moved to back away from them just making her slip ever closer to the center of the room. Even master Adam was beginning to slide closer, the floor around them beginning to tear away in chunks.

Suddenly there was a surge, rips in space that tore open all around them as more and more people wearing the coloured dusters of masters came out of nowhere.

As each one arrived more and more flowing barriers of debris and energy formed around the tiny black void.

Emily watched as massive blocks of strange material formed, drawn from all around them. Each slab was black and inky deep and fit into the next, a ring of them forming as a device began to form around the miniature black hole. The whole thing began to spin, faster and faster, and as it spun it began to hum. A second ring formed, and a third, and another, and another. Finally, the room was filled with spinning rings that formed a ball that looked almost seamless as it spun. It spun and hummed, and the world grew quiet again, the black hole somehow contained by the spinning rings.

Emily stared at the masters there, so many. She didn't even know that this many existed who wore the coat. They all seemed to speak in hushed tones, quietly talking. Not one seemed concerned, none looked at her either, they seemed so… distant.

Emily had never thought about how dangerous it all could be, she had just thought it was exciting. A gift to be born with the power to shape the world.

She could feel hot tears welling up, blurring her eyes as she stared at the spot where Smith had stood. His body was there, and he was still breathing, but what was there could never have passed for the once handsome show-off. He may have been a bully, but the wheezing husk that clawed the air didn't even look human anymore.

She tried to move but a master she didn't recognize was suddenly there over her. They pushed her back down and she sat hard. "Sorry little miss," he said with a deep rumbling voice, "But I need you to sit still. You've seen a lot today, but the Black Order is here now."

She looked up at him, and though her glasses were lost she felt she almost knew the man's voice. His black robes fluttered as his hand came up to her face.

She backed away, but he held her tight if gently. She begged him, "Please, I have to find Wally! Tell me he's okay?!"

The man nodded, his deep cowl flopping about, "He's going to be fine Ms. Emily, I promise, and when you wake up, you will be too."

She squinted hard, trying to recall the man who held her. "Who are you?"

His hand came back up to her eye level, bright pinkish sparks snapping at his fingertips. His voice was soft and soothing, and her eyes suddenly felt heavy, "I'm just a janitor…"

****

The weeks following the incident at the school went by with little pause. In no time flat, the regular day-to-day school life seems to be back, and it seemed everyone had forgotten all about it, though Wally had no idea how anyone could have.

He wasn't good with people, and he knew that emotions were difficult for him, but he did try, it was just awkward. Even now as he walked with everyone, their intense chatter just made him feel even more separated from them. They went on about this or that bit of gossip, and some new show the theatre was planning. Yet, all Wally got was a buzzing from it all.

They came to where the two Teachers were on the street. Thick snow blanketed the old city street, making everything look like some old movie in black and white.

Today was a power lesson, a class on controlling the two fundamentals of psychokinesis. The students and teachers were responsible for this because the masters had their own agendas. But it was easy enough, all they did was work outward from the outer wall, going street by street clearing away the old houses and scrap.

Anything useful like electronics and books had been scavenged long ago so now it was just a matter of continuing what the big three had started. Building the school with the materials scavenged, and reclaiming the wastes.

Their class had been partnered up with the class Smith had been in. He was still out healing from the accident but they seemed in good spirits. Even Smith's cronies had barely said a word to Wally as their classes had walked down from the trolley together.

"Come on, come on, get friendly." Called out Teacher Cindy, a matronly woman, with silver-grey hair, and a genuine smile. She waved her arms at the class as they gathered drawing them closer. "No one here bites… hard…" There was a polite round of chuckles from the others, but Wally didn't get it.

He stepped in closer.

"Ouch!" Emily had been right beside him as he moved and he trod on her foot with his heel.

Wally jumped away, "Oh, Emily, are you okay?"

She stood awkwardly, one hand on her friend's shoulder but was smiling. "Yeah I'm okay," she said looking up at him, "Just got too close I guess."

He tried to say he was sorry; wanted to try and make her laugh instead, but nothing came out right in his head. His mind was a whirlwind of what's and what not's, and in the end…

"Aren't you going to say sorry at least?" Her friend Karen said with a haughty tone, her glare speaking levels of dislike.

He started to stammer a bit but a shrill whistle cut him off, and he whipped around.

Teacher Cindy's partner held his hand up a long blade of what looked like grass held between two fingers making a shrill tone. Wally didn't know the man's name, but he had a grey coat which meant he was uncentered. Powerful enough to have gained his stripes though. A cursory glance at his arm showed five different coloured lines, each one meant he had passed one of the master's tests of control over one of the nine arts.

Wally would have liked to ask, but the man was already talking.

"So, we're going to be breaking into groups. Each class already has three units so line up in your usual groups." His voice was strong and commanding, despite his frail appearance. He was tall but looked lean, and tired, with dark circles around his eyes. He looked like he badly needed a sandwich and a nap.

Wally and the rest of his class lined up with him and Emily at the head of the line, but something felt off. He looked around and leaned into Emily's ear whispering, "Since when do I stand this high in the class?"

She chuckled, giving him a nudge so he stepped back, "Shhh…," she looked at the other class head. That would have been Smith had he not been injured, but Alexie was their head of class. It made Wally sick to think someone dumber than Smith was still in control of an upper-class group.

He shook his head, he was higher up than most of them in the class; wasn't he? For real though, he thought, even his own feet had brought him to this spot. He felt a little foggy suddenly and shook his head, the Teacher's voice bringing him around.

"Alright students, four and four, class heads, split them up." He turned to Teacher Cindy, "You're taking the west side of the street, the last one to Bruce avenue buys dinner." He smiled and looked at the students, "Alright everyone we have fourteen houses to go, then we can call this side of Albany street done. After that, the mundane can come and collect the supplies."

Teacher Cindy was known for her competitiveness, and her frown only grew as he had spoken. "As Teacher Lucas said, only fourteen to go," she crossed her arms and turned on her heel beckoning for her group to follow.

Wally watched as Emily and the other group left, his group gathering around Alexie.

Alexis wasn't as suave or put together as Smith was, but he was almost as powerful, so everyone followed behind him as they made their way to the first house. It was tucked up behind a copse of overgrown trees, one of which had Fallen in a storm and crushed in the roof. Teacher Lucas stood at the head of the driveway, "Alright two groups, I'm sure you can guess. One Breaker, one Builder, and one Conduit please."

The whole group split up quickly, it wasn't their first time doing this exercise. However, it wasn't as easy as usual, as it was the first time doing this with people from a different class. Mixed with the others, it meant familiar pairings weren't possible. So it took a moment but after a while, six groups formed. Teacher Lucas nodded to them, "Alright, link up now Conduit's, and pass the connection to me."

Wally placed his hand on the shoulders of the two in his group. Both were from the other class, and neither looked particularly pleased with him. He didn't care though and drew aether through them both forming a psychic link.

Telepathy was a simple trick for him, most of the mind-works were. While others had a hard time around him forming a first-time link, the minds of Sammy, and Davis opened up to him like a book. It wasn't like a fight, here it was like a handshake. Their minds were just there and he took them in his hands.

When he opened his eyes he could see light forming at the corners of his eyes, white shimmers, and flecks that danced about. Davis was sturdy and proud in his mind, his brown-green eyes turning like gears. While Sammy was shy but self-centred, her own eyes a bright yellow-blue like a swarm of fluttering wings.

Their hearts and minds opened to him and he found their power calling to him too, it was a struggle to resist the temptation to take control of the link.

He let it go to Sammy as the breaker of the group, he could see the swirl in her eyes intensify as he did, the green-brown and crystal flecks of Davis and his nearly clear flow of colourless aether flooded her.

Davis stepped up beside Wally and looked at him, "I always heard you were weak, but I have to admit you have serious control." He pointed over at the others, most of whom looked to be struggling still or unexpectedly fighting for control of the link.

Wally smiled briefly, "Thanks, I practice a lot."

Sammy scowled, but he could feel her mind in awe through the link, "You sure you don't want to lead? I'm just a cannon, all I'm good at is breaking."

He shuffled a bit, feeling a bit uncomfortable, "No; but I'll help though, I'm good at moderating. So I can keep your power levels in check if you're alright with me shadowing in your mind?"

"You can mindwwalk?"

"Yeah, and I can pass the link to Davis when we're ready to reconstruct the raw materials."

Sammy nodded and Davis stepped back, both had a pleased feeling emanating from them.

Teacher Lucas received their link and turned to them with a deadpan stare, but a very happy feeling flowing back through their link. He looked at the others.

"Well everyone, had this been combat you'd all be dead already. Except for group six. Top shelf performance you three." He pointed out down the street, "Well… what're you waiting for? Get on it, and take group one. Maybe you can help them form a link faster. Start at the end, it's the biggest house."

They nodded and all six of them started at a trot down the street, though the other three didn't look too happy. Teacher Lucas was right, even without his aether sense, Wally could have told that all three of them were too stubborn to give up control.

They came to the house and he stopped for a moment, "Did you want me to help… form a link I mean?"

Alexie turned his nose up, "We don't need your help, Weenie, we can get this on our own if these two would just back down."

Duane, and Lee, were both from his class, and neither was happy being talked to like children.

Duane stepped over to Wally though and nodded, "Don't listen to him, Wally."

Duane and Wally had linked before, so he knew Wally's talent for it. Lee wasn't really in his fan club though, not since the incident with Smith whom she held a major crush. Yet, albeit reluctantly, she too held out her hand.

Davis walked over to Alexie and spoke quietly to him. Alexie didn't look too happy still, but after a second he also came over.

Wally first opened himself up like he always did, he knew Duane would right away seek control but in this link, Wally was in control.

It wasn't a fault of Duane's, it was just his nature, forcing the aether at your opponent to wrestle their power into your control also left you open to being redirected. Those with more power instinctively sought more, it was like a reflex, so Wally had learned to limit his internal power, and instead rely upon the flow of aether around him. He tweaked the energy coming from Duane, and next Lee, finally turning the link over to Alexie.

Wally looked at them as he watched their aether sync and their eyes take on that telltale sign of the link.

Wally nodded to the others, “Okay, let's get…”

Alexie pushed him aside, “Don’t think because you’re smart you call the shots.”

“Alexie!” Duane shouted.

Even outside the link now Wally could feel their connection falter.

“I don’t care who leads," Wally said blandly, "I just want to get this done.” He pulled his coat tight against a heavy bone-chilling wind, “That and I’m cold.”

Alexie scoffed and silently motioned for his group to head to the back, though Duane did stop a moment.

"Thanks, Wall-man."

Wally faked a smile and gave him a little nod.

They took up positions all around the house, his connection with Sammy and Davis letting them move almost perfectly in sync. They waited for the others until finally, they got their signal.

“Three!” Alexie's voice.

Wally felt a surge of power drawn through him, his hands raising on instinct.

“Two!”

The power gathered at his fingertips and flowed through his body, shared between the three of them.

“Break!”

The House seemed to scream and groan as the combined force from them all was released at once. The walls buckled and shattered inward then exploded all at once. Debris flying out in all directions flowed around the barrier that Davis focused on creating around them. A plume of dust and smoke began to swirl as they channelled it all upward into the sky to be blown away. When the smoke and dust were gone all that was left was the raw material. Shards of wood and metal, bits of the house and all, all of it hanging in place.

The tiniest splinter floated in front of his nose, and Wally blew on it gently making it start to slowly spin.

He smiled, this was probably the only time he ever really felt happy, using powers on this level was surreal, he could never have done this alone. The link radiated with good feelings as his improved mood flooded into the other two.

He retook control of the link, sliding in behind Sammy's consciousness and gently shifting it to Davis. He held the link only long enough to get a feel for the debris they held in the air. All of it, down to the smallest grain of glass. It was like having a snow globe shaken up that then froze mid-shake.

He looked around the crater that was where the basement had been, to see where the other three had gone. Chunks of concrete and wood floating here and there hiding them from sight. He could feel them though, their pulsing life forces calling out to him. He found Lee first, her brown long coat standing out against the snowbank behind her.

He smiled, and she smiled back. Then the snow behind her began to move.

At first, he wasn't sure what he was seeing. The snow separated from the ground slowly, a massive thing that looked like a pile of black rubber cords standing up. It swung its whole body, thick ropey arms forming into a huge creature. Before she or anyone else could react, it lunged, and in the blink of an eye, Lee was gone. All around him the world snapped, shattered rubble falling to the ground as the link he had felt before popped like a balloon.

Still one with Davis and Sammy, Wally pulled control to himself in a rush of aether using not the power inside him but the potential energy of the debris still falling. He didn't think, only acted, reaching out and catching Lee as her broken body fell from the sky where she had been launched. He caught her up gently in a net of telekinetic energies and brought her down to Davis. Meanwhile, Sammy was already launching a barrage of stones at the creature as it shambled up out of a pit in the ground.

Wally looked at it closer, and everything around them, he was looking for any sign of Alexie or Duane, but he couldn't see them. He did however notice what the creature was as it stood and a half-consumed body flopped out from inside it.

Openings appeared in its ropey frame as it swung its arms and body about trying to block Sammy's attacks. It was pulling hard to get free of the ground, pulling up its roots and thrashing about, reaching for something near it.

Wally focused his power and let out probing threads as Master Adam had shown them. Only his were more like telekinetic threads fine as spider silk and twice as strong. He guided them and laid down a mass of kinetic lines until one touched a person. Wally tugged the threads he laid down and lifted himself across the empty hole in the ground in a massive leap. He had never done this before but did it now on instinct alone, the threads he had laid down allowing him to move about faster. It was like riding the waves of aether, the flow of power all around him heightened his senses through his link to the others. The creature lashed out suddenly as he neared it, the end of its arm opening up in a starburst of massive flowers and gnashing teeth wreathed in wriggling tentacles. He pulled on his threads in a flash and was pulled to the side out of its reach.

He had always had good senses but now in the heat of the moment, he felt faster than ever. Wally landed hard skidding to a stop over a body in the snow, Duane had been hit and was out cold. He grabbed him up in his threads and tossed him over to Davis who was ready for him. Davis' hands swung up and the trees around them reached out, catching Duane and bringing him to the ground gently. The branches bent down and twisted together and formed a cage around Davis and the other two.

Sammy was still on the assault, she had run out of things large enough to throw and changed tactics. Now that they were out of the way she was trying to force the creature back into the pit. Huge whirlwinds forming around her arms became like a pair of massive clawed hands pushing it back. But it wasn't enough.

Where was Alexie?

Wally leaped back into the air again over to Sammy's side.

"Can you hold it?" He shouted, barely heard over the sound of the winds.

She smiled and nodded, "I got this, find Alexie!" He wanted to believe her, but through their link, she couldn't lie, she was tiring out quickly using the power from her own body.

He tried to draw more power from around him to feed the link between all of them, but it was no use. There was just so little life around them. He focused further and further out, his searching threads catching on anything they could.

His threads touched on the presence of a person again and in a flash, he was off. Up and over the tree hedge he landed in a pile of snow and found him. Alexie just sat there, staring at the raging monster. He barely even looked at Wally as he landed beside him, his eyes fixed in place.

"Alexie… are you hurt?" He asked, but he already knew the answer. Alexie didn't speak, didn't move, he was terrified… and he had run. Wally reached out to take his shoulder, "Come on man, we need you. Sammy and you are our only attackers. His hand closed on Alexie and the feeling of fear washed over him, so strong it nearly broke his link.

Alexie looked at Wally, tears filling his eyes, "I can't do it… please… don't make me… I-I don't, w-want to die." He tore free of Wally's grip and scrambled away on all fours, kicking up the snow, getting up, and bolting off as fast as he could get to his feet.

A sudden shift in the link between him and the others made Wally look back. He could see the creature where Sammy was still fighting but he couldn't see her. It was clear from the link though she was hurt. Wally knew he couldn't waste time and he jumped up over the hedge and back into the fight.

The monstrous Bloom creature had pulled itself out of the pit finally and was now attacking the tree cage. Thankfully Sammy had retreated behind the dome, but she was clutching her arm and was hurt badly.

Wally cast out his threads again, he needed more power, and he wanted to help. The link between them screamed in his head, he wanted to help but the more power he tried to divert to them the more it seemed he was failing.

The creature hadn't noticed Wally yet so he snuck around to get behind it. His hope was maybe he could distract it long enough for the others to get away. But before he could even attack it the mass of grey-black vines parted on its back and a Bloom flower the size of a truck tire came out screaming at him. All over its body, Bloom flowers pushed themselves to the surface. Six in all, gnashing, roaring flowers on the ends of muscled vines. It looked like some kind of hydra made of vines as it tried to get at them all at once.

It screamed a long wailing howl, a call that was echoed all too quickly by the wails of other bloom's.

Wally's mind was reeling, how many more were there? How could they stop them?

It all seemed so hopeless, but he wasn't Alexie, Wally couldn't just run.

There was only one thing left to do.

He had promised Geoff he would never try to do what he was about to do alone again. Geoff told him he wasn't ready, but Wally didn't have a choice.

He jumped away to the far end of the pit and calmed his mind as best he could. He closed his eyes and imagined a flame, burning hot, warmth filling him. He focused on it hard, fed the flames with his will till he could see it glowing. He held out his hands, felt the energy burning in his palms, he opened his eyes…

But nothing happened.

"DAMMIT! Why won't it work?! I'm doing it exactly like the Teachers always say to do it, I can feel it, but the fire won't come to me!" He shouted at the creature as if it could understand. But it just screamed back at Wally and began to crawl toward him.

Wally still didn't back down, filled with energy and rage for his worthlessness. He struck at it again and again, lashing it down with threads of kinetic power, imagining steel wires that cut into its flesh. The creature struggled hard against its bonds, oozing murky blood as it pulled against his barrier.

He was feeling the strain of the power on his body and tied the anchors off. A neat trick Geoff had shown him, like tying off the end of a fishing line. He then tagged it again with even more threads till it was forced down into the old remains of the basement. He tied those lines off too and stumbled back as exhaustion washed over him. He looked up to see both Davis and Sammy slumped over, Lee and Duane huddled beside them. He had been pulling so much through the link, he had tapped them as well for aether.

Still, he knew the creature wouldn't be trapped down there forever, and now he was totally alone.

"*Sweet child… are you okay?*" The soft cooing voice came from beside Wally, a lithe red-haired woman in a white dress, suddenly at his side.

He had never been so happy to see another living person, "If you're a kinetic please help us, please I'm begging you… my classmates are hurt, and I…"

She raised her hand and pet his head slowly, "*We are sorry child, but we're afraid we can't help you. You have to help yourself…*"

Wally was shocked, "B-but, I haven't even found my center, I'm not strong enough."

She frowned looking him over with swirling red eyes that looked more like they were filled with ink than energy. She put one hand on her hip, and one on his forehead, "*That's not true. You have such potential…*"

"But I haven't even found my center, I can't make fire, I can't control any of the elements." He was at a loss, why wouldn't she help him?

She made a chortling sound and shoved him playfully, "*Fire… Who needs fire? Fire burns and kills, you don't need the power of death.*" Her smile made him feel a little calmer, "*What you need is the power of life itself…*"

He pointed at the creature trying to free itself, "But the Blooms are only scared of the heat, nothing else works."

She spread her hands wide in an odd gesture, "*Face it, you're trying to make fire but it's not working. It's not because the fire isn't in you, it's because your power is too great for such mundane things as fire. You're made of something hotter than fire… And a flame that burns so hot will only gutter out. No, you must take what fate gave us, and make yours what gave the first fire life.*"

He looked at her, and asked curiously, "What's hotter than fire?"

Her snow-white smile and soft pale lips curled into a beautiful smile. As if he had said the funniest thing ever. She took his hand and he felt the power inside her, "*Pure energy sweet child. Do you not feel the power, it's everywhere, in everything, and it's calling to you, I can feel it. Make it yours, control it…*"

She was right, Wally could feel it, the power was all around him. But it was like trying to grasp water with your fingers, the harder he tried the more it just slipped away from him; he was just too tired.

She stepped behind him and he felt a tingle washing over him, her arms around him he could feel the flows suddenly like they had always been there.

"*Feel that spark of life, that breath of energy.*"

He closed his eyes and focused on her voice.

"*Just let us in, we will show you. Let the aether suffuse your body, let it burst from your every cell, call it into you from everywhere around you, become one with the energy of the Void itself.*"

He did as she said and there it was, like a little spark deep in his gut. Following her guiding light he reached for it and found it with such ease he didn't know how he had ever missed it. It grew rapidly just like she said, his whole body alive with so much power it almost hurt. He opened his eyes and could see the sparks dancing off of him, arms glowing as snaps of plasma arced between his outstretched limbs. But something felt wrong, it was too much, he had never felt this much power even when linked. He panicked and felt the surge intensified by his will and emotion.

"I-I don't think I can control it!"

She wrapped her arms around him resting her chin on his shoulder, and though she spoke he noticed her breath never misted the air like his.

She pet his cheek and cooed to him sweetly, "*Oh child, that's your problem, you're trying to control it. You don't control the Void, the powerful don't truly control aether, they feel it, embrace it. Let it flow through you, then you can guide it better.*"

Wally knew this, he had been guiding power like this for as long as he knew he had these powers. He felt the flows around him, knew they were there, now he knew where they led.

He nodded and opened his eyes, the spots gone, he felt like he was opening his eyes for the first time, the world backlit by the flows of life energy that fueled it all.

"Then," she whispered, *"Then, you can wash away the sins of this world with righteous fury!"* She wrapped her wrists around his and he felt again as that tingle took him. A deep calm that made his mind feel blank, and killed the scream of danger. His thoughts fell silent, and he let the power he held free, didn't constrain it to his will but moulded his will to its design.

He called out lighting from the snowy sky striking the ground all around them, eruptions of earth and shattered stone flying through the air. As waves of concussions ripped the world apart he felt a sudden pop, and he knew it was his center, like the flowing waters of a dam suddenly unmuddied as the dam broke, flowing free with clean waters. The power living within him awake and calling for him, he shaped the lightning called it to his hands into bolts of pure plasma. Then he compressed them down tightly into shining needles of light. He opened his hands and the needles rocketed through the air with pinpoint accuracy, each one striking deep into the Blooms many flowers, the compressed energy releasing with a shrieking pop like the crack of a whip right in your ear.

And he didn't stop, till the creature was still.

He stepped back and marveled at how he could control it now, so easily too. Watched as the energy dissipated back into the flow of aether around them. He held his hand out and watched the energy dance between the hairs on his arm as it fled his body, but even though it was gone he didn't feel weak. Laughing as with a simple flex of his hand the sparks grew in intensity with just a thought. It was his now.

The woman still hugged him tightly and he rested back in her arms completely exhausted.

"Thank you, thank you so much; I couldn't have done that without you."

"*Of course you could have, child,*" she purred, hugging him back against her bosom. "*But it's not over yet,*" she pointed to the creature's remains.

He looked at it, no longer whole it did still squirm and twitch now and then. He felt the power welling up inside him and looked at the creature, knowing what it had done, all the pain it had caused… his classmates?

He looked around in a panic, "Where are the others?!"

"*Others?*" The strange woman said, sounding rather confused.

Wally pulled away from her, crossing the grounds around the sunken basement of the old house. The tree that had been guarding them was smashed to bits. Sammy and Davis, Lee and Duane, all four were gone.

Again the strange woman was at his side, "*Ah, those others. They are safe, they are ready for our gift, and will be more happy with us…*"

The hiss in her voice stung him and Wally turned at the ready, but he was too late. The moment he moved against her she was on top of him, delicate fingers like cold iron holding him down, her sweet smile mere inches from his face. He tried to use his powers but she already had him. The moment he tried to touch the aether in him it drained away.

She leaned in and kissed his forehead, "*Dear sweet Wally, you have our thanks. These walking graves are so hard to subdue, but we can still make good use of it. We had only planned to take the children, but to have found them; what a perfect surprise.*" She still had not moved and though she was not much bigger than him she felt heavy as a horse.

"So, you're the one who's been taking them?!" Wally spat the words angrily, still twisting to be free.

She nodded, "*A mother wants what is best for their children,*" she said to him softly. She came down to meet him eye to eye, "*They have told you the bloom are monsters, but you are all being misled. But we will free you all…*" Her hands closed on his wrists tighter and he felt her mindwork let him go. She looked at him curiously, "*You are not ready though, no. Fate's grip is strong, and I cannot deny Azure a piece such as you, though it may be me. I will see you in my garden soon enough though,*" she raised her head to the sky. Her dress front parted as her flesh opened up, the Bloom inside her chest pushing its way between them hissing angrily.

It was like none he had ever seen in science class, massive and pale like a white silk cloth it seemed to flow on the wind. Each of its nine petals moved about then would suddenly freeze, then drift about more as they flexed long steely black fangs.

Wally was so scared he didn't even sense it as others approached.

Twisted smiling faces walking out of the snowstorm, they jumped down into the old basement and back out carrying pieces of the still wriggling creature.

She stood up but pushed him back down, then she leaned in and whispered to him. "*Don't move, my children are young, and focused. But if they sense you they will not hesitate to turn you whether or not I forbid it.*"

He laid back in the snow shivering from both the cold and fear, looking up at the worsening storm, wondering all the while; where was everyone? Where were the masters? Or the Teachers? Why was she sparing him? He opened his mouth to ask but closed it right away as one of the smiling Bloom suddenly slowed and looked down at her.

The man looked familiar to Wally, and he remembered right away. It was Andrew, a former Teacher who they said had disappeared.

His smile slipped and he spoke quietly, "*Mother Hazel, I can sense others coming.*"

He looked around but his eyes were so consumed by inky blackness that he must have been blind. He made a hissing sound and his Bloom came slithering out of his empty left arm socket. Thick and woody looking it was like a serpent, head knob like bulbs on the end clicking against each other. It snapped its petals open and closed with an audible clacking noise. Bright flashes of fleshy looking yellow petals with clusters of silvery bards at their heart the source of the hiss as they rattled in their shells.

"*I can sense one more, close too,*" he said suddenly, "*But it must have the power to hide, should we search for it?*"

"*No.*" The woman he called mother looked down at Wally and put her fingers to her lips, then looked back to Andrew. "*Go, take the walking grave and spread it to the children, it will make them stronger.*"

"*B-but the last child…,*" he stammered.

She waved her hand and Wally felt as her power slammed Andrew into the ground with the sound of snapping bone. She stood up and took her hand off Wally's chest, "*I believe I already gave you a task you ugly toy. Remember, we saved you, we can end you!*"

He hissed and clawed the ground as his bloom twisted around him, body bending in unnatural ways with a snapping sound as his limbs twisted back into place.

Wally was stunned.

When Andrew stopped moving, he rose to his knees slowly, a petulant tone in his voice,

"*Yes, I'm so sorry Mother.*"

His Bloom reared up above his head and let out a loud scream. Other bloom picked up the call and doubled their pace emptying the pit of the remaining vines.

Andrew stood, stopping only a moment above Wally before huffing the air and running off into the storm.

Wally looked up at the sky, unable to speak or even move. Waiting all the while for the sensation of that woman's aether to leave his mind, to no avail. As sleep took him before that feeling ever let him go.

****

When they had found Wally out in the snow he was almost frozen, covered over in a thin layer of snow. Geoff had gone right away to find him in the medical ward. It seemed the boy's healing had kept him from the worst of it though he had lost a pinky to the frost clutching his coat closed.

When Geoff left the hospital room though he could hardly believe all that the boy had told him. It had been really hard to have to take Wally's memories again.

He opened his belt pouch and slipped the vial with Wally's taken memories into the velvet-lined sleeve, the crystallized shard glowing faintly jingling in it's new home.

Geoff walked to the reception hall and sat down hard looking up at Lucas. The man had brought Wally home in his arms, carrying him the whole way leading the survivors back. Only a handful of them had even made it, it seemed the Fallen were far greater in number than the Masters were letting on. Thirty-eight people had left that morning on an exercise, most of them no more than children. A simple supply run and only eleven of them had returned.

Two of the students had burnt themselves out, he supposed it was better than becoming a Fallen, but was still saddened by it, they were still being counselled, but they would live.

Small victories, he told himself.

He shook his head and looked away from Lucas, "You saved a lot of kids today, Cindy, too. Has she woken up yet?"

Lucas was still a little dazed but he nodded, "Yeah, she's tough, her sister Susan is in there now too."

Geoff nodded, "Do you know me? What they call me around here, Teacher Lucas? Or what I do around here?"

Lucas looked down at Geoff with a guilty look, "Um… well I, I've heard them call you things before Mr. Black, but I'm not so young that I put stock in rumours." He seemed so nervous suddenly, shifting his footing.

Geoff smiled, "Humor me, please?"

Lucas sighed, "They call you, the Black Highlighter.

"Yes," Geoff nodded, "The Black Highlighter," he reached into his cargo shorts and pulled a black marker out of its usual pocket. The same marker that had started it all. "It's because someone asked me for a highlighter once, and I tossed them a black marker instead." Geoff shrugged and slipped it back into his coat pocket, "I just did it because I didn't think he'd remember what he was hoping to highlight. Not even if he did use a highlighter."

Lucas looked more than a little confused, "And now you're explaining this to me?"

"Because it doesn't matter if you know."

Lucas paused and sighed, "Because I won't be remembering this, will I?"

Geoff stood and closed his hand around his belt pouch clicking shut the clasp on it. "I'm grateful for you saving my boy, so I promise; I'm going to make you the hero of the day."

He could feel the man's defences rise but it was too late, even a mindworks prodigy like Lucas was no match for him. His hand came up in front of the poor man grabbing Lucas's wrist, the contact and his powerful weaves of aether too much for almost anyone to withstand.

It took three hours to modify the memories of all those involved, and when Geoff was done he was more than a little exhausted.

He took one of his little memory vials and opened the top absorbing the power from a happily made memory. It wasn't enough to bring him back, more like just a cup of coffee for his soul.

He walked into the room where Wally was fast asleep and took a seat. He leaned back and enjoyed the aftereffect of the memory he had absorbed. He must have been humming the song because he heard Wally shift and the boy suddenly sat up.

He rubbed his eyes sleepily with a bandaged hand, and yawned, "What song is that?"

Geoff sputtered, "You don't know, Ted Nugent's: Stranglehold?"

Wally shook his head.

"Oh boy, get comfy and let your old man teach you something." This moment was why he worked so hard, these times when he could make a happy memory, instead of taking bad ones away.

He hoped this memory was one that Wally cherished, because it was getting harder and harder to take bad memories from him.

****

The library had been quiet today, it was the weekend and the only ones here were Wally and herself. Anna could see the deep concern in Wally's eyes as he sat down across from her, "Well sir, you look like you have something more than a book return on your mind, what's eatin ya?"

She set aside the text he had brought to her and looked at the cover: Advanced theory of Kinetic focus and the Center, written by the seer, Master Neil. Anna frowned and slid it further away. She had read it once, but she found he rambled too much for her liking. There was a whole chapter on how the appeal of peanut butter and ham as a diversionary tactic was lost on the earlier generation of kinetics; who rambles like that?

There was no wonder Wally was confused, seers like master Neil were often considered confusing. She handed him a copy of an old bit of fiction she had liked as a young woman.

"Here, just for a laugh, a little imagination can help a kinetic find their center, at least better than an odd man's dusty theories."

He looked up from the book she had slid him in exchange, meant purely for fun. He wrinkled his nose a bit, he wasn't a little kid anymore, she sometimes forgot. They almost looked the same age now. She had not aged in the last decade since she came into her powers.

He still aged normally, and she had watched him grow into the handsome young man he was now. She often felt like his older sister, so she felt she knew him. Geoff had taken care of her too for a long time, it was only because of him they had survived the event all those years ago. But Wally was not the kind of young man who liked fun, he was all businesses. So Anna was always making him read old books she found funny, to try and remind him to slow down.

Wally was just to smart, it rankled others his age. Especially those in his classes. He had not yet found his center, yet he could shut down anyone who tried to spar against him.

Wally finally slipped the book into his bag and continued to press her, despite her attempt to jump the rails on the conversation.

"I don't get what this has to do with me; I wanted to know about my powers, why am I so different." He had only one of the tattoos on his arm still, others in his class had three of the four already.

She sighed, "It has to do with how we control our powers Wally. You see, we kinetics tap that energy, to control the primal elements, solid matter, liquid matter, gaseous matter, and plasmic matter…," she could see his jaw work and held up her hand. "Let me finish. You know that the energy inside yourself is the first step. People like the masters got fast-forwarded because of the same virus that made the bloom…"

He huffed a little indignantly, "I know this already. It's the Fever virus, it turned on powers in some, and in others laid dormant for years and was passed on to their children. Then… there's the bloom."

Anna nodded, "Yes. Just having the ability to sense aether does not make you a kinetic." She tapped her desktop and brought the screen to life. The image emitters in the corners bringing up her screen. She quickly filed through till she found some more references for him. Wally was like a dog with a bone though and barreled on.

"So why can't every pyrokinetic make lightning? But almost every kinetic who isn't pyrokinetic can make fire? None of it makes sense."

"I'm not really sure. They may all have the potential but as with all powers we are limited by our mental limitations. The aether in our bodies has a harmony that resonates with the cosmos. Fire is birthed by a combination of altered states, so anyone who grasps the core concepts of aether, and has found their center can find their inner flame and make psire." She opened her hand and let a little purple-green flame come into being in her palms. It wasn't much, she was no pyrokinetic either herself, but like all kinetics who were raised to Teacher level, she had mastered the ability to make psire. She smiled and made the little flame dance, "An aerokinetic needs to know the right way to breathe life into a heat source, terrakinetics, how to make fuel and friction feed a flame, even a hydrokinetic like me can manipulate a fire if they can feel the accelerant and find the flow of the aether to work it." She closed her hand around the fire putting it out, "I know you'll find your center one day."

Wally crossed his arms, "But I wanted to know more about electricity. Actual heat, lightning, real plasma!"

"I know," she said slowly. "I'm getting to that," she chuckled. There was no one around so she patted the bench seat beside her for him. He sighed but came around to sit down beside her. She gave his shoulders a little squeeze, "Look, Wally. Only when one's aether is truly in harmony with their state can we manifest it at will. Only when I'm at my calmest can I pull water from nothing, I have to really focus. Plasma is the most primal of all elements, it's in everything, but is the hardest to manifest. The masters who can call down lightning still only use it as a last resort simply because of how terribly taxing it is."

Wally nodded, "But most of the masters aren't actually pyrokinetic."

Anna nodded, it was true, only masters who had black coats were.

"We learn to harness the state which resonates with us the best. Whether that's aerokinetic's, terrakinetic's or hydrokinetics. All can call on and manipulate fire, some better than others. Some seem to hear the whisper of their inner flame the greatest and so we call them a pyrokinetic. But even they are truly not what they are called. Only those who can generate electricity – not just manipulate it, but truly manifest it – are true pyrokinetic's. It is such a rare talent Wally," Anna herself had only ever met three actual pyrokinetic's.

That didn't seem to be enough for Wally.

She shrugged, "I guess using pure energy to do anything is dangerous like that. Only the Big Three, or maybe master Adam could answer that. Some who can learn it find themselves blocking their gifts, or worse, burning out."

He looked down at his feet, "You mean if I feel it, I shouldn't try? That, it's dangerous or something?"

She leaned over and bumped his shoulder, "It's fine, just remember, don't force it, feel it. The surest way to endanger yourself is to rush it. If you feel the lightning within you maybe doubt is what's blocking it. I for one think you'd look great in a black duster, out in the wastes, defending the innocent, answering only to Azure… Pretty nifty little brother."

He suddenly opened his hand, a snap of light shining in his palm, it was quick, and Anna almost missed it. He stood up and stepped away from her, "Nifty, well what if I can make static, I mean, like whenever I want?"

She was shocked, and stood up too, walking over to him, "Make static, what do you mean?"

"Well it's like you said; it's so pure, and it kinda hurts like it's burning me back."

She was amazed but afraid, she knew what that meant, "Static, you haven't used it though, right?"

He had his back to her, and she could see he was shaking as he spoke, "It was an accident. I got mad at Ralph, he was shoving me around, teasing me. But when he pushed Emily because she tried to stop him, I lost control, and… I…"

"Wally, you didn't?"

"I said it was an accident, nobody cared that he had hurt Emily, it was all how I had gone too far." Wally punched the bookcase a glowing arc of crackling static jumping through the shelves. "Then, nothing, it was like it never happened. No one even remembered what he did, what I did. They all just thought he had been hurt in an accident. That's when I realized it, someone had messed with my head too. But it wasn't like psi-work stuff. I can break any kind of mental wall, these people's memories were just… gone!"

"Ralph nearly died, Wally, he was seriously hurt and still is. If you did that," she reached out to him, but he pulled away.

"I didn't do it, he burnt himself out. But was there, when the masters lashed out at the black hole to secure it. I saw how they did it, and I joined in! Me!"

"I mean we have to fix this Wally, this is serious, you have to tell Geoff, he could help you, or Master Adam, he's a true pyrokinetic."

"Don't you think I tried to tell them? You said it yourself, powers like this are dangerous. They already treat me like a freak!" Anna could see his eyes taking on a deep glow, and she felt the air as it began to crackle.

"If they hadn't messed with my head, maybe I could have learned faster. Maybe I could be stronger. Maybe they would still be here," he growled, each word dripping venomously.

She reached out to him, but a snap of energy leapt up from him and made her hand go numb.

"Wally, ow… oh Wally; I know it's awful, but you can't blame yourself."

"I tell one of those Teachers, they'll shred my mind just like they did the others." He coughed suddenly, a painful-sounding hack that doubled him over.

"They wouldn't do that Wally, you're just a student, They only mind wipe criminals, those they can't save."

"NO! You can't help me, I only told you because I needed to tell someone I can trust, but it's too much. I can't put this on you, Anna, I'm sorry." He turned to her and she could feel him inside her head already. Feelings of calm and silence welling up inside her.

She tried to resist, but it was too late. She had never felt so weak.

"Wally, what are you doing? I don't feel… What is this?"

The power around Wally was building and she could feel him losing himself. She had seen it before, her best friend's mother had burnt herself out trying to control what wasn't hers to.

Anna pulled aether to her in a flood of anger and jumped at him shrugging off his mental tap on her. She wrapped her arms tight around him and drove him to the ground.

"You idiot!" She shouted at him, "You're gonna just let the bullies win! Burn yourself out, run away, do you think that'll fix it, Wally?!"

"Let go of me Anna, it's too much, you're right!" His skin was burning hot, eyes glowing so bright she could see them even when he blinked.

She shook him roughly as they thrashed wildly, his power was growing too quickly now. Tears streamed from his eyes, floating like molten stars in the air. One touched her arm and she shrieked as where it hit her burned and turned her skin to ash.

He was burning from the inside now and hid flesh turning into vapour as energy swirled around them. Snaps of lightning, like nothing she had ever seen a kinetic make, shooting out from Wally.

"I couldn't save them, so why do I deserve saving!"

She understood that so much, she had struggled with that before the event had made her what they were now. Her clothes burned away from the intense bursts of plasma that were now raging all around them in the library. She saw the scars that crisscrossed the insides of her arms, the remnants of her haunting youth. Jagged tatters, smooth slashes, all long since healed. Permanently etched on her flesh, reminders that pain begets pain.

Anna hugged Wally tight, wrapping herself around him. She truly wished she had met him when she was younger. The thought that knowing she wasn't alone then may have made it easier. But here he was, hurting so much.

"I know Wally…"

She hugged him as the world burned around them, her power barely able to keep them alive as she tried with every ounce of her being to syphon his explosive power away. She hugged him till the world went dark and she slipped into a vast light that filled her sight brighter than the sun.

****

She had heard everything again.

Geoff shook his head as she finished her story, then he opened his belt pouch and pulled out an empty vial, handing it to the nurse.

"Apprentice Madison, you're dismissed, please wait in the hall."

Madison nodded and took the vial, her eyes still glazed over as she took the tiny glass bottle and walked away. His compulsion was subtle and she did as he asked though no more than a trick, she wouldn't remember anything Emily had said.

Geoff turned back to Emily with a smile, "Go on little miss, was there anything else?"

She shuffled a bit in the cot, but shook her head, "That's all I remember, Mr. Black. At least till that medic woman, and someone from the Black Order woke me up carrying me here." she said sleepily. Telling Geoff what she had heard looked to have taken a lot out of her. She smiled though, and she sat back against the pillows on the cot.

Geoff nodded, and pet her head, "That's quite a good memory you have there Ms. Emily, really good. You heard all that, did you? Did you see anything too?" He was worried for her, it had been very traumatic, and it was all his boy's fault again.

She shook a little, "I didn't see anything. The selves were between us, till the static started. When it jumped all over the place, that's when I tried to get to them, but I guess I got hit."

Geoffrey sat on the end of the cot looking at the burns she had gotten they would never heal, not pure aether wrought like they were. Geoff sighed thinking about the other two. The slight burns she had gotten were nothing compared to the state Anna was in, she was lucky to be alive. Wally also had yet to even wake up, though just like Geoff there was little if anything that could leave a scar on that boy.

One thing had been bugging Geoff though. He cleared his throat and turned a little to see Emily better, "So… why were you there anyway?"

Emily blushed, "I-I, ah… followed Wally. He's been so angry lately, and I've been worried about him. The accident at the training hall. Then the whole thing with surviving the bloom attack." She coloured deeper as she went on, "You know Wally Mr. Black. He's smart, talented, handsome." She looked down at her hands suddenly, she couldn't lie while he was there. "He's just bullied a lot because he's not like the other guys." She grabbed the sheets and pulled them up as if hiding her face made it easier.

Geoff nodded, "You like him then…?"

She hesitated, but nodded.

"Even after what happened?" He asked slowly.

She nodded again and let the covers go. Her mouth opened and closed a few times like a carp, but nothing came out.

He didn't want to force her, so he let his grip on his power go. He sighed and ran his hand across his shaved scalp, "Just like when I was a kid. It's funny to find the things that haven't changed since my time." He patted her foot and stood up, "Girls and boys still have no idea how to tell each other how they feel." He knew Wally very well and had always tried to do right by him. Sure Geoff wasn't Wally's real father, but he had tried to at least be there for him. He wished that Wally talked to him more, but he just wasn't that kind of kid.

Geoff smiled and stepped to the side of the bed, "Well that'll do for questions I think. We have all we need. You can rest easy now kid, this matter is for the Order to deal with."

She nodded, "Thanks Mr. Black, you're the best. I know if anyone can make this better it's you."

"Yeah, I always had a knack for seeing the space that's not there." He felt a pang of regret, knowing how to make this better didn't make it easier. "Making things fit just right."

She looked confused, "But, what about the Black Or-"

He reached out to her, a shot of quick pink sparks leaping out from his fingertips. The lights danced across her eyes leaving the faint smell of a candle snuffed out as wispy tendrils of white light streamed from the corners of her eyes starting to glow faintly. Tiny liquid sundrops floating from her as he drew the memories into another one of his tiny glass vials.

When it was done she stared blankly, he shook the vial, watching the glowing liquid roll about till it formed a tiny crystalline shard. He then opened the pouch at his hip and slipped it in with the other vials.

He looked down at the girl with a sigh, her placid eyes staring at the wall. He truly regretted taking her memories again, but rules were rules. Anyone involved – and not of the Black Order – could not be allowed to remember what those with true pyrokinesis were capable of.

He cleared his throat loudly and Emily looked up at him, "You're very lucky Emily," he said softly. "Had you and Ms. Anna both been standing under that faulty light when it fell…"

Her eyes suddenly seemed to focus and she looked about as if lost, "What... I'm sorry… Mr. Black? Oh… My head hurts. Were we talking about something?" A look of panic washed over her, "Is Wally okay, I-I was looking for him, but that's all I can…"

He smiled at her, "It's alright kid, he's fine. You can thank young Wally when you both return to class, he just had a rough time stopping the fire before help came." He put his hand on her shoulder and leaned her back into bed. A little tap on her forehead and a spark of compulsion and she drifted right back into sleep.

Geoff stood up and left the room and found Madison staring off into space in the hall. He took the little bottle from her and she suddenly came too.

"Mr. Black? What's going to happen to Wally? Now that they know he's a true pyro I mean, is he going to train with the Ord…"

The spark was fast and her eyes clouded over as she tried to mentally resist. He drew the memories out though and she leaned back against the wall.

He snapped his fingers and she jumped, "Sorry Madison, I just wanted to make sure Wally's friend was okay."

She looked dazed but came too quickly, "Ah… yeah. She's okay, or she will be. Man, it's so weird it's only been a few weeks since that nasty burnout. Your boy's going to be okay right?"

Geoff nodded, "Yeah, Wally's tougher than he looks." He slipped the little vial into his pouch. "Maybe it was wrong to push him back into training. A few weeks off won't hurt his studies."

Madison quirked an eyebrow at him, "What's that stuff?" She asked, pointing at the case on his waist.

He looked at it and back to her, "Just some cleaning supplies."

She crossed her arms under her ample bosom and leaned in, "Really, cause it looks like a nineties party starter."

"You know I haven't even had a drink since twenty-nineteen… God… It's been a long time." He laughed at that and closed the pouch.

Madison just chuckled, but she still looked a serious eye up at him.

"I know Wally is an underclassman, but I was super impressed how he stood up to that bully in front of half the school, then fighting bloom, now stopping a fire! You tell him when he's back on his feet that if he ever needs anything he can talk to me." Her eyes took on a mischievous glint, "Unless that little Emily girl would take offense?"

Geoff just laughed, "Thanks Maddie, you're a peach. I may just tell him to come to you if he wants to or not. He needs to know he's not alone, and if I'm not mistaken it took you quite a few years to find your center?"

She nodded, "Seven years almost."

"And now look at you now, head of your class, and you'll make Teacher for sure, once you go for the test."

"Tomorrow night," she said, with a beaming smile. "I meant to ask Mr. Black, I always see you around here, and I know they say you work for the Masters, what do you do?"

"Me, I'm just a janitor Maddie…" He said it with a smile and took his leave after that. He knew who he was, and what he did, to some it may have seemed trivial, but someone needed to clean up around here.

He walked off around the corner but suddenly felt a tug. It was like a thread pulled, and made him turn down one of the halls that led to a wing of the hospital not often used. The hall here was lit by soft glowing lines of lights that ran along the ceiling and floors that seemed to cast no shadows. It was why he knew right away he wasn't alone when he saw one coming from behind him. So Geoff stopped and waited.

The voice that greeted him was one he knew all too well, and still sent a shiver down his spine. "**You're still telling everyone you're just a janitor, Geoffrey?**" The sound of countless whispering voices always made Geoff feel off. But Adam was still a good friend.

Geoff turned with a smile, "Well I do just clean up after everyone. What's happening, Adam? You back for business? Or something personal?"

Adam shrugged, "**Something personal, and something business**."

Geoff hadn't seen Adam since the incident with Wally those few months back. He wasn't one of the more common faces around the school. Adam spent most of his time not even on the planet.

So Geoff was curious, "So… what can I do for you?"

Adam looked up at Geoff, the smile on his face never reaching his cold blue eyes. This time though the voice that spoke was a little boy's voice, Adam's real voice.

"Well, I had heard my father's gone missing. I thought I owed him that much to find out if anyone has any newer info. Only to hear, your son ran into him."

Geoff shook his head, "Sorry, yeah, he's one of them now. Andrew went out with a full party to find Nancy and bring her home. They were fully set, two groups, four Swords and four Shields, with Andrew. Only one came back, and he was a gibbering mess." Geoff crossed his arms and avoided Adam's eyes, "It doesn't look good Adam. By the time we realized the boy was turned, he disappeared and took six others with him too."

Adam's voice was as cold as his eyes, "So, my father has Fallen."

Geoff didn't know what else to say, "Are you going to be okay?"

Adam didn't even flinch, he just went on in that same flat tone, "It is what it is, but thank you, for asking." He opened his coat placed his hands on his hips and shook his head. It revealed the strange clothes he wore beneath, alien-looking gear, like it was made of tree bark but woven to fit him.

Geoff looked at him solemnly, he was still waiting for the business. "So…"

"It's done Geoff," Adam said quickly, cutting him off.

Geoff took a step back, "What's that Adam?"

Adam looked up at him and rolled his eyes, for once looking his age. He tapped his foot impatiently, "The boy Geoff, you know he's ready," he waved his hand and drew an effigy to him from the wall. "We have watched him for a long time, his center is clear, he is one of us," he let the effigy step about before calling it to him.

Geoff let more of his searching threads spread out, the walls were tingling with energy. He realized too late the trap Adam had laid.

"I have no damn say in any of this? I'm the boy's guardian." He reached down and opened his pouch, the vials inside packed with so many memories and raw emotions. That much power may well give him an edge if this went south.

Adam stepped into the middle of the hallway and pulled out a rod of black steel from his sleeve. Geoff had never seen anything like it, but it resonated with a massive amount of aether.

"I've been to see Azure, and he told me it's time. Wally is no longer your charge. I'll be taking the boy with me." He let the rod touch the ground and pulled up on it, the short rod suddenly growing till Adam held a long spear. He grounded the tip, the spear near twice the boy's height. "War is coming Geoffrey, and we will need every soldier we can get. The best of us for that job are kinetics like us and that boy. How many lives will you trade for one boy? He must be ready." The walls seemed alive now crackling effigies separating from the paint, peeling away to fill the hall around them both.

Geoff filled himself with power, the bright pink glow filling his vision as snaps of plasma arced about him. "I've not raised a weapon for Azure. He needs to be trained to control his gift, not to be thrown in with the Order's dogs of war!" Some of the energy that flowed around him touched on the memories inside Adam's effigies. His mind raced as his power touched them, pain, sadness, love, longing, so much powerful emotion. As his power surged through the effigies around him he drew their strength to him, their blue light changing a bright pink. Geoff blinked a few times as a hot tear escaped his eye to roll down his cheek. "I'm not done yet, I'm not going to just give up on them…"

Adam looked at him, "Them?"

Geoff closed his hand around the vial of memory he kept at his neck, "Anyone Adam. I know we have to win no matter what. But we need people, not heartless machines."

Adam shifted his stance, his probes of aether already skittering across Geoff's mental wards. Adam sighed lightly, "So then, you'll fight me…?"

Geoff took a fistful of the memory vials in his hand, "If that's what it takes!"

"*It won't,*" The sudden voice behind him made Geoff jump. But a hand closed gently around his wrist before he could crush the vials and release their power.

Geoff looked back to see the mountain of a man with the smiling face and swirling galaxy blue eyes.

"Azure?! What are you?"

Azure's smile grew wider still and suddenly there was a pinch between Geoff's eyes as his mental wards were pushed aside.

Geoff blinked as he looked around the all too familiar room he was in, a strange construct it looked like a massive warehouse. He stood at a counter with a package in his hands, packing tape beside him, it was so surreal to be back here. Azure was there too, wearing old dusty-looking clothes and a sweater with tool logos all over it. He looked around as if curious, but Geoff wasn't.

Geoff slid the box aside, and Azure turned to face him as if seeing him for the first time. "Hey... oh, hi. Geoff, you should open that," Azure said pointing to the box.

Geoff scowled at it, "Why, so you can trap me in my head. I know we're in the Dreamscape, I'll get out of here, you can't trap me in my head like some mundane person."

Azure looked at Geoff with a frown, suddenly pulling a tall bar stool out of nowhere and taking a seat. "Who said we were in your head buddy?" Azure took the box and slid it back to Geoff.

Geoff looked at the box and took it, a box cutter appearing in his hand long enough to cut the tape then vanishing before he put it down. He opened the lid and looked inside, "It's empty…"

Azure looked inside the box, then up at Geoff, "Are you sure, look at that." He reached in – packing peanuts that hadn't been there a moment before spilling out of the box – and pulled out a small vial. He handed it over to Geoff, "It's just a little gift."

Geoff took the vial, "This isn't real Azure, so it won't work."

The world shook and splintered, cracks appearing in the walls and floor. Only the desk stayed in place as everything began to flake and fall apart as if burning like paper in a fire. In moments they stood alone in the real Dreamscape. A blasted flat land of glassy smooth ground like a blue mirror stretched out in all directions. Only the desk stood there between them.

Azure looked around and sighed, "You know, it's hard on people, this new world. We have all the problems of the old world and add to that all the new problems." He leaned over the counter his weight making the wood creak. Geoff knew it wasn't real, but in here the mind made it feel real.

Geoff rolled the vial about in his hand, "So what's in this?"

Azure shifted in the seat making it groan under his heavy frame, "It's a memory, one of mine, and one of yours. A memory that we haven't made yet."

The air grew still, and Geoff tossed the vial aside, "No deal… not ever. You can't buy me, I'm not one of the flunkies who follow you blindly. I followed you because I believed you wanted to help. I have been here for fifteen years, taking care of these students. I'm sick of turning a blind eye, blanking memories, twisting fates, and for what?!"

Azure stared at Geoff, and Geoff glared back at him, then Azure started to laugh.

Geoff couldn't believe the smug punk, "What's so funny?!"

Azure chuckled a bit more, but sat up, "Do you know how many people talk to me like this? I'll tell you, it's not a lot. I like it. Reminds me I'm still human." The desk disappeared between them and Azure stood to face him. "You're the first person to ever say no. I paired a lot of guardians with potentials that day. Everything was burning down around us, the world in chaos, Seed running wild, the Bloom starting to rise. Yet all I knew was the brighter future. All these children, all those with the potential to grow. I found guardians for them all, pushed survivors who had the potential themselves to become masters to seek those children out." A long duster appeared in his hands, the gold quill of a master on its shoulder. "Looks like I was right about you… Master Black."

Geoff blinked his focus gone, he suddenly felt the tug of his body and stumbled back. As he caught his footing he found himself beside Azure, with Adam still looking ready to fight. But as soon as he recovered Azure was already laughing, and Adam instantly relaxed.

Geoff turned and without hesitation tried to slug Azure in the jaw. His fist never made contact though, the man simply staring at him as Geoff's fist passed by. "You're a real prick, you know that?"

Azure nodded, "I have to be certain what we do is the right thing, there are many possible outcomes in the world. It's the job of the three to figure those out. The masters need to be the best they can be, to execute the plans we lay. Do you think I'd trust someone who'd just hand over a child without question?"

Geoff didn't know what he thought anymore.

"It was your choice to raise that boy, and you raised him well. Sure he's had some rough spots, that's undeniable. But he's not a bad kid, he just can't control his power yet. I think it's time we stop pretending he doesn't have a center though. Training pyrokinetics isn't easy, to begin with, let's stop making it harder. So what do you say about that Geoff, want to help bring your boy up to snuff yourself?"

Geoff was stunned but nodded.

Azure nodded too, "Excellent. Well then, check in with Taylor, she handles all the coat alterations for the Masters, she does amazing things with a thread and needles. Your new post as a master is a bit more demanding, you're going to do great though… Headmaster Black. Nice ring to it, don't you think?"

Geoff looked at Azure, right in his stupid smiling face.

"Ha! Are you kidding?"

From the look, Azure gave him he wasn't.

Geoff smiled but couldn't help a dry chuckle.

"Have you ever raised a kid? I bet you haven't. So I'm not gonna make it worse, but I can say I have. I raised a boy of my own, long before all this, raising Wally and Anna was about as tame and made all the worse knowing why I was being told to do it. You're a monster." He snatched the coat from Azure. "I know what this coat means, dangled like a Christmas bonus. You're messed up. I won't take the job, I've got enough shit going on around here already. But I will take this coat, the respect boost is at least a little compensation for the crap I've already endured."

Azure just chuckled, petting Geoff on the shoulder. "You know, Adam was right about you Geoff. And yeah, you're right, I am messed up. But, for good reason." Azure's eyes shimmered and his stare wavered off to the wall. "There's a war coming Geoff, soon we won't have a choice who fights. It'll be all or none, and I hope I never have to live that potential future."

HOLLOW MOTHER

9yrs A.E. Central Canada

"A POWERFUL DRAUGHT, brewed from wych-hazel, to awaken the dead!"

The voice on the television called out loudly rousing Nancy from her sleep, opening her eyes to stare at the ceiling fan above her. She sat up fast, knocking a book on the floor, and looking around her living room. She'd been waiting for work to call her back and dozed off watching an old zombie movie.

She rolled slowly to her feet, her stomach upset still since dinner. She looked at the table in the dining room, her half-eaten plate staring back at her. She just had no appetite these last few weeks. She hadn't been feeling good but the doctors had said she was coming along fine, she would be a new mother in only a few months.

She leaned back, carefully reaching down to pick up the latest mommy and me junk book Dave had brought home for her. She picked it up and saw the post-it note right away.

Love you, see you after work

His writing was awful, but he really did care.

"Oh, ooooh ow," she fell back on the couch as pain rocked her. She looked down at her stomach, heavy even for thirty-six weeks. She rubbed her stomach gently.

"Sorry, little lady."

Nancy pet herself gently, and felt the baby move. She smiled, she hadn't felt much movement today.

She tried to get up again, but again pain shot up her back and Nancy fell back onto the couch. She clutched her sides and rolled back and forth trying not to cry out.

"Oooo, baby, you are - Ah - testing m-"

She froze as looked at her belly peeking out from under the hem of her shirt and saw her skin move.

She ripped up her shirt, but nothing moved, her skin was taut, stretch marks creeping up her sides. But nothing moved. She ran her hands across her tummy gently, the faintest sensation of movement. But nothing moved. She couldn't shake the feeling though so she kept feeling and touching. But-

"Something moved!"

The main character in her movie suddenly shouted, making her jump.

She grabbed up the remote from the end table and clicked it off.

"Stupid movie."

She wiggled her toes against the carpet and reached up to stretch, and found her back to be really stiff still.

"Okay baby, I know you don't want to, but I need to move now so you behave."

She put her hands down and pushed up hard, the heavy pain returning as she did. A tight tug pulled at her back, it felt like little needles poking down the back of her legs. She really couldn't move, it just hurt too much. She couldn't even reach her phone, she had left it to charge in the bedroom.

"Alright, okay," she was starting to feel a little panicked now, "I got this. Come on Nancy, get, UP!"

She pushed herself up, a feeling like her skin was tearing rushing up her back and sides. She ran her hands down her legs as she fell forward, the pain like nothing she had ever experienced. She rolled over quickly desperate to check herself over, the pain shooting through her back, but oddly enough, not her stomach. She looked up, tears streaming down her cheeks. She crawled forward through the dirt and debris across the floor pulling herself over the shattered remains of the coffee table.

It was dark, the only light coming from the crackling tv,

just enough to show her face in the mirror's reflection.

Bent over, arms twisted, her fingers blackened, she could only scream at the sight of her own reflection. Twisting creepers sprouting from her back twitched and shivered; the shape of her body still imprinted in the couch, her veins turned into creepers worming their way through flesh and fabric. Her stomach dragging on the floor squirmed, and Nancy felt the bloom inside her twist her guts, made her whole body shift and move against her will.

The pain was excruciating, so much so her vision dimmed, and she blacked out.

THE MARK OF MASTERY

18yrs A.E. Central Canada

"Savera!"

Hearing her name she came back to the moment, the sudden noise snapping her out of her own little world. Savera looked around to remind herself what she was doing there and stood up.

"You alright girl?"

Savera looked at Carly as she spoke.

"Yeah, just daydreaming."

She petted her friend on the shoulder, then got up and hurried to the door on the other side of the long hall, and the guy who called her.

Two people in scribe's robes stood there, smiles on their faces. She smiled back at them and stepped through following them, closing the door behind them.

The room beyond was spacious enough, all the amenities of the scribes at hand with its shelves stacked floor to ceiling with books. A large desk along the far wall stacked high with paperwork took up the greatest amount of space, the clawed feet looking awkwardly splayed out under its load. The rest of the room stood mostly empty, not even any other chairs, just the one that looked like an old barbershop recliner that sat in the middle of the floor.

The man who had called her was someone she had never met before, but who Savera knew by reputation well. Master Eric, a high-level kinetic with a very unique talent, was kind of a rockstar around the school.

His assistant, another scribe with her quill tattoo emblazoned on her collarbone, stepped around the desk and waved her hand absently as she fussed at the desk. A stack of books from one corner of the room began rising and flapping their way to her like an odd flock of birds, stacking up to form a stool she sat at to begin scribbling away.

"Hi Savera, how are you?" Master Eric asked, his voice again coming as a shock.

"A little nervous," she replied, "If I'm being honest."

He nodded and patted the comfy-looking chair in the middle of the room.

Savera looked at the chair, then at him.

He had a calming aura around him, his energy seeming to rise like a happy cloud. She had always been good at reading people, and though this gift was not her power it came in real handy, something she assumed she had learned from her father. This man was so personable, he gave off as much threat as a daisy; and yet.

"It's fine hon, nothing to worry about. We're just gonna chat a bit, and decide where you want your marks of mastery. If you want this, that is." Again he smiled, and it was like the world flexed around him. "No one says you have to get it, it's just a regulation for those joining the fighting ranks. If you're still having doubts about it, you can take time and decide."

Master Eric was beyond powerful, like many of the masters who wore the black robes, she couldn't imagine how one man could hold all the power she felt from him.

She shook her head as she stepped up.

"I'm not backing out, my powers are just like my dad's, I'm a fighter."

"Oh?" He seemed amused, not insulting, more just curious. "Show me then."

She cracked a wry smile and flexed her senses, a quick wash of energy around the room, mostly wood, and steel. It was her wheelhouse for sure, but the obvious way wasn't always the best.

Savera felt like showing off.

She drew vaporous motes of dust from all around the room, pages of paper ruffling releasing trapped bits of pencil lead, grains of sand hidden in the corners swept there by errant chore work coming to her call. The smallest bits of solid matter she could gather swirled to her flowing like water into a stream that circled her.

"Impressive, and useful." He paused and shifted his robe, "Skill like that could be useful to the scribes guild."

She chuckled and then flexed her control, the ring of loose matter suddenly flattening and splitting into two long curved swords of glowing glass.

He looked impressed now, raising his hand she felt his power wash over the blades.

"Held together with excellent control, but;" he closed his mouth and she felt pressure between her eyes as he tried to invade her. It was a light attempt, not meant to break her, and was repelled with ease.

"Very good, you've got real skill hon." He opened his fingers and a flame came to life in the palm of his hand. White-blue in colour the flames danced, "What about Psire?"

She wasn't as good at making flames, but she had learned a trick. She let the matter from her blades dissipate but held the particles loosely. She turned up the heat like Carly had shown her by vibrating the particles quicker and quicker using the water in the air to up the pressure, and just like that-

There was a pop and a ball of green-blue fire shot off like a bullet, straight at Master Eric. He lived up to his title though and simply caught it like she had thrown a baseball. The flames absorbed into his own.

"Eric! What the shit?!"

The woman at the desk had stood up and did not look happy.

"Sorry I -"

"No worries," Master Eric shook his hand and let his flames extinguish. "I can barely make psire. Definitely can't shoot it off like that." He laughed and sat back the air itself catching him in a shimmer as he sat back on a chair made of air. "Useless in combat really, I saw enough death the night of the event, things I won't soon forget, or ever wish to relive. That's why I took the scribe's life, the flower of life was my calling. I'm just here to help you find you, and present you with your mark of mastery."

He raised his arm letting his wide black sleeve fall back to his shoulder. His forearm was a mass of wide black bands, and up his shoulder was his tattooed quill with nine bands of coloured ink. She had seen others with the nine bands, but never the black.

He must have seen her eyes linger on it.

"From before the Event," he rolled up his other sleeve to reveal a similar image. The same lines mirrored inversely the thick black bands on his right arm broken with small lines, were on the other arm in thin black lines that looked like they would fit in the gaps.

"What are they?"

He chuckled and waved his hand, a series of circles made of arcing lightning. Thin crackling circles that formed began to overlap filling the space between them till they formed a massive symbol of energy.

"The harmony of the circle, the unbroken line that is life, that comes around as we are reborn again and how we overlap to affect those around us still just in our being." He tapped one circle and changed its colour from blue to green. "A circle is an interesting thing. These bands represent the rings of mighty Saturn."

She marvelled at them as she saw it now, having seen them in astronomy class.

"So cool. I always wanted a tattoo."

Master Eric stretched his arms high over his head so the sleeves of his coat fell back to his shoulders.

He seemed to almost be seeing them for the first time. The same look she had seen a dozen times.

"My dad used to have that same look whenever he came home with a new one."

There weren't any places like the tattoo parlours of old in Winnipeg anymore, life was hard, and the people grew harder every day. Artists needed to pick through scrap or work in mills to keep their homes warm and food on their plates. She couldn't even remember the last time she heard music outside of the school. Down in the city the arts were being left behind in favour of survival.

"Savera?" Master Eric had leaned in and was staring at her with a cheeky grin. "Floating away on me?"

"No," Savera shook her head and sat down on the edge of the chair. "Just thinking; I just wish that things had been different. I always hoped my first tattoo would be something fun. Not…" She trailed off, she wasn't sure what she thought.

Master Eric just nodded and stepped up to the chair's shoulder.

"I mean, it's been almost eighteen years. I haven't aged a day since that night, but I'm older, I've changed inside. I was with my mum that day it happened, got caught in the mists, it all went sideways from there, like, I don't get why. But like, it did, and now it's all work, all the time. My dad took care of me since I came into my powers, but I mean, shouldn't we be worried about more than just surviving? What if we forget what it means to be human? I don't want to forget art and music." She trailed off seeing his smile had slipped, he looked concerned now his hands paused over a tray of powders and liquids. "Sorry Master Eric, guess I'm just more nervous than I thought I was. I just don't want to forget all the cool things my dad showed me, I don't want it to disappear because so few of us remember it."

"Of course," he waved his hand and let the tray float away back to settle on the edge of his desk. "Change has come, and we best be ready for it. The words of the poets tell us that; there is peace in the end, but till the end keep peace at hand."

Savera giggled.

"What?"

"Isn't that a song lyric from Gorillaz?" She asked.

Eric looked up as if trying to recall then slapped his sides laughing.

"Oh God, you're totally right, kid. Well, I'm glad your dad taught you well in music. Classic," his gleaming slime made the whole world feel warmer.

"Yeah," Savera sat back in the chair.

"Your dad would be proud of you hon, as long as you remember what he taught you, you can pass it on. The arts and religion may change, but there will always be people in need of music and art, at least so long as we protect this world. So we should all make sure that the things our parents taught us are never lost." He waved his hand at the desk and the little tray floated to him again. "So, when I'm done with your marks of mastery, want me to get Tamara here to play with the ink for you? Bet she could put your dad's name on your shoulder or something, in his honour."

Savera blinked, then started to laugh.

"Oh, shit, uh yeah, my dad's not dead," she laughed.

"Oh, I just assumed from how you were talking that maybe… oof, this is awkward." He turned away sheepishly, his arms falling to his sides, sleeves falling forward as he began to laugh. "I mean you mentioned how he had always wanted to be here for your first tattoo, so I assumed he wasn't with us anymore."

"Naw, he just started going on about how proud he was of me, next I knew he was tearing up, and I started tearing up. Gah, it was so weird, I mean, he's such a tough guy, but with me, well. So I told him I'd see him after it was done and came with Maddison, she's also getting her mark today. She's going into the Order of the Shield."

Master Eric turned back to her, his smile lighting up as he floated on his invisible stool to her right side.

"Well then, I have a lineup it seems, so let's get you ladies your mark so you can go show off." He rolled back his sleeves again with a flourish, waving his fingers. "Alright, my sweet Tamara, may I ask for your attention?"

The woman he called Tamara stood up and came around the desk, her eyes lighting up red and blue, her iris twisting into diamond-shaped edges that began to tick slowly in on itself like a clock turning itself inside out.

Savera had seen many combinations of kinetic powers make many different forms of eyes, this was one she had never seen, and it was hard to look away from them. But Tamara had just as sweet a look on her dark chocolate cheeks, her gleaming smile settling Savera.

"Sit back sweetie," Tamara asked, "This isn't as comfortable for some, as it is for everyone."

Savera nodded and sat back resting her wrist face up on the arm of the chair.

Tamara sat sideways on a pile of books that slid to meet up under her. As she did she held her hand up over the ink tray Master Eric had been tending to.

"I'm ready."

Eric nodded and raised his hands over the ink tray.

Savera watched as hair-thin threads of ink slowly flowed up her fingertips trailing liquid from the tray. They swirled around her hand glowing faintly as the bits of glittering paint mixed, powder and liquid mixing in a slow-motion vortex of colours.

Thin points of ink caught in a state of constant motion drew down over her arm and Savera had to fight her urge to try and resist as they pierced her skin. Driving into her flesh the threads stitched down deep, more than any tattoo she had ever heard of. Each time the threads dove down and surfaced she watched with grit teeth as the bands of colour took on form. Each one felt white-hot as it struck, and she realized why.

"Does… this… go to… Ah, the… bone?"

Tamara nodded as she dipped her fingers carefully back into the ink.

"Sure does, a mark that is both permanent and easy to hide. Only another kinetic shown how to find the mark could find it if you wanted to hide it, and only the three people who invented the process know how that is."

Savera watched as Tamara leaned in closer, her glowing eyes so focused and intense on one spot as she worked another line into the pattern of rings. Beads of sweat forming despite the cold didn't fall though, instead, they seemed to rise up and away, as if the other woman's control over the ink was refracting gravity in some way. The ink itself was still glowing, steaming tendrils of misty air rising over the tray master Eric intently watched.

He had yet to use his powers, other than to harass her, she noticed, and she wondered if he was doing anything at all. She was just about to ask when he suddenly sat up and cleared his throat making Tamara jump a little.

"Tamara, take a break. Don't have to do it all at once." He pet her shoulder and Tamara finished her line, both of them then sat back and began to check the work.

It was quite interesting to see it.

"They're so pretty. I'm gonna miss classes," she stroked her arm as she realized it was like graduating high school all over again. That same feeling of accomplishing something that had taken so much time to master. "I always loved learning to use my powers."

"It's never over honestly," Tamara added, "I'm always learning how to stretch my pattern control." She then took a towel from Master Eric, dabbing her brow.

Savera liked that, but she was too focused to say much, watching instead the still glowing ink. One large red line, one thin one for completing her training in internal forces, one thick green one for mastering the basics of bridged powers, and lastly-

"Oh crap, I smudged it!'

She had just meant to touch the line to check the semicircle of blues ink. Somehow though as she had moved the flesh of her forearm, the ink had shifted to leaving a smudge on her skin.

Tamara took the towel off her face, at first a smirk on her face. But her smile soon faded as she saw what Savera meant.

Where she had grabbed her arm to see the unfinished side on the back of her arm the line had indeed shifted and now looked like it had taken on her thumbprint.

"Now, how did you do that?"

Master Eric leaned over her arm, pulling her this way and that as he looked it over. His eyes now glowing again she noticed they had begun to shift and move like Tamara's, cascading inward while they spun in that strange funnel-like way.

"Well, it seems again I need to insist you join the scribes. You're an Inkwell."

Savera had never heard of anything like that before, and clearly, Tamara was amused by the look on Savera's face, as she chuckled before she spoke too.

"This is no ordinary ink, it's tuned with kinetic power and diamond dust. Each grain of don't is inscribed with a code only a few kinetics can manipulate. Who did you say your father is?"

"Raymond Richards."

"Ha!" Master Eric's sudden guttural burst of laughter made even Tamara jump. "No wonder, he's only one stage below you, Tamara. His ability to move earth and water earned him the nickname Skinwalker. And let me guess you can move water too?"

Savera nodded.

"There you go. Why doesn't it say that in your file?" He didn't look mad, but his tone said it all, and Savera felt like she was sixteen all over again, being caught skipping class.

"I'm not good at it, I mean, not really. I can manipulate fine particles of solid matter, but water alone is almost as impossible. But mix them and it gets so much easier." She tried to consciously force the ink back into place but it was no good. "So did I screw it up?"

"HA!" Again, Master Eric's laugh echoed loudly. "Hardly, have you seen your father's mark? He said he was itchy, so we paused, he scratched up under his arm where we had just finished and now the lines are less liney there." Both Tamara and he had a good laugh, then he turned back to her. "I suppose just like your dad though, you'd rather be out there in the world fighting the good fight."

There was no hint of a question in his tone despite how he had worded it, but still, Savera nodded.

Master Eric nodded too.

"Well then, a drip of water for me and we can get back to it. Maybe see if we can make that little thumbprint pop a bit?"

Tamara nodded and tapped Savera on the wrist.

"Turn your arm over hon, almost done."

Savera smiled and held out her arm.

The rest of the inking went quicker it seemed. They chatted about her classes, her friends, everything. Then as they finished up, they talked about the two of them.

"Met Tamara as the world was ending."

Tamara's smile grew even wider.

"He was right in the road, no shirt on, throwing lightning bolts about the street at the seed beasts. Like a mini Thor." She turned her gaze for a moment and blew Master Eric a kiss.

Savera couldn't believe what she had heard though, lightning, that meant he was one of the elite. More powerful for sure than she had ever heard.

"My fighting days are over for now though, and fate has other plans for me." He played with his sleeve and waved his hand at the tray making it float away. "A voila!"

Tamar turned over Savera's arm so she could look at the final piece that had been added, but right away she noticed something.

"Two blue lines?"

Tamara nodded, but Master Eric spoke up.

"What are the external forces, Savera?"

She thought for a moment, then pulled the answer from memory.

"Finding our center, the elemental state of matter that is our focus. Then, the balance, finding the correlation between two states that allows one to become another." She raised her hand and pulled dust from the floor where she had let it settle. "And lastly void mastery, the ninth seal."

"Right, but you never told your teachers that you can move liquids like you can, so that means your training wasn't tailored right." He winked, "Keep practicing and you'll have it down in no time. Besides, we can't change it now, so if you don't train hard and master it, you'll make a liar out of us. You wouldn't want that would you?"

Savera stood up and walked over to the desk and stared down at the coloured liquids in their tray. The longer she focused she thought about it and opened herself to the power she felt inside her. The ink shifted and swirled and she twirled her finger, the parts and particles moving as she willed it, but as they moved she let her focus spread and she felt as the density shifted, separating the heavier parts from the liquid. It didn't stay apart long, but long enough for her to get the feel of it.

"I've never moved just a liquid before."

"But you are starting to see how it works. The heavy metals we use, the method of bonding kinetic energy to them, it was like highlighting it for you to see. Ferromagnetic liquids work really well with kinetics."

Master Eric stood beside her and held his arm out.

"Defensively, and offensively," suddenly she felt as the tray shifted and realized what she had been seeing as she sent more of the ink from his arm out to catch it up. The ink on his arms was what was moving it, threads of black so fine she only caught it now because she was open to her source. He let it go and let all the ink flow out around him, ivy vines that blossomed with red-black flowers.

"Yeah, it's so subtle," Savera could feel it, she wasn't sure how he did it yet, but she saw it now. "I think I get it though."

"Guess we did need to add that second line then."

He held out his hand to her.

Savera was so overwhelmed she just higher him instead.

She hadn't noticed he was so short that as she did his head was under her chin. He just laughed and hugged her back.

She couldn't wait to show her dad.

But as with all things in life, fate is rarely accommodating.

First bell.

It was six in the morning already. Tamara looked at the window, the sky still mostly black.

Master Eric shuffled back to the chair and propped it up all the way.

"Well, it seems we have to pick up the pace, don't we?"

"It does indeed," Tamara added, "Three more before you meet with, the Azure."

Savera still had so many questions, but she truly believed she had all the time in the world.

She left the office and walked over to where Carly was talking to the tall long-haired boy from their class.

Carly waved her over.

"Savvy, you know Wally?"

"Kinda, we don't really talk much," she said, trying not to make it sound as awkward as it felt.

"No worries," he added with a chuckle, "Emily tells me all the time I need to stop being such a wallflower. Mark of mastery? Let's see." He paused as if realizing what he was asking, "I mean, if it's not somewhere-"

"Calm down," she held up her wrist for him to see, "What were you so worried about?"

He heaved a sigh of relief, then thumbed the air in Maddison's direction.

Carly just smirked.

"What?"

"Emily got hers on her thigh, high on her hip almost." Her smile was almost too wicked for words. Wally here got excited and asked her too."

"And?"

Wally coughed, almost seeming to choke, but again Carly filled in the blank.

"Oh, she showed him."

"What?!"

"What, what?" He squeaked.

"Oh, it's not that big a deal man. You're just a prude. I don't know why, but he's saving himself for marriage," she laughed and wound up, punching Wally in the arm so hard he almost fell over.

The three laughed and chatted like that till the familiar creak of the heavy door at the end of the hall made them all turn.

"Maddison?" Master Eric called.

Carly smiled, hugged Savera, and turned to Wally.

"Wanna see my mark later?"

He frowned and shoved her towards the door.

"Get out of here you pervert."

They watched as Carly walked away, another set of footsteps approaching echoing up the stairs. No doubt the last of those who were getting their mark this morning.

"Hey, Wally?"

"Yeah?"

"Did you ever want to get a tattoo before?"

He shook his head. I'm younger than you all, grew up after the Event. My dad never liked tattoos, so I guess I never saw the need for them. I see them all the time. Lots of the masters have them." He wrapped his arms around himself, fingers pensively tapping his shoulders. "Guess this is the only one I ever thought about."

She nodded then looked at her mark.

"I always wanted to get one in honour of my dog, Pac, he was awesome."

"Pac? What's that?"

"That was his name, Tupac, he was my dog."

"Oh," he hummed a bit, "Never had a dog either. You don't really see many pets in the upper city I guess."

"Yeah, not a lot of them survived the Event. But Tupac never even saw that, thankfully too, I've seen what that chemical did to animals." Savera shivered. "I think though," she paused again, still thinking about Tupac, the spots on his face, his soft white fur. "One day, I want a tattoo that has meaning, more than just a status symbol."

Wally smiled and Savera flushed, no wonder a woman like Emily was hot for him. He was quite handsome.

She nodded her head to him.

"I better get going. I report to the spears guildhall at nine, apparently, it's a big day today."

"Yeah, the seers pushed the council to have all our final testing wrapped up by the last bell yesterday." He flipped his coat collar open to reveal the edge of a scribe's insignia. "My dad says it's been a rough year. Lots of people without their spears and shields missing, without any accounting for them."

She had heard that too, her dad had said much the same when she had told him she was joining the spears too, proud as he may be, he was also worried.

"Hey Wally, thanks."

He gave her a curious look.

"Just for talking?"

He shrugged, then chuckled, "No problem."

She wasn't sure why she had said it really, but she felt she owed him, it was an odd feeling, something deep inside her.

She waved and turned before it got even more awkward and started down the hall to the elevator. She had a while still before she needed to report to the guildhall, and that feeling in her stomach was growing louder the further away she got.

Maybe breakfast would help?

Tilting at a Loss

9yrs A.E. Eastern Canada

She sat up quickly, the stupid dream about the bloom again making her head spin, she hated these dumb visions. She looked around and found her book under the edge of the bed and picked it up. An old copy of Don Quixote, she had picked it up at a rummage sale.

Wait, wasn't she just outside? She felt cold, looking around for the breeze.

"Moooom! Amy pulled my hair again," came a shrill cry from down the hall. Nancy jumped at the sudden noise, standing and walking over to her girls. There Nancy found the eldest of her daughters with eyes full of petulant tears.

Nancy planted her hands on her hips, "What did I say about fighting, girls? Mom's waiting for work to call, they...."

Her daughter pouted, "But she pulled my hair!"

A shout of protest from down the hall called back, "I didn't! She's lying!" Amy shouted joining the argument.

Nancy put her hand to her face, "Alright you two, break it up! And no more yelling. Mummy had a bad dream, and she isn't feeling good." She rubbed her temple. A strong throb was growing between her eyes. She needed some coffee. The world rocked and she stumbled into her nightstand. Amy and Madison were staring at her now, they looked worried, "It's okay, mummy's fine, she's just tired." He checked her watch, "Where is that sitter?"

Nancy took Amy by the hand and walked into the kitchen, she grabbed a pair of mugs from the cupboard and poured herself a tall glass of water. She was just starting to relax when she heard a knock at the door. She set down her glass and walked to the main entrance.

"That must be Sarah, hope you girls are good for her tonight, I don't want to hear…," the doorstep was empty. She turned left and right, staring out across the lawn. Nothing moved in the dusky light, the street was empty on both sides, all the way down the hill.

Nancy stepped back in and closed the door, she looked down at Amy. "Did you hear the door?"

Amy shook her head.

"I swear I-"

Knocking cut her off as again the door vibrated.

Nancy froze and peered through the peephole, but no one was there. She stepped back from the door and turned to go back to the kitchen when the knock came again. Nancy frowned looking at the door and waited, and again the knock came. This time she was fast and she peered through the peephole.

Still, no one was there.

"Mum, what's wrong?" Nancy jumped in spite of herself. It was just Madison. "Who's at the door?"

Nancy shook her head, and said, "No one. Pranksters I think?"

Amy came into view, still holding the glass of water. She looked so much like Nancy. "Are we gonna watch a movie? Madison wants to pick."

"Yeah, that sounds..."

A knock at the door rang out.

Nancy looked back at the door.

"Just ignore it mum and come watch the movie." The sternness in her daughter's voice made Nancy look at her.

Again, the mystery knocker made their rapping loud and clear. Nancy turned to the door and grabbed the knob.

Amy's sweet voice was suddenly right beside her, "Mommy, what are you doing? I thought we were gonna watch a movie?" Madison now stood with her sister. Both looked so sad.

"I just have to see who's at the door sweetie, then we'll pick a movie," her head twinges again. She rubbed her temples as memories returned. Wasn't she waiting for work to call?

The phone rang in the living room.

The faces of her daughters changed from sad to angry so fast it scared her. They both stood very still, staring at her. Their eyes seemed to bore into her.

"Amy? Maddie? What's wrong?" Nancy had never seen them like this. Her memories of her girls were all a mess though, the harder she thought the more painful the images that came to her.

Amy; wasn't she the older one?

Nancy stepped back from the girls in front of her, "Who-no, what are you? Where are my daughters?!"

They didn't speak. They just stood there staring. They didn't blink, they didn't even seem to breathe.

As still as statues, they stood frozen, their eyes tinged with a deep look of hate.

Nancy turned to the door, to run, to be away from here, but her hand was frozen to the knob. She pulled and pulled, but the ice was growing thicker. She looked down at the snow flowing in around her, and when she looked up her home was gone.

"ANSWER ME!"

But they couldn't, the things standing before her were not her daughters. Instead a pair of manakins faced her down, their blank faces staring back at her from the other side of the security fence in front of the mall store window.

The hall around her was empty, everything snow-covered as far as she could see. Shops she didn't recognize were crammed side by side. No idea where she was, the glass ceiling long since collapsed letting the light snow drift down on her.

Her hand was gripped tight to a chain-link fence, wet snow and ice freezing her to the spot. Nancy stared at the black mark on her arm, the once beautiful tattoo of a red coral tear scorched off in a fit of rage. She could barely move, not even to force herself to look away from her own snarling reflection in the broken widow's remains.

She wanted to cry, but she had no tears to give, her face frozen, her skin cracked, her eyes sunken and dark. The world was hollow, and all she could do was scream till she had no energy left.

IN NAME ONLY

18yrs A.E. Paris, France

The dimly lit hallway coming off the plane opened up into the airport terminal to a flood of buzzing fluorescent lights. Stepping through the doors, the music changed suddenly in a rush of noise. It was quite jarring to Jack, coming out of the mostly silent corridor from the plane.

He looked around as a woman's voice piped up over the loudspeakers, an announcement in French, about watching your bags and other standard things with travel, but Jack barely looked up. He did glance out the bright white-lit glass window to his left, the cloudy skies hiding the morning light. He yawned a little, feigning tired and rubbing his eyes. Then put on an oversized pair of shades despite the lack of sun. He then pulled his cap low and shouldered his bag and slowly slumped through the terminal.

He was fully awake but needed to keep a low profile as he went through security. It was a trick people in his line of work used often. Look tired, bored, or gruff, make yourself seen, but forgettable, an expert at being the most visible shadow in a sea of black.

He slipped in with a gaggle of yammering American refugees, talking briefly with an older man about how long the flight was. Then Jack got him talking to the woman next to him about the weather and as the two picked up the chatter, Jack slipped away down a side hall.

The trip had been a long one, and people coming in were all in a state of disarray. From the sound of it, he had made it just in time too, this plane was the last one he knew would ever be coming from the states to this airport. A humanitarian effort by the United Nations to try and evacuate civilians. Trying to keep civilians out of the path of the Seed, and the other things going bump in the night these days. Jack could hardly believe it when he had landed in New York with the military presence choking every street, heavily armed soldiers ushering people onto ships or planes roughly. But as hard as it had been to get into the U.S., it had been even harder to leave.

Their military was getting slammed, and so even children willing to work could find a job in the service. So it was that, as he had been pressed at every corner by women and children with posters and flyers. Flashy things that showed men and women in powered armours saying things like, "*Enlist Now!*" And, "*Save the Country!*" It was all propaganda though, there was no salvation from the beasts now. He had seen military forecasts, in weeks the Seed would be gnawing down the walls of the Brooklyn barricades.

It wasn't a matter of if anymore, but when?

Even here in Paris the war on the Seed and the Kinetics waged on. Though it seemed that the people didn't see it, or more accurately said, played at being oblivious. Here at least the virus seemed contained, no more people randomly exploding into fits of energy from nowhere. But the war wasn't over, the intel he had, had made that clear. The kinetics they captured in the U.S. had talked, and what they all said was grim. A war was coming, and soon. But none knew more than that it seemed. Thankfully they had found out that most recently a cell of Kinetic terrorists was plotting something from here in France, so their mission had changed and his unit was redeployed to Paris.

Jack stepped up to the counter to check in, slapping his carry-on on the counter. He pulled out his passport and slid it over to the woman. She smiled and snapped him out of his funk almost instantly, he hadn't seen such beauty in weeks. Her painted red lips had a pouty twist as she smiled, and her sweet voice reminded him of bird-song.

"Bonjour monsieur, comment puis-je vous aider?"

Jack smiled and tapped his passport, slipping into his best American accent.

"Sorry miss. I don't understand French."

"Ah," her smile slipped for only a moment as she sat back a little more from the counter. She nodded though and went on.

"I was jus asking ow I can elp, but I can assume zat you are immigrating?"

"No," he shook his head, "I won't be staying, just a layover for a few days. Once I and the family have met up, we plan to head to Portugal. Sounds like a lot of work is going on there?" He posed it like a question, but she didn't even look up from her screen.

As she eyed her screen her features became less soft, and her eyes took on a dark light. Her smile never slipped, but it was clear from her eyes something had changed. He was good at his job, and he noticed these things. He looked at his bag, tapping the button on the hidden compartment and slipped his hidden gun from behind his back into the stash.

She didn't skip a beat though and waved her hand at the holographic screen, and spun it to face him. His ID was already transposed to the screen.

"Can you confirm zis is in fact, you sir?" She asked, her tone, darker than her look.

He nodded and removed his glasses slowly.

"As you can see, it is, is there a problem, miss?"

She nodded and tapped a few keys, a second image coming up of a very similar-looking I.D. layout but from Russia.

"You ave already been ere, at least according to ze computers." She tapped away at the keys, "Can you explain zis?"

He looked it over, it looked like one of his, the alias he used, but while he would normally use a different name as the last name this one was the same as he used for his American passport, the last name December.

"W-well now," he sputtered as if confused but it seemed he may have been burned so he backed up a bit. "I-I-I don't really know. See I'm..."

She raised her hand and snapped her fingers at a pair of guards, which brought the men to his side in seconds. Neither laid a hand on him but it was clear that he was in no place to sneak by now.

"Now hold on, there guys, look, we can talk this out alright," he said, feigning a fearful tone.

"Venez avec nous s'il vous plait," the stone-faced man on the left of him said. He didn't look like your average airport security either, neither did. Both men had the Axon logo on their uniforms, their hands on their tasers. Jack was in no position to act here, it was too soon to blow his cover, provided he hadn't already, and the terminal was now all abuzz with gawkers and looky-loos.

So, Jack acted sensibly, he raised his hands slowly and let himself be led along through a pair of double doors.

Again, the phonebook hit Jack in the ribs.

"QUI ETES VOUS?! OO ARE YOU?!'

It was a good punch, he gave the guy credit, but it was hardly necessary. Using the phonebook trick meant they could have hit him much harder than they were, so he wondered why the guy was holding back.

"Come on mate, enough of the love taps hit me like you mean it, or let me go, we'll just call this all a little misunderstanding."

He wasn't playing dumb anymore, but he wasn't talking either, and it made these guys mad. He braced himself as if to take the hit, but as the burly bloke punched the phonebook Jack instead relaxed. He let his body move and absorbed most of the force. It was a good punch indeed, but it was wasted effort on someone who knew how to take a hit.

The bigger guy who had been doing the punching stepped back and rubbed his hands. Clearly, he wasn't used to punching people, he had wrapped his knuckles too loosely.

Jack was just starting to enjoy the tenderizing though when the door on the far side of the room opened.

He was more than shocked, and felt as a ball of ice dropped into his gut, his grin slipping as a man he knew all too well came scowling towards the desk.

He looked much older than the last time Jack had bumped into Agent Gilbert, but that mug was unmistakable. His hair was greyer, and his skin looked pale – as if he spent his days indoors now. But the heavily muscled D.G.S.I. operative still looked like a force of nature. The French counterpart to Mi6, the two of them had butted heads more than once. Yet on occasion an ally in the field, Gil, unfortunately, had never taken to Jack's methods. This made it tough to work together. Jack just found Gil too uptight, maybe not as friendly as government murderers could be.

Gil walked over and sat down on the other side of the table, and the two Axon guards stepped back. Jack looked up at them and rubbed his wrists, having already slipped his cuffs. The Axon guys both went for their weapons but Gil just raised his hand and they backed off again.

"Out, fools."

The two men both looked rather sour, but they stalked out the door silently.

Gil pulled a pack of little cigarillos out and held one out to Jack, but Jack just waved it off. Gil frowned even deeper.

"Do you mind if I smoke at least? It has been a long day."

"Of course not, Gil," Jack said with a chuckle, "Mind if I ask you something though? Before we get on with whatever this is."

Gil nodded.

"When did you start working in town?"

Gil tapped the desk, "I'm not sure you would ave urd zis, but ze agency is no more." He took a long drag from his smoke and exhaled slowly, "Even yours. Mi6 is gone, and we are old men. What are you, fifty now? Why are you still in ze field?"

"You know me, Gil, I like to travel," Jack had to bite his tongue as he replied, trying to keep the snap of sarcasm from his voice.

"Ze people in ze city, zis ere, is Axon's concern now." He grumbled as he finished his tiny smoke and put it out on the corner of the table, his face still looked stern. "So, now I ave anozer question," his eyes narrowed. He gestured at Jack stabbing the air with a pointed finger, anger burning in his voice, "What ze fuck are you doing in my country, Jacque?"

Jack leaned back in his seat, hands spread wide to stave the other man off.

"I can't get into the details, Gil. You know I can't. But as soon as I can, I promise to bring you into the loop."

Gil slammed the table.

"Don't throw me such merde, you are here to shit in my backyard. Ze English ave no jurisdiction ere, we ave told your Black Knight and ze Crown to shove zer so-called, *Humanitarian Efforts*." He slid a drive onto the table and a display popped up photos showing scenes Jack knew all too well. Men and women, left for dead, one from Monaco, another from Iran, and China, and on and on. All high target hits confirmed or rumoured, some even his, it was still concerning how informed he was. Gil waved his hand at the images cycling by. "Zis is ze legacy you leave behind, ze Crown doesn't send a group of zer Grim Reapers to peace keep." He tapped the drive, the images disappearing and pocketed the black steel box. His eyes never left Jack as he spoke, "Ou is ze mark?"

"It's not like that Gil, I…," Jack trailed off, he didn't want to lie to the man. He looked at his watch, then at Gil, then back to his watch. He was never alone anymore, the Royal Knight's spooks were always listening.

Gil caught the look and pulled out paper and pen, and held it up.

"I want a list Jacque, ou are you working wiss?"

He wrote on the paper, "*Two taps Yes, one tap No,*" and slid it slowly across the table.

Jack took it and tapped the page twice, "I won't do that Gil, as it stands you can't hold me now that you know who I am. Let me go and I will go."

Gil smiled and nodded, "I am internal affairs, I can hold you as long as I need to. Are you here to kill a politician?"

Jack tapped the page once, "I'm not at liberty to speak of the mission. But as soon as…"

"No more bullshit! Who is ze target? Is it a diplomat? A drug dealer? Some scumbag war criminal? A dictator in hiding? A fuckin alien?! Who is it?!"

Jack tapped the page over and over, then paused at the end and tapped twice. Jack supposed that Kinetics counted as the latter, they weren't human. "I'm not at liberty to speak of the mission," Jack said and drew a little pyramid on the scrap of paper.

Gil slammed the table and stood up, he knew the deal, whether Jack pulled the trigger or not, the deed was sealed. He walked around and slammed his hand down in front of Jack. "You are on ze next plane back to London, if I see you in my country again Jacque, I will not be so kind." Gil then stood up and banged the holding room door. The Axon guards came in in a flash and grabbing Jack by his shoulders dragged him to the door.

Jack held back a second nodding to Gil, and his old rival nodded back.

Men like the two of them were a dying breed, they were warriors, killers. But here they were, both chained by bureaucratic red tape.

"See you around Gil," he said with a smile.

"I hope not," Gil replied solemnly.

From the office, Jack was escorted back out to the main terminal. His bags, tossed unceremoniously at his heel, surprisingly hadn't cut up, or tossed out, it even looked like they hadn't searched any of the compartments for hidden gear. Seemed kind of a shoddy shakedown really, the guards just watching him the whole time. But they eyed him like wolves in winter, keeping him close even as he approached the counter to arrange his flight home.

The man at the counter was a tall Indian man, Sikh from the bright white and blue turban to match his uniform, and the large metal bangle at his wrist as he waved Jack over. The man smiled broadly and reached for Jack's passport without hesitation, his bangle clattering on the counter as he slid the papers over to read them.

"Good morning sir, and welcome to Air London. How can we help you?"

Jack smiled, "Send me home, it appears I'm not welcome in Paris anymore."

"Expired visa? Or-" he glanced at the two men behind Jack, but he barely flinched. "A spot of trouble? Well from one Queens man to another I will happily see you home my friend. The Queen needs all the support she can have right now." He began to type away at his desktop, but Jack suddenly got a great idea.

"You're a Queens man?" He asked slowly, making sure to keep his tone down.

"Of course, as my father before me, and his before him. It is why I work for Air London at this airline, while so many have abandoned the Crown. I know it is not the fault of our Queen that this war rages on."

At last, Jack felt a glimmer of hope, "Well if I told you, that it is of the utmost importance? That these bags are sent to the right people, that they need them… today?"

The man nodded and handed Jack his ticket with a huge smile.

"Then I would tell you, your flight leaves at twelve a.m. and unfortunately no sooner."

Jack looked at the man, checking his name tag, "Thank you, Solomon."

The man nodded, “Please, call me Sol.”

Jack nodded back, “Sol it is. Thank you again.”

He made a vague waving gesture at Jack, “Oh my friend, think nothing of it. They could not replace me here anyways, if I get caught what is the worst that could happen?”

Jack laughed but inside he cringed, in these times who could say what the penalty was for minor treason? But Jack had a job to do.

He showed the ticket to the guards when he returned to them, they grumbled, but there were no other options. They confiscated his passport, still not his real one anyway, and then walked him to the main doors. There they flagged a cab and gave the woman driver specific instructions while Jack loaded up his bags.

“No detours American…,” the one man said to the driver. The other guard was still glaring at Jack, he had been the one who had been punching him.

Jack nodded to him, “See you in the morning lads. Oh and don’t worry, I’ll not soon forget the lesson you’ve taught me,” he patted his gut and winced jokingly.

The man snarled something in French that Jack didn’t catch, then turned and stormed back inside with his partner.

Jack hopped in the car checking the driver's I.D. in the little screen behind her head and tapped the window. “I’m all loaded up, driver.”

She turned and slid the window open, her hair a half-shaved rainbow of bright purple hues braided into a ponytail. “Driver? Buddy, in my cab we’re all friends. I’m Pamela.

****

The cab drove away from the parking lot with a squeal of tires, people all around staring as the vehicle ripped out and around another cab and out to the road. Those same people went right back to milling about, a kicked-up ant would have seemed less chaotic, yet it was much more organized to the trained eye.

Gil was not as strong as Georgia, his powers were more based on enhancing himself physically. So as she stood next to him and looked down at the parking lot he shivered a little at her control. Every person below was being controlled, at a quick count, there were more than two hundred at least, dancing to her tune. Georgia was not like some who meddle with minds, she just put them to sleep and puppeteered their bodies.

The tingle of her power faded to a dull throb, and the people in the street suddenly came back to themselves, most of them abandoning whatever thing they had been doing and heading about their day none the wiser. Though he noticed a few who stopped and looked about as if wondering what they were doing there. But even those walked away after a wave of her hand. She had used them as a screen to make it seem more legit why he got the cab they wanted at such a busy print, but still, Gil didn't understand.

"Why Jacque?" He stepped over to his desk and took a seat pulling out another cigarillo. He tried to light it, but his lighter failed him yet again. He pulled energy to his finger and called a little flame to life lighting it and giving a short pull. He stared at her but she just stood there.

"Georgia?"

She trembled and Gil felt as the power she held released making the pressure pop like a soap bubble. She turned to him, her green-grey dress flowing and flexing. She ran her hands down her sides and smoothed it down before stepping over to sit on the edge of his desk. She grinned and swished her fingers with a snipping motion and his smoke fell in two.

He loved to see her smile but hated when she messed with his bad habits.

"You didn't answer ze question."

“I can not talk to you when you look like zat…," she said with a grin.

Gil touched his cheeks and smiled, he forgot he was still wearing his old man face. A little sweep of aether welled up at his neck and washed up and under his skin, till it tingled out to the tips of his hair, age washing away as he returned to how he looked when he gained his powers.

She smiled and patted his cheek, “Jus like ze day we met.” Which meant he was back to looking like he had eighteen years ago when he became a Kinetic.

He kissed her fingertips, then brushed the remains of his smoke into the bin. He had very little power truly – he could hardly float a pencil – but he was a master of the physical powers. Healing and body modification was a snap to him. He wished he had, had these powers when he was still a field agent, the things he could have done for his country.

But that life was behind him, now Gil worked with the Kinetics, but he didn’t take orders well. It was why he was often not brought into the loop.

She sighed and looked him in the eyes, “You know I appreciate your help, but zis mission, I can not tell you much of. All I can say is zat you were meant to be here for zis.”

He nodded, he knew how it went, nearly twenty years now and fifteen working for the D.G.S.I. had trained him well. He had no problems working with them, especially with Georgia.

“So long as you know mon amour, ze people are my concern first. Zis Black Orchard your masters speak of, it is not zer war. So make sure zat green-eyed prick knows where I stand,” he tapped his desk.

She looked down, the French flag emblazoned on a plaque set below the glass top.

“Flags, like countries, have borders." She whispered tracing the outline of the flag, "But ze coming war is not one which will care about ze imaginary lines made by men,” she hopped down and came around the desk. She gave him a quick peck of a kiss, then she looked to the corner of the room and nodded.

The tall Asian woman who stood back in the shadows of the office walked over, "Are you ready to go?"

Gil looked at her, "Bring er back to me Ms. Yuuki."

Yuuki nodded and waved her hand in the air, "I always do." The tattoos on her arm shimmered as her fingers trailed the air. She had more than him now, four bands to his three. He made a mental note to ask her later which of the trials she had passed.

She pulled her bangs low to hide her missing eye and closed her other eye as if she was searching for something by feel. After a second the air flexed and bulged as space seemed to twist and ripple outward, a hole opening in front of her. Shreds of reality flapping into the vortex making it look like a whirlpool at the edges. Gil didn't recognize the shadow-filled hall it opened to. Georgia stopped long enough to walk back to him and give him another kiss, whispering sweetly how much she loved him in his ear. He kissed her back and nodded, then she stepped on through the gate followed by Yuuki who closed it with another wave.

The silence in the room was stifling, and Gil felt the urge to be away from there. He got up and ran his fingers across his face feeling that same tingle as before, his face going to its older-looking self. He gathered his papers and put them into his attaché case, and grabbed his coat before heading out. In the hall, he bumped into a small man standing beside the door, the poor TSA agent whose office he had commandeered.

"Can I get you anything, sir?" The man asked slowly, as if because he spoke in English Gil might not understand him.

Gil shook his head, "I'm done wiz yer office, Axon appreciates yer compliance."

The man looked around, "What about your partner? Will she not be joining you?"

Gil had forgotten that Yuuki had posed as his partner to get in here so she had some new gate points. He just looked at the young man with a deadpan look and practically snarled, "What partner?"

The young man nodded and retreated into his office, practically slamming the door.

Gil shrugged and walked away. Making his way down through the airport to the main car park to his car, he was ready to call it a day. All this talk of late, this so-called coming war. That feeling of uncertainty crept up from his chest, clawing at the back of his mind like a hungry vulture. He turned on the radio with the hope of calming his troubled thoughts, but the music was off, instead a woman's voice was translating for some dignitary.

"*And with this a historic day, we put our foot down and say 'NO', we will not be bullied. The United Nations will stan…*" the air went dead.

A moment later a different voice came on, a man's voice crackling into life, "*Je suis désolé, il semble que nous ayons perdu la connexion avec notre correspondance…*"

Gil flicked off the radio, he had had enough of politics today.

****

Jack held on tight as his driver swerved about through the cars on the road. Obviously familiar with the roads, she was daring, maybe even a bit risky, which made Jack a little tense. Several times he found himself having to grab the handle above him to keep from being flung about. Needless to say it was more than he bargained for.

His cab driver, a woman as crass as the worst of Americans he had ever met, was for sure a strange one. Her guitar, riding in the passenger seat, buckled in like one might a child or pet. Her outfit was less than professional too, all leather and steel studs.

Yet he couldn't deny her knowledge, as for some odd reason felt the need to point out all the little details of the quarantined city's landmarks. She knew the history of the city better than he did, and he had studied French architecture and art at Cambridge.

France had not changed much on the whole, not like some places in the world. Even still, the Seed had hit France harder than anywhere in Europe, and the virus that spawned the plant zombies was still a problem too. But despite aliens, and revolutions, the people of the city of love endured.

The city's penchant for xenophobia had kept many advancements at bay here, the council that ran the city refusing to alter the city's artistic airs. Not even to shore its defences. But despite that the city thrived, commerce flowed, and one could almost forget the silent war fought on almost every street.

It had been almost twenty years, and things were finally going back to rights. The streets were lively, and the people seemed happy, but the city was not at all safe.

As his cab neared the city center he could see the Eiffel Tower. The A.I.-directed dirigibles flying in for the morning were quite a sight. The military had revamped the tower after the Seed attacks. It still functioned as a radio tower but now was specifically for the airships that patrolled the air. So many places in the world had learned quickly enough that fighting the Seed head-on was folly. The airships over France were a great means to combat the creatures as they seemed ground-locked for the most part.

The tower was still a tourist attraction only now the upper level was set up as docks used for the military ships. The second and third-floor observation decks still let people up, only now it was under guard. He had planned to go see it but a drive-by was all he was going to get it seemed.

Towers two, three, and four were also built, though not as visible from where his cab was now, and Jack had heard that by next year three more similar towers were to be finished. These newer towers were nowhere near as tall but had been modelled as duplicates of the original. It seemed it was as far as the city council would let the military go.

As the government wrestled back control from the Seed they built them as outposts, the six built around the city center to give their drones range across the breadth of Paris.

They stopped at a traffic light and Jack looked up through the sunroof as a shadow passed slowly over them. It was like a fat dragon, long and slender with little thrusters on both sides like wings. One of the blimps up close was on patrol, scanning lasers sweeping a building nearby. It slowed to a stop, a hatch opening on its belly and hovered in place, a long rack dropping down with what looked like eggs in little cradles from inside. The eggs started to drop and Jack lost sight of them as they fell onto a rooftop out of his line of sight.

He was curious so he tapped the plexiglass window, "Miss, the drones the French use, have you seen them?"

She didn't hear him though, as he noticed she had earphones in.

Jack shook his head and sat back, this trip was seeming to be all for nothing.

The light turned green and she took off again and they came along the river. "So! Ever been to Gay Paris before mister?" She suddenly shouted.

Jack nodded, "Yes, a long time ago."

She held her hand up to her ear, "What?!"

He reached through the little window in the plexiglass and tapped her earpiece.

"OH! SHIT!" She pulled her earbud out and laughed. "They fit so nice I sometimes forget I'm not just listening to the radio. So yeah, we're coming up on one of the big tourist spots in Paris," she pointed out the window to the right.

He looked and noticed he recognized the area for sure. They were close to the Louvre. The square was off-limits, pillars and guards staking about. But that glass pyramid could only be one thing. The front doors were gated, with huge metal bars across the windows in stark contrast to the rest of its aesthetic. It made him more than sure it was the perfect place to be hiding. Such a heavily guarded building and for what? They said it was because of the virus, but his sources said otherwise.

"You know, they say that some infected got in there. I think it's a hoax though. I think they just wanna hide the fact that the art in there was all stolen during the riots after the Event, and the place is actually empty." She slowed to a stop at another light and rolled down her window.

"Yeah, seems fishy right?" She chuckled.

Jack nodded, "It sure does seem odd."

"Hey, those Axon guys told me to take you straight to this hotel on the south side." She shifted about in her seat to look at him better. "You wanna stop anywhere before that?"

He looked at her with his best charming smile, "Could we? I mean, I don't want to get you in trouble?"

She shrugged, "Hey, what do I care. Do I seem like the 'follow orders' kind of gal?"

He chuckled at that, "I suppose not."

She smiled and gave him a wink, "Well then, where to, Jack?"

After a few detours to make sure that one of those blimps wasn't following them Jack pretended to finally catch his bearings. He then directed her to the hotel that was originally to be the muster point for his team. He got out and went for his bags. The car door opened and the woman got out. Taller than he expected she had a few inches on him if not a solid foot.

"Need a hand?" She asked, making him turn to her.

"No I…," Jack stopped and stammered.

She had just propped her boot up on the back door of the car and was adjusting her sock, though only her sock came all the way up her thigh. Her pant leg had been torn off, it seemed on purpose too, and she fumbled with a garter that seemed to have loosened, synching up the tiny pink slip of fabric.

She didn't pay him any mind at all so he turned back to the trunk and grabbed up his suitcase.

"No miss, I think I'm fine. Just need to pop in and drop off my things, I have friends in town here waiting for me."

"Well here, that's my card." She was suddenly stuck out her hand, her calf muscles flexing as she leaned in towards him. "You need a ride anywhere, silver fox, just give me a ring."

He smiled and slipped her card into his back pocket. Boorish or not, a gentleman never said no to a reasonable request from a lady.

"I will, thanks."

So with that, he stepped up to the curb, and she got back into her cab and screeched off. He shook his head, Americans never changed, even the ones who didn't live in America.

He entered the front hall of the dinky little hotel and quickly checked in. The others were already here but they didn't have long, he was sure. When he failed to check in at the hotel Gil had sent him to he knew they would scour the city for him. So he made his way up to the room and slipped his key card into the lock and pushed the door open.

But after the morning he was having he wasn't surprised when the click of a gun at his temple greeted him.

His hand snapped up and he caught the barrel, ripping forward on the receiver and pulling the entire barrel from the grip. He turned on his assailant and using his case slammed the masked man into the wall. A flash of steel made him back off catching the blade of his attacker with his pilfered gun part. He parried it aside and brought his knee to bear on the man's wrist, his knife falling from his limp hand to again pin him against the wall using his case.

"Dammit Baker, stand down!" Came a shout from the other side of the room, "It's Jack!"

Jack pulled the mask off the scrawny guy he had pinned to the wall to find Baker, one of the six from the team he was here to meet.

"What the hell Baker, ye ponce, I could have killed you?" Jack growled, stepping back and letting go of the smaller man.

"What took you so long, old man?" Baker coughed, shoving Jack back. "Fall asleep in a park feeding birds somewhere waiting for the KGB?"

A younger agent, he was clearly sour at being so easily disarmed, his petulant glare making that abundantly clear.

"I heard your mother was in town and decided I'd pay her a visit first actually." He sniped back.

Tom, the one who had called out earlier, laughed and stood up. For a mountain of a man he was so soft-spoken and had a knack for being overlooked despite his size.

"Good to see you, Jack, what was keeping you though?"

Jack noticed that Tom kept his other hand hidden behind a newspaper, and that meant he too was no more trusting. It made him hopeful for the future of his craft. Both these men were inexperienced for sure, and Baker lacked tact at times, but both of them were good.

Jack dropped the gun parts in his hand and set his case down.

He shook his head, "I've been burned. Someone tipped off Axon, and the French secret service was waiting, or rather an old friend showed up. So, we have to move now, by noon the whole city will be looking for me."

Baker kicked the wall, "Shit! I told you, Tom, I knew something was up!"

Jack looked back and forth between them, "What do you mean?"

Tom's hand came out holding a silenced gun, slipping it behind his back.

"The city has been on high alert all day. I was second to land, been here for three days, Carter was next with Ashley. But after the ladies showed up things got weird. Baker and

Smith showed up yesterday and already they had doubled the number of drones flying over. This morning that had doubled again."

"Kinetics," Jack shook his head, "They've got their claws deep into this city's still beating heart. They must have tipped off the police, whatever this Black Orchard is that's coming, someone here knows something." He popped the catch on his suitcase and grabbed his tablet from under his clothes. "Here, send the call, get the others here and meet on the roof. We are not done yet, the mission isn't over till we're home having a pint."

Tom took the tablet and put his hand on the screen, it beeped and turned on. He walked back to the kitchen table, set it up, and began typing away.

Baker picked up the bits of his sidearm and smoothly reassembled it.

"I'll go get Ashley, she's just down the hall."

"Be quick," Jack said," we're on a tighter marker than we were before."

Baker just nodded and ducked out the door.

"Message sent," Tom called over to Jack, "Just need your handprint to deliver the payload."

Jack walked over and placed his hand on the screen, a sweep of blue light flashing across his palm. It beeped, and Tom tossed the thing in the trash as a sizzle of electricity surged and wiped the device.

"Alright, let's get to the roof," Jack said with a grin.

Tom nodded and stood up, and together they made their way up to the roof to wait for the others.

On the roof, they found their cache marker and activated it. It was disguised to mimic a standard Amazon drone so their stash of weapons and gear could go anywhere. Ashley and Baker showed up right away, a half-hour later followed by Carter and Smith.

All six of them gathered, waiting in silence till the buzz of a heavy drone overhead brought them about.

The drone was large, big enough that two people could actually get in it and sit comfortably. Jack walked over and swiped his palm past the scanner, the locks on the cargo disengaged dropping the large crate, and the drone took off again.

"Guess the intel was right. They are a hundred percent autonomous," Tom said, watching the machine fly away. "Now we need to find out how hard it is to crack one of those," he said pointing at one of the blimp drones a block over.

Baker popped the crate and began handing out the heavy-looking cases inside. Each of their teammates was tasked with a job, so each one had their own case. Baker was their master in arms so his case had their weapons. He pulled out a set of four sleek square looking P90 assault rifles handing them to Ashley. He slid a rack of six SIG Sauer P226 snub-nosed pistols out next, immediately going to work checking them one by one. Ashley behind him opened the case of ammo and began unloading and inspecting a few of the clips. They were using special rounds packed with armour piercing rounds and a little thermite for some pop. He had seen how quickly some kinetics could heal so he had requisitioned these. It wasn't humane, but neither were some of the ways intel showed them that kinetics used too.

The thought was always triggering, memories of a recording sent by one of the knight's stationed in Japan when the kinetic's had begun their coup. A man freezing to death in a room filled with lava was hard to forget as parts of him evaporated into mist as fast as he froze.

Jack shivered.

"Getting cold gramps? Want me to go grab you a sweater an a earl grey?" Baker laughed at his own joke, but he was the only one.

"Shut it you twat," Tom hissed.

Tom, and Carter, as their techs, had begun to unload the computers they needed. With the shrinking timeframe, shrinking tempers as well, they only had a few minutes to capture one of the blimps, and get it into position, or risk having to try and grab one further away and pull attention they didn't need as a blimp left its route.

Baker knew the risks, he just was still sour about being shown up by a man near twice his age. So he shrugged, and just returned to his work, which left Smith and Jack with the final task.

"Let's go," he said with a nod to her.

Smith nodded back and came over to the crate, taking the handles on either side and lifting the massive device inside. It may have seemed odd, but though it looked like a larger than average king-can beer, what it was, was far more impressive. They set it down and Jack went to work checking the screen on the flip-up handle and inputting his codes.

"We're in er," Carter said, piping up. He had to think before he nodded, her thick accent not always the easiest to understand for him being she was from Kerry and he had done his bit to stay out of the south of Ireland. Despite that, Tom nodded and rushed over to Jack.

"We have forty-five, give-or-take five minutes. After that they'll know for sure they're not in control. As long as we watch for the command prompts, this blimp here, G32Parra, its flight path goes right over the Louvre."

"Alright then, suit up knights!" Jack cracked the release on the top handle and the cans dropped. He quickly handed them out, rolling two over to Ashley and Baker who in turn tossed him one of the SIGs.

Jack put the gun down and set his other gun with it then stepped over the can and gripped it with his feet. With a quick twist of the handle on top he pulled up and the suit billowed up. It was much like the larger Royal Knight's suits. Made of a kind of graphene steel, and meshed with nano-machines. It quickly enveloped his whole body except his head, the steel body of the housing coming apart to be caught up by the liquid-like metal to form a helmet that slid down between his shoulders that could be deployed in a heartbeat.

They all flexed and shifted, patting themselves down to calibrate the suits as it prompted them. He then picked up a brick dislodging it from the edge of the roof and crushed it to powder.

Jack was the lead here so he knew the full details of the brief, he called everyone over and they gathered their gear as they suited up.

"So, the target is the Joyeuse, the so-called sword of Charlemagne. We don't know why but whatever this Black Orchard event, the kinetics keep mentioning is, the Joyeuse is connected. We take it back, and eliminate any kinetics in our way." He looked around at the others, "Any questions?"

The silence in the group was heavy, not a one had a problem with this. The Kinetics, and the Event from eighteen years ago, had taken a toll on more than one of them. This was just another chance to take a shot back. So they worked quickly and suited up so that by the time the ship was overhead, they were all calibrated and ready to go.

The blimp pulled low over the hotel, and they lined up to get on. Jack set the timer on the payload, the cases all set to go up in a poof of phosphorus. He then stooped down and picked up both of his guns and flipped them back, by his hips. The suit reacting to his command, nanotech threads reaching out and catching and holstering his guns.

He looked up as the hangar bay on the blimp opened slowly.

"Everyone onboar-"

"Hold up Jack," Tom called out, "Mind you avoid the drop drones. They're not active but we could only get us on as emergency inflight repair technicians. So as long as we don't touch them we should be fine. But wake them up and we will not have time to hack that many before they link to command and go live feed on us."

Jack looked around, "You heard him. Look, but don't touch." They all nodded and one by one made the jump up into the blimp.

The suit's capabilities always made him smile, it was like his college days, only, even then he could never make a six foot vertical jump. Now he cleared the jump like no one's business, landing on the gangplank above. He quickly moved next to the rack of sleeping egg-shaped drones so Baker could clamber up. The others joined him quickly, Tom and Carter hooking up right away to the system hardwired to keep their signal footprints down.

The hangar doors closed beneath them and Jack turned to his partner.

"Smith?"

She looked up from checking her rifle,

"What's up Jack?"

"Bit'o outside work please," Jack pointed to a hatch heading up, "Head on a swivel an all. Don't need to be caught with our pants down."

Smith nodded and headed up to the top of the blimp for the rest of the short ride..

Though it felt like an eternity, the slow ship plodded along on its route. Soon they were over the target. They opened the hatch as they came low initiating a scan. And as the ship finished its process they jumped out onto the roof of the main building. He looked at the others and tapped the spot on his neck helmet sliding up and clicking into place with an audible snap.

He waved his hand as if cutting the air and the others went for the door. It was covered by a high-tech looking contraption like the other buildings under quarantine. Tom skidded his hand down the frame and found a port plugging into it, and after a few seconds the door lock hissed open. The bars across the frame swung out of the way and it released from the frame, the whole frame lock drawing back pulling the yellow tarp covering off too. Sealed down Carter produced a can from her hip pouch and stepped up spraying a vibrant blue foam on the door hinges, and then around the knob, then she secured a pair of magnetic clamps to the door front. Tom was still watching his tiny monitor and held up three fingers, then two, one. He closed his fist and Carter pulled the door off the frame, metal hinges and lock dripping melted metal and superheated foam. They set it aside inside, then sprayed it down with an orange spray that seemed to freeze the metal in a snap.

Smith took point, Jack right behind her hand on her shoulder his side arm pointed at the ready. They made their way down two floors from the service door and into a long stretch of hall. The signs on the wall pointed left and said requisitions and elevator, and to the right indicating server room and security.

"Hall clear…," came Smith's whisper in his com.

"Copy," came back repeated by the others, Jack and Smith took position in the hall while the others filed down to join them.

Ashley and Baker held at the stairs while the others followed Jack down towards the servers. After several doors of offices though they found a junction box on the wall instead. Tom popped the case in a snap and tried to plug in but just shrugged after a moment. "No good, power is cut to everything except external alarm systems. Going to over-watch," he quickly nodded to Carter. Both of them pulled frisbee sized devices off their backs and tossed them out down the hall. The sleek black discs stopped in mid-flight as tiny rotors in their middle spun up quietly as they came to life.

Tom put his hand on Carters' shoulder.

"I've got control, lead me to the evac point and I'll hold over-watch with Ashley." The drones zipped off ahead down the hall and a small infrared feed came up in the corner of Jack's vizor.

"I've got your eyes," Jack replied, and tapped Smith on the shoulder.

She stood to a low crouch and started off in the direction the drones had flown back the way they had come from. As the drones flew past the stairs Baker fell in behind Jack as they passed. Ashley slipped into the shadows to hold their evac point, and Tom, being focused on the drones, retreated up the stairs behind her.

The drones hummed along leading them down the hall to the elevator, but even with a little force they pried the doors only to find it was stopped above them a few floors up.

Smith looked up, and then down, "Intel on the target puts it three floors down. I recommend the two of us scale down while the others secure the stairs for evac route. Two floors down, two floors up?"

He was inclined to agree with her but before he could agree Baker stepped around and jumped in and grabbed the line, "Too slow teacher's pet." And with a chuckle disappeared into the dark.

Jack shook his head but looked at the others."Any of you know what the Joyeuse even looks like?"

Carter and Smith shook their heads. "Great... Looks like I'm babysitting then. Well Smith take lower level Carter you take the stairs up top. Either of you see so much as a shift in the dust you radio in and get your ass back to evac, I want no surprises."

Both women nodded and in a flash were through the fire escape door behind them and gone. Jack gave a little sigh and motioned to the drones, "Tom, be a dear and find our friend Baker please."

"Copy," was all he said and both drones disappeared down the shaft.

Jack then waited till their displays in his heads up display showed they were out in the light and followed after. The open doors were open to the right floor at least, coming out cautiously onto the floor of the service hall looking around.

The hall here was much like the one above only there were not as many doors. If schematics were right the doors here were a kind of service line, hidden passages built behind the exhibits for the former staff to travel about when the museum had been open. He noted one of the drones had stayed back and instead checked the other feed. It had the cam hovering in the middle of a hall of statues and in the middle of them a strange scene like nothing he could have imagined.

Jack bent low and ran his fingers over the ground in the hall, his finger even in the suit could feel the spongy texture.

Baker was beside him, and he seemed confused too from how he stared.

Jack stood up and held up a bit of the mushy material in between his fingers.

"What are we looking at here Tom?" He asked.

The drone above them gave a beep and a scan passed over it, then a small pincer came out from the edge of the disc and took a pinch.

"Spectrometer says it's organic but it's hot, radioactive hot. Good thing these suits are sealed, that sample is giving off the same signature as the Seed." Jack froze and looked all around, the walls, the floor, the ceiling. Everywhere you looked black slimy patches of grassy looking mold crept slowly claiming dominion. That meant that the air would be brimming with spores. He touched the mic at his ear, "Smith, Carter, call back..."

A second later Smith came back, "Copy," her deep breathy whisper steadying him a little.

"Carter, call back," but the line was silent. He looked back at Baker, "You and Tom get your asses to the fire escape, now!" He shoved Baker back towards the elevator.

The disgruntled young agent turned back at him, "What do you think you're gonna do old man?"

Jack reached down and his pistol came to hand, "My job, now you get up there and make sure I still have a team to extract at the end of this." He tapped his com again, "Tom track down Carter and keep an eye on my back."

"Copy, drone two set to follow assist," The drone above him suddenly hovered low, a little arm coming down from under it. Jack placed the SIG from his hip into the cradle and clicked it into place. A beep from the drone and only its feed was in his h.u.d.. "You have fire control Jack," Tom said quickly.

Jack looked around and watched as the display in the corner of his visor now followed where he looked, with the little green laser on the gun sweeping the hall.

"Chuck us a nightcap Baker," Jack whispered.

Baker grabbed his own sidearm and tossed it to Jack.

The second drone that had been scouting returned suddenly, and zipped past them both and back up the elevator.

Baker stopped and turned to him, "Hey Jack?"

Jack looked up from checking the clip and caught the extra clip Baker tossed,

"Thanks."

"Yeah, just never mind, and don't go gettin killed yet, grandad," and with that, Baker turned and headed to the elevator.

Jack watched the drone feed till he was sure Baker was up the shaft. He watched as he slowly opened the door to the fire escape to find Smith was already there. She nodded up at the drone, and the two were gone.

"I got this Tom, just keep a door open for me,"

Knowing they were fine, he flipped his feed back to his drone, and Jack slipped through the door into the exhibit hall.

****

The stairs were dark but with infrared on Smith had no issue seeing. She had been down two floors, the thick mist and heavy moisture still clinging to her suit. She now realized it was probably spores and it made her skin crawl. But the thought that Jack was going into that alone made her even more worried. She had worked with him several times now and though she knew he was good, he could be reckless.

It was all for the mission

Or so he would say, as she was pulling out a bullet from his shoulder, or bandaging up burns. But the Seed weren't like people, they didn't leave survivors.

Smith paused at the service door that would take them back to the others.

Baker paused as well, looking back at her, "What's up mama?"

She didn't bother exerting the effort to frown; he couldn't see her face. But she let the venom in her words drip heavily.

"Unlike Jack who chuckles when you call him Grandfather, I'll just shoot you when your usefulness is up, boy." She looked up the stairs but nodded to the door, "Go on ahead. I'm going to make one sweep for Carter."

Tom's voice was suddenly in her ear, "Jack's orders were to pull back to evac."

Smith looked up at the drone, "And we will. All of us. I'm sending Baker back to you."

Baker didn't argue this time, he just nodded, turned, and opened the door for the drone and took off.

She wasted no time either, barring anything she didn't have the time for. She needed to get to evac before Jack. She had to find out what had happened to Carter fast.

The stairs above were much like the next floor. The door was barred so she left it alone, the next floor up too. But that was where Carter should have been, so Smith took a quick look about.

There were a few scuff marks along the rail she noticed as she scanned the area. So Smith leaned back and brought her rifle up and flicked on her target sights. The mark on the rail indicated something had been dragged up over the edge and up through the center. She stayed back from the rail after that, hugging the wall and walked slowly up to the next level.

The walls here looked slick like they had below, a grey mold creeping along the walls and ceiling, the floor too felt almost like it bounced under her steps. Strands of what looked like grass blowing in a breeze reached out from the walls as she passed, but as she checked her ambient air, her suit said there was no breeze. That made Smith stop. She knelt down and touched the floor gingerly. The ground was definitely colder, the low temperature over the hotter ceiling temperature making a little rush of air that made it sway and move.

Smith came around the next set of steps and onto the landing. The door here had been torn clean off the hinges and lay in pieces all over covered in vines. One of the strange flowers had broken through from a vent above her, the corpse remains of a woman half stuck up in the ceiling. She had clearly been trying to escape the gas and died anyway.

The air from the hall was much colder, but that didn't make any sense. Tom had said that the power was out.

Scanning the area Smith found more scrapes in the ground. It seemed as if something, or someone, had been dragged here.

She slowly slipped into the hall keeping down, "Tom, you copy?"

"Copy Smith," he said right away.

She scanned the hall gun up and alert, listening for even the tiniest sound. "I thought you said the doors were all closed up? I've got power to the air conditioner up here and an open door.

He was quiet at first but spoke up after a moment. "I'm showing no power still Smith, I'm sending the drone back up to you, stay put."

"Cop…"

She took a half a step and pitched forward, the world falling away beneath her. She spun and threw her arms out to try and catch anything to arrest her fall but hitting something mid fall she cracked her head and spun backwards. The suit's self preservation mode kicked in and like a cat twisted her about so she landed safely, but the force of scrambling as she fell had knocked her rifle from her grip.

Pushing up off the floor from all fours she looked around slowly.

A heavy ice-fog blankets the room here, it was so thick it filled the room and billowed up to the floor above which was how she had missed it. Not even a glimmer of light pierced the lightly glowing green icy mist.

The ringing in her ears from the rush of adrenaline subsiding Smith noticed a buzzing sound. Her com had taken a hit it seemed, and shaking her head in an attempt right it did little good. In cracks and spits though a voice came through after a moment, she could hear Tom's voice, feverish and panicked.

"Smith? Smith? Do you copy? Where are you?!"

His shouts were frantic, and she felt a pang of regret for not listening to him.

"I copy… Sorry. Fell through a hole," she mumbled looking around. The room she had Fallen into must have been huge, she couldn't even see the ceiling, or where the green light was coming from, the fog obscured everything.

The suit was registering below zero temperatures around her, but the fog in the air still beaded on her h.u.d.. She tapped her helmet and switched to thermal and froze. The room was lit top to bottom in heat signatures, squirmed with activity everywhere she turned. Writhing human forms crawling about the walls, hanging from the ceiling. She wasn't safe on the ground either though with some just swaying gently around her. Everywhere she looked the bodies filled the room on her h.u.d.'s display.

The room was below freezing despite the body's temperature. Huge black patches of icicles hanging down like spikes from the ceiling. Smith couldn't see why, but somehow the power here was still pumping cold air.

She had seen these zombified people before, they were stupid, and strong. They seemed to be sleeping though, so she picked her way carefully around them. Like flowers in a field they spaced out in even rows, but she had to avoid vines from ones who had taken root.

Smith checked her heads up again, it was under minus ten degrees. She changed her display, running through the different spectrums, and that was when she found her. A black smudge that flickered against the sea of yellow and white.

"Carter," Smith hissed through her teeth. She could see the other woman dangling from the ceiling. Her suit, though designed to blend her temperature, was breached. Held in the flower-like jaws of one of the zombies on the wall. Clearly, from how she kicked now and then but was quiet, she was past stage one already, that meant she was either stage two or later, trapped in a deep sleep. She would be past the recovery point and would wake from her comatose state one of them in only a matter of hours. The only cure from here was more of a mercy than anything else.

Smith cursed their luck but then breathed in a sigh, only a few feet away was Carter's gun. It must have Fallen while she struggled or been pulled from her. Which meant Smith at least had a chance.

She slowly picked her way to the gun and picked it up. Her suit interfaced and the safety disengaged for her too, a second stroke of luck. It was almost empty, but she still had two full clips of her own. Smith wasn't worried about the ammo though, these things were asleep it seemed. So Smith turned on the krypton laser on the guns sights and swept it through the fog.

As she did it passed over the objects and creatures in the room, working better than the thermal. She swept it around The room at waist height and after only a few passes caught a glimmer of reflection back. Smith ducked and dipped through the frosty jungle of flower faced monsters. Careful to avoid the flowers at all cost. Finally to the wall she found what had made the laser reflect. As she had hoped it was a doorknob, she tried it slowly. It creaked. Smith froze. But none of the monsters around her moved more than to sway as they did anyway.

She knew she'd have only one chance. Smith looked back up at the ceiling and found Carter. The suits they wore all had safeties in them. Certain modifiers so that if need be they could avoid capture. That in the case of an agents death, the Knights tech, wouldn't fall into enemy hands.

Smith took aim, the head, the only guarantee at stage two to kill an infected. Smith cursed silently, knowing there was no other way. After all, if their positions were reversed she'd have wanted Carter to finish her off quickly too. The gun felt heavy in her hands suddenly, the trigger like a lead weight. She tried to pull the trigger, but she couldn't do it.

It was a twinge in her side. Smith looked down to see what it was, then up into the face of a man. "What did you…," Smith retched inside her suit. The mask opened and she grabbed at the flower latched onto her ribs. She hadn't felt it bite her.

The man stepped closer and wrapped his arms around her, "An English woman. So beautiful, so strong, but ungifted. Se non problem. You will only add to my garden ere." His eyes were glowing brightly in the fog, beaming with joy at her, a strange mix of bright green and purple-black that lit his chiseled features in nightshade hues.

He was rather handsome, oh but she was tired…

Stage one.

The thought hit Smith like a train, she had always known this job would get her killed some day. She was a government assassin. She just never thought it would be this job in particular. She pulled her side arm and pointed it at the kinetic who held her.

He chuckled mirthlessly, "Mon couer, zat will not kill me."

She laughed back, spitting blood in his face, "Its not for you Pig!" She aimed and fired, the explosive round hitting Carter in the head. In seconds her suit began to glow as the nanites that made it up began to melt down. A rapid conversion activating to convert their components to thermite. The flames were instantly so hot the creatures around her burst into flames.

The creature holding her hissed loudly lifting her off her feet. "You foolish bitch, you'll ruin ma art!"

She smiled but tapped her com, "Tom?!

The kinetic looked up at her confused, "Qui?"

Tom's voice was suddenly in her ear though, "Smith, where are you?! Carter's signal just flat-lined!"

A cool tear trickled down Smith's cheek. She had no idea what awaited murderers like her in the afterlife, but she wasn't afraid. Smith only had one regret. "Tom, tell Jack I tried…"

"Smith, you're not making any sense," his voice was panicked. She could hear the others in the com too now. Anders and Baker were both shouting for her location.

Smith just killed her com and tossed her gun aside. She knew this monster wasn't going to let her get a second round off.

His eyes swimming with energy his grip on her gut loose, he didn't move. But from the way he stared at the flames, and the strange way the fire seemed to bubble it was clear he was doing something. He was so focused, but so was she.

Smith could feel her body going numb, onset stage two symptoms, she had no idea it could progress so quickly. But she leaned in and grabbed the kinetics collar.

"Oi! Cunt!"

"WHAT?!" His head twisted unnaturally to face her, spitting in rage as he screamed at her.

Grinning at his angry face Smith dropped the pins from all her grenades down his shirt from, and with a last chuckle, hugged his face into her chest.

"Cheers mate!"

****

The blast rocked the whole wing of the building so hard Tom and the others felt it two floors down. He looked at the others as the notification in his visor popped up to show Smith had flat-lined too. In his readouts the building was all a mess. The floors above them had fire alarms going off. Main floor alarms were going off in all corners, and still Jack was quiet.

"We're pulling back now," he nodded up the stairs.

Anders nodded and made her way up, while Baker still watched the hall.

Tom called the drone back and once in sight set himself as the follow target. It zipped faster to him and he shut off his direct feed and followed after Anders.

He came around the bend of the stairs up to the fire escape. Moonlight spilling down from above illuminated Anders as she came to the upper hall. The whistle of a strong wind picking up. Turning she looked down barely raising her hand and the whistle of wind became a roar. A hail of machinegun fire tore through the doorway hammering Anders sideways. She was flung back falling down the stairs and into his arms. Thankfully the armour had taken the brunt, but the impact had knocked her out. Small caliber rounds weren't enough to penetrate the nanomachine enforced mesh that made up the fabric, let alone the kinetic plating of their armour. Unfortunately falling down two flights of stairs after getting peppered by machine gun fire was.

The silver-blue shine of the moon reflecting off white caught Tom as he looked up. One of the French drones now standing in the door. It stood on four legs, its rounded body and a myriad of red eyes glaring about. As merciless as a spider it gave no warning, and made no demands for surrender. Two panels opened on it's back and an already whistling minigun spun up ready and began to fire.

With Anders in his arms he pitched back down the stairs landing hard on the level below. Quickly he tossed her aside and pulled a grenade tossing it back up the stairs. The drone came around the corner just in time as the explosion went off blasting a huge section of the stairs to smithereens.

It was far from enough though, as three more dropped down through the gap above ready and firing.

Baker was beside him with a rifle in hand, and the two of them laid into the mechanical walkers. Thankfully the drones weren't very tough and the explosive rounds were. Their shots tore limbs from bodies, and shredded the machines apart like swiss cheese. But for each they destroyed there was still more that came. Three more fell making a nice blockade, but in a moment the sound of metal being dragged could be heard and two more dropped down from above.

Baker tossed a grenade up the stairwell and grabbed Tom, Tom grabbed Anders, and all three tumbled back down to the floor they had come from.

The stairwell above collapsed and caved in on top of the drones. Tom couldn't see anything and switched through the spectrums on his visor to get line of sight on anything in the smoke. It seemed no more drones were coming so both men relaxed and lowered their guns.

"What was that about?" Baker asked suddenly, cutting the silence, "I thought we had two hours till a second patrol would be in range?" He kicked the door, power suited foot smashing right through the metal frame.

Tom shrugged, "We did, but they must have had a change in their routine."

Andrea suddenly tapped his back and Tom slowed enough in his run to bank a corner for cover setting her down.

"You okay to walk?"

"I'm fookin great," she slurred, holding her head. "Evac was a boost. Sa where to now?"

Tom didn't know.

Baker, who had been watching the hall suddenly leaned back around.

"Well whatever we decide, we better hurry it up." He quickly backed up and shoved the two down as a laser swept the hall. "We can't hide in here."

Tom quickly reloaded and did a check on ammo. They weren't looking good.

"We better go down. Find Jack. Can't be worse than this toffee pie."

****

Thick slime slathered the walls and ceilings everywhere Jack looked. Constantly wiping at the condensation beading on his helmet made him switch his suit to a lower temperature so he could see without having to switch spectrums. It was a slow crawl wading through the accumulating muck in the museum. But odder still than where the water was was something else. The exhibits were untouched.

Art on the walls, pieces hanging in the air, even the sculptures submerged like he was, all of it, dry.

He couldn't have explained it if he didn't know the answer.

Someone was doing this on purpose.

He passed another dead seed, it's body sprouting flowers that looked like angry red trumpets. Only on their bodies were signs of rot, sunken eyes leeched out, bodies swollen and brown but hard as driftwood. They had obviously died in a fight, many missing arms or legs, heads split like melons on the beach.

He crept along the hall, sticking close to the walls, careful to avoid anywhere that looked like they were being protected from the water. It seemed a safer bet to slosh as quietly as possible through the still waters than to disturb the dry spots that remained untouched.

He checked the maps as he went, signs pointing to the room where the sword of Charlemagne should have been, but as he neared the room he found the display empty.

"Tom copy," no reply. "Tom, do you copy?"

Jack had already been on edge, the warzone of a museum, the flooded halls, now this. It wasn't like Tom to-

The building shook with such force that cracks above his head rained plaster down like a heavy snowfall, a layer of white settling on the surface of the water all throughout the hall.

"What the fu-"

"This way…"

The sudden shock of the voice behind him made Jack spin about gun up at the ready.

The room was empty still, but there in the gloom a glimmer of light flitted away down a side hall and out of sight.

Jack wasn't stupid.

He took only a quick moment to think back to the map of the rooms on this floor, where the speck of light could be going. The hall there would twist going up to the second floor or around to the grand hall beneath the glass pyramid. The likelihood that who, or whatever was going up was likely, but it posed no points to ambush with the close quarters hall there. So he backtracked one room and hung left heading towards the grand hall from the far side.

He moved slow and carefully through the waters, no chance of stealth. The sound of the water might as well have been a dinner bell to these alien beasts, so he set his drone to over-watch and let it scan the room so he may at least have warning. It zipped through the open doors to what had once been the main entrance to one of the grandest museums in all the world, its cameras sweeping the whole room to reveal a perpetually flowing waterfall that fell from the top of the pyramid. The room had been leveled, the tall stairs up were gone and lay in chunks of concrete and twisted metal. The bits of Fallen stone made tiny islands in the lake in the center. The light of a full moon from above shone down on eerily calm waters.

Jack looked up to where the waters poured from and shivered. A dark hole opened into an ever-flowing abyss pouring waters into the room. But Jack had driven past it that day, the pyramid had been sealed in steel, yet here he was standing under a moon filled starry sky.

"Well that's unsettling," he mumbled quietly.

"*Is it?*"

Jack spun but the hall behind him was empty.

"*I just thought it was so beautiful. I miss the sky.*"

The voice was behind him again but this time he used his drone instead to scan the room.

"Quit playing kinetic," the drone locked on right away to movement in the water. "You can't hide you witch."

"*A witch couldn't, but I am no witch. I am an immortal, and hiding is what the Fae do best. Nimue taught me, and only Nimue can be here. You are not Nimue, so you aren't welcome, NONE OF YOU!*"

Pillars of water shot up all around Jack, bursting up from the depths like an octopus' arms, tentacles wrapping around his body before he could react. The tentacles formed hands closing around Jack's wrists and locking down on him in an iron grip. They took his gun from him with ease and surrounded him in a cage of water dragging him to face the woman as she bobbed in the water.

He thought to call the drone, but it was hit too before he could and the connection was cut, its view going to static.

"*Fuck off!*" The woman's voice screamed, "*Leave this place!*" The many hands dragged at his armor, as if trying to find a way inside, "*Stop yelling at me!*"

Jack was shaken and pulled around violently, but even through that he hadn't said a word since she grabbed him, so it made him wonder.

"Wait, I didn't say anything," he called out, "And you're the one yelling."

"*Not you, them!*" She gestured aimlessly at the room around them, "*They never stop!*" Jack looked around, but aside from them there was no one.

"We're the only ones here," he said, trying to see if anything might make her grip loosen.

"*Oh?*" She paused for a long moment, "*We are?*" She seemed very confused as she floated towards him, "*Right, sorry, you're right.*" She flinched as if hit by something, holding her head, "*No, why am I sorry? I can't always be sorry to no one. And no one can be here, I'm alone, you're just in my head too,*" her eyes grew wide, a deep sadness as tears flowed down her cheeks, "*Aren't you?*"

"No, I'm here."

"*No, you can't be here.*"

"I promise... I'm very real."

"*I told you all to fuck off! Now get out of my HEAD! Only Nimue can be here!*"

"You're a mite bit nutters aren't you, love?" He asked, leaning towards her.

"*No, no, no, NO LOVE! I had love, children, husband, they loved me, no, they still love me. You, you have no love! I can't feel it, that suit makes you hollow. You knight's. Nimue tells me you're the ones, one of you could love again, but I think you're F'd. You can't love. But Nimue says she wants to talk to you, so-*"

"Wait, who's Nim-"

She didn't wait to hear his question though, waving her arm she sent Jack spinning, thrown about inside his prison of water. Rolled about till up or down didn't matter as the whole of his vision became a blue-grey glowing blur.

When finally it did stop he was kneeling, but Jack wasn't where he had been before.

The ground under him was smooth as glass but rippled like water at his touch. It reflected the light of a bright setting sun and as he looked up he could see a single tree far off in the distance that looked like it may be massive.

It was like nowhere Jack had ever seen.

"*I don't like bringing you here.*"

Jack rolled away from the voice beside him coming to his feet in a fighting stance. The woman who sat beside him with her knees to her chest was not the same woman he had seen. She was thinner with long silver hair that flowed down into the ground around her as if one with the waters that made up her silvery dress.

"I don't much like it myself, love?" He smarmily replied as he gathered his wits, "I can't say being kidnapped is high on my things to do list." He said with a chuckle. He looked down at his clothes to see he was no longer dressed in his gear. Instead he wore a knight's armour, heavy scale plate clinking as he moved. "I do like the renaissance fair remodel though."

The woman glared at him.

"*Kidnapped? No, all we have done is save you from yourself.*"

"Saved me?"

She fixed him with a gaze that made him almost back up, her bright white-blue eyes glowing like swirling waves.

He cleared his throat.

She sighed and stood up, floating towards him across the water, her feet never coaching the ground.

"*You've been chosen, and that false knight's attire was stripped away. Your heart has been weighed, and now you will find yourself pressed to service.*"

Jack tried to back away, but this woman was quicker than he was. She grabbed his jaw and held him tightly looking down on him.

"*And you will do this, I promise.*"

"You can't make me do anything you monster! I serve the Queen! And I will never betray her or her people. I will deny you to the end, puppet my body if you would but know I will never give in. So long as there is good in the world, I will fight to see freedom and peace!"

She froze in her tracks.

"*Then you serve the people like a good knight would.*" She released him then and he fell back. "*Rise Artri, reclaim your fate in your own hands.*

"Oh I- Wait; what? How do you-?"

"*I have seen your heart and mind laid bare here, your name was known to me long ago as the one who would carry the blade of the gods to the only ones strong enough to wild it without going mad.*" She smiled and bowed, the flows of glassy water releasing around her. "*Here in this world we cannot lie. We are bound to oath, to speak only truths. Had any of what you said been a lie, your true words would have come out.*"

"And you?" He felt oddly calm as he asked her, despite that he knew. He thought it better not to push the narrative though and instead stepped back and squared off.

"Who are you, really, why are you here?"

Her eyes glazed over, blue glow now black as a moonless night sky, her head rolling back, her whole body going rigid.

"*I am the lady Nimue! Trapped within this place so long I felt the stir and have held these blades here for those who would claim them. A guardian of the power they hold.*"

She seemed to return to herself then, looking down at him, her face somber, eyes a bit darker than before, but the sky cleared in a blink, the clouds were gone. The snaps and cracks of distant thunder faded, and soon Jack felt his chest begin to burn. He exhaled heavily, not realizing he had been holding his breath, he had never been one to feel fear, but things felt differently here, like he couldn't hold back his feelings here.

"No, you're not some fairy, you're a monster, an alien from another world who brought war and plague on an innocent world."

"*You have no idea, space is vast, intelligence without end, I have seen countless worlds like this blue gem fall like so much wheat before the storm. You call me alien, this word hurts no more than breath can. Different is all you call me, and yes I am. But is that such a crime, I think not,*" she whispered those last words so he had to strain to hear them.

"Why am I here?"

"*I told you, you are here for this.*"

She raised her hand and the world around him swirled and twisted, when it stopped they were at the base of the distant tree he had seen before. There, sitting back against the tree was a strange shard of steely-looking material in the rough shape of a sword, like no picture of Charlemagne' sword he had ever seen, it radiated a power even he could feel..

"What is it?" Jack couldn't understand it, but he couldn't look away from it, the thing called to him like a siren's song.

"*This is your test, handed to me by Merlin himself-*"

Jack wanted to laugh, he wanted to spit at her, call her a fool, call her a liar, but he couldn't.

"Merlin is just a myth," he stammered, still slowly walking towards the blade and the tree.

"*A title of sorts, a great man of many names, he was a story teller with power beyond mortals blessed to him by his bloodline.*" Her voice echoed in his head.

The thing in front of him looked like no sword of kings he would ever have imagined, more like a fragment of a bigger piece, or steel scrap hammered roughly together.

"Excalibur?"

"*Known also by many names it is not some thing of fanciful tales. To hold this does not make a man a king, nor even a leader. The one who will wield it will only bring death. A sword is not a gift that brings life, it is a curse on your enemies that can bring death.*"

He turned and looked at the woman, but he could find no more words.

"*So what would you do with it? Would you seek to rule? Cast it into the pits for all eternity?*" Her rage grew as he remained silent, her final words spit at him in a rage that shook the world anew. "*WHAT?!*"

He turned away, he knew he was no man fit enough for anything but to kill, a murderer, but even he didn't deserve to be cast yo that fate.

"Nothing. I don't want it! I don't want to kill anyone, no more." He knew that words were true, he had never wanted to be a killer, an orphan raised in the military he had set himself apart not because of his violence but his valour. But decades of service had stained his hands in blood, and how was he to know who was innocent or guilty. His commanders had made him a weapon, to be pointed and set upon the world to soak the soil in crimson justice.

Now he stood here crying, heart torn open, past lain before him to see like a tapestry of some monster.

She nodded, floating to the object and picked it up then stepped back towards the water and slowly began to disappear. With each slow gliding step she sank further below the water's surface till only a shadow fading away left any proof she had been there.

"*Poke*!"

Jack spun about to find himself face to face with the crazy woman from before, back again in the halls beneath the Louvre knee deep in flowing water.

He stared a moment, blinking away tears as he looked around.

"What-?"

"*You're worthy.*"

Jack scrubbed his eyes with the back of his hand looking down to find he was no longer clad in armour of any kind. In fact his clothes were gone completely.

"Where are my clothes? And my armour?"

She looked at him

"*Nimue said it would kill you, so all I can give you is this Artri.*" She waved her hands over the waters and a bright glowing ring appeared beneath the surface. That same slender blade made of twisted metal rising up from under the water.

Her hand held high till it floated in the air, she then took hold of the blade by the hilt and held it out across her arm. Laid out for him to take Jack stepped close then stopped.

He had been Jack for so long, but that was who he had been, not who he really was.

"No one has called me Artri since I was a kid. Some nun named me that at the orphanage, son of a bear or something I think it meant? So for now, I think I'll just stick with Jack"

He gave a little chuckle as he sloshed towards her through the water.

"*If you must. But it also means, warrior king,*" she giggled a little at that. "*I like the bear thing though. I love animals, Kodiaks are fun don't you think?*"

He nodded.

Hand poised to take the blade he had no idea why he even wanted it anymore, he reached for it anyway, knew he needed it.

But so did the armour.

Black fingers lacking the body behind it, skeletal looking steel twisted and grabbed hold of Jack and threw him across the room. Jack did his best to control his fall but he hit the wall hard and fell harder choking in gulps of our water as he plunged below the flowing waters that flooded the hall.

Jack stood up aching all over to see the woman in the water fighting back against the suit. Unfettered by a physical form though the suit attacked like a raging beast, slashing and stabbing at its target.

She fought back as best she could it seemed, but any attempts to restrain the nano machines just saw them slip apart and reform to strike at her again. The blade still in her hands she cradled it to her chest as she screamed back at her attacker, but flying profanities did nothing to halt the powerful tech and soon she was being pushed back.

Jack had a plan though.

"Nimue?! Can you get it to stand still a moment?!"

She didn't respond at first but a sudden surge of waves and wind pushed a wall of water across the room, scooping up the armour and washing it back.

"*We can, but for only a moment!*"

"That's all I need," he rushed in to her side, "So what's the plan?"

She smiled sadly.

"This…," in that second her voice lost all resonance, only her voice came through her eyes no longer glowing orange but instead deep brown, and filled with tears.

As she released whatever hold on the water she had had the armour surged at her, arms like blades driven home through her chest as it wrapped around her wrestling the blade from her grip.

Blade in hand it tossed her aside, limp body falling onto the stone islands beneath the waterfall.

It stepped back and turned to Jack, the visor flickering as a crackling voice came echoing up from inside the suit..

"Jack, Jack, Jack, I had hoped we could trust you."

"Baker?"

The slosh of water from behind him made him turn to find Baker there.

"Where is ev-"

"They're DEAD! All of them Jacky, all dead, and you will be too." He scratched at his neck, a bulge shifting under his suit. "Now, get your naked ass out of my way."

Jack stepped to the side, keeping his hands down at his side.

"You don't have to do this Baker. They were giving it to me."

"Oh?" Baker's helmet opened and he turned to look at Jack. "See, I don't think that makes a fat lick of good." He walked over to the suit and reached out to the blade pausing to look down at a ripple in the water, a thin wire line on the waters surface.

Plink

As the pin pulled the grenade blew, designed to give no chance to react, the white phosphorus ripped through the armour and Baker alike. Like molten light the world burned hot a flash that burned even the water and cast Jack back into the hall in a rush of steam and flame.

When he opened his eyes he gasped as the air burned at his lungs, the world was still burning, all traces of water gone and so were the doors to the entrance. The room was still a wreck, no small space spared the carnage pitted smoldering holes still burning. Not even a kinetic could heal from that.

The thought made sense return, and without thought for his own safety he ran to where he had seen Nimue fall. But as he searched he could find no trace of her, despite finding bits of Baker and the suits smoking remains everywhere.

He coughed and heaved trying his best to stay below the smoke. Stumbling back and forth was getting him nowhere though so he turned back to the doorway. He staggered a bit, bare feet squishing wetly across bits of stone and glass that bit at his soles and left red smeared footprints.

He was in such pain though that it barely registered, it may as well have been someone else's body he was piloting for how it felt.

He sat down hard as he cleared the room, a chunk of stone that had once been a bench. Split in two he looked at what had felled the solid marble seat and almost laughed.

Sunk almost to the crossbar was the sword.

Silvery metal already cool to the touch, he ran his fingers along the twisting curves, and let the thrum of energy it held flow into him in turn. It wiggled in its stone sheath as he pulled it out and held it up high. It was lighter than he had thought it might be. Words of wisdom gleaned from his favourite author echoed in his mind and he shivered as he remembered how death was lighter than a feather, and in that he knew it was he felt his duty weigh down on him like the proverbial mountain.

"You found it?"

The sudden sound made him turn, the hazy image of a woman in the shadows appearing as he blinked. But it was not smoke or his eyes, she really had a haze about her, a veil that kept his eyes from focusing on her.

"Who are you?" He had no strength left to fight, his body felt weak, but he wasn't going to die lying down if this one was here for blood too.

"I'm a messenger, that's all. I'm here to deliver something."

Her accent was light, but he recognized it right away, he had been to Japan enough times before not too.

"You're a Kinetic? Or-"

"Hush man."

She placed her hand on his head and a rush of heat tore a gasp from him as he felt his body twist back muscles bunching along his spine folding him over the wrong way. As the shock left him though he felt his pain ebb away too, not a scratch or bruise or burn left on him, at least none that hadn't turned to a scar long ago.

As his eyesight cleared he was left still starting at the hazy figured woman. Though now accurately aware how cold it was in here.

"That's some delivery," he added jokingly.

She made a sniffing sound and turned away from him.

"Where was that when your friend was in danger." He didn't let the words hang there either, as she turned he followed. "What, don't want to know how she died? Did her life mean that little Kinetic?"

She raised her hand and he was pushed back in a burst of snapping electricity that lit the room in blue light.

"You don't know anything," her voice dripped in acrid tones as she rounded on him, "You think talking makes you smart, but your words are empty. She was keeping us away. While she was here we couldn't get ten feet into this place without finding ourselves miles away with no idea how we got there. That sword is more important than you can imagine, and more dangerous than anyone could ever express." She crossed her arms making her form waver violently. "So before you pass judgement remember you were here. What did you do?"

Jack hung his head.

"I did what I could." He looked down at his fingers, he could almost feel the ages of blood soaked days slipping like silk from him the more he gave up on acceptance.

"Us too."

"Yeah," he nodded. "Any chance you have a spare pair of pants on you there? Not that I'm not used to being in a pretty woman's presence buck naked, I jus-"

"Oh for- just shut up." She suddenly struck the air with a sound like a gong, a kettle bell toll that shook the hall causing little rivulets of dust to rain down around them. The effect left cracks in mid air, pieces of reality fracturing inward on itself opening into a swirling vortex of crackling energy. She reached into the void and pulled something out he recognised right away, his bag from the apartment, the bag he knew should have burned to ash hours ago.

"How did you-? No, never mind." He took the bag from her and nodded, "Thanks."

She sniffed again, then she spoke.

"What did she say when she gave it to you?"

He looked at her, and then at the sword as he changed.

"Well, lots actually. But basically, that it needs to go to the right person. Know anyone that fits that description?"

"Would you believe me if I said, I do?"

"No," he shook his head and pulled out one of his spare guns from the bag. She looked no more phased than if she were watching a man hold a banana so he spared her the attempt to look tough and just shoved it in the back of his pants.

He stood up straight, checked its contents one more time, shoved all he needed into his bum-bag and tossed the old suitcase into one of the still burning fires to burn.

Then he paused, she was still watching him.

"What?" He asked heatedly. "Do you want this?" He stepped towards her with the blade held out, but as he expected she backed off practically tripping over her own feet in the attempt. She stood up and her foggy physique shifted as she appeared to pat herself down.

She made that same sniff of disapproval.

"I thought so, so then, what do you want? Delivery done, you brought me my gear."

"I'm not here to deliver anything to you, fool." She giggled suddenly, but not a cutesy little chuckle, a dark malicious little titter that made his hackles rise as she crossed her arms. "I'm delivering you to where you need to be." With that her already hazy form seemed to melt into the shadows, her cheshire grin the last thing he saw before that newly familiar gonging sounded behind him and he turned to see reality crack again.

The inside rippled and for a moment he recognised the interior of what he saw, the room was a guard station he knew well. The office inside-

"Buckingham?"

"Hold your breath," her voice whispered in his ear, "Or your heart will implode."

Her words made him gasp as with a heavy shove he was thrown forward into the rippling window and spun about. He closed his eyes and felt reality stretch as his body was squeezed under pressure till he felt he may pop. The feeling lasted only a moment but suddenly it was like he was pulled and the feeling went in reverse till a split second later he opened his eyes and was standing in the office he had been looking at.

He looked around and gave a quick cough, realizing as he did he had in fact held his breath.

He waited till she was through to pull his gun, the muzzle coming to rest between her eyes as she stepped through. She didn't look surprised, or even move away, she just tapped his worst aside.

"We don't have time for this. I can't be here for long or they will notice my energy and be down on us." She was still hard to see but her posture spoke of unease, she also wasn't wrong.

Jack knew all too well the securities put in place to defend the queen and the rest of the royal family. Sniffers who couldn't use powers but could sense others who did were always on guard at every corner of every building.

But something wasn't right.

The room was empty.

The monitors across the far wall showed every square inch of the interior main floor. A second bank of glowing screens across from that showed the grounds. The door across from the holding cells stood open leading out into the palace halls, and the cabinets where the weapons should have been were empty, more gear than any one night crew would have ever needed short of a war breaking out in the halls here. Usually there would be eight or more of the royal guard in here watching these monitors, but no one was here.

Jack frowned and stepped around a chair to the desk and began scanning through the monitors.

"What are you doing?"

Jack looked up.

"It makes no sense, where are they all? The Grenadier, Coldstream, not a single Guardsmen is here."

"Then it may be too late already," she stepped up behind him and turned him around in the chair. "I warned you, I have to go, so here it is. Your queen is in danger, her life is measured in hours," she paused to look at her wrist, "Three hours to be exact."

She stepped back and walked to one of the street monitors from the grounds where a shadow slipped slowly down the street.

"The knights are on the move. The coup has begun."

"You're joking, right…?"

Her matter-of-fact stance said she wasn't.

"But why? Why would any of the Knight's do this?"

"I don't have time to explain, all I know is that the queen is still here. The seers are in agreement, which I will say is very rare, what will happen here tonight will be felt centuries from now in the greatest way." She reached into her coat and pulled a folded up paper and placed it into Jack's hand. "That's a map, you have to be at that spot in the sub-basement before midnight. I will open a gate there at exactly five minutes to the hour, and I will only hold it open for that one minute."

Jack glared at the woman.

"None of this makes sense. You're not making any sense." He sighed heavily, his world was secrets, always looking for the answers, never the question. "But then, this is hardly my first rodeo." He took another deep breath and stepped back. "Well, time to get on the job I guess."

"Just like that?"

Jack nodded, walking around her to the shelves. "just like that. We are the keepers of that which is unsaid, Semper Occultus."

"Always secret," she nodded to him as if she too now understood. "Tell no one, and assume everyone is your enemy. The seers say only two make it out tonight." She slammed her first against the air like before, and reached through she pulled out a strange knife and handed it to him. A fancy looking thing, it was sleek black and double edged. "Take this, no locked door with that on you." She turned to step through, but paused. "Oh, and, don't drop it."

Jack nodded, and the kinetic woman was gone. He looked at the straight blade, looping the ring on the butt end on his finger and started at it. The blade was so thin he felt he might break it if he relaxed too hard. But to his surprise as he gave it a test swing a click made him look down.

On the floor was a triangular bit of metal.

He leaned down and picked it up, standing up he turned it about. Then he saw the edge of the desk. The bit in his hand fitting onto the corner.

He looked at the small combat knife with well deserved respect, and not too little, an amount of awe, and was just about to say something out loud when the sound of heavy boots echoed from down the hall. Jack had never been so glad to hear the sound of approaching boots, and he rushed to see, but as he almost cleared the door he realized what this night had been like he decided instead that caution was still key.

The heavy steps of boots echoed through the halls through the open door, so he quickly shut it, taking only a cursory glance at the cameras before baring it too. The camera feeds revealed twelve well-armed queen's guards were the source of the sound, all in standard two-by-two formation, their hats were gone but that distinct red coat a few of them wore could still be seen under the body armour they had on.

They were all on edge, clear from the way they moved. Four of them suddenly stopped and broke off heading right to cover the hallway that intersected the one they were in. While they did that the second group passed, heading still in his direction of the security office they were in perfect sync.

At least, that was at first.

A sudden commotion in the hall sent two of the four men flying back into the other two, one man rag dolled so hard his head snapped back, neither got back up. The two survivors scrambled for only a moment, flipping a table in a flash to get some cover. The table jolted and both men backed down the hall walking the table with them and pulling their Fallen men with them too. Clearing the corner they only stopped long enough to clear their Fallen comrades' things then continued backing up with their makeshift shield.

They fired their rifles only once the whole time Jack watched, a quick burst fired blindly. It made Jack wonder why at first but even as he watched he noticed no one else in the hall. It was as if they had been shot at by ghosts.

Jack looked around to find a mic, a touch screen to the side of one of the keyboards had a glowing volume up symbol, but nothing that looked like a way to call out. He hit the button immediately anyway, the speakers in front of him blaring to life with a dozen voices all at once. Panicked men and women asking for backup, the stoic few whose replies grew fainter between squelching sounds as their sound cut in and out, and the ones clearly just trying to survive. Soldiers, people, all of them losing hope.

But where were they all?

Other than the ten right about to come knocking he couldn't see anything, and none of these men were talking at all.

The guardsmen now with their backs to the door huddled behind their makeshift cover, they didn't seem worried about what they may find here, but rather what had found them down the hall. And though Jack was not looking forward to walking into whatever this was, he went to the door anyway. Figuring that having to answer some hard questions was better than leaving them to their fate, he just hoped he was helping the right side by doing it, but then, it wouldn't be the first time he wasn't sure which side that was.

The moment he popped the latch the two in back saw right away and pushed in, none said a word, just grabbed him as they did. Two more turned and covered the door and the other four filed in and set up to cover the two as they ducked low and dove in just as a series of metallic tings rang off the door following the last two in as they slammed it shut.

They bared and latched it tight and looked around at each other, and then at the one man of their group who stood apart.

Jack was still held by the two who had rushed in first, his head held down, forced down to his knees, but even he thought something was off.

"Fack'n ell boss. E's dead."

"I got eyes dun I."

"You got this'n?" Asked one of the guys who held Jack.

"I sir," the other murmured softly.

Though the room seemed tense, Jack couldn't resist, "What's go-"

Crack

"Doyle, what cha do that fer?"

As Jack had tried to speak, the side of a pistol had caught him hard on the back of the head. His head reeling and vision blurred Jack barely kept his wits.

Thankfully, this wasn't just glazed over.

"E ain't a bloody seal ye ape, ye can keep em quiet without clubbing em," another man hissed. Lights spinning and the world reduced to a narrow hole Jack regretted his choice right now.

The guards' boots all shuffled about in his line of narrowed sight and huddled as they began to mumble.

The guy holding him then switched off with another less heavy-handed of the men and joined the others, several taking turns holding him in check, and though he wasn't hit again, the feel of cold steel pressed against the base of his skull was all too real.

According to his watch blinking up at him, it was a good twenty minutes before he was given a gentle shake. "If you're still awake mate, keep ye mouth shut," he whispered, "When the cap'ns ready, e'll ask is questions of you. But fer now, ears wide as he says is peace."

Jack just nodded but looked up to see what was going on.

The man they had been gathered around was no longer on his feet, but he was also not laying down. Three long spikes had been the source of the metallic ringing, long spines, one of which had punched through the man's skull pinning him to the wall behind him.

Jack quickly checked the monitors, but there was nothing in the halls.

"An, who is this now?" The one who spoke caught Jack's attention right away, an older guard long in years to some he had the hard set of a guardian of the old days. He sat back on his heels coming down to eye level with Jack. "You look like a tourist mate, so what're ye doin ere?"

Jack thought to play it, but this man didn't look like no ones fool. "Designation Mr. December. Agent number, yankee, three, sierra, mike, alpha, november, zero."

The bulk of the guards stepped back, weapons coming up, but the guard in front of him didn't even flinch.

"Why are you helping us then?" He asked slowly, "Why didn't you let the black knight's dogs take us down?"

Jack looked around at them, he couldn't believe what he was hearing, and clearly, it showed.

"You don't know? Then, mate, you're out of the loop. Cut em loose Parker," he stood up, knuckling the small of his back. But when Jack wasn't let go right away he squared off. "Did I stutter soldier?"

"Sir, he's a knight."

"Do you see armour on him? No. He's not an inside man. Besides, if he had wanted to, he'd have either left that door shuttered to see us all pinned up like Sam ere, or ended us emself." He nodded to Jack, "I've heard your code before mate. The Yesman, Jack'O'December, himself."

Jack slipped the man's wrist hold and stood up bringing the man who had held him up with him. He let the guy go and stepped back, hands up, he closed the knife he still held so no one got the wrong idea and tucked it beneath his watch.

"Twice in a day my reputation has preceded me. I need to cover my tracks better." He nodded to the captain, "Thank you."

The captain waved his hand.

"You lot said this is the knight's work? What's going on?" Jack had heard it from the kinetic, but hearing it from one of his own felt different, like hearing the words had made it more real.

"Two o'clock this marnin almost every guard was either dismissed or reassigned to the knight's detail." He looked sour, "The Smithe family, my family, we ave been loyal Queens men for ten generations Me own son is a knight, pilotin one ot'hem suits. An today, I was dishonorably discharged," he looked at them all around him. "All of us were. Sent home as a potential threat. So six knight's set up camp on the edge of the castle grounds and the queen was ordered to remain in her chambers under guard. Only, even other knights are asking why now too. So this doesn't sit well with me, no. So I calls up the boys, only again, half o'them didn't answer." He looked off to the side and punched at his armoured chest. "Me neighbor, Mike, we served together for twelve years, an I walked in on the thing what killed em."

"Thing?" Jack was curious, "Was it a kinetic?"

"No, it was not human. Had a bright yellow flower out it's throat, like one o'them bloom things. Only it's not cold out so it shouldn't be here. It was lightning fast but I knew where Mike kept his ol whinney. Took both barrels to the chest and still started to get up before I took its head off with an old cavalry saber Mikey had on his wall. Then the things blood turned it brittle as glass. It was so cold it burned me." He took a moment to show his hand, heavy eyes red and misted he coughed lightly. "I ain't never seen the likes, you hear me. Next I knew I was roundin up any as not already dead and got us here. But it's no good, there's more of those things, an when they don't want you too, you ain't see 'em till they's on top o you."

Jack nodded and pulled out his gun. The collective twitch in the room said they still didn't trust him, but at least no one tried to shoot.

"We can't just sit here. The queen is in danger, I have a way out, but it's in the basement." He thumbed the air towards the table and the map he had left there. "If we can get down there to where the queen is, we will have one minute to get out."

The captain walked over and eyed the map.

"Ain't never seen these tunnels." The old vet lamented.

"Sir," one of the others piped up. "I have, it's an old war tunnel leading to the tower." The young guy who spoke looked it over then pointed to a monitor that showed a set of lifts. "The elevator in maintenance will take us down. Was down there once looking for a kid that got lost from his tour group. It pretty much ends in a giant door that's been sealed for ever and a day."

Jack nodded, it sounded like they knew what they were doing. But there was an issue, the circle on the map was on the other side of that door.

He reached for his knife then and flicked the switch so the blade came out, a cheeky smile forming on his face.

"I've got the door if you boys can get us there."

"Wha? Wit tha thing?"

A few guys chuckled along, obviously enjoying the thought. But Jack just slid the knife carefully into the desktop and lopped off a large section of it so it fell heavily to the ground.

All eyes on him he clicked the knife and tucked it away. He pulled out his gun and turned to the other desk where the monitors still showed hall after empty hall.

"So, we have unknown contacts, unknown numbers. But they also think we're afraid and trapped. In my line if I can't see my target, I make sure they can't see me either." He tapped a few keys and found what he needed, switching the cameras between the spectrums. Night vision, and thermal didn't work but then he switched to one that showed something strange. "What's all this then?"

The captain came over.

"Magnetic distortions, it helps detect optical camp like those Asian spooks use. So they're out there but it won't help, we got plenty o'gear, but no helmets or heads-up goggles." He spit off to the side, "Won't elp us none just knowin this is the Japanese. An the gear is been stripped outta ere, no way we'll see me before they pin us up like bugs too."

Jack walked over to the panel on the wall.

"Well, firstly, this isn't the Japanese, they're purests, no kinetics or monsters, just robots and ninjas. Second-like, let's make it easier."

He walked to a bank of computer terminals and found the panel he needed and flipped the first row of switches on the power line. The halls on the monitors were cut with a pop, the lights going out hall by hall. He kept the power to the room and engaged the security doors on the main floor, magnetic locks shutting the doors of every door on the main floor.

"We just straight shot it through the halls. From here it's back up the hall, one right and then two lefts to the lift in the service hall." He looked over one of their rifles, "You got krypton beams on those? If they're usin some bending the light trick thing, the lasers will bend, or at least distort.."

There was not a murmur of descent from the lot, they all switched on beams in a moment, green lasers sweeping the room as they checked their sights. The sound of a couple test clip changes from men with their eyes closed made him proud as each of them made sure they were ready.

"Captain, I hope you won't mind I won't take point. I have-"

"Rye ye grunts, laces up, sights on a swivel. It lights up, it dies, an I want no wasted shots, aim for the head just like we done. An you spook, you got the noodle, so keep it down, keep that map an direct the line from the rear."

Jack nodded and grabbed the long case he had left leaning up against the wall, still so surprisingly light.

"Some kinda secret weapon in'air, Spook?" One of the older guards asked in a gruff tone.

Jack just looked at the strap and slung it over his back. "I sure hope so." Jack nodded to him, "And please, call me Jack."

The man shrugged and grabbed one of the others by his pack pulling a sleek looking device out from the guy's pack. He checked it and handed it to Jack.

Jack looked it over and smiled, "A cornershot, that's handy mate."

The grumpy looking guy just shrugged and got into position.

"A'right then grunts," the door locks whispered open.

Jack quickly snapped his pistol into the carriage and checked it, flipping the pistol left and right before the two men ahead of him entered the hall. Jack clicked on the built in laser then nodded to the captain. Ready and set they popped the door and tossed a flashbang grenade out into the hall. Mouths open, eyes averted, and ears plugged the bang shook them, but not more than the collective scream that followed.

Chilling to the bone, vicerally wet and wailing, it was like knives slicing through meat on a cutting board made of slate.

Two men rushed the hall laser guided sights up; they caught the points where the light reflected and split like a light show, and a short burst of rounds peppered the strange shadows. The creatures that appeared hit the ground writhing and gnashing at the air as their camouflage failed them, but they were far from done. More lasers from the others swept the hall catching more of the creatures, some trying to maintain their invisibility, others standing stock still as if paralyzed by the flash bang.

"Move you wankers, push on."

Jack followed, doing his best with his tiny laser to at least spot the creatures if he could, but as they cornered the main hall their laser split off into a thousand shards of green they lost two men in a heartbeat. Both men were pinned to the wall and floor, torn to shreds by needles as long as Jack's forearm.

The group pulled back and threw a second grenade. Thanking their luck the blast this time caused even more screaming than before. The blasts didn't seem to stun them long, but the creatures had also grown more stupid it seemed. Several shambled right into the lasers of the men holding the gap, lit up for all to see they went down in a hail of gunfire.

Jack tried to grab one of the guns from the downed guard but to no use. The second he touched the grip it locked him out and the trigger wouldn't squeeze.

Instead he took the ammo from both men and the knives from their belts as they pushed again into the hall.

Burst fire on, the men gained headway and the shifting shadow beasts seemed to fall back.

Jack took a moment to grab the men's tags, and grabbed the flashbang off the belt of the one named Doyle.

He caught up as they finally pushed to the front hall. The lift on the other side looked like it may have been as far away as the moon though.

The front hall was completely open, with no cover at all and a gallery above.

The creatures had already proven capable of climbing the walls, so the likelihood was low that they wouldn't take advantage of that.

"Captain?!"

The man whipped around, one eye covered in blood, a gash running from the corner bleeding heavily down his cheek.

"How many shocks you all got?" Jack held up the two he had picked up.

The grizzled man smiled and Jack was passed the lot. Eight in all, he tied them together using a belt, then in a dash pulled the pins. The long end of the belt in hand he swung the load with all his might and heaved them high just as a rain of needles shot around his feet and down from above.

He let loose the bundle just in time and fell back into the hall opening his mouth and exhaling hard as the blast rocked the room.

The heavy thudding of bodies couldn't be heard over the sound of the ringing in his ears, but the creature's screaming was like nothing else. It vibrated in his core and he stood on shaky legs and killed three that had Fallen around him just to deaden the mind scrambling shrieks. His explosive rounds made quick work at short range like this, blowing their flowery heads clean off in a splatter of glowing orange liquid that left a cool mist in the air as their blood froze over in fractal icy lacework.

The other guardsmen were not far behind him, sweeping in with precision they dispatched another ten. Then rushed on to hit the emergency panel on the wall, the captain pulled out a key from around his neck. He gave it a twist in the lock and the power returned to the elevator opening the door. They filed in quickly, turning to cover the ones still limping in. Not a one had escaped unscathed, only Jack had thought he had escaped till he felt a twinge when one of the guards passing him nudged him by accident.

"Oi, am I hit?" He shouted over the ringing in his ear. "Mop! Mop! Crap, I can hear nothin mates, sorry!"

The lot of them seemed to be laughing at that though, and one turned him around and there was a slight popping feeling as Jack felt as he was touched. Hot pain shot through him in a flash and made him grind his teeth. The man held up a needle. It hadn't gone all the way through his side and again he was thankful for military grade armour that looked like civilian clothes. The plates in his shirt had kept him from getting speared. They all laughed and poked at his clothes laughing still but obviously impressed he had survived.

After a minute of kneeling in the clutch of the howling ringing noise, sound started to return slowly.

The ding of the fancy elevator doors opening up to a utility hall lined on one side in pipes. The bare white concrete walls seemed stark and haunting after the decadent grandeur of the upper levels, echoing whistling sounds coming up from the bowls.

They exited the elevator in standard form again, the lasers had been highly effective so the hope remained they may work here too. They scanned the halls and made their way onward till the long hall turned.

Being that he was nearly deaf he almost didn't notice except he was in the middle, a good idea he thought too, until a hand came to rest on his shoulder making him turn grabbing one of the guardsmen.

They had all stopped, the soldiers behind him checking gear as if to set up a defense line, now pausing to rest.

"Captain," Jack mumbled trying to stay quiet, "We can't stop, we don't have enough time. We hav-"

The captain waved his hand, cutting Jack off, and ending the conversation. His words came quietly through the racking scream in Jack's ears, but it was clear.

Jack looked at the men gathered at the corner, this was it for them. Blood dripped from two of them in a steady flow that left crimson smears in a trail down the hall. Smeared by the steps of those who had tried to keep them going it was clear few of them were still bleeding, almost as if they couldn't stop it. The dark rags wrapped around wounds and the worsening looks on the faces of those who were hurt spoke to the toxicity too, as he locked eye with the now one-eyed captain it was made even clearer. The blood oozed from under a bandana he had tried to use to hold cloth to it, thick veins pulsing darkly seemed to be spreading out almost to his other eye already.

"Captain, boys. If you stay, you will die, I have an out, maybe they-."

The looks of laughter and the bubbling sound made Jack madder still.

The lot of them were fools.

But he knew better than to argue a fool, he had rarely let anyone win over his stupidity either.

"Get your men to this point on time captain. It will be your only evac." Jack grimaced and grabbed the man by the collar as he started to laugh too. He turned the man's collar and pulled his chain out from inside his shirt holding up the man's tag. "What about these, huh? Should you not make sure you get these where they need to be Captain Daniels?" He then shoved the tags he had pulled off the Fallen in the hall. Silvery, round steel glinting in the fluorescent lighting looked like little stars in the man's hand.

A name to the face the man didn't change his pace he instead took off his and shoved them back into Jack's chest. The look on his face, a mix of pain, and pride. Wincing as he turned and pulled a claymore from one of the other men's packs.

One by one the others came to him and handed him their tags. They seemed to know, or at least had decided, this was it.

He took a moment as he walked away to hang them all around his neck. There was more than for the men he had met; realizing as he saw the names that they had already lost so many more.

The long hall went on with no other side halls, the hum around him made all the more unbearable by the buzzing pipes running power and water all around him.

At least his hearing was coming back.

Jack was careful to keep an eye out ahead, even the slightest sound beyond his footsteps and he froze. Side halls were easier at least, the flip grip on his gun let him peek around and see if his laser reflected.

He paused now and then to look back but no one was at his back anymore. With only two ways down to this area he knew that he mostly had to worry about what may be ahead of him, but it didn't stop him from worrying.

Finally coming to the end of the hall he found the heavy doors that led to the Tower of London side, at their pace that meant he had roughly a half-hour to the extraction. Thankfully he had a time saver.

Jack looked over the large double doors, thick reinforced steel, he could tell it was thicker than his blade was long so he instead rechecked the lock. Heavy bars slid through the frame, so it was at least mechanical and not powered or computer-controlled, but it meant he was not getting through that way.

That was when he saw the hinges and got a great idea.

He pulled the knife out and clicked the button, the slender blade sliding out with a faint whisking sound. He drew the knife down the heavy hinge on the left, catching them carefully so they didn't hit the floor. Once all three were off from one door he then heaved with all his strength and pulled the heavy door open a crack.

He dropped his back against the wall and flipped the hinge on his gun through into the hall on the other side. He didn't need the light, it was just as bright, and just as seemingly empty, but it also was not as long as he had imagined, ending not twenty feet away in a second door like this one.

The lift down to the bunker was indeed there. But so were more dead bodies. He carefully swept the laser into all the more obvious spots to hide in the small room before he pried the door a little further to slip in. He crossed to the body on the floor to find one of his own, an SiS brat in full Knight gear. No obvious sign how they had died, the suit had already melted down to prevent capture. The inside of the suit would be no more than a charcoal mass crumbling to dust.

Jack knew not to touch the suit still, no need for it to blow up all together, but the weapon on the ground was too tempting. He carefully picked it up but was quickly disappointed, this weapon was locked. He had already been removed from SiS active duty it seemed.

He sighed and hung his head, it meant he was never expected to come back. Or worse still, that it had been planned that he wouldn't.

He checked the clips, it looked like similar rounds to what he was using, and was at least the same caliber. He popped out his nearly empty clip, and popped out the last few rounds, slipping them into the extended clip he had just picked up. He then grabbed the last two from the other man's corpse, pocketed those, and slipped the mag into his gun. He checked the balance and ran a quick drill to familiarize himself with the weight for good measure.

There was precious little time left to get stuck with a useless weapon so he carefully popped off one round from each clip. Certain they weren't going to cause an issue he stepped over the two and into the lift.

The short trip down made his ears finally pop, the ringing subsiding just in time for a humming sound to fill the void of silence. He brought his gun up just as the bell dinged and the door opened to find six more Knights in full gear. They had set up behind a barricade in the hall, but their backs were to him, not guarding the door, but laying siege to the door to the bunker.

Their focus fully on two heavily armoured gold giants down the end of the hall, they never even heard Jack as he disembarked.

Gunfire and blasts of light shot back and forth, and Jack had to duck back to avoid a blast of light that caved in the back wall of the elevator in a fractured pattern that looked like a spider's web.

He rushed for the corner wall in a momentary lull coming up behind one of the Knight's, a woman, he took her around the neck and pulled his gun on her.

"Alright love, I know you can hear me. Tell them to stop firing, or I start."

He knew he wasn't a match for her strength in her suit, but she didn't, and right away her arms were up. The others stopped too, turning almost in unison to Jack and his human shield.

Odder still though, as they stopped firing, so had the two giants at the far end of the hall.

He still had his gun to her throat angled up under her helmet at the weak spot as she fidgeted,

"None of that now," he jabbed her hard. "Which o'ye fools is in charge?"

The helmet on one opened and Jack was face to face with his own commander.

Luis Thatcher, a veteran of the last twenty five years, he was a glorified desk jockey, yet here he was smiling like the cat who had caught the crow.

"Ello Jack'o. What're you doing here?" Despite the wording he spit each letter like an insult.

Jack felt stunned, he hadn't seen his boss in over a year, and it had done the man good. The suits only did so much, and Luis looked like he had lost fifty pounds.

"I should ask you the same thing, sir. Since when do the knights operate on the queen's land?" Luis didn't move a muscle, his weapon and those of the others trained on him unwaveringly. "Nothing to say to that, fine, drop your weapons, or I'll be forced to drop you."

"You first trai-"

Jack's aim was perfect, the man who spoke took the round in-between the eyes and his still hot weapon was pressed back to his prisoners neck before any could react.

"Anyone else wanna call me a traitor, last I saw, I wasn't the one openly firing on a door that leads to the queen's bunker." Jack pulled all the tighter till he felt her throat bulge as she swallowed. "So, I say again; last time mind ye; dropem. I mean, get your shit together, this is London. SiS doesn't operate inside the country, and we don't fight our own."

Luis snorted a laugh, "Those look like humans to you? They're the monsters here, they have even taken the queen's face."

It was Jack's turn to laugh now, but he had to think a moment, it may have made sense.

"She isn't even the real Queen Jack. The Black Knight has finally gotten the proof and we are ending it tonight. You've been following an imposter the last twenty years Jack, but we in the know, we are woken."

"Look," Jack snarled, "I've been SiS for twenty-five years Luis. Tonight has been one of those days, I've seen things, and I tell you, the only thing that doesn't make sense here is the Black Knight calling the shots. Sending SiS into the Queens home. Killing loyal Queens men."

"Those monsters killed the queen," he spat back pointing off with his gun to where the suited giants had been standing, "They're the ones pitting countrymen against one another."

Jack let go of the woman and raised his hands, "If they're such monsters, then why haven't they taken the shot?"

The giants were right there, their weapons near as large as the men they were pointed at. For being as large as they were they walked stealthily on heavy mechanical legs and snuck up. Moving with ease to disarm all of the agents, but it was not so easy, the theme of Jack's whole day.

Even as the SiS agents dropped their weapons their suits began to glow, and the men and the one woman in them began to scream. Even Luis' suit snapped shut suddenly, white light shining from inside the cracks and crevices as they melted down taking the agent with them. The outside of the suit squeezed tight as the phosphorus did its job, glowing hot, leaving smouldering marks on the ground as they curled and twisted under the heat.

The golden armour-clad giant came close and relieved Jack of his gun, gently despite his size too. Overlapping plates of scale armour made no sound not even a click as they waved their hand for him to follow.

"What are you?" Jack asked, breaking the heavy silence. "I mean," he looked over the strange alone design of their armour again, "You aren't using Knight tech."

The one beside Jack stooped low, his mask parting like the petals of a flower to reveal a very serpentine, yet oddly human face. Thin slit like nostrils down where their chin was and no visible mouth, its viper-like yellow eyes narrowing as it regarded him skeptically.

"We," it started, speaking through what sounded like an artificial voice box, "Are the last guard. We have been consultants to the crown for a millennia, but when the Black Knight rose we were betrayed." It leaned in further, "And what of you human? You don't seem to fear us?"

Jack spread his hands wide, "Well the shit I've seen has been eye opening to say the least. An army of lizardmen in the catacombs below Buckingham palace does not seem so strange any."

"Army," it made a strange face and started to cackle. "We are only two, no army I fear, not that one would help your kind survive what is incoming." He nudged Jack forward, through the ajar bunker door. "Come, the queen does not fare well."

He couldn't believe it, but these things, these people, they were the good guys.

He let himself be led down the hall past many doors, brought out into a sterile-looking medical room. Even here the doors and ceiling seemed to have been built with the height of these two in mind. The other one also opened the mask on their armour, the same serpentine face regarding him closely. This one did not seem as trusting though, and even as it seemed to stand at ease by the door it caressed its weapon with a lover's consideration.

A wracking cough followed by a child's sobs from a curtained off end of the room made Jack look away. He looked at the first lizard man and they just nodded towards the curtain.

Jack crossed quickly to the far end and pushed aside the curtain to find who he had been sent to get. The young woman sat up in a bed, long red hair falling in ringlet curls that looked to have seen better days, her sharp green eyes were on him. She was pale as a ghost, bloody gauze wrapped tight in her hand held to her side.

"Your majesty," torn between his urge to leave, and his reflex to kneel, he instead bobbed in place like a broken toy soldier. "We have to get you-"

"Stop," she suddenly shouted. Her hand coming up with an alien looking pistol in her grip, he was shocked how well she held it together. Her aim was steady and if this smaller weapon was anything like the rifles those two had, this one would easily end him.

Jack nodded, keeping his hands up, "My queen, I'm here to protect you," he checked his watch, "And we are running out of time."

"Oh? Really," she growled, "That was what the last one of you SiS blokes said too. I'll tell you the same thing he never got to hear as Fa'brik crushed his head. I'm safe right here." She flicked her gun sideways, "Off wit you then." The young queen was not well indeed, but she was not desperate either. But again, Jack had been sent here to do a job.

The curtain parted again before he could say a word though and the first lizardman stepped in. "Your majesty, Ta'lean says this one is the emissary. The scent of the kinetic we contracted is on him. She promised to send one of Alexander's own to save the boy, and while I am not so trusting of one who reeks of death as this one, I have to agree, he does have a trace of her scent."

Jack nodded, "Thanks mate, I take it, you're Fabric, was it?"

They nodded and offered his fist forward, "Fa'brick," he put a heavier lean on the Fa sound and then bobbed his head again, "Lown Home Guard."

Jack bumped his fist against the others, "Lone home guard? Never heard of you, but for guarding the Queen, you have my thanks."

Fa'brick shook his head, "No, not lone, low-en, that is our peoples name. But never mind, we have little time, and it will not matter."

Jack put his hand up, slowly pulling out the map as Fa'brick eyed him suspiciously. "It's fine, the woman, the kinetic, she gave me this, told me to be here and a door would open to get us out." He spread it out on a table beside the Queen. "We just have to get to this room here in, ten minutes. We can make it. And don't assume I don't care how you pronounce your peoples name, I speak eighteen languages, and might I add well enough to pass as a native in just about any country," he sighed, "At least when my cover isn't blown."

Fa'brick chuckled, but it was the other one, Ta'lean who spoke.

"My brother meant no insult; he only means as the last of our kind remembering who and what we are is a moot point. We will be here to the end, and the Queen has more important things than our state to cause you worry." She then turned him back towards the Queen.

She looked to be holding it together well despite it all and he returned to her side.

"We need to move-"

"I can not move, this body is done for now."

"My queen, I-I- Wait? Did you-"

She nodded sadly, "This body is not mine, for eons my kind have done their best to guide the rulers, but for a long time we were pushed away, I'm afraid that our insistence that the fate of this one world did not matter, well, we were wrong." She coughed, a bit of blood spit up landing on the white sheets. The blood was near to black.

"What are you?"

She sighed and sat back. "If only we had time, but we do not. The only thing that matters is protecting the true heir to the throne." She waved her hand and as if out of thin air a young boy appeared. "This is Count Andrew, first in line to the throne of England, and future king regent of all of the holdings of the future empire."

The young boy looked nothing like he had expected. His hair was dark, his nose sharp, with hazel eyes, but the longer he looked he recognized the boy. He looked like every statue he had ever seen of Alexander the great.

Jack coughed a small laugh, "This is hardly the time to joke your majesty. Who is this boy? Really?"

She said not a word, her head rolling to the side, "Please. Promise me that he will be safe. One day this boy will be a mage to rival those misguided ones in Canada, and only a power like that can wield the mighty weapon Caliburn." She coughed again, a racking cough that doubled her over. "Please, he must retrieve Caliburn from the Black Knight one day. Few else would ever dare, and those who would, will never live to speak of the Black Knights true origin."

"And what is that?"

"That he is no better than me, a parasite of energy, a demon if their we're ever such a thing. One of we Ari who has fallen. He seeks a way to rebuild his ranks, he will stop at nothing. But I fear that it has all been for nothing."

Fa'brick nodded, "Three days hence, the Black Knight found what he had been searching for. He has Caliburn, the sword of control. Like the piece you carry only a few can wield it, but with his expendable army of mages he will be able to activate the power of Avalon once more."

"Avalon! This is madness! You all expect me to believe this-this mystic hogwash!" He slammed his fist down against the rail of the bed. "How many people have died today for the delusions you alien freaks have wrought?"

She looked sad, but not angry, her hand gently coming to rest on his. "Whether you believe or not does not matter, you are a soldier, I have seen that look in your eyes countless times in others. I have; and I know you will do the right thing." She took the boy Andrew by the hand and led him to

Jack's side, "Go now. Ta'lean, Fa'brick, go, take them to where they must go."

"Wait, I-"

"There is no time," she looked up to the ceiling as if her eyes could pierce the walls, a far off gaze that spoke levels of pain. "Go, please. It is coming."

"What?" He begged.

Her eyes locked onto his and he found himself staring into a milk white expanse of starry light, golden flecks swirling in a vast void. She smiled as she pet his cheek, a weight of the ages that he saw in those depth pushing him to run. He almost ran into the lizardfolk as they carried young Andrew under their arm. And he almost didn't hear her last words. Really wished he hadn't heard, two whispered words that spurred him faster still.

"The end."

****

The air felt tight, like a frog ready to jump, sitting in her palms. Yuuki had sat here all night wondering how things were going, her farsight still blocked by the coiling of such grinding and unavoidable events.

Fate was like that.

But still she sat there, unable to not worry. She knew that something would happen, knew it was almost time.

She checked her watch again.

Eleven fifty-eight.

It was as people always said, a watched pot never boils.

So focused was she though, that she almost missed the faint popping sound heralding another. She wheeled on him as he walked around the rocks along the rocky coastline coming eyes to chest with a mountain of a man.

"You're not who I was expecting," she knew the man called Azure only by reputation, but seeing him she was less surprised now. If anything it seemed people didn't give the man enough stature. She felt heat rising in her cheeks, "Where is Luse?'

"Oh, were you expecting him?" His tone was so mischievous, it made his smile seem devilish.

She nodded, but then shook her head covering her hair across her bad eye. "I mean, I thought I was, I just knew that a powerful kinetic would be here to witness this with me."

"So you know what is happening tonight?"

She nodded again, "But I-"

"Look, we can't save everyone, but today sets the next piece on the board for a chess game eons in the making." He sighed and looked off into the sky, but his glowing eyes spoke to the truth that he wasn't even here. "When we try to save the world we damn countless more to a fate worse than destruction. I know," he locked eyes with her and his smile looked so much sadder. "We don't know the full breadth of what we do, even the three of us Immortals. Power makes us more accountable for the things we do, if only those in power had learned the lesson before they damned the world to this fate. But then if they had, then we would never have been present to help guide fate. Then what would have happened?"

The sky grew light in the west, the second time in her life she had seen such a thing happen.

Her heart stopped she looked at her watch, "No! I'm too late!"

"Are you?"

She looked up but Azure was gone in a pop, the sky back to dusky black in a blink.

She looked at her watch as panic made her heart slam against her ribs.

Eleven fifty-eight.

No.

The digital numbers blinked and in a flash she punched the air. Focusing her power she found the curves of the wormhole connecting from here to the depths of the bunker under the Tower of London. Twisting in a flash the air shattered and spun inward like a whirlpool connecting with a crackle.

Staring into the white light lit hall beyond she saw the sky begin to glow on the horizon just like when Azure had stood there. This time she was ready.

Jack tumbled through her portal, followed by a child thrown through into his arms, the Lown woman stepped back and Yuuki closed the gate.

Jack stared at the spot where the air was pulling itself back together.

"What are you doing!" he lunged back trying to reach back through, but Yuuki grabbed him before the portal closed and cost him his arm.

He grabbed her and threw her to the ground, but he had no time left as the air suddenly popped. A massive force of energy blasting all of them back, she watched as Jack was hurled over her. She grabbed the young boy, trying as she could to throw up a shield but there was no stopping what was happening, and even she blacked out as the air in her lungs felt like it was sucked away.

****

Jack stood on shaking legs, holding his arm which was now at a right angle, the pain making him cringe.

Ears ringing again.

The kinetic woman was suddenly at his side, her hands on his chest. A strange feeling suddenly burned through him, like a match lit at the end of every nerve in his body burning through him and he felt his arm even more. He flipped back and hit the ground rolling up avoiding his other arm, knife in hand, but no sooner was he up than he realized he felt fine.

"What did you do to me?"

She didn't even bother with him though, just gave him a derisive sniff and turned to Andrew, she made to lay her hands on him too, but she paused and stood.

"I healed you," she stood and turned to him, "The boy will be fine though," she smiled, "He's special, like me. In his own way."

Jack moved before he even thought about what he would do. "He is nothing like you, you monster!" He grabbed her and pointed her towards the west, "Your kind do things like this to innocent people!"

Her one eye stared at him the glow bright in their core as her eye changed. She removed his grip from her with ease but just stepped back.

He was enraged now, "Why are so many willing to die martyrs, than to live?"

She tossed her long hair back, "Sometimes living is harder. What would you know of sacrifice?"

He wanted to throttle the little tart, "What would I know? I have lived only to serve the greater good all my life! Living is always hard! That's life! But dying like they did, that's just giving up!"

"Our choices make us who we are, so do our sacrifices, and sometimes we must sacrifice everything to protect what we care for most." She turned from him then, and paced back towards the cliff.

"Nothing to say about this either then? This okay to you?" He spit the words with every ounce of venom he could muster through the pain. Looking out at the sea where the cliffs of the English coastline should have been.

She looked out there too, as if searching for an answer in the haze. "That was not us."

"What was that then?"

"Their reason for retaliation," she pointed out over the water, there should have been waves, tsunamis crashing against the coast, instead the water was boiling, a huge landmass rising from the turbid waters like a shadowy crescent moon. Massive marble white rings rising up from the parting waters to free whatever this thing was.

"Avalon, Atlantis, Agartha, whatever you call it. This is how the earth ends." She said quietly as they looked at the thing.

"You really aren't a part of this?" He asked, dumbstruck.

She shook her head, "No, but you were." She rounded on him, "This is the endgame that Sal'Da, the Black Knight sought."

Jack was still trying to wrap his head around what he was seeing, "What?"

There was a polite cough from behind them then and they both looked to where Andrew now stood.

"Prince An-"

"Sal'Da, the real name of the Black Knight. My Aunt told me everything." He choked a bit, obviously trying to be brave and hold back tears, but he went on. "I know she wasn't really my aunt, but she never lied to me either." He looked at the kinetic woman. "No one could anyway, right Ms. Yuuki?"

"I suppose not," Yuuki said, shrugging.

Jack looked back and forth between them. "Well, are you going to tell me what happens next?"

They both looked at each other, a long gaze that seemed like a conversation was taking place beyond him.

"If this is some kind of kinetic crap, cut it now, I'm done with this." He took the case off his shoulder and was about to pitch it when a gust of air waved aside the mist over the sea. There was nothing left, it was really gone.

Jack had spent years, no, his whole life, protecting his queen and country. He had never really known what from, the enemy, terrorists, the world abroad. He was just the bullet, and the ministry the gun, they just pointed him at the threat, and he made it dead. Decades spent on the favoured side of violence, an angel of death to his target. But here in the end his country had been reduced to ash not by some foreign threat, and Jack had never seen it coming.

"Where would you go, spy man?"

Jack turned to her, he didn't know. "Anywhere I want for once," he looked at Andrew and smiled, "What about you my boy? You really want to become some kind of king, and play puppet to these kinetics?"

Andrew smiled back, but shook his head, "Sorry to disappoint you sir, but I already know I will never become king, well, not really. But I know I have a role to play." He reached into his pocket and fished out a folded bit of paper, he unfolded it carefully and handed it to Jack. "But I do know you won't let me go it alone. You have one last mission, Knight."

Jack took the bit of paper and started to laugh, "Boy, you are good. I see a long life of court intrigue and manipulations of political figures in your future."

Andrew chuckled dryly, "Oh, I know."

"Boy," Jack looked at him, then back at Yuuki and frowned, shouldering the case holding the sword again. "This stays with me till I say so. Try and take it and-"

She snorted and suddenly moved with lightning speed, so fast he could only block her, taking the full force of her kick and falling back. He felt a familiar pull from behind and curled his body around the case as he was thrown into a portal again.

****

Andrew laughed seeing Jack get sucked away. "He won't like that, Miss Yuuki."

"What? Oh, well we don't have all day. Besides, he'll get over it." She allowed herself a smile before flicking her hair about. "Come on, boy, uh, Andrew."

He nodded and stepped into her portal and was whisked away too.

She paused a moment hearing a pop and looked up to see Azure standing there holding the paper Andrew had given Jack.

"What is it?"

Azure's smile was happier this time as he held out a picture, a crudely drawn picture of a man in slacks and a Hawaiian shirt holding a sword in one hand, and a boy's hand with the other. The picture was coloured carefully, the lines no better than a stick figure, but it was the words at the bottom that made her laugh.

Me, and Uncle December

"So, will the weapon work Azure, can we stop Sal'da?"

Azure shook his head, "It's not our place to stop him, that's for others to do. But path we set can because it will help us save humanity."

Yuuki could see that he was hiding something, not that he was lying, only not saying everything.

"Your poker face is garbage, you know that?"

"I know," he said chuckling, "I never liked subterfuge, maybe I'll take a page out of our friend's book. But war is coming, and I don't have the luxury of putting all my cards face up just yet."

She nodded, she trusted him, trusted the three Immortals greatly, and without another word stepped through her portal whisking herself back to Canada.

Back to where the real fight was.

A Mother Knows

9yrs A.E. Eastern Canada

Her eyes shot open. She had Fallen asleep at her desk again, waiting for her girls to get home. What time was it? The clock on the wall must be wrong. She had only been sleeping there for a few minutes since she had last looked at it.

She shook her computer mouse and woke up the screen, turning on a TV show to give her some noise in the background. She fiddled with the mouse for another moment. It never seemed to work. This new tablet that controlled the whole thing was confusing. When she was a kid you had a remote for each device, or if you were lucky a universal one that controlled a few at once. No matter what button she tapped, or the app she swiped, they all seemed to not be working. She checked her phone but had no signal with it either.

She got up and stretched, and felt something move that shouldn't have. She grabbed at her chest and felt as something moved, her ribs seemed to pulse. She was about to scream when she remembered; the bloom.

She sat back in her chair again with a heavy sigh. What a dumb dream, her bloom was nothing like that. Was it?

She needed to clear her head, so Nancy walked to the door to see if going outside could help her. Walking through the house she grabbed a cup of coffee from the kitchen and made her way to the patio. She pulled on her coat, slipped her feet into some slippers and opened the back door, but what she saw, she couldn't understand.

There on the deck sat Amy and Madison, and beside them Ben, they were all laughing, smiling and chatting up a storm.

Nancy slid the glass door open and stepped out into the raucous. “Were you guys here the whole time?”

Ben Stood up and hugged her, “Yeah, your lovely daughters here said you were asleep at your desk again. So we came outside to sit under the wych-hazel, so we didn’t wake you.” The lovely little tree was in full bloom, despite the summer evening. Stark white bark studded by starbursts of pale orange and red blossoms.

“Hey Mum,” Amy piped in, “Isn’t it gorgeous, it’s like it's blooming just for us!”

Madison waved too, “Come on, sit down, dinner got cold, but it's your fave pizza so it’s good cold.”

Nancy looked at the table, a box of pizza with a little wizard on the top, and the heavy aroma of cheese. She did love a cold slice of pepperoni pizza, especially with a…

“Beer…?” Ben held out the frosty mug to her as if pulled from thin air.

His wide smile creeped her out, and she backed up a bit. Was he…

“Reading your mind, of course. The bloom connects all of us, hon.” He stepped closer and hugged her tight, and pulled her to a seat. The feeling as something in his chest squirmed against her side made her cringe.

Right, she almost forgot because of that stupid dream. Everyone has a bloom, that’s why everything was so peaceful.

Her daughters smiled, and Ben smiled, but it felt wrong.

It was their eyes. Sad eyes filled with fear. You couldn't hide that, eyes were the window to the soul.

Nancy had had enough, “This is all wrong, all of this! What’s going on?!”

A blast of air rocked the world suddenly, the little buds on the tree shrivelling up and turning to dust that made her cough. The whole horizon lit like dawn and began getting brighter.

She looked at the faces of her daughter, and her friend, no more smiles, just dead eyes. The bloom's inside them burst out from them, flesh and bone crumbling to dust as screaming deathbloom's rose to tower over her.

"This is all in my head! This isn't real! **GET OUT OF MY HEAD**!!!"

When Nancy opened her eyes they were gone, but the feeling of squirming, like snakes in her chest, was growing. She looked off over the fence at the sky, watching as it turned shades of yellow and orange. Off to the southwest, the light faded from the summer sky. Now as she looked at the snow falling all around her, she felt so, wrong.

The Longest Road

18yrs A.E. South Central Japan

The brightly lit buildings towering over the city streets, signs flashing neon colours. LED screens proclaiming their multitude of wares and exotic local attractions. Akihabara square was as bustling as it ever had been before the Event.

The famous intersection was filled with cars and people, with street lights changing, and people crossing. One of the busiest street corners in the world, in a world many wondered still stood. It seemed to blur if one watched long enough, the people milling about like ants, going about their lives, blissfully unaware, or ignorantly satisfied with the current status quo. They were just so focused on just being normal.

An outside observer would almost say, it was as staged as a rakugo show. A play with two sides played by one person, it flowed in tempo, thinly veiled to distract the senses. But if you watched for long enough a keen eye could see the truth. Just one such observer quietly stepped out from a shimmering gate glowing against a wall.

Luse looked around to make sure he had not been seen. No more than a sliver of light from his gate could be seen, but he still wanted to be sure. He watched the crowd carefully, but no one even looked up. So Luse went unnoticed as he joined the throng, heading to his first stop at the immigration office.

Japan was very different from his last visit, but that had been nearly eight years before the Event. Twenty years had seen the country jump in advancement. The first thing that hit him was not the airships in the sky with turbines providing the city with unlimited power. It wasn't even the men and women who walked by sporting mechanical limbs. No, it was the security. It was heavier, even more than in other places Luse had been of late.

Large mechs rolling through the street alongside the cars were everywhere. A new kind of military tank, they were very advanced. They looked like black steel crabs, rolling along the streets or parked huddled in alcoves. Glowing eyes ever watching scanning the roads. The heavy-bodied beasts were built to traverse all terrains, large turrets built onto their shoulders and what looked like some kind of mortar on their backs.

A group of four of them rolled by, clawed feet clutching heavy-looking rubber balls. They were not fast, but they were very maneuverable. He reached out with threads of aether hoping to get a peek at what made them tick. The moment they touched the beastly bot the threads turned away though as if the armour repelled his attempts. Luse made a mental note to avoid them if he could.

When the chaos of the Event had broken, the world fell apart. The police presence was paramount on this side of the world. Floods of people left with nowhere to go fled the uncontrollable Seed and the Pod ships.

So it was that everywhere Luse looked, armed soldiers in full gear stalked the crowds. Looking like green-eyed metal golems in the same black plate armour as the tanks. They openly carried machine guns, and they looked ready for anything. This had once been such a friendly place, it made Luse sad how oppressive it felt now.

He turned a corner and came up to where a man knelt on a tatami mat. It was nice to see that this still was here, as a kid he had loved to listen to rakugo with his mother. The man was reciting the words to a popular rendition of Teresuko. He held his fan, imitating a woman's voice, then moved the fan aside, turning to speak in a deep man's voice in a sing-song fashion. Luse was surprised the man had not drawn a crowd, his voices were great, and he had great timing. Yet the people here passed the man by without a glance. Luse paused only long enough to toss a few coins into the man's collection bowl. But he didn't linger despite how much he loved the comical story of the fisherman catching the strange fish.

A group of soldiers walked behind Luse followed by no less than three drones. The things looked like arrowheads zipping around above the crowd, they didn't have any visible guns but looked viciously sharp. They seemed to be searching for something, for who or what they looked for Luse didn't know. He also didn't need to know either, he was here for a different reason. So he dallied no more and made his way to gather information.

Luse checked the old phone he brought with him, pulling up the map to the immigration office. It was close now, two more blocks and he was there.

The plain-looking government building seemed newer than most, sitting back beside a tall police station. The police station looked more like a military outpost. Two tanks flanked the door to a garage entrance, and drones flew every which way from the roof. A large airship-sized drone sitting on the roof suddenly lit up and took off. Luse checked the time on his phone again, clearly, his distraction was on time.

The doors opened and Luse walked in pulling back his hood. He looked around as he stepped inside, people from all walks of life filling the waiting room. It seemed no one was turned away, but it also seemed it was very busy. They were so efficient here though in no time he was in front of a service window.

Luse looked at the teller, "Evenin miss, do you speak English?"

She nodded, smiling, "Yes, of course, sir," she said with a giggle, "You, are Irish?" Her accent was perfect, her giggle so disarming, the act was perfect, as he looked her in the eyes he saw the levels of stress.

Luse kept it calm and nodded, "From great mother Ireland. I certainly am, my lovely. Perhaps ya could do me a favour?" He looked around quickly to make sure no one was looking and with a slight push of aether shadowed her mind. It was not something that he liked to do, but the longer he could stay off the radar the better. Just gating here had already put a target on his back. Others would be looking for him now, at least if his visions were to be believed. Being caught without papers would bring the soldiers down on him, which he couldn't risk so soon.

The young woman nodded absently and pulled a blank I.D. over to her. She pulled out her seal, put her mark on the papers, then filled it out. She then looked up above him and the glass between them turned a shade of grey from his side. In her mind, as he was he could see the screen projected on the window. Her eyes saw only what he wanted, and he filled his life in her mind. Then when it was done he released her mind and she snapped back to herself.

She looked down at the paperwork, "Your travel papers appear to be in order, what a lovely name, Luse, Mc-Mcloughlin? Did I say that right?"

Luse nodded "Beautiful, simply beautiful, you have a way with words Luv." He reached through the gap in the glass and took the papers from her.

She bowed her head a little, "Thank you, sir, thank you. Luse, like a, like Green?"

He nodded, "Indeed it is Mandarin, mother was French-Chinese, and my father a potato pickin Irishman. But they met and had me in Kyoto, military brats, you know the story."

She giggled again, this time a little more genuinely as she responded, "That sounds lovely. And what is your reason for your visit to Japan Mr. McLaughlin?"

He held his hand to his chest and smiled, "Why, I'm here looking for Luv."

She laughed again, this time snorting a little. This brought a glare from a passing woman behind her.

The woman stopped and tapped her shoulder, "Suga mi-san wa manā o ki ni shimasu." The woman then stalked off with another scowl for Luse.

She pushed her glasses up on her nose and her fake smile returned. "I would love to recommend some resorts then. Many in the country cater to single men and women. Do you know how long you plan to be in the country?"

Luse shrugged and pointed up at the billboard on the wall. A picturesque view of a gorgeous mountain range dominating the wall, "Not really, but you could help me now, do any of those resorts have a good view of Mount Fuji?"

She nodded, "Of course sir, I have all these trip plans here. There are many resorts that look out at the sacred mountain." She tapped the glass and flipped her screen to his side of the glass and showed him. The Chou main line was the quickest to get there, and there were over seven resorts. But as she went on he noticed all lines ended quite abruptly well before the mountain.

He tapped the screen, "So sorry to ask, but I'm just curious why all the lines stop or divert here? Isn't it a really popular thing to go up the mountain's summit? I mean…" He hadn't wanted to cause a problem, but the mountain was where his visions were drawing him. He should have guessed he had pushed too far, her eyes filled with dread despite her smile. She had already pushed the button under her counter.

She shook her head, "Royal decree sir, by order of the emperor – may he live forever – the mountain, it is taboo to go there. Konohanasakuya-hime must not be disturbed."

He waved his hand, a jolt of electricity jumping to her and her eyes clouded over. A trickle of light leaked from the corners of her eyes as her memories of him faded on the breeze. He looked up to find the camera behind her, he knew his face was already obscured, an odd trick of the kinetics. Conventional cameras would only see his eyes; anyone looking at his face would see only the glow and forget any feature of his Irish mug.

"Thank you miss, you've been a great help," Luse said cheerfully, and turned away from her window.

The response time of the police was impeccable. He could hear a hum already as two drones came into the large room.

"Please, you will show I.D. and get down on the floor."

The message repeated in Japanese then again in Russian, and on again in more languages than Luse knew, the drones hovering just inside the doorway. Luse watched as everyone who heard the drones all got down on their knees, pushing their faces to the floor tiles. As the drones flew over them the people held their passports up or slid them in front of them. They made sure to keep the Q.R. scan bar visible for the drones. He dropped down and followed suit, trying to not look up, but unable to resist. Two soldiers stopped just inside the door rifles held at the ready, and two more followed the one leading them.

That one's appearance stood out from the rest, slightly larger for one thing, obviously an enhancement suit. The suit itself was a stylized samurai with a demonic theme; horns on its helm, a snarling dragon's mouth and whiskers under its glowing eyes. That one carried no gun but had a strange device on their shoulder that scanned the room as the drones did.

Danger vibes came off the suited soldier in waves, one hand casually resting on the hilts of two katanas at their hip.

The soldier was speaking in Japanese making Luse have to focus to catch what was said. "We were alerted to a disturbance. Why was your terminal alerted?" Said the large soldier in a mechanical voice.

The woman at the counter stammered, "I-I must have bumped it… I did not mean to. I humbly apologize…" Luse couldn't see her but he could tell she was in tears from the sound of her voice.

"You will report for retraining, the Daimyo expects better of you. Government agents are privileged, take your duties more seriously." The soldier who spoke turned and joined the others, and both walked out following their drones as they hummed through the air.

Everyone started to mill about, so Luse stood up too. He turned to the window, but the woman was already gone. He felt bad not being able to do anything, but he knew he couldn't, and he hated knowing that he knew it, more than anything.

The whole room was a buzz, the soldiers had seemed to loosen tongues. A dozen different languages in just as many dialects all at once, made his head hurt as his powers tried to compensate and make sense of it all, he gathered himself up though and left for the street.

He walked back through the city in a short time and made his way back to Akihabara square. There he made his way down to the subway and found himself at the Chuo Line platform. Drones still buzzed everywhere, even down here. Luse did his best to avoid them, but the more he did, the more that came. It was clear they were onto something amiss, he hoped his diversion hadn't gone as bad as all this.

He would just divert one drone and two more would appear from out of nowhere. He was beginning to get worried when a voice on the speaker system announced the arrival of the train. Rather than wait he stepped around a pillar and blinked onto the track. The train speeding along he blinked again, through the cars to the only one that was mostly empty.

Mostly at least.

The people around him seemed stunned and he didn't let them think about it. With a quick jolt, he connected with every person looking at him. A quick little gesture and sparks leapt out to them all and he stole the memory of him in a flash. He held the little gems giving them a little toss in the air. He looked down at the one person whose mind he didn't touch, a little girl who looked up at him with a stunned look. He put a finger to his lips and closed his hand around the gems, then opened his hand to reveal a glowing marble. He handed it to the girl and she smiled at it, "A little memory of real magic for you," he said with a wink.

She held the little marble and put it into her pocket, "Arigato, misutā."

He ruffled her hair as he sat down, "Your very welcome kiddo."

The people snapped too as he sat down and they all looked about, but no one questioned his appearance. To them, he had always been there, and so he laid back in his seat, in relative comfort for the trip.

There were televisions up along the sides of the ceilings, flashing news and commercials. The recent events were quite troubling along the borders of China it seemed, and it had come to Japan to step in. He watched the subtitles carefully reading as the government-sponsored news expressed the joys of the people. The union of the Empress of China to the new Emperor of Japan seemed to be the greatest thing since sliced bread, at least as the people he pulled the truth from felt. Hoping to bring a rise to a new more powerful Asia, even the generals in control of United Korea began to see the benefits of their reign.

The erection of the Japanese-designed defence grid had already proven effective. No planes could pass it nor anyone on the ground.

Some kind of electromagnetic generator the towers prevented anything bigger than a mouse from passing. That was why he had had to gate in. Blinking in had been a flop, the range of the defence grid was beyond the range of a single blink.

The news of the union of Japan and China didn't come as a surprise. Luse had known it would happen eventually, but Azure and Rojas both agreed something had accelerated the event. Time was not flowing right here, and Luse's visions of the mountain were their only clue. If he didn't find the fox before the end of the week in the shadow of Mount Fuji, the war would be lost.

Even Azure couldn't say what war that was, which meant that it was bigger than even his seemingly cosmic power, and that worried them. Luse didn't know how he could stop something he didn't know about, but that was his job now it seemed.

Luse waved his hand and switched the channel, which was to say, to another newscast. This one in Chinese, and how their glorious Empress Xin, could not be any more amazing. Also how smart she was, for taking Emperor Takeo for a husband that was.

He sighed and sat sideways, kicking up his heel onto the seat next to him. He was just getting comfy, his eyes getting heavy, when a dream all too familiar crept into his head.

Luse could see it like before, a mountain rising out of a sea of glass. There were trees all around him like spindly goblin's claws reaching into the sky. Stretched out before him was a shadow, long and shifting as if the stark black mountain cast a woman's shape. She reached out to Luse her hands touching his shadow and he felt her need. He tried to reach out to her too but was stuck as he was, arms folded across his chest where he sat his seat. He knew he saw this all in his head, knew that should he open his eyes he would lose this vision. It broke his heart knowing he was so close here in the Dreamscape that he could almost touch her. Yet so far, that he could not help, not yet.

"*I'm coming little fox…,*" he whispered in his mind. Luse felt as her presence fluttered. He was closer now than ever before in his visions, the mountain so close. He turned his head towards a flurry of motion, as a pair of eyes were suddenly beside him. Bright blue and alive with sparkles flooding them, Luse almost thought it was Azure but they belonged to a shadowy form that took hold of his shoulders giving him a little shake.

Luse opened his eyes in the waking world and found the little girl was beside him. Her eyes were hazed with blue smoke as if shadowed by another, but he could sense no evil in them. She said not a word but pointed to the head of the train car where a soldier and a drone were approaching. She pointed to his boots up on the seat and wagged her finger as if to say it was bad.

He put his feet down but he had already been seen.

The soldier approached and spoke, "Ima no robun!"

Luse looked at the girl but she had already sat down. Her mother beside her held the girl tight and looked ready to flee at any moment.

He looked back at the soldier, "Sorry, what?"

The drone scanned him again, then spoke instead in its mechanical voice.

"*Papers, now.*"

Luse held up his papers quickly, the eyes on the soldier's helmet narrowing. The drone scanned the paperwork, then his face, then drew closer. It backed up and tried again, but then flashed red. The soldier raised his gun and spoke into the mic on his shoulder and the drone put itself between them.

"*Kinetic detected. You are under arrest, by order of the Emperor. Do not resist.*"

It finished and spun backwards.

Luse just smiled. He reached out with a thread of aether but he couldn't shadow the soldier. He frowned a little at that, he hadn't seen anti-kinetic metals anywhere in Asia. Only-

No, it couldn't be, the suit was just tamper-proof somehow was all.

The drone just kept repeating, so Luse held up his hands and kept his smile, the speakers on the train calling the stop, and again in English.

"*Next stop, Uneohara Station. Last stop Otsuki.*"

"Well, that's me anyhow boyo," with a quick burst of aether he pushed the soldier back. The suit resisted but was no match for Luse. With a flicker of thought, he pulled the gun away from the soldier, crushing it and his drone just by closing his hand. He pushed up hard on the soldier, bending the bars from the handholds on the ceiling and wrapping them around his arms and legs. "Been a slice, but I'm off," he gave a little nod to the little girl, then blinked off the train. The blink took him to the edge of the treeline far back from the track. The sight of the station just around the corner, and the town's lights behind it. He then blinked up into a nearby house with a window overlooking the station building.

The sight was something else for sure, a half dozen soldiers storming the train weapons drawn. Drones swarmed like angry bees, their red scanner lights sweeping the area and every person they passed.

Soldiers grabbed every person as they were forced off the train. The anger in their voices was audible while holding them. Drones scanned every face, it seemed that they had learned this way to detect kinetics. It was at least something easily hidden, but no less troubling that they had a nearly definite way to detect any unsuspecting kinetics.

Many kinetics just wanted to live their lives and be normal. Catching some like this may be a bad idea too, many more may not be as gentle as Luse with those who cornered them.

He was still watching the scene, hoping for the soldiers to just leave the innocent people alone, when he noticed something at the edge of it all. He wasn't looking for something so odd but then he saw a flash of red light from a circling drone pass over the edge of the roof. At first, he thought he saw a woman sitting at the edge of the corrugated steel peak. But as the drone fluttered off he saw the silhouette against the lights of the city, a long, fluffed tail, and pointed ears.

"A fox?" It was only there for a heartbeat and gone in a flash. Luse scanned the station and the platform, people being shoved about by angrily shouting soldiers, but no fox. The lights flickered in the train car where he had pinned the soldier. A flicker of red, there, on the roof. Luse blinked to the roof of the station and caught sight of a red tail going off the front end of the train. He blinked again towards it and caught sight of it on the track.

It was just sitting there. Watching him?

It sat there on the track before the stalled train, huge sharp-looking eyes staring up to where Luse stood.

A flash of lights came up over the edge of the roof of the platform making Luse look up. Drones again making a sweep. He looked and the fox was gone again.

Luse blinked out of sight down the track, nearly appearing right on top of the little red beast. It jumped and vanished into the shadows. He blinked again, and again it was ahead of him, he stopped and looked back down the track. He couldn't see the train or the lights, shrunken to no more than a mere glow on the clouds. He looked and found the fox again, it stood off the track now. It walked lazily up a small set of stone steps towards the top of the hill. He followed behind it and found himself on a road, a small highway from the look of it. Lights coming up from the west heading towards Uneohara. He wrapped the shadows around himself, bending the lights of the streetlamps, and watched the trucks pass. More military transports, again followed by their crabby-looking tanks.

When they passed he released the darkness and let his shadows fall back. He looked down as something brushed his leg. The fox sat staring up at him, glowing blue smoke swirling in its eyes.

He smiled at it, "Well, lead on."

As if it understood him it trotted off down the road, its fluffy red tail swishing back and forth as it picked up speed and faded into the night.

The moon was getting higher in the sky when again he caught up to the fox, sitting next to a sign.

Luse looked up at it, Otsuki, at the end of the line.

When he looked down the fox had again disappeared, the town was all but dark and the fluffy little beast was nowhere in sight.

"*Hehehehe…*," the child-like giggle carried on the wind and startled him.

He drew psire from the aether and cast a glowing orb behind him for light. He let his senses range out, but nothing was there, not even the fox.

He extinguished the psire and flooded his vision with aether instead. He looked about and found footprints in the grass nearby. They were small, and human from the look of them.

"*Hehehe…*," again the giggle, just behind him.

He didn't overreact this time, and instead, let his senses reach out. He felt something and turned and found a path.

It was a small path that led up a hill away from the town and into the trees. It led off a way, then began to climb up higher. Soon stone steps cropped up out of the trodden earth, and up ahead an ancient-looking arch. It had been red once, but it looked like it had Fallen out of care. Luse bent down and ran his fingers over one of the stone steps. They felt old, a deep memory of ages of travellers past welling up. People who had felt faith so deeply left a mark on a place. His fingers found what he sought, a paw print. It was set in the stone, lightly pressed into it, but the memory it held was fresh.

He turned back and looked up at Mount Fuji, it stood so stark in the night, the stars in the sky lighting its silhouette against the night's inky majesty. The moon behind him pierced the clouds that had hidden it and split the heavens.

He looked back up at the shrine arch and saw the fox pass the pillar, and stood shocked as a little girl stepped out the other side. The moon disappeared behind a cloud again and the shadows swallowed the child up.

Luse ran up the stairs now, his mind a race as his feet tried to keep up. He didn't try to blink forward, somehow he knew it wouldn't work. That he had to make the top on his own. He knew it though, the sense of knowing was so strong it pulled him like puppet strings. His dream pulled him to the mountain, but fate was pulling him up this hill.

The pillars grew more frequent as he climbed too, each one looking more and more well kept, each adorned with hanging baubles, or lanterns lit with bluish flames.

He ran and ran, and soon the hill grew flat and he burst from the woods into a courtyard. It was lit all around with more blue-flame lamps and candles. It was mostly an open yard of cobblestones, but at the back sat a small shrine. It was tall, made of wood, and built in a very traditional Japanese style with the piqued roof built with wooden shingles. The door to the shrine was open, the rice paper screen lit from within by a pulsing yellow glow.

Luse stepped towards it but froze. Again, the moon crept out from the clouds, the moonlight spilling across the yard to reveal he was not as alone as he thought.

Everywhere he looked stood temple priestesses in Shinto Miko robes, long red and white robes cut straight with high belts. They stood stalk still but not a one looked pleased to see him. Several held bows with arrows knocked ready to loose. Just as many though just stood there holding fans or rods that ended in loops with rings. Though the breeze blew here none seemed to move, not a hair strayed out of place, the only sound coming from the trinkets that hung from the arches as they jingled together.

"Ehem…," the cough came from up above, and Luse looked up to the shrine roof where an old man sat in the lotus position balancing on just two fingers.

Luse looked at the old man, he looked like an egg on a skeleton's body. His robes hanging from him loosely fell off his shoulders almost lazily. He stretched his head up high and exhaled a plume of smoke before settling back down on the edge of the roof. He slipped to the ground lightly gliding to the ground as if made of wind himself. He brought a long old pipe to his lips and took a long pull exhaling another plume of spicy-smelling smoke.

Luse moved to step forward but heard the tension of bows pulled tighter. He froze again, "I come…"

"In peace," the old man mimicked in Luse's voice.

Luse shivered and nodded, he could feel the aether pulled about him, whatever this man and these women were, they were not human. But they were not kinetics either.

The old man came to stand before Luse then flopped down to the ground. One of the Miko was suddenly at his side and set a pillow down for him. He sprawled out and reached out and patted the ground in front of him. Luse looked down, the man patted the ground again, and so Luse sat. Slowly, making no quick motions, and keeping his hands visible he got comfortable.

The old man had a kind look to his face, a kind smile and wise eyes, and somehow he looked familiar. Luse was trying to place the reason why as a moonbeam passed over the man, the flow of aether twisted, and the man's features changed. Long flowing tails twisted in the darkness, hidden only in the moonlight's embrace, till the shadows lifted and the moon bathed them in its cold blue light, their illusions returning them to human form. Only now Luse sat across from himself.

"You're a giant fox?" Luse couldn't believe it.

The man nodded back at him, "I am, and I'm not. I am only me, as you are you. A traveller," he pointed up to the sky with his pipe.

Luse knew about the Mirri and their Seed, but he had never met the like Azure and Adam had.

"What are you?"

The man chuckled, "Old, and running out of time. But if you must call me something, you may call me Inari." He coughed hard, curling in on himself clutching his side with his free hand. One of the Miko was there in a flash and handed him a large silver flask that sparked faintly. The silvery metal was etched with strange scrawling lines and was inlaid with moonstones carved to resemble the moon phases. Inari uncorked the lid and pet the young Miko's cheek before unstopping the lid with a resounding pop. A flood of pure aether poured up from it and filled the air, raw and wild it made Luse's senses go wild. Inari's face changed, eyes narrowing into a bestial vulpine form and he drank the pure power from the flask. His jaws opened and he inhaled the sparkling cloud, then closed it up and his face returned to that of Luse's again.

"This mana will not keep me alive much longer. The rise of your kind has seen the flow of mana return to its rightful heirs. For seventeen years I have dreaded this day, but I'm afraid I gaze now upon my last full moon."

The Miko seated near him began to cry, soundlessly sobbing as if her voice was beyond Luse's ears to comprehend.

The man saw Luse's look and reached out and handed the woman his flask, "My daughters. They have no voice to give words, but they are more expressive than any who has ever held breath to let pass lips."

Luse leaned forward, "I never believed in aliens and the like, I never even believed in myth. But here I am, talking to a living myth, a fox spirit, from space? Because I became this, a kinetic, now dreams plague me, and I see foxes in my sleep, innocence hiding in the shadow of ancient mountains. An somthin tells me, ye know what it means?"

"Often we find ourselves faced with choices. "Inari said nodding, "Do I believe in the dream? Do you follow what you see? What is real? The intangible belief, or what you hold in your hands? Do you stay content with what you know to be true? Or risk it all on hope? All of these things bog down our mind, yours most of all." He rolled back to look up at the sky, "Long before your kind had ever rolled a stone and called it a wheel. My kind were slaves to beings who called themselves gods, the Ari. They came and took us from our home, used us as beasts to fight their wars knowing we fed on the very essence that made them powerful. But no matter what, we held our beliefs." He exhaled a plume of smoke and its shape formed a crescent moon-shaped thing. "They brought us here and made us their weapons in their civil war. But I survived and lived to see their fall, crushed by the power of true gods. I have never seen your kind interact well, you humans are as divided as night and day. Yet who you seek is one who can restore a tenuous balance, I can feel it." He jabbed the smoky crescent, it floated up into the sky and disappeared in the wind. "You are here to fix this imbalance, three have risen, six more shall follow, and by three more nine shall be the balance less one," he paused, looking at Luse, "That is prophecy if you wish to write that down?"

"Like a steel trap this noodle," Luse chuckled and tapped his temple.

"I am so overjoyed to have gotten to witness the rise of your people. So I would like to offer you an exchange of sorts."

Luse was no less confused than when he had come here, but he knew he had to accept. That gnawing feeling of the knowing digging at his chest, and the feeling of twisting fates. Luse nodded and shuffled closer.

Inari waved his pipe as he smoked, "Your task, the dream that brought you here. It is true, a fox does lie within the mountain, and so much more. The child is human, or mostly. But her bloodline can be traced to one of my daughters and is very strong. She is human, but she is like you now. But so are those who have been giving help to the new emperor, dark children, like yourself… yet, not like yourself." The smoke he exhaled this time took on the shape of a lotus with long thorns tipping every petal.

"The bloom?" Luse paused, looking hard at the shape, "No, a Fallen. Does he know what the bloom are?" Luse had not for a moment thought that it was the Fallen who were behind the recent burst in Japan's progress. Rouge kinetics were abundant since the Event and were well known to interfere wherever they wanted to. But the bloom and the Fallen, they were just monsters. He looked up at the smoke, "What are they doing?"

Inari shook his head sadly, "I have no idea. All I know is that I have heard whispers, the humans and their demons are planning something. The island shakes daily and still they build their weapons, and march on their brothers and sisters." He grinned wickedly, "They never learned to let sleeping dragons lay."

Inari held up his hand and one of the Miko came to Luse's side, making him jump. He could see her now, they all seemed to care less about hiding their appearance, her large ears twitching, long red tail swishing about. She held a pillow in her hands and nestled on it the flask. It still sparked faintly, and the overflowing power in it was intense. Inari looked at Luse expectantly so Luse picked it up.

He smiled broadly as Luse took the flask and sat up, "So here is my bargain immortal."

Luse looked up in surprise, he had never said he was immortal, how had Inari known?

Inari just smiled, "Don't look so shocked, you're hardly the first of your kind. My nose senses the ages haven't touched you, and I doubt they ever will." He chuckled and reached out with his pipe and jabbed Luse, "So, my bargain?"

Luse shook, and nodded, "Yes. I mean to say, what is it that you want?"

"I will give you that, to aid you in your quest. In return I ask for only one thing," Inari looked sombre for the first time. He came to a kneeling pose and placed his forehead on the ground, "Please save all of my children?" Several of the Miko rushed over to him and tried to tug him up. Their faces and gestures were all ones of shock and sadness at his prostration.

He shooed them off and remained face down till Luse himself called out to him, "Please Inari, please stop. I swear on my word, I will protect them with my life. Just please stop this."

Inari sat up and looked Luse in the eye, "It is not protection they need, it is freedom, child." He looked up at the sky, "I want these poor children to see the cosmos, it is the only thing that has kept me alive all these days. We are trapped here without any hope, there are none who would help my kind, too much bad blood is held against us. Those with the means to leave this world would never help my kind, which will make this world our tomb." He coughed a little, "Promise me that you will help them leave this world, help them see the stars one day."

Luse didn't even have to think, he handed back the flask. "You don't have to bribe me, these lovely lasses will see the stars."

Inari pushed the flask back at him, "You will need that more than me immortal. It is not a bribe, it is my end of the bargain, I have seen it in the stars." He coughed again, this time harder than before, he smiled when he sat up silver blood trickling down from the corner of his mouth. Again he pushed the flask away, "Thanks, but it'll do me no good. For years I fed on the mana, it has prolonged my life many times beyond the norm even for my kind." One of the Miko handed him a cloth, "I wasn't jesting when I said this is my last full moon. Just go, and know the blessing of a fox spirit from space isn't as funny as it sounds." Inari broke off into a wracking cough again but didn't stop. He coughed, and the Miko cried. There was a huge welling of power as Inari stood up, his body changing. His arms and legs grew long, face again becoming that of a fox. His skin became white fur, glowing faintly as he rose to tower over the temple roof. His tails thrashed about and the ground around them shook as waves of kinetic power lashed out. The aether screamed as his coughs became howls of pain.

Luse stood up and reached out with his power, but before he could do anything the Miko's around him acted faster, blocking him with ringed metal staves that on touch made his control of his powers slip away like a fish in a rain barrel.

"What are you doin, let me help!" He pleaded, but they pressed forward and pinned Luse down, the metal seeming to leech away his power.

Inari clutched his chest and finally settled back, his silver-white fur growing duller. He looked at Luse with those smoke blue eyes, so still, so peaceful. He smiled one last time, and just like that he was gone, the light within his eyes fading.

The Miko around the clearing all began to cry, most dropped their weapons weeping silently. Some lost all control, turning into what Luse assumed were their true forms. Thin humanoid foxes with long tails, their bodies covered in red or gold fur. They made no noise as they cried, but it was so true what Inari had said. Truly, Luse had never known anyone so deeply expressive. How they called to each other without a word, gave solace, and showed their loss. Luse had only once before felt anything so deeply sorrowful, in all his life.

Luse sat there for what felt like a long time as the Miko went about interning Inari's remains. When they were done one of the Miko who had taken on her true form walked over to him. She was a bright golden colour, her fur seeming to be made of sunlight from how she shone with aether. Fox's eyes met his and he stared back at her. She raised her hand and mimed an action, but he was not sure what to do. He paused a moment then reached his hand out.

"I don't know how to sign, but if you let me in for just a moment?"

She didn't even hesitate for a second, just ducked her head under his hand, her mind opening to him like a lotus. He quickly found what he needed gleaning the knowledge of their sign language, her mind like a deep ocean of feelings. Like her father, she drank a bit of his power, a shared feeling of joy emanating through the link.

It was a fraction of a second, but it felt much longer and he stepped back shaking his hand and signing to her.

"*Thanks.*"

She clapped her hands, and signed back, "*Can you make fire?*"

A small flame danced to life at the fingertip of a white-haired Miko beside her.

Luse nodded and raised his hand and conjured a ball of green psire to his palm. She nodded and turned to where Inari's remains lay wrapped on a pyre. She and a few others who also had pale or gold fur stepped into a rough circle with Luse. Most returned to their human form but all of them followed him. He felt the flows of power around each one as they conjured tiny white and blue flames, no more than a candle's size. They threw the flames at the kindling around Inari and Luse cast out his flame as well.

He could have lit the body alone, but it seemed rude, so he held back.

The fires lit the pyre instantly and in no time a blazing fire consumed his corpse. The Miko all threw flowers and little things into the fire, but Luse didn't know what to do.

Luse stepped back from the fire and walked to the archway leading down the hillside. He stopped only long enough to find the Miko who had come to him. She was in a human form now and leaned heavily on her staff near the arch with a little smile on her face. She stood up straight when he came over and reached back to straighten out the fur of her tail as he neared. It seemed a nervous thing and she waved as he came close.

"*Thank you again immortal,*" she signed.

Luse shook his head, "I'm not even sure I did anything. I'm not even sure what to do now." He shrugged, "And please, call me Luse."

She held up a fold of leather that looked familiar. She leaned her chin on her staff humming softly as she looked at it.

"*Not Jean-Guy?*"

He looked at what she had, and checked his pocket, frowning. He attempted to snatch back his wallet but she was quick, she flipped her hand again now holding his fake passport too.

"*Luse? Odd name…*"

"Sneaky little blighter. No, not Jean-Guy, I keep trying to leave that name behind me. It's easier for some of my friends, I guess. But…"

He opened his hand wide, the passport and wallet jumping to him. Then he paused. Even now about to slip his old life back into his pocket, he looked at the fold of leather and the fox woman. He watched as they burned little mementos and such, then tossed the wallet and papers into the fire to burn with Inari.

"I'm Luse."

"*I'm called, Fond.*" She signed so quickly and fluidly it was like watching her hands dance. "*The path that's easy is never one worth travelling anyway. You truly honour our father with such an offering,*" she lunged forward and hugged him suddenly then. Without a free hand, he just hugged her back. When she stepped back he could tell she was crying again, but she smiled all the same. Her hands already signing quickly again, "*Thank you again, and please take the staff. It is made to combat people like us, those gifted with the voids mana will find themselves unable to cast for a short time after being struck by it.*" She must have understood the look on his face because she giggled soundlessly. She tapped the stones embedded in the metal with one hand as she signed with the other. Each time she brushed the stone her glamour faded and she became a fox, before turning human again. In the end, she settled on something in between, a human form but with her fox tail and ears. "*The stones are a false diamond. So those with the gift like you, and ourselves lose power when touched by them. Many man-made materials become hungry for mana, and devour abilities.*"

Luse nodded, he had noticed this too but had never seen one so powerful. Azure made devices using diamonds like these, machines powered by aether. So few people were capable of copying his technique though, despite his attempts to train others. Most of the devices could be used for no more than batteries to store aether. Like smaller versions of the flask, he had been given.

"I promise to return for all of you, I will." He stepped closer to Fond carefully.

She slipped the flask into a bag, and handed it to him, he hadn't even seen her take it.

"*It's fine, we are not without our means, our father just wants us to dream bigger. None of us have known the wonders of the stars as he did, and it is not possible for most of us to live as long as he had, so we know that it may not be our fate to leave this world. So for now this is home,*" she pet his cheek, then playfully tweaked his nose. "*Besides, humans are fun to tease,*" he noticed one of the little ones nearby pointing at the bag in his hands and giggling.

He held it up and noticed the bag's design for the first time. A sour-looking pink cat with big eyes meant for a little girl or boy.

"Oh, it'll take more than that to get me, lass," he shouldered the bag and struck a pose. There was a smattering of clapping and he did blush a bit this time despite himself. Luse looked through the clearing in the trees, the mountain far away illuminated by the bright full moon.

"I wish I knew what I was doing, instead of just knowing I have to do something."

Fond nodded. She then stepped around him so that the mountain framed her and began to sign again, her delicate fingers nimbly flying through verse,

"*Our father often said, not knowing one's own fate is a gift because it gives us the illusion of choice. But I believe, to know one's fate, and go to it, not a willing cow, but a hopeful bird will see you soar to new heights.*"

He paused as she finished, watching her hands as again her tail came around her and she nervously petted it.

He smiled and nodded, "You're right, you are lass. You fox people are truly incredible."

Fond flushed red in the cheeks and pulled her tail up in front of her. He noticed for the first time too that she had more than one tail, the tips of her tails clutched in front of her as if to shield her while a third wagged happily from his praise.

One of her sisters, a bright red-haired girl walked up beside her with a devilish smirk and signed to him.

"*I bet she read that on a fortune cookie, she's usually as deep as a mud puddle.*" She leaned in to Find and nuzzled her ear affectionately.

Fond looked up angrily at her, looked at Luse, and turned all the redder still and suddenly vanished altogether. It was like the shadows just reached up and swallowed her whole.

Luse stared at where she had been, her sister, as well as a few others, walking over. They all seemed to be having a good laugh, it was nice to see their smiles breaking through on their tear-streaked cheeks. It made Luse feel better, the air filled with a happy aura. A few still gathered around the pyre, but even they smiled with a genuine glow.

He looked around for Fond, but the silver-furred fox seemed to be gone. He walked to the edge of the clearing and turned back to the Miko who were still gathered. He hiked his little pink pack up on his shoulder, he then opened a little gate and slipped the staff into it.

He bowed deeply to the foxes, "I promise I'll be back, I'll come back for all of you. Also, I wanted to say thank you Fond, I promise I'll try hard to fly." And with that, he walked off, back down the path towards town.

****

In Akihabara, the streets of the city were still in chaos below Bekka. She sat on the edge of a building kicking her feet in time to the music playing in her earbuds. The rooftop was windy, and the air was cool for winter in Japan. From her perch atop the tall building, she could still see the soldiers on the ground, and their drones buzzing about. She folded back a lock of her purple hair into her hood and pulled it lower over her eyes. It wasn't like anyone but her spotter could see her, she made sure of that, and she wasn't cold. No, Bekka just liked how the style of it made her feel like some vigilante hero on patrol.

But, she was getting bored of waiting.

Two hours later and she was still waiting, but two hours more and she was getting worried.

It had been four hours and they had had no sign from Luse at all. He had explained his plan to her, where he was going, and how long it should take. But as she watched the clock on her old smartphone she shook her head. Two minutes and he would officially be late.

The streets were still filled to bursting, and she had only made a small distraction. No one was any the wiser.

The wrecked mech was still in the streets, a small wall of barricades around it. It was still smoking from the hole where its power core had been too. She had blown it out herself, though it had not been easy. Luse had forgotten to mention these crab tanks could not be touched by aether.

Bekka was not good at combat, she was a shield, not a spear. Her abilities lay in illusion and defence, though she was a good shot with ol'Sparky

Bekka leaned back against Sparky – an old PVC tube she used as a makeshift forced air cannon – it rattled and clinked, and she adjusted her skirts.

The mech had not expected to have a burst of lighting punch it across the street, the shot of plasma tearing its power core clean out. Her spotter David had gated her out of there so fast, no one had ever seen her do it.

Her phone beeped and she looked at it, eleven o'clock, time to pull out.

She looked at the sky, it was still early, and the moon was only just beginning to dip past the zenith. She let aether flood her vision and looked across to where David would be. She flashed a quick psire signal and looked down at the street. Bekka wasn't good with following orders, but they did need to leave the area. She looked down and took note of the people on the street, a few soldiers, but nothing she couldn't avoid. She grabbed Sparky's strap and picked it up. She hugged it tight and tipped forward into the air.

The rush of the air was always what she loved the most. The way the world sang as she fell through the sky was exhilarating. The lights flew past her in a blur, and the ground rushed up to meet her.

Bekka did this all the time, air and heat wrapping around her as she formed a mirage. To anyone looking she was no more than a shimmer. So she pushed a burst of air downwards and dropped to the street like a feather, the ruffles of her long black skirt fluttering about.

So quiet, and wrapped in a shimmer no one saw her till she joined a group of tourists. They were all talking and looking around for what could have caused such a strange breeze. She mumbled about a big drone, and they all together walked on, no one even questioning her presence.

David would have seen her jump for sure so she made her way to the crosswalk, and sure enough there he was. She waited to cross and joined him as he stepped under a corner noodle shop and ordered some noodles. He stepped over beside her as she passed with a smile, and nudged her, "You got some kind of death wish there Beck."

She shrugged and nudged him back. "No worse than you with all that spicy food, it'll kill your gut one day you know."

David just shrugged, "So, are we headed to extraction then?" He shovelled a bit of noodle into his mouth and slurped noisily, making Bekka cringe.

She shook her head though, "I've got a bad feeling Davey. Somethings up…," she mumbled that last bit, adjusting the hood of her coat again.

He nodded, "Yeah, something feels off, the aether is… I don't know, it feels all… twisty."

They turned towards the hotel district, a less traced area, or at least a more discreet area. It was quiet here, the place they went to was a kind of safe-house for kinetics. When they walked in she nodded to the guard, but she noticed that there were a few keys still missing from the hooks. So the others had either left or were still out. David returned their key and they went up to their meeting room.

David went to the minibar and grabbed a drink, a Canadian rye he preferred. While he rummaged for something else, Bekka walked over to one of the couches. She was exhausted, having had a hard time sleeping during the day she had now been up for over twenty hours. "Hey Davey, you mind if we don't head home right away?"

David stood up noodles in one hand – now covered in some kind of chilli sauce – a tall drink in his other. He chewed quickly and swallowed, "S-sorry," he coughed, "You okay?"

Bekka nodded, "I'm fine and trust me, I want to head home. I want to see my kids so badly. I'm just exhausted, mind if I catch a few hours of Z's?"

David nodded, "Yeah, that's fine. I was going to go pick up something anyway. I'll just finish this on the move."

"Oh don't worry, you can eat here," she didn't want him to have to run away.

But he waved her off, "Already leaving partner." With hands full he didn't even bother with the door, instead, he just blinked away. There was a slight pop, seeming to just disappear in an instant, his body suddenly sucked into what looked like a pinhole of darkness.

Bekka envied people who could move like that, she was fast even for a kinetic. But people who could gate or blink… or both, they always seemed so free-willed. She had tried to learn but it was just not something she could wrap her head around. Something about wormholes being around us all the time, just unable to see them for how small they were. People who could blink could travel those wormholes and seemed to move faster. The difference between quick-stepping like she did, and real blinking was major. While she was just moving faster than the normal eye could follow, she was still constrained by obstacles. People like David could move meters, but there was more to what they did. Having to know where the wormholes were, and where they led to was a serious skill.

She had decided it was not worth the risk. She had a family to live for. Luse often said it was that fear that held her back though. Bekka liked to joke though that it wasn't fear, but common sense.

She made herself busy so that when she got up she could just grab her things and go. Something was making her feel off. Despite the fact the operation had been a total success, her stomach still twisted. She couldn't explain it, but it was like her aether was coiling in her chest.

She sat down in front of the mirror in the bath, slowly taking out the hairpins that held her new wig on. She pulled off the multihued purple wig and shook it out, fraying at the seams, and ready to fall apart already, it was cheap but so pretty. She ran her fingers through her short blond hair and sighed. She would borrow some thread and material from another wig and fix it later. It was hard to focus for some reason still. She pet the lovely purple wig and placed it in her bag safely.

Her phone beeped again, already midnight, she needed to sleep. It just felt like she was missing something though and she couldn't figure out what.

As she lay there a tremor shook the building and she looked up. A massive surge of aether, but it was so strange. It was as if the energy was returning to the earth.

She felt something cold touch her hand and looked down. She touched her cheek, realizing she was crying. It was so odd, she didn't know why.

****

Fond had watched Luse as he left, all the way down the hill till he left the barrier. She had then gone back to her duties, but try as she might she could not rid her mind of him. For a human, he was something special. Never before had a human made her feel like such a giddy little schoolgirl. She was still blushing as she walked away into the woods away from the fire. She knew she should be sad, but she couldn't be. Her father was ancient, he had been ready for this for a long time. She was happy to see him at peace now.

She was nearly eighty years old and in all her years her father had never allowed her more than passing interactions with a human – trips to town to gather offerings for the temple, and such. He was never cruel to them, just afraid of the humans finding out their secret. Nowadays a person unable to speak was not so strange in society, three of her daughters had led good lives in the human world till the Event. Only her eldest had come home when called though, so she was still worried for the other two. Both were very capable girls, but; a mother would worry.

A sense of malice floated on the breeze making her nose wrinkle. It smelt heavily of anger still and ready to strike from beneath a calm crisp winter lake, a scent she knew all too well, the scent of one of her brothers.

Male Fenix could live for thousands of years longer than Fenix women, they also grew much bigger and had stronger powers. Matters made worse, Oosta and Cammu, her oldest brothers, were the eldest of Inari's children. At one time the temple guardians, but age, and time amongst the humans had made them hateful. Countless years older than she was, she could sense one was close, and it made her fur bristle.

Her brothers were the only other males besides her father she had ever met. A product of breeding Inari said, only a male and female Fenix could produce a male for some reason. So it was that the scent grew stronger as she came to the edge of the woods, and she grew more concerned.

She said a small prayer for her father again, a hope that his burden did not weigh his soul on his journey back to the void.

She had not seen either of her brothers in ten years though it was for the best she assumed. With Inari gone, not many here could have controlled those two. She hated to think what those violent fools were doing now, especially now that their father was gone.

Their lives had Fallen apart as fast as the human world had in the turmoil of the last decade. Inari had sold all his companies off, liquidated all his assets after the Event and never looked back.

He had been a major mogul in the human world. He was smart, with the backing of ages, and knowledge of tech beyond human know-how. But he was cruel, he had ruined many lives and used his powers to become a major player in human society.

Then just up and disappeared.

Her brothers had refused to give up their wealth and power, so Inari's last act was to destroy both sons' businesses ruthlessly too.

Inari had wanted them home, to be safe, to guard their home as was the plan. The Fenix had been trapped here since the fall of the Ari eons ago, long before her time, but her father had never stopped talking about it. The potential to finally go home was theirs at last. To see if any of their race still lived other than them, and if not, to try to not become the end of their people. So when these strange human Immortals began to venture out, he began to teach them more, and venture out less.

When her brothers had vanished Inari then used most of his power to reactivate the Ari's technology here. Without his sons to guard the temple, Inari had raised a barrier around the shrine so no human could come here.

That was over fifteen years ago, till today, walking through it as if it did not exist.

And oh what a human.

She blushed again and stroked her tail, thinking about his accent and especially his eyes, like swirling green star-filled galaxies.

She shivered and walked on towards the barrier waving her hand across one of the ward stones there. It lit up and a display glimmered to life at her touch. She monitored the readings as Inari had shown her, then altered them a little. The barrier consumed so much, the defences so little, so she transferred power to the defences so that if the barrier failed then they would at least not be caught without help. She walked to the strange-looking tree amongst the others. Its silvery trunk was stark and straight, climbing up above the treeline.

The crown of the tree looked like a colossal ball-shaped birdcage, swarms of silvery creatures silently watching her as she stepped close. She held her hand up the bangle on her wrist paired to the defences and watched as a small flock of the creatures responded to her will. They flew down and one perched on her hand, the others flapping about her too. She petted the one on her hand, its seemingly liquid body humming with power as its beaked face scanned the area.

Fond looked off towards the temple, the familiar feeling as her sisters began calling for her. She shook the bird off letting it return to its cage and made her way back up to the temple. She stopped a few more times but headed back, checking the trees along the way. That human's presence, though nice, did trouble her. Luse, what an odd name, for such an interesting man.

When she came into the clearing she found her sisters mostly spread out, many still tending their father's pyre. She grabbed a few more sheets of paper and tossed them in with her wishes. Several of her sisters still cried and sobbed. She dabbed her eyes with her sleeve too. He may have been a rigid old fool, but he had always been a good father, at least to them.

"Sssssssso, the old man is dead," came a hiss on the wind.

Fond drew her fan hiding her bangle and activated it, she knew that voice. A shadow crept up from the trees, the massive form of her brother Cammu stalking forward. She lowered her fan as he drew near, this was only an illusion. The barrier was still active, he was outside it somewhere though. From how ghostly the image was he could have been anywhere in the countryside.

Cammu sat down near the fire, many of the sisters clutching their daughters and slinking off into the shadows. He smiled a toothy grin, the human voice hissing through his bared teeth. "Sssssisters, nieces, I have returned. Yet you look ssssso sad, fear not, I have come back to guide you." His smile was stained with shadows as he looked up at the sky, "Ssssssome night, perfect for a happy reunion, yes?"

It was clear he had stolen the voice from how it hissed. Even their father had only ever done it twice in all her life, to take the voice of a living person was considered taboo.

Tonight was different, she could tell, Inari had been ready to kill Luse had he not liked the man's answers. She stepped up to Cammu and shook her head, without knowing where he was out in the woods she could only communicate this way. She was not happy to see her older brother, his presence meant he was here for their treasures.

His eyes glimmered darkly, "Sssssuch insolence from a pup. Inari must have never taught you manners. It's fine, sssssssoon this barrier will fall, and I will come home to reclaim the technology sssstored in the temple." He chuckled a little, his long clawed fingers dancing through the fires.

Fond glared at her brother, he had no right to be here after how he left.

"*Leave*," she signed to him.

But he didn't even look at her, he just hissed a little then continued with a smile, "Our loving father ssssssssso disapproved of my actions, he can't ssstop me now. Oosta was always the rebellious one, I only wanted to help us all. But my poor brother's death is on him." His shade shook with laughter, "He should have gone overseas as I told him to. With Inari gone, it falls to me to protect us all now." He sighed and stood up walking towards the shrine on his hind legs.

Fond moved to stand between him and the temple, fixing him with a stern look.

"Why must you vex me, child," he mumbled quietly. He then looked up, staring off at the mountain, large ears swishing as if he could hear something. His lips peeled back in a snarl, "And who are you…?" He did not ask anyone in the clearing, more seeming to speak to the mountain instead.

The moon suddenly peeked out from behind the clouds washing over him and in a glimmer of foxfire the shadowy illusion vanished.

Fond looked to her sisters who wore the bangle as she did and activated them. The tower defences coming alive took to the sky but she quickly recalled them. The barrier would hold, at least for as long as she needed it to.

Many of the sisters looked as horrified as she did. Their home was no longer safe,

****

Luse marched on through the woods, his mind swimming to the brink of drowning in this sea of new information. He still couldn't wrap his mind around it all, more travellers, foxes, or at least something like a fox. Aliens he knew, but what were these Ari, Inari had spoken of?

Luse was beginning to feel unwell.

Luse looked up at the mountain ahead of him, Mount Fuji towering ominously above the clouds.

A flash of light made him turn back, blue sparks and a crackle of power that lingered in the air. He looked for the arch he had just stepped through though, but it was gone. The path was gone, the stairs gone, all of it, gone.

No turning back he supposed, he instead continued onwards down the hillside, and eventually back to the town of Otsuki.

The town was as dead and empty as he had thought it may be. He walked down the streets following the signs for the quickest route back out to the highway. At one point he had to hide, seeing lights coming around a corner behind him. Quickly he blinked inside a nearby house avoiding a trio of drones sweeping the streets. A moment later the windows began to shake and he watched as one of the crab tanks passed too. It was making its way along behind the drones and a jeep truck filled with soldiers. A second tank behind the truck came next pulling a huge crawler unit by chains. The crawler looked like a centipede being led on a leash, its square mechanical body snaking along the road in that way that centipedes did on all those legs. It was carrying cargo on each of its six segments, heavily laden, its clawed feet even left gouges in the asphalt road. Luse waited for its tail end to come up and blinked onto the second last segment. It was harder on a moving target and he stumbled. The crawler paused and he quickly threw up a glamour like he had seen the foxes do. He bent the light from the moon around him making it appear he was no more than a box. A soldier came down the line looking along at the cargo, but thankfully never climbed up. After a minute the same soldier came down the other side, everything was clear to him though, and he walked past and soon the crawler's legs shuddered and they began to move again.

From their route, he could tell they were heading towards the mountain. The so-called sacred Mount Fuji and whatever was there.

The convoy made its way down the road, through the town and back out into the countryside. They did not attempt to hide their path, they owned this country. Drones flew about the fields in the distance, passing more tanks on the road heading in the other direction with similar cargo haulers. It seemed they were one of many supply trains moving at night. It seemed odd to move so much this late at night, but he wasn't surprised.

Luse made a point of checking into a few crates on the crawling barge he was on. They were all electronics, crates filled with computer parts and other odd wiring units. He couldn't have said for what, but he imagined they were for more drones. He heavily considered destroying the lot, but with the number of haulers he saw heading back towards the city, he had a feeling it wouldn't matter.

In the end, he settled for just being happy he was making good time. This was far less conspicuous than it would have been to blink in and potentially get caught, cause an issue, or worse hurt someone innocent.

Luse could feel the pull of the mountain like nothing else. Every time he closed his eyes, he could see the fox, and sometimes a woman he had never met before. So, when they came to the mountain and turned off onto a side road that led up to the mountain, he finally understood why the tanks and haulers had legs. The road ended and they headed off roads, up towards an old bus path that had seen better days. The hauler bulled along the path, its cargo staying stable as the legs turned to adjust so its body stayed mostly level. They came up to a huge gate on the side of the mountain carved out for a tower that now stood there. The gate opened as they came near and they headed into the side of the mountain, an underground bunker built into it.

Before they could disappear inside he made a note of the surrounding area. Far off to south and north in both directions Luse spied more towers like the one above the gate, floodlights blanketing the area giving no place for him to hide. Cannons loomed down from the tower top large robotic-looking eyes scanning everything. A hatch near the top opened, and the drones that had been following them flew towards it. There they were snatched up by arms that pulled the drones inside the tower.

The place was a fortress, but it was clearly not impregnable.

As soon as they passed inside the shadow of the bunker he noticed his glamour fade away, without the moonlight he had to think quickly. In a rush, Luse reached out with his senses and found a soldier nearby. The man had just removed his helmet and Luse dropped him with a quick pulse of air. He would wake up with a headache but would be fine.

Luse hopped off the hauler as it turned and made his way into the little office where he had sensed the man he had knocked out. The soldier hung propped against the wall, a half-smoked cigarette in his hand. He looked as if he had just Fallen asleep. Luse quickly stripped the man and stashed him in a crate tying him up and gagging him. He then got into the man's suit and made his way further down the path into the mountain.

The bunker here was very different from what he had expected. It was clean and well lit with only the floors unfinished, the walls and ceilings were all clean whitewashed concrete, well lit with lights built into little cages in the walls. There was venting here too, though it was still very warm.

He noticed it more as he walked further into the base that cold fresh air was being pumped through grates in the ceiling.

He left the little room, the sign on the door reading, "Smoking room." He took a quick look to check if the coast was clear, then left to follow the path ahead.

Luse could feel his goal was now at hand, a heavy pull called to him down here. It was like a rope tied to his chest drawing him into the heart of the volcano.

He passed several others in armour, but few even did more than nod. The disguise was working great, his path seemed clear, and he felt he was almost home free.

He followed the feelings and let go of his concern, letting only fate steer his path, and threw caution to the wind. The path winding downward branched off many times, but none of these side paths mattered. His goal was below, so close he felt it Like a second heartbeat. He almost felt if he closed his eyes he could have reached out and taken the string of fate that tugged his heart in hand.

It was getting warmer the further he went, the suit's sensors reading external temperatures at almost forty degrees. He stopped and removed one of his gauntlets, putting his hand on the wall. It was cool to the touch, but the air was like a furnace. He put his glove back on and walked around into the next chamber. His curiosity was too much to deny anymore. The room was a vast factory, brightly lit robotic arms pumping liquid metal through tubes. It was like a car factory powered by lava. They appeared to be 3D printing parts for something, something big.

He walked to where a strange-looking piece was being fabricated. It was like a finger, or a claw, only as big as he was tall. The screen near the line didn't show much more than that. He couldn't imagine what they were planning, maybe something to combat the English and their superweapons.

He turned and walked back out through the door. He paused as he noticed a group of soldiers approaching. Luse waited till they were in line with him then fell into line at the rear. They marched on for a while though they turned off from his path, turning towards a different tunnel. He turned to go the other way. Only this other path was not empty.

A group of soldiers stood with guns at the ready, a large samurai commander in the back. His angry-looking dragon-faced mask grinning, made him look happier than he sounded.

"Yameru!" The man shouted suddenly.

Luse heard a shuffle behind him and turned, the soldiers had all turned, guns at the ready. The samurai stood holding a sheathed sword pointed at Luse.

"So, you at least understand some Japanese, outsider?"

It was clear his cover was blown and so Luse raised his hands slowly. He removed his helmet and let it fall, "Enough to be polite. You have a fantastic grasp of English yourself."

"Not polite, you are deceitful," he said with a thick accent. A device came up off his back, a red line laser scanning over Luse's suit, "We track all suits. You stole this! Then you are a criminal. We wanted to know what you were doing, you did not wander till you came to that lab. What have you come for, thief? What have you stolen?!"

Luse smiled, "Nothing, I'm just searching for someone. So if you let me go, I will be on my way…," it was a generous offer. He counted eleven soldiers in total, barely enough to stop him, though it would be harder in those anti-kinetic armours of theirs.

None of the soldiers flinched, their commander holding up his sword held it as if to unsheathe it.

"Take him!"

Their leader shouted, and two soldiers rushed forward. Luse was ready though and quickly put up a barrier, turning the water in the air solid. The air shimmered for a moment, and both men slowed to a crawl as it turned to gel around them. The soldiers behind him opened fire too, again the air shimmered and the bullets slowed as they crawled through his barrier. He reached out with tendrils of aether, the concrete and metal used to make the tunnel turn to clay under his control. He walked over to the wall and touched it and it flowed like liquid, forming a thick wall of sharp spikes blocking their path. He then turned back to where the new group stood behind his barrier of congealed air, the two soldiers trapped like flies in amber.

He pushed toward the soldiers that were blocking his way. The wall of aerosol gel moving with him stopped more bullets, but not all things were going so smoothly.

Suddenly the samurai with the shoulder-mounted weapon stepped up, the device on his shoulder opening like a tiger lily firing a dart. It cut right through the gel and nearly hit Luse. Thankfully the shot went wide, the gel must have affected its targeting.

Luse stopped and snatched the dart up. A strange thing it was full of a bright orange liquid he imagined was something unpleasant.

Luse smiled and held the dart up, "Hey, asshole, you dropped this!" He opened a quick hole in the wall and sent it right back at the launcher. It smashed the flower-shaped thing to pieces, blowing it apart even as it seemed to be reloading. The strange violent neon orange chemical exploded all over his armour and began smoking and hissing right away. The weapon quickly ejected off his armour though, and he immediately sprayed a foam all over himself too. The chemical seemed to be eating away at the heavy armour plate of his suit already. It looked like fine cracks and it seemed to be cracking.

Luse shook his head and continued forward, "You should have let me pass!"

The soldier waved his sword at his men, "Buki o teniireru!" He shouted, and two of the men ran off.

"Send your fellas there to get all the weapons you got! Bring 'em on big boy, I ain't afraid to scrap," Luse shouted with a chuckle. The truth was he didn't want to fight, but it was too late for that. His best option now was to distract them enough and hope they'd never see his real play coming.

His wall of gel pressed forward and the men moved back. They were coming up onto a huge set of doors as big as the hallway now.

"Kare o oshimodosu," the samurai suddenly stepped forward. He grabbed two of the men and threw them into the gel wall, only to watch as they sank into its murky depths.

He snapped and savagely raged, and his men stepped back to either side. The Samurai shouted and they retreated behind him, lowering their weapons, and holstering them on their hip. They then lined up, drawing out short swords from sheaths on their backs.

Luse blinked, he had assumed this thing on his back was merely an antenna. He looked a little more at the armour he wore; then at the armour the samurai wore.

The armour the samurai was wearing was servo-assisted, which meant he was easily twice or more stronger than an average human. Most likely he was fast too, so he wasn't surprised as the samurai soldier held up his sword in one hand. One of his men knelt, holding the sheath as he drew it out. The samurai reached up and took hold of his mask, a hiss of air releasing as the faceplate split and slid back into the helmet, "Outsider, no more of your heretic magic, fight me! Or, are you a coward?!"

Luse pushed the four men he had trapped up against the wall, fusing their suits into the concrete. "I'm no coward, but I'm also no fool, make no mistake, break your word and I will bring this whole tunnel down on you." To emphasize his point Luse squeezed his hands shut making the tunnel walls groan, cracks shooting every which way. "So, it's a deal boyo, I want this all to end peacefully. But you lot have someone here against their will. So let's see what you got?" Luse tossed the gun at his hip aside and reached back and drew the short sword. For the first time realizing why Azure insisted they all learn to fight with a weapon, Luse was shit with a sword, but it would do for the moment. He felt the weight in his right hand as he checked the blade, it was finely crafted.

The samurai smiled and took hold of his fancy sword, and drew it out slowly, a shower of sparks erupting from the blade as it was drawn. Bright red hot flames intensified into a glowing white jet along the edge of the massive katana. The sword seemed to be drawing power from the suit, sputtering only when he lifted it from one hand to the other. It was at least six feet long with the curve, which gave the samurai an advantage of reach. Luse wasn't worried though.

The samurai smirked and waved the glowing, laser-edged sword twirling it about in wide sweeping arcs that left a trail in the air, and a hum in the ear.

Try as hard as he did to be intimidating though Luse couldn't help but chuckle. Most of the soldiers seemed to waver, even the kneeling soldier, dutifully holding the samurai's scabbard, looked up.

The samurai slowed his showboating and glared at Luse, "What is so funny, outsider?"

Luse held up his hand, "It's just… I mean, you have a laser sword. Like a real laser sword, how much power does that even take to use? An no wonder you have to wear that fancy armour, I can feel the heat from here. You must be cooking," Luse hit a button on his suit and disengaged the armour, the heavy plate loosening up. He shook it off and let it hit the ground with a resounding clang. Then he looked up at his opponent, "I am Luse, known as the green immortal, and barer of the Emerald Flame. Who are you that challenges me?"

The samurai stepped forward, his men retreating down the hall a short ways away. He glared down at Luse with a sneer as he spoke, "I am Yasuhiko, Kai, of the Yunshinkan dojo. Master of Tombo style…," he reached to his hip with his off hand and drew his second blade. It was less of a blade, more of a small fiery jet of a plasma torch.

Luse chuckled again, then waved his little sword about comically, "So does this thing have an on button? Guess not? Well then, guess I'll fix that…," Luse knelt and drew aether to the tips of his fingers on his left hand. Drawing on the ground, he made a rough outline of what he wanted.

"What are you doing?" Yasuhiko asked.

Luse just looked up and winked, then pushed down on the ground. The stone floor began moving like sand under his fingers. He then stood up and kicked the bits of armour, and the gun, into the kite-shaped hole. The metal hissed and screamed, melting in the pit. Luse held his hand over the hole and a bright, glowing hot shield floated up to his hand. It cooled as it rose to him, the dark-black carbonized surface seeming to absorb the light. Luse looked at Yasuhiko.

"Figured a fair fight was only fair if we both have our own fighting style advantage," Luse said with a nod.

Yasuhiko nodded, then raised his longsword high, his short sword out to the side. He then strutted forward in a stance Luse remembered seeing Azure use once.

Luse strapped the shield to his left arm and held the sword out forward, "We had our chance to end this peacefully."

Yasuhiko's mask closed with a snap, his words coming back sharply with a mechanical growl, "This is the only way for peace!"

The massive sword came at Luse so fast he had to dodge rather than block, a wide sweeping arc that came down like a hammer on an anvil, cutting the air and leaving a glowing trail As it sliced down into the floor. Luse had no time to breathe though, as just as fast the second blade came up following it. The smaller blade came glancing off the shield, the heat making Luse want to close his eyes.

He struck back without thought, stabbing forward through his guard to try and catch his opponent's side.

But Yasuhiko was as fast as Luse had assumed. Sidestepping and bringing his massive katana up using his knee on the back of the sword to swing it up even quicker.

It struck the shield, carbon steel, and plasma arcing and screaming as they skittered against one another. Luse pushed hard and sent Yasuhiko backwards a few steps. But the man just planted his sword butts on his hip, turning sideways and walking forward again, slow and menacingly.

Luse looked at his shield, a thin steaming grove cut into it where the metal had just evaporated from the intensity of the plasma. The sword in his hand felt suddenly heavy in his right hand. Luse could feel fates pull as if time were running out.

Luse raised his hand and Yasuhiko paused, "I feel I was too cock-sure mate. Yer a good fighter, even without that suit I dare bet you'd be a better swordsman than myself. Mind you I'm shite as a swordsman."

Yasuhiko didn't move, but his men were shifting in their stances. No doubt the thought came to many of them that their boss was about to win. Yasuhiko widened his stance, "I was born to the sword. It is my family's legacy to live by the sword. My daughters lived by the sword. My father and his father before him, lived by the sword. The sword is life and death…"

Luse nodded, noting the sadness in the man's voice when he spoke of his daughters. "Then I will do you the honour of not holding back mate, and take this fight seriously." Luse gripped his blade in his teeth and switched the shield to his right hand, then took the blade in his left and gave it a twirl, "And use my proper sword hand." He still wished it was somewhat heavier, a mace or club, but it felt better at least to hold the weapon in his dominant hand.

Yasuhiko just began to advance slowly again, and rushed the gap between them and brought his sword around.

Luse stepped quickly, moving in closer, careful of the short blade in the man's other hand. His shield came up hard, the edge slamming into the man's helmet knocking Yasuhiko's head back hard.

Just paused for a breath, hoping high this had done it, but it barely fazed him as he slashed at Luse across the side. Luse deflected the blow, spinning around inside the man's arms to bring them front to back. His sword caught Yasuhiko on the arm, glancing off his armour but forcing his arm down, and his blade off its mark.

Yasuhiko tried to kick Luse but missed, his powerful strike carrying him past. He didn't turn or even look, just swung his heavy blade wide. The sword caught Luse's shield again and sent him skidding back against the wall.

Luse moved to dodge, but something had him, he turned to see one of the soldiers he had fused to the wall had grabbed him. Yasuhiko's blade came down and met Luse's shield with a deafening wail, sparks flying wildly about.

Luse kicked up, shoving Yasuhiko back with incredible force, his sword sent flying, taken away as Yasuhiko was sent sprawling. With only his shield still in hand, Luse glared at the soldier in the wall.

"So, this is how you fight fair is it?"

Luse tore free of the soldier and walked over to where Yasuhiko was picking himself up. A quick pulse of aether through his body gave Luse all the strength he needed as he grabbed hold of the blazing katana with his bare hand.

The other man stopped, staring at Luse's smoking flesh, the sizzling pops as the meat of Luse's open hand cooked but did not give.

"Laser swords," Luse scoffed, "Silly things of fancy to the likes of me. What good is a weapon of light and fire when any child with kinetic power can be taught to bend such forms of matter to their will."

Yasuhiko tried in vain to wrest the sword away from Luse, but he held on tight. His fingers gripped the spine of the blade and he began to twist. The blade now sputtering guttered once more and went out. The energy arcing through Luse's arm flashed as the weapon crumpled in his grip like it was made of tin foil.

He heard the soldiers move, their blades piercing through him, hot steel separating flesh and muscle as they stabbed at him. Still holding their leader pinned down. He turned to the soldier next to him, the man's sword plunging towards his face glancing off unable to pierce Luse's indestructible diamond bones.

They stabbed and slashed, hacked and chopped, but he just healed and smiled. Several stopped trying and went for their guns, obviously no longer caring their superior was still in the way. Luse stood dragging Yasuhiko with him as a shield, holding the man up in front of him, and took hold of his shoulder crushing the armour with a vice-like grip.

"Tell your men to put their guns down, or this gets messy!"

Yasuhiko was quiet except for grunts and the whine of his suit as he strained to be free.

"TELL THEM!" Luse was done being subtle, his voice shaking the walls.

Yasuhiko waved his hand, motioning for them to put down their weapons. The men slowly lowered their guns and tossed down their swords, backing up against the walls near their comrades.

Luse reached down inside his well of aether and sent threads through the power armour to find the core to the samurai's suit, a round disc on his lower back emitting a ton of power. Luse tore it out, and the suit collapsed, the armour opening up ejecting Yasuhiko.

He was not nearly as tall as he seemed in the armour, long grey hair tied up in a bun. Luse walked around the suit slipping the power core into his backpack. He looked down at the man, his shoulder a mass of blue bruises, he stared up at Luse with hate-filled eyes, but still said nothing.

"Yeah, well, that's what you get. For the rest of you, when you're being told to stop me again, remember this, right here, this moment, an remember, how amazingly well that plan worked out for your friend here."

He turned to walk away, having left the path down towards the doors open. But stopped as he watched Yasuhiko slowly crawl over to a sword.

"Give it up brother, you can't beat me that easily, an I won't be falling for your fair fight crap twice."

Yasuhiko didn't stop though, he crept on towards the sword and picked it up. Coming to a kneeling position and tried one-handed to steady his blade.

Luse looked down at him, he knew this moment, and let his voice fill with power.

"***Stop!***"

Out of his armour, Yasuhiko was no longer immune to Luse and his power, and the man froze like a statue.

"What are you doing? Just because you lost?" Luse walked back and sat down beside him and took the blade from his hands.

"You could never understand, outsider." Yasuhiko looked even more furious, "You have already claimed victory. So why must you deny me my honourable death…"

Luse turned the blade over in his hands, the other soldiers who weren't still stuck in the wall had already fled. They had lost their will to fight.

"Go ahead then. Take the easy way out. But remember this, there are those who you mean something, whether you realize it or not. And when you're gone, who will fight for them?" Luse rolled up to his feet the other men there looking like blinking robots in their armour pasted to the wall. "I'm going to tear whatever evil bastard is responsible for all this chaos out of here, like a bad spud, roots and all. Someone will have to keep the peace." Luse turned, a final look back at Yasuhiko, the man sat still just looking at the blade. It made Luse think about Jackie, he let the feelings fill him up with new energy. With a little pulse of aether, he found Yasuhiko's thoughts, delved into his memory and found what he sought. A day in the man's mind that stuck out as two beautiful young women were being wrapped in funeral wrappings. A third woman screamed and beat on his chest, shoving him away. A feeling of conviction to find those who had claimed his daughters was all he knew, Luse let the images play over and over in the man's mind. Luse knew what it was like to blame yourself for another's death, "It is better to go on in grief than give up in defeat. So maybe ask yourself this, what would your daughters want you to do…?"

Luse walked off to the end of the hall, chased by the sound of the other man's cries of sorrow.

This was why kinetics like him were so feared. It wasn't the power to crush a fighter's body, no, it was their ability to break their mind and destroy their very will to fight.

Luse stood before the double doors as they opened into a massive elevator big enough for one of their haulers. Over two dozen soldiers stood there, weapons at the ready.

Luse just smiled and closed his eyes. He heard the weapons fire and opened himself to the aether around him.

As he opened his eyes the air shimmered and the bullets stopped. He blinked past the lot of them to the center of the room and rested his hands on the floor. A jolt of aether and the floor beneath him tore open, the metal twisting like a screw downward. He dropped down into the shaft below the elevator and as he did crushed the tracks for the lift on both sides so they couldn't follow.

He fell into the abyss, dimly lit by lights along the walls. The feeling he was close growing with every footfall. There was something else though, a new feeling, deep and pervasive, that he had not felt before.

Malice, and an intent to kill.

****

The bunker was designed to not shake even in the case of eruptions, but the water in his glass was rippling as he felt the tremor. He checked his phone, and the alert showed a minor breach on level five. So as Takeo sat, listening to the Englishman at the other end of the table drone on about results, he swiped off the message. He turned off his alerts and slid his phone under his arm.

The Englishman, Sir Smithe, was a peculiar sort. A knight of some kind so he said, he was also a bureaucrat, his rumbling voice so deep it made Takeo tired just listening to him. It was like watching a stick bug grumbling in a bear's voice.

Instead, Takeo looked across to where the young empress sat, her face as unreadable as ever. His bride-to-be looked so much like a doll, with smooth pale skin, long black hair braided down her shoulder, and perfect almond-shaped dark eyes. She was dressed in a suit, though she wore a skirt. It was hardly customary, but he had to admit, it fit her well.

The new Empress of China, Jin Xin, lived up to her title for sure, she emanated an aura of captivating beauty and power that Takeo just didn't feel he deserved.

His cousin would have made an excellent empress to Japan. Why she had abdicated from the throne he didn't know, but he had promised to lead with honour in her place. He had never led anyone before, he felt inappropriately prepared all the time. His advisors just bowed and scraped and gave him his reports, now this fool was here.

Takeo turned his attention back to the scrawny little white man sent from England. As much as his voice was grating, Takeo needed to keep them at bay, that meant learning from them as much as he could. Takeo had spent over twenty years in America, ten of those in law school. But England was nothing like America, the queen had wrested control back after the events in France and Canada. The queen's representatives said it was not a land grab, but Takeo couldn't help but notice that their holdings had doubled in the last ten years. Even more so in the last two.

Takeo looked down at his notes to find where they were in the briefing. His ears suddenly piqued at something the speaker said.

"As soon as your shipment of power cells is received your majesty we…," a gentle cough silenced the room.

Takeo looked over to where Empress Xin sat. The whole room had gone silent at such a slight sound, her ability to govern the room was truly amazing. It was no wonder she had managed to rise without opposition as her people's leader.

She leaned over to her secretary, a minister whose name escaped him, the man just nodded, then spoke.

"The Empress would like to remind you, that at this time those power cells are still the property of the Eastern Empire. They will not be sent anywhere without the needs of the people of this empire being met first. With all due respect, Mr. Smith.

"That's Sir Smithe… not Smith. And I would remind her majesty that this is why we are negotiating here." He gestured widely, a holographic display appearing across the table showing the map that outlined the current domain of China and Japan. "My Queen has graciously sent me, one of her own Royal Knights, as a representative, a gesture of good faith. We have brought you many new gifts, and have helped your two great nations ahead since the Event." Smithe, barely inclined his head, his arrogance irked Takeo greatly. But it was true, the new technology from England was amazing, at least a little, the kinetic blocking tech at least.

When Takeo had come to the throne he had learned they were not alone in this world. That the weapon the Americans had used was alien in nature, not man-made. Then again he found out that the three treasures of the royal family were too. It was a pity they had been stolen by their caretakers. Yet he had learned that seeking them out was not futile.

Takeo glanced over to the far wall where Cammu stood with Takeo's security detail. His form was just an illusion, the whole group of people in that corner were. They hid Cammu's true form from the humans in the room. The child of Inari was a fox demon, a Fenix as they called themselves, and had shared much with Takeo these last few years. When Takeo had appointed him his personal guard, Cammu had given Takeo no reason to distrust the Fenix. He knew his sisters and daughters had taken the three relics but said that made them safer. Told Takeo everything about his people, where they came from, and how they got here. How his family had manipulated Japanese stocks for generations.

So when Cammu said he didn't like the smell of Smithe, Takeo trusted him.

The whole room murmured for a moment as Takeo felt it too. Again the vibrations were rumbling the whole bunker. He looked to Cammu, but the Fenix had not moved in almost an hour. Takeo rapped his knuckles on the table, "Please, everyone, our guest is still speaking." He nodded to Smithe, and the man barely inclined his head.

Such arrogance, even in the face of one openly trying to be accommodating.

Smithe then fixed his coat and continued, "As I was trying to say. We have done our best to bring you aid. Your technology is amazing, this is true, but the Crown of England has backing beyond human comprehension. But unlike those who were helping the Americans, our allies only want to see us succeed." Smithe waved a hand over his map, the image of a chess knight appearing on the field between China's border and Mongolia.

Takeo noticed that some of what had once been Russia was marked the same colour as Mongolia. "Have the barbarians already gone so far? I was led to believe we had already pushed into the Fevralsk region?"

One of Empress Xin's generals nodded, "We had, but since the arrival of the new gods in Russia we were forced to back off." His hand tapped the table, the man did not like to speak in English, and Takeo could tell. But it had been made a rule that as no one could decide on proceedings to be held in Chinese or Japanese, then it would be English.

Unlike Takeo who had lived in America a long time, not one other here had left their own countries that he knew of.

The man still looked at Takeo as if expecting something. Takeo nodded, not knowing what else to do, and turned to Smithe.

Smithe again gestured to where he had set his piece on the map. "We will deploy Royal Knights here… and here," a second one appeared close to Pakistan. Smithe smiled, "The government of India has already agreed that British rule is better than bowing to some irrational snake charmer."

Takeo knew the son of the current prime minister of India. They had studied together at Princeton, and he still considered the man a friend. He had not heard from him in over a year though. He jotted down a note to do so and slipped it to his secretary to take it down.

Smithe coughed, "Passing notes my young Emperor?"

Takeo gave the man a deadpan stare, "A reminder."

Smithe nodded, "Ah, yes of course. Do take notes then, for this is how we will win this war."

Takeo heard that a lot of late. War, he still did not understand what it meant.

"Why do you say that? I don't recall when this became a war. Or who it is exactly, you think we are at war with? I want no part in any war. I only wish to protect my people…," he said, straightening his tie. He looked at Empress Xin, his wife-to-be, "Our people."

She looked at him then smiled, a true smile, he could feel it. He had never seen her smile outside of photographs, she truly was radiant.

Smithe looked like he was bristling, "You don't want war, but war will have you. You don't understand what it's like… or maybe you do. But you are ignorant to the facts."

His tone alone was enough that two samurai stepped out from their posts, weapons going active as laser reticles targeted his head, their hands slowly going to their hilts. As much as Takeo would have loved to see this man cut down, he raised his hand and the two soldiers returned to their posts. Though he noticed neither man deactivated their weapons.

Takeo stood up, not a tall man by any standing but he had always been fit. His father had him train every day in their family style of aikido. Now in his forties, he still never went a day without training. So as this pompous fop may be taller, Takeo was not afraid of him.

He placed his hands on the table and leaned forward, "I believe you need to remember your place, Mr. Smithe. Neither of our empires came to you, you have come to us. So if you came to garner our aid in your war, you are going the wrong way to establish a relationship that would see any of our generals send our people to war."

Smithe sighed and seemed to deflate as he slouched forward a little, "Does no one in this country understand the emphasis on title? I try, I truly do, so, please… I am one of her Majesty's Royal Knights. My title is Sir, not, mister." His hand came up to his temple rubbing at it as if to release himself from some headache. "You don't understand Emperor Takeo…, but proper etiquette is critical. It sets us apart from these heathens. People who plop out genetic mutants out of tubes and call them gods." He leaned heavily on the table, "Do you think the freaks, mutants, and monsters will just stop at your borders if you build a wall?" He rounded on Empress Xin, "Look at history. Building the biggest wall never stopped the Mongol hordes. It didn't help the Americans keep out immigrants. So I say why hide behind a wall, take the fight to them!"

Again Takeo didn't understand, "You speak as if you know of some great plot. These mutated people are not some unified threat. We have dealt with many…," he looked down at his phone and wished again his cousin was here. "Some have monstrous powers, but they are not unified."

Smithe smirked, "Aren't they?" He tapped the map image and it shifted, this time showing a map of Canada. He pointed to the middle where the name Winnipeg stood out. "This city has been our target for nearly five years now. Every year their spies range out snatching people away to turn into weapons. They still resist us in France, though at least most of those monsters they made are dead from the cold. Only the Royal Knights can truly seem to defeat them. But you have seen their powers for yourself, Emperor."

Takeo nodded, "And we have made sure our soldiers are ready to fight them."

Smithe nodded, taking his seat, "Yes. I meant to ask you about that. You figured out how the armour is able to resist their telepathy, and even somewhat their telekinesis. When do you plan to ship this promised information?"

Takeo was no fool, "We agreed to make your armour, once the order is complete it will ship. As to the properties, we already know that even their kind cannot make material so strong that a stronger one of their kind cannot break it. So till they figure out a way through our armour I will not release the compound and risk its secrets."

Smithe's smirk grew wider, "Ahhh, the age-old question of God's impotence. Yes, we have seen likewise effects with our collared ones. They cannot exceed certain limits, though they can train to grow stronger apparently. Some even become too strong and can break collars, though it is rare. Many beg to be recollared anyway if trained right."

Takeo looked at the map, "And as to this city of monsters. If they stay where they are and leave us alone, I will do the same."

"Make no mistake Emperor Takeo, they have no intentions of leaving you or anyone else alone." Smithe shuffled some papers and slipped the device emitting the hologram back into his attaché case. "We could work out a deal? Our collar tech, for your alloy compound? It would benefit us both…"

Takeo had considered it, at this point all they could do was scare off kinetics or kill them. But to capture or control them, that would be perfect. He shook his head, "For now we will continue to show force and deter them as we have."

Smithe shrugged. "It is an offer others have already taken, and one I will keep open for your cabinet too." He sat back in his seat and slid the papers he had signed over to the nearest secretary. "Well then, I presume that is all we had on the docket for today? If so, I will begin preparations to mobilize the third fleet and see to it that my Royal Knights are deployed to the north and west. Th…"

A sudden clatter in the hall made both samurai guards at the door move. The one stepped out into the hall while the other approached Takeo's shoulder. "Great Emperor, and Empress, we must move you now."

The empress's secretary was the first to speak up, "What is the meaning of this?"

Takeo checked his phone, ten missed alerts, "The breach, I thought it was contained?"

The samurai bowed deeply, "The intruder has evaded capture, it is a kinetic. They breached the elevator, and are heading towards the operations centre."

Takeo looked to where Empress Xin sat, her face again an unreadable mask. He quickly stored his phone and stood, "We will make for the monorail. From there we can decide how to proceed."

The sound of clapping suddenly silenced the rest of the room, all eyes turning to Smithe. He looked rather pleased, clapping heartily, "This is perfect." He pushed back in his chair and stood up snapping his fingers.

The shadows suddenly peeled away from the wall behind him, a man and woman in full-body suits stepping up beside him, dropping onto all fours like dogs. They wore seamless grey suits that clung to their form. Bright gold collars around their necks struck through with an odd-looking blue-green circuitry. They were emaciated to the point that as they rubbed up against Smithe's legs their bones could be seen through their suit.

The samurai moved to put himself between the strange pair and Takeo, but Takeo pushed him towards Xin. Throwing the table aside the samurai moved as he was directed. He pulled the Empress back and into Takeo's arms and drew his sword.

The table flew up towards Smithe but stopped in mid-flight. His laugh became a bit unnerving but he stepped around the table. The table squealed and flexed and suddenly shattered into splinters, the bits frozen in place in a rough sphere around the two and their master.

The pieces became like rain and fell to the ground, and Smithe just stepped through. "Please, allow me to take care of this kinetic for you, your majesties." Smithe suddenly bowed deeply, "I know how you both feel about their kind," he gestured to his followers and the two both stood up. Smithe looked at them both, a dark gleam in his eye. "My dear Empress Xin, this kinetic filth is only good to serve less they think themselves above god."

Empress Xin stood up, but she held onto Takeo closely. It made Takeo feel stronger, even in the eye of this. But it wasn't Xin who Smithe was watching.

He eyed Takeo like a hungry man might watch an apple dangled before him.

"What about you Emperor Takeo… Your poor cousin lost everything, everyone. Her mother, father, and siblings. Even her husband and their son were butchered. As I heard little more than skeletons were left of them. All because a kinetic believed that a male heir would bring war to your people. You only lived because you're so far removed from the family line that the kinetic didn't see you as a threat." He reached down and grabbed the collar of one of his strange pets, "But your cousin couldn't handle the power, and you have brought nothing but peace. These things are the ones who will bring us war! They are nothing but vile MUTANTS!"As he shouted at them he swung the frail-looking man around like a ragdoll. His grip on the collar made the things head flail about.

Takeo looked at Smithe, he thought for the first time, truly seeing him. The man was unhinged, and Takeo didn't feel he could go on with this.

"What do you want?" Xin asked, suddenly squeezing Takeo's hand.

Smithe let go of the collar, dropping the kinetic to the floor. His smile went ten levels of crazy to sweet, "To show you how we deal with kinetic scum in Great Britain…"

****

Luse met no more opposition as he dropped down to the bottom of the elevator shaft.

He found a small service vent below the shaft and opened the hatch. It was freezing cold so he raised his body temp and stepped inside. He was even closer than before to his goal bow. He could feel the pull. Yet as he grew closer that same feeling of malice had grown too.

He was walking through the vent when he felt the air change, and the pull intensified.

He found a vent cover above him, but it was too small. He let his senses flow out around him, searching the area around the vent. The path he needed went in towards the mysterious malice and whoever he sought. But the vent didn't go that way. The hall above him seemed empty, but something was off.

He decided the risk was worth it and blinked into the hallway anyway. He blinked into mid-air and lightly dropped onto the ground making no sound on the stone floors.

The hall turned as he had sensed and he followed it onwards.

Further down he came to a doorway with a keypad. He touched the keys and let his senses guide him. He typed in the pass to the last key entered and the door opened.

The moment the door opened he was hit with the stench of fear and human filth. He looked around at the round room as it went up three floors. Made up of holding cells the whole room was made of metal and hot enough that it made a mirage where vents pumped in the air.

The metal here was black and as he touched it Luse realized why it was he hadn't sensed the people here. The moment his fingers touched it the aether in his body began draining away. Prolonged contact would strip a kinetic of their powers. Everything here was made of it too, chairs, walls, even the food trays stacked by the door were made of the same metal.

There was a guard on the catwalk above and one on the third floor. Neither wore much for armour, and neither seemed to have noticed his entry, or care at least. Luse was still wearing the uniform if not the armour so he assumed maybe that was why. He grabbed a pair of trays and checked the numbers on the tags on each tray. He walked along and found the door that matched and tapped the bars.

Luse tried to not look away but wished he could have.

The man was stripped naked, except for a pair of manacles keeping his wrists to his chest. He was hobbled too, manacles around his ankles.

He looked up at Luse and came to the door slowly. He coughed but looked at Luse as he spoke, "Anatahadare? Hoka no gādo wa doko desu ka?"

Luse looked up to where one of the other guards was walking back towards the stairs. He then turned back to the man in his cell and put his finger to his lips. He let the light within him show his vision flooding with green light. The man immediately began to cry, whispering, "Arigato…," over and over. Luse put the food tray on through the slot and the man began to eat. He wept but he ate and smiled all the while.

He quickly made his pace over to the next cell with the other tray. He nodded to the other guard as they passed, a quick pulse of aether to fool the man's mind he was a friend. The man stopped and Luse handed him a smoke from his pocket, and just like that walked on.

He could feel the pull on his heart even stronger now, whoever it was he was here to find was here. Right above him now he felt that if he looked up he might be dragged through the walls to them.

The fox was here, in this miserable dungeon.

The hairs on his neck stood up all of a sudden as a tussle of air announced the door opening. Only by the grace of the aether did he manage to dodge a barrage of shrapnel.

There in the doorway to the hall stood a trio that could not have looked odder. Two tall slender, bony-looking people dressed in gimp suits, the third in a suit of golden armour.

Luse looked them over, the auras from the two in grey said to him they were kinetics, but there was something about that knight too.

"Oi, arsehole… you missed!"

The man in the armour raised one ungloved hand and snapped his fingers. Both of the kinetics dropped to all fours, gold collars on their necks going from flashing red to solid green lights. They then began to charge themselves full of aether, their reserves seemingly endless. It was dangerous to hold that much power, yet these two were holding enough to have powered a small town.

The knight then spoke in an oily slick English voice, "Donner, Sable… make the mongrel sit."

Both kinetics lashed out from across the room, fine lines of aether like spider silk firing out from them both with lightning speed.

Luse let out a field of aether around him, the energy meant to draw in their assault. The lines of aether entangled with his and he began to push back at them.

To the mundane this all must have looked so odd, one guard even stood between them. The lines of aether swimming around him through the air were invisible to them. But not to Luse, or these two.

Neither fought with any style or thought though, they just lashed out, again and again, growling like animals their wild aether had no shape or colour. Their powers were incredible but it was clear both had been cut off from their center. He couldn't imagine what that must be like, it made sense why they clutched onto every drop of aether they could get.

Luse felt a shift in the field between them as one of them all of a sudden went on the offence. The two Japanese soldiers saw this and the one on the catwalk above went for a panel on the wall. The poor fool didn't even seem to notice what happened. Didn't feel as the tray passed through him. But his step faltered and his legs hit the wall in time with his torso hitting the floor.

The tables and trays faltered a little as the material resisted their control a little. But soon anything not bolted down rose and twisted like octopus legs. The wild limbs lashing out was different with telekinesis than it was with using one's center. Exerting your will over an object was harder and more taxing, but required less practice or thought. These two attacked with the sheer force of will, and they were very willful.

But Luse was not so easy a target.

As the two kinetics attacked him, the air itself became Luse's shield. Shifting the molecules allowed him to adjust the airflow's density. So just as with the soldiers before, these kinetics attacks were forced to a crawl.

The knight tapped his foot impatiently, "What is taking you cretins so long?! You are two, he is one, he cannot be that much stronger!" The knight reached out and took the one by his collar and dragged him back, whispering to him. The kinetic made no sign it had heard over the squealing of twisting metal as its partner continued to attack. Though Luse was sure he had, as it changed from defence to offence as well.

Now with both of them attacking Luse spread his defences wide. He tried hard to push them back but it was clear they held so much power that it would not be that easy. He drew as much power from around him as he could, but the metal here was cutting him off. His own reserves were not limitless either and soon defending was becoming a strain. He was beginning to lose his patience.

He quickly took stock of the cells here, half full, he folk in them exhausted from the drain of the place. Whoever needed him was so close he could barely focus on the fight. These growling beasts were too well guarded to break into their minds.

Luse had hoped that from the moment they had attacked that this place would wear them down too, but whatever those collars were they were so full of aether they were not giving up anytime soon. He could feel it from where he stood, and it pained him to have to do this.

"I'm gettin tired here ya jackeen…"

The knight snapped his fingers again and in a flash both kinetics stopped. Their aether faded, and they crawled back to their master's side. The knight nodded.

"I am glad to see you can be reasonable, mongrel. This fight is over then…"

Luse nodded and crossed his arms, "Then I accept yer surrender."

The knight's hand came up fast, "WHY YOU INSOLENT LITTLE!"

Luse reached out with waves of pure aether, the force of it crushing all three with a gristly snapping sound, done in a second. He squeezed the very fabric of space around them, the pressure rising till he could see flesh and bone tear through their clothing as their limbs turned to glass inside his bubble of intensified gravity.

Luse let his hand fall to his side, their bodies falling wetly to the ground. He sighed and walked over. The Englishman was still alive, if barely, but all he did was choke and spit. His armour wasn't like the Japanese soldier's armour so it had done nothing to stop Luse. The kinetics bodies were trying to heal as he stepped over them. A quick pulse of aether at the base of their skull ended that though, their severed heads falling to the floor.

Luse reached down and put his hand on their chests, first one then the other. Kinetics forced to such madness deserved better than this end. He set their corpses ablaze but glared down at the crumpled armour of the knight.

"You brought this on herself. I wanted no fight here, but what your people are doin," Luse pulled the man away from the flames. He set the man down and turned away from him, "You'll have time to burn where yer goin…"

Luse started to walk away, but a sound from the Knight made him look back, he was laughing. At what, Luse had no idea though. Luse reached out with a thread of aether to try and get into his mind, but the man's mind wasn't just empty, it wasn't there. Either he was good at walling off his thoughts, or he was already brain dead.

The feeling from the cells above was still there, but he knew he couldn't just run up there. He made his way up to where the two halves of the guard still lay, stepping around him to find the panel on the wall and accessed the cell doors and opened them all. The cell on the end was where he had to go, but he took his time and got others out as he went along. He ushered the people to the stairs and slowly made his way to the last cell.

There he found a woman sprawled on the floor, her hands manacled like the others. She seemed in better health, and even as he stepped to her side he could tell she was different from the others. Her body was still full of aether, a deep pink aura around her. Her mind however was blank too, she was in the Dreamscape.

Open to that much power there was no wonder why she was still brimming with aether. Touching the Void directly was how kinetics learned to gate, which also meant this woman was a true pyrokinetic. Now he understood why fate was pulling him to her.

He knelt beside her and opened himself up to the Dreamscape too. He would have to bring her out if he was to move her safely. But going into her mind carried its risks, so he steeled himself. Took a breath. And slowly reached out, and touched her forehead.

The land around Luse was the same as every other time he had ever come to the Dreamscape, that same flat land of glass rippling like water. As always it stood dotted with strange trees pulsing with raw aether, that same old strange sky that seemed at once a roiling sea of clouds without sun or moon, and the next moment a blue, warm, and vibrant midday summer.

Here though as in the past when he had entered the minds of others, there was a piece out of place.

He spun about noting the occasional tree, but on his fourth spin there it was. As if it had always stood there, a wall of uneven flat river stone appeared. There was no gate, just this section of wall. Luse could hear the sound of running water, followed by the occasional click of wood on stone. He walked around the wall, but there was nothing there.

He paused for a moment and looked up, the wall wasn't high. He held out his hand and closed it, he felt a flutter in his palm and opened it up again. There, a little firefly sat. A trickle of memory in it he sent off, a little message to Azure and Rojas.

He found footing in the wall easily enough and climbed up. At the top, he pulled himself up and sat on the edge of the wall. He looked around a huge garden, surrounded by the wall stretching off through the center of a city. He recognized it as Kyoto at once, the unmistakable Kyoto tower in the background. But he had never seen a wall like this in the city before.

He sighed and dropped down into the garden and felt his mind become hazy. It was never easy to keep your wits when you stepped into another's dream. Thankfully he had done this enough times he was ready. As the dream tried to sweep him up he steeled himself and accepted it rather than resisting. To resist made the dream stronger, accepting his role here was to wake her made himself a part of it. He looked down at the fine robes he now wore, a yukata if he wasn't mistaken. Very finely cut and formal looking, he felt like some kind of nobleman.

The grounds of the garden were wide and filled with bamboo and rocks in decorative patches. There was a small stream off to the left of him that ran towards a house up a hill.

The reality around Luse flickered, water flowing uphill, making his mind question the place. He shook his head and remembered he was looking for someone, but there was a taint here, a wrongness that crept into his bones like an icy chill.

He walked up the hill following a rock-lined path that wound between the groves of bamboo. Nearer to the house he came to a large patch of sand that had been raked into intricate flowers. The finesse and time of this place made him realize she had been here a long time. No mere retreat from pain, this was a whole world to whoever this woman was.

The house was again a very traditional Japanese design, wide and low roofed with black tiles, the walls made of wood with sliding walls for doors. The whole thing was surrounded by a huge deck with fancy dragon-carved pillars at the corners.

As Luse approached the steps he stopped, he could hear someone running. He paused there as a little boy came running around the side of the house. He stopped when he saw Luse, and when Luse smiled the boy waved back.

Luse stepped back to the bottom of the steps, "Hello there little man, are your parents home?"

The little boy nodded, "My mummy is making lunch," he exclaimed happily.

"Well isn't that fantastic," Luse said, crossing his arms inside his sleeves. "Can you maybe, go get her for me?"

The little boy nodded and ran to the door and disappeared inside. A few minutes later returning with a tall pretty woman beside him. He tugged her arm and pointed to where Luse stood.

Luse had never seen her before in his life, but the moment he did he knew her. He bowed as she came to the top of the stairs, "Good day Empress. May I come in?"

Her face became a thundercloud as he spoke her title and Luse felt a sudden pressure as she hissed at him. "You may not! You will leave me be! This is my place!"

So she was aware at least, that made some of this easier for Luse.

The boy tugged at the long sleeve of her shirt, "Mummy, who is he? He sounds funny."

She smiled at her son, "No one Yuudai." She closed her fist and a swirl of energy grew around her. She looked down at Luse, "He's leaving anyways."

Luse shook his head, "Afraid I can't do that Empress. I'm here to rescue ya."

She was shaking with rage, waves of anger radiating off of her. "I don't want your help, you can't make me leave!"

Little Yuudai looked up, suddenly worried, hugging his mother's hip.

"You're leaving?"

She dropped to her knees beside her son and hugged him tight, "Mummy's not going anywhere precious." She hugged him tight but Luse could tell what was going on, this was no dream. She had made this place a prison, the sky growing dark as the world changed.

The world around him flickered, and Luse was suddenly standing amid flames. Spears of stone rose through the house, the bodies of people hanging from them floating in the air. Heavy snow fell all around them. Flowers like nothing Luse had ever seen sprouted all around the yard. Like six-foot-tall tiger lilies made of glowing blue glass. Little rivulets of fire poured from a few that leaned forward.

Luse looked back up at the house. A man stood over her now holding her shoulders and shaking the young empress.

"WHY YUUKI, WHY DID YOU KILL THEM?!" He shouted in her face, "WHY? HE WAS OUR SON?!" As he shook her the look in her eyes was crazed. People stood around her and Luse recognized the swirl of power as the fires consumed the man too.

The memory, something was off. The flowers around them weren't some construct of the dreams. He reached out and tried to touch one and it recoiled from him.

So that was it, "YUUKI, IT'S NOT REAL!" Luse shouted to be heard over the sound of the fire, "NONE OF THIS, IS HAPPENING!"

She shook her head, "No, I did this, I did THIS!" The roof collapsed and a cloud of smoke engulfed them all and the light faded. The world went still and quiet like someone had hit mute.

Luse stood in the choking darkness, "Please Yuuki, you have to stop this!" His voice felt hollow but Luse tried again, "Yuuki, please. You have to stop this torture," he said as he walked a few steps forward. "Even if this was real, it's done. You don't have to put yourself through this over, and over like this!"

Yuuki's soft voice echoed through the fog, "Leave me alone… please. I just want to be left alone… it's my fault, they're all dead. I killed them." A deep sorrow filled the air thicker than the cloud of noxious smoke.

Luse coughed, but kept going to her, "It wasn't you! I can prove it!" Luse found himself struggling to stand as waves of self-loathing washed over him, the dream trying to force him down. He reached out and stepped forward till his hand found her though. Yuuki struggled to be free but he held on to her wrist.

"STOP!" The fog cleared around them and he stood there with her. The flames had frozen in place, the smoke had stopped too. The only thing that moved was them, and the flowers.

"Here," he said, pointing to the flower beside them. The thing recoiled from his touch but rooted as it was it could not resist. He forced her hand to touch the glowing blue flower. As they did the scene around them changed, the place the flower stood replaced by a man. His arms held wide he had flaming orange droplets of aether dripping from the bloom that was pushed out through his throat, eyes swirling black and blue as he invaded her mind. He howled like a beast at her, filling her mind with rage and hate.

Yuuki tore her hand away from Luse, the moment of contact broke the image of the man disappearing again.

The pulsing blue lily quivered beside her once more, "What is that? What did you do?"

He waved his hand and cleared the smoke from around them more.

"I didn't do anything, they did it." As the smoke disappeared a field of blooming, blue, glassy lilies appeared, a strain of bloom Luse had never seen before. He counted more than thirty, a frightful thought so many could live beyond the cold. He touched another and found its true form revealed, a woman with another one of these new bloom. It tangled through her hair, coming out from the back of her neck.

"These monsters made you do this, and from the look of it… it took a lot of them too." He grabbed the flower and pulled but it was Yuuki who cried out.

He held up his hands apologetically, "This is what happens when a kinetic touches the mind of another, we leave a little of ourselves with whomever it is, and in the Dreamscape can see it all. It's usually different depending on the kinetic," he knew just how to help. He inhaled deeply and the smoke and fire were extinguished, revealing all of the flowers.

"You need to realize this was their doing, see them for who they are. Find the lie, face the truth," each one was the mark of a Fallen. "All of these monsters, just to take you to the brink, to make you do something so horrible." Luse walked around the bloom to the edge of the house, "I'm sorry you have had to live with this luv. But we can fix this."

Yuuki was crying now, but her eyes were aglow with aether, "Yes we can. I will kill them all!" She screamed the words at the nearest one, and it shrank back. Her rage grew stronger than her sadness, she used aether to tear the bloom up, she screamed in pain but kept at it. One after another, they were torn up. But the harder she pushed, the harder it grew. The bloom whispered to her, and Luse could tell she was failing fast.

"Why are you stopping now?"

She fell to her knees, "What does it matter? I was still the one who did it," she pulled on her hair till her knuckles were white. She hid her face in her lap as she curled up on the ground sobbing hard. The bloom's control was so strong, one at a time was impossible, she had to do it all at once.

Luse hated this, but he had to push harder, or he knew he would lose her. "Then quit! Ye seemed content before? Maybe ye can just go back to reliving killing yer family!"

Yuuki growled but didn't look up, "You have no idea what you're talking about! You don't even know me!"

Luse scoffed at her, "Oh I know exactly who you are, girly, but do you know who you are?!"

"I'm a murderer! And if you don't leave me alone, I will kill you too!" Her anger bubbled like magma within her, the ground around her beginning to smoulder and burn.

Luse looked down and spat on the ground, "What? You're angry? Good! Be angry, emotions feed us, staying calm and being rational is all well and good but if we don't allow ourselves to feel, what are we?"

She lunged to her feet and shoved Luse, sending him flying. "JUST GET OUT OF MY HEAD!" The force cast him back so hard he hit the stone wall he had climbed to get in. She flickered from where she was getting closer, and for the first time, he saw her face, how she really looked. She was still fiercely beautiful, but the whole right side of her face was a scarred mess.

"I'm nothing but a monster!"

Flashes of memory flickered about as her mind was drawn to sorrow again, the flowers singing deepening as Yuuki gave into despair.

Luse shook his head, "You're not a monster! You're a coward, you think you're the only one! Nine hells, you're not even the first person today I've fought who lost loved ones to these shite monsters!"

She screamed and her eyes changed, the one like any kinetics began to twist and change bright blue light consuming it as it turned in on itself in a cascade of jagged swirls. But her other eye, devoured by the light, burned away. It was strange, Luse had never known a kinetic to have only one eye but as she pinned him to the wall with flows of aether he got a good look.

Missing completely the eye socket sparked as she fueled her gifts with the Dreamscape's raw power.

Luse bared his teeth at her, snarling through the pain as his bones creaked.

"I know what it's like too, imagine knowing you're not even supposed to exist!" He pressed back at her bindings and felt them loosen, so he kept going. "You remember, don't you?! On the day of the Event, you heard a voice! It told you what to do. How your life was needed, and fate had a plan for you!"

She stopped her screaming, her single-eyed glare staring daggers at him. But he could tell he was right.

"That whisper is a gift we call the Knowing, the three Immortals, they spread the word before they even came to power. Their gifts were so strong it transcended time itself with their will to alter the fate of reality." He had never mentioned this to anyone, many already knew it anyway.

The ground around her feet was beginning to melt now, the glassy terrain of the Dreamscape overtaking her purgatory.

She stood up straight, "That's nothing new, so what does this have to do with anything?"

He smiled at her. "That's easy… I never did…," he said, chuckling through the pain. "I've seen it, the countless iterations of our current timeline. Not one was I a part of. Only Rojas and Azure were meant to be fates chosen; and Jackie. I have watched the lines of aether and seen nothing of my fate. Azure was so happy to see that in all those times I ceased to exist. I was never meant to be the green immortal that I am." He wept openly now, he didn't care, his lovely Jackie was the one fate had called. "So I was risen. If you want to talk about being fooled by fate, answer me that one. Cause this mad sexy spud wrangler was a no-one. I knew nothin, was nothin. I thought it was noble to give up your life for another, especially someone you love. So instead she used her knowledge to pass her gift to me, to make me into the immortal she was supposed to be."

Her powers let up and Luse dropped to the ground, Yuuki staring at him, tears flowing down her cheek from her good eye. "They're all gone! All of them… and whether it was me or not they're still gone!"

He stood up slowly, "I know that! And every day you're gonna ask yourself; why did it have to be them? How do I go on?" Luse was crying now, "But it's because we have to!" He looked at her now, really seeing her. "Every person who survived the Event asks these same questions every day. Hell, most of humanity has asked these same questions since we crawled outta the mires of darkness and into the light."

She looked at the flowers around them, "I'm afraid, what if I hurt someone else?"

Luse laughed, "You're afraid, well surprise, surprise, we all are. Look, you've been given a gift, one that so many will never know. So few of us ever know what our place in this world is, or ever was. It's not till those whose lives we touched by our deeds speak up that we learn who we truly are." He loomed over one of the flowers, its roots smouldering. She was almost free of them, "It's time you left this nightmare…"

Yuuki looked around her at the crumbling world and sighed. As she let it go, the whole thing popped like a soap bubble, the sparkling remnants clinging where the flowers held on. She watched them fade and snarled, "I want revenge."

As the fractured reality fell away they were left standing on the plains of the Dreamscape.

Luse reached out his hand to Yuuki, "Then it's time we go."

She hesitated, looking at his hand, but took it causing a surge of power, both of them cast back to the waking world.

Coming back to the waking world Luse was acutely aware of the pain in his body. He cringed and stretched as he lamented how the Dreamscape was dangerous like that. Pain in there had a way of being more dangerous to a kinetic than anything in the waking world.

Yuuki was already to her knees retching onto the floor. Her face pressed against the steel she sobbed and rocked back and forth mumbling.

Luse reached out and pet her head and she recoiled against the back wall. "Who… oh… it's you. You are real… right?"

Luse nodded and beckoned her over, "It's true, I'm real. Come here, let me get those off of you," he said motioning to the restraints.

She nodded and slid forward on her knees. He worked quickly finding that it was a magnetic lock. He just matched the polarity and they clicked open and fell off of her. The ones on her ankles were even easier, and when she was free she smiled. It made the scars pull tight and she grimaced, pulling her hair across that side of her face.

Luse stood up and stepped back creating a small gate back to where he stashed his bag. He grabbed it and reached inside and pulled out the shirt he had been wearing earlier. He brushed it off, "Sorry, I'll get you something proper to wear once we leave. But we can't have them folks there seeing you like this."

She grabbed the shirt and slipped it on, "I'm long past the point of shame… but, thank you." She buttoned it up, "Can you find my cousin? This place is huge, but he has to know he's in danger."

Luse gave her a quizzical look, "What do you mean?"

"That man, the one with the flower in his mouth. I remember his face," her fists clenched till her knuckles went white. "That man was one of my father's high-ranked generals, and that woman beside him, that was my secretary. That means they're both high enough clearance that they could pull this all off."

Luse nodded, it was all beginning to make a lot more sense. He gave her a thumbs up and turned, "If you have an idea where, we can try to find him, but remember my top priority is you."

She nodded, and together they left her cell. They found a key with a magnetic release on the guard's body. Luse rested the halves of the man back together trying to be kind. They then walked down to where the other kinetics were gathered and worked together to free them all.

With all that had gone on here, no more guards had shown up. The knight and his pet kinetics were still there where he had left them, the flames still burning away. But the room was quiet and the hall outside silent.

Once all of the prisoners were free though Luse opened a gate, a large one to one of his safe-houses. He anchored the gate so it would stay open and turned to them.

"Alright now, everyone through to freedom, and watch your step, there's a bit of a drop." He stepped back but only two people even moved and both of them stepped around it and went to check the door. The one hit a button on the wall, and the other a similar panel on the other side. Luse was confused and turned to Yuuki.

The man from earlier came forward, "We have decided to stay. We are not ready to give up on Japan… this is our home."

Luse looked around at them all, "You all understand what that means? You may not even survive this."

Yuuki stepped forward, "These Fallen are going to learn they messed with the wrong person. They took my family, but they should not have stopped with that. I will make them wish they had killed me too."

Luse reached through the gate with threads of aether and pulled through clothes. They were all suits and slacks from his wardrobe, but functional. He handed them out to everyone, even to Yuuki. "Well, you might as well look good while you take your country back then." They all thanked Luse as they changed and when they were dressed he used a little aether to alter the outfits. When he was done all eight of them looked more than a little dapper. The fine-cut suits made them look, "You guys look like badasses!"

That elicited a few weak laughs, Luse snapped his fingers, the military jumper he was wearing changing into a nice black suit.

The bits of armour that were resistant to his powers fell to the floor with a clatter. He reached down and slipped them into his little pink bag, then pulled out the slightly glowing flask. He tossed the bag through his gate and looked at them, "Last chance to get out of here?"

Yuuki shook her head, "Not yet, I have to…"

"Find your cousin," he smiled, closing the gate, and slipped the flask inside his coat. He gave a little flip to his collar and smoothed out his lapel. "Well that feels much better, and just in time it seems."

He had been wondering when the alarm would be raised. Luse raised his hand just as the doors to the prison block blew open. Bits of steel and concrete flew inward but stopped suddenly. Luse looked at his hand, he hadn't done that.

He looked and saw that the others had formed a wall much like his own. Of them, only Yuuki had control of their center but not one was without some skill. They followed the lead of the other and mustered all they had, Yuuki herself feeding them power through a rough one-way link.

Soldiers on the other side of the shattered doors paused only a moment. Seeing them all here though the soldiers opened fire. A barrage of bullets sailed the gap, though most were stopped by the barrier. Luse took the opportunity to reach out and catch the bullets and absorb the energy of their flight for himself. A few of the others saw what he was doing and dropped the bits of the door and did what he did. Incoming bullets simply fell out of the air their kinetic energy drawn away and absorbed replenishing them rather than draining themselves.

It was going alright till he saw the flash of laser sights. Luse dodged just in time, the shot meant for his head narrowly missing him. The dart took one of the kinetics with him in the chest and threw her back across the room. Luse didn't have to look, he knew she was dead. He kept his focus on the two samurai in the back, one readying to launch a second round while the other took aim.

Luse ripped a bit of concrete out from the wall and turned it into a spear. The sliver of stone flew straight and almost reached the man. In the last seconds though it suddenly veered up and buried itself into the ceiling. The second dart at least didn't hit anyone, a bit of stone catching it in mid-flight.

Luse turned to see who had stopped him from taking out the samurai and found Yuuki beside him. "Why did you stop me? He could have killed another one of us!" He hollered at her, but he saw the tears in her eyes. The kinetic woman who had been hit by the dart was mostly gone, her body melted by the acid.

She glared at him though as if he was in the wrong, "Those are my people too! I won't kill if I don't have to!"

Luse turned away from her and drew as much aether as he could. "Well let's hope when you have to, that you can pull the trigger," the metal here was still draining him. He huffed a little with the effort and let his threads burrow into the concrete of the hall. There he found the power lines draining electricity into himself. It leapt from the walls in snapping blue arcs and slowly replenished him. He then turned the flow back and turned the walls to liquid stone. The soldiers were so busy firing at them, they didn't see as Luse suddenly unleashed thousands of tentacles of stone. Luse grabbed the soldiers or pinned them to the walls, tearing weapons from their hands. He didn't miss one as they turned and tried to defend themselves.

When he was done the whole hall was filled with struggling men in black armour. Not one of them could do more than twitch, and spit curses. Even the two samurai stood rooted by spikes piercing the frame of their powered armour.

Luse looked over to the wall where the figure of the woman lay. The hole in her chest smoked as if burning, her clothes dissolving in the bright orange chemical. But it was her flesh that was the curious sight, her skin had turned a grey-black colour still creeping further as he examined her. Sizzling blue frost was still creeping up her throat spreading through her insides. The orange glowing goo was some kind of freezing chemical. The effects of which were lethal even to a kinetic.

Luse turned around, jabbing an accusatory finger inches from Yuuki's face, "Remember why we are here. You chose to stay, you want to play at being leader, get others involved? Fine! But…," he then pointed at the nearby body of that poor kinetic woman. "You're here to fight, you said it yourself, so remember that sight. They won't hold back just because you are Empress, they will kill you!" Luse let out a sigh, and fixed her petulant glare, with a glare all his own. "I'm here to save you, so if that means I have to truss you up like a lamb. I will toss your ass through a gate to somewheres safe, so fast all you see is the floorboards hitting you in the nose. Count on it!"

He could feel it still, the twisting of fate so strong now it was like a knife in his gut. Every moment they were here reality itself felt balanced on a knife's edge.

"Let's go," Luse left the room, making his way through the prone soldiers. As he went along he collected up a few swords, "Take a blade, and take as few risks as you can," he tossed a sword to one of the others.

He was passing by the samurai when one of them suddenly shouted at him, "Coward! You monsters have no honour!"

Luse stopped, "You wouldn't know honour if it bit you in the arse. You fools have had your rightful empress locked in a dungeon, and the only reason you're even alive right now is because she still chose to stop me from ending yer miserable lives." Luse grabbed the shorter sword from the man's hip, "I'll take this though. You're not going to be needing it."

He drew the blade and checked the dull as a stick edge. It was like the other one, intended to be powered to form a laser edge, but it was strong though and was much longer than the other blades. He sheathed the sword again and knocked a knuckle on the helmet, "Hold the fort down will you…" The samurai raged inside his suit wordlessly screaming. Luse just chuckled and motioned for everyone to follow.

The lot of them moved on down the hall, staying in a tight formation. It still made him curious though, there was still no kind of alarm or anything. Yet it was clear from the presence of drones though, that they were no longer being taken lightly.

Yuuki looked at Luse sadly, "I'm sorry, I just don't want to be the cause of any more death. I swear I will fight tooth and nail Luse. I can do this."

It made him wary, but the plan still stood. Get her cousin Takeo out, kill an unknown number of potentially powerful Fallen, and get Yuuki to safety, without hurting any of these soldiers too badly.

Luse sighed, "Yeah, easy peasy Luv"

****

The shockwaves had stopped but Takeo felt almost worse now. It was the waiting, the not knowing what was happening gnawed like a ravenous beast.

It wasn't till Cammu stirred though that Takeo truly began to worry, one of his illusory forms stepping towards him.

"My Emperor, we need to speak… in private."

Takeo nodded and stood up, "Well, while Smithe takes care of our unwanted guests we should make our way to the upper level."

One of the samurai stepped up, he leaned in and whispered to Takeo the news.

Takeo frowned, "And when was I to be informed?" The man just looked down and flashed a glance, his robotic eyes settling on general Kemin, his cousin's most trusted advisor. "General Kemin, why was I not informed the facility had taken so much damage?"

The empress's secretary was the first to speak up, "Is there a problem, Emperor?"

General Kemin waved his hands, "No, no, there is no problem. Our men can handle this," he then stood and looked over at his retinue and the lot of them stood and they left. This left Takeo and Cammu alone, with the Empress and her entourage. He had been nervous enough as it was, this made it worse.

Again he heard the whisper in his ear, "This is very important, I suggest you send her to the helipad."

Takeo nodded, changing to speak in Chinese, "My council speaks wisely. Empress, I believe it is time we depart. It seems that there is nowhere safe from these kinetic monsters… yet."

She nodded, and Xin stood gracing him with a little smile. She looked to Cammu's illusion beside him and nodded to him.

Cammu bowed deeply, "Empress if it pleases you? Follow the soldiers to the helipad. Emperor Takeo's private craft will be ready for you." She nodded to both of them and the rest of her party rose and they followed the samurai.

Once clear of the room Cammu rose from where he had lain. He stalked over to the door with a silent sneering snarl on his jaws. His tail reached out and closed the door, "No respect. Close the door when you leave the room….," he growled.

Takeo had known Cammu for some time now, but his true form still left him a little awestruck. That all too human body with his fox's head, and the six long tails. Cammu's fur was bristling, and the way his tails whipped like ribbons in a strong wind his friend was angry.

"You're worried too, aren't you Cammu?" Takeo said, taking his seat.

He walked over to the long couch by the wall and sat back on it crossing his legs.

"Something about all of this reeks," he growled. He stroked his jaw, looking off to the far wall, "I have been wondering for some time what is going to happen. This world is a sinking ship Takeo, and we are going with it. But there are options, I have sent you the papers. My fath-" he paused mid-sentence and coughed. Then suddenly he wrapped an illusion around himself and he was talking as Cammu the human. "Inari, umm, he passed today."

Takeo stepped forward but Cammu put up his hand.

"It's… No, I'm fine."

"My father was also a controlling man, Cammu. He never approved of my actions either. You and your brother did well to help me, I am only sorry your brother did not approve of where it was leading."

Cammu nodded, "Unfortunate is true, my brother was older than all of your human history. Yet he could not see past the end of his nose…"

Takeo remembered all too well the fight between them, if not for Cammu, Takeo would have been killed for his very voice. He shivered to think about it.

"Do you…?"

Cammu coughed and stood up and walked over, "Look Takeo, I have been here for you. So you know when I say you have managed to surround yourself with fools and traitors. I can't even say I'm not trying to be rude. I am betting on the short runner with you, you have potential, I see that."

Takeo sighed heavily and sat back on the edge of the table, "I know. I'm not the first choice… what was I, the thirty-second. But I will see this through…"

A commotion in the hall made both men look off to the door. The doors burst open and one of the samurai stepped through the door and collapsed.

Takeo rushed to the man, "What's happened?!"

The man rose to one knee, his suit was destroyed, one arm little more than tatters torn off to hang from wires. His leg on the right was also locked up too, a long thin metallic bath longer than his hand stuck pierced in his hip.

The samurai reached up and tore his helmet off, "I am sorry my Emperor! They took Empress Xin!"

"Who, who took her?!" Takeo asked as he shoved his coat into the man's arm wound to staunch the blood flow.

Cammu was there with water at the man's side in a flash. The injured man tried to choke some down, but just coughed and spit up blood.

He grabbed at Takeo, the look in his eyes filled with horror, "Kinetics took her. They attacked us from behind and stole her away."

Takeo looked at Cammu, "That pompous fool Smithe, shows how useful he and his pets were. They could only have gone one way though, right?"

Cammu shook his head, "I have heard they can move like no other beings. But if they are trying to get a large group out… then maybe. They may still be going for your ship. The hangar is guarded, I will radio ahead to have them delay the launch. If need be we can fire up the E.M.P. wall and keep them from leaving."

Takeo grabbed the man's shoulder to thank him. But as he rested his hand on the man's shoulder he slumped forward.

Takeo looked up from the dead samurai to look at his friend, "Cammu…?"

"Say no more. My Emperor…," and with that Cammu all but vanished. The doors to the room burst open as a dark shadow raced off down the halls.

Takeo looked around him, the whole room empty, but for the hum of the lights and him. He stared at the wall and walked over to where a set of swords rested on brackets in a little alcove. He loosened his belt and slid the sheathes in by his hip, and behind his back.

Takeo was never a politician, he had always been a free spirit, but he was done waiting for some would-be assassin. If they wanted to kill him, he was not going to just lie down and let them.

****

Luse and the others worked together well. His new allies even seemed to be getting stronger by the minute. They learned quickly, and though they couldn't match him in every way, they were creative and intuitive. But the fight dragged on for what felt like hours, security unrelenting through corridor after corridor, the group making their way towards the heart of the facility.

Yuuki explained to him that the elevator he had destroyed was the service line. Without it, the lower levels of the bunker were cut off till it was repaired. That meant that the only way in or out of the bunker was the helipad. So that was where they would be taking her cousin.

Thankfully Yuuki had been privy to the layout, and knew it well, so she led the way. He could see why she had been next in line. She was smart and strong, and a natural-born leader.

They burned a path straight through the complex to the bunker's secured section. They fought through more soldiers and samurai but finally, they came to the end of the line.

The hallway opened up into a large hall, a set of huge double doors at the far end. Yuuki grabbed Luse by the arm as they entered though, he turned and saw the look on her face.

"What's wrong?"

She was shivering like a leaf, her hand pointing to the far end, but there was nothing…

The attack came so fast even Luse didn't see it, like a hot knife something cut into the side of his neck opening his throat wide. He looked down at his hands, the front of his suit already red with blood. His leg gave out, severed nearly in two if not for the bone, and he toppled forward hitting the floor.

Yuuki managed to dodge the attack but two of the others were not so lucky. They were cut down as the beast materialized in the middle of the room.

Laying as he was, Luse could just see it as it walked forward, a Fenix man like Inari, but a bit smaller.

His expression was not what Luse had expected to see though as the creature spoke.

"Kõgõ Yuuki?! What are you doing here? What have they done to you?!" He growled and his tails reached out like tendrils towards the five kinetics who still stood.

"Cammu STOP! You don't understand…," she rushed to him and grabbed him around his waist.

He stopped but he did not show any remorse, "Stay behind me, I will protect you. Kinetics, where is the Empress Consort? Where is Lady Xin? By order of the Emperor, I demand you produce her… NOW!"

His fur bristled and he held his ground, but the others were stunned.

Luse checked a little cough and began to sit up, "Well… that stings." He sat up and turned his leg around the right way, cut to the bone, the green diamond within shone brightly, the flesh knit in moments and he stood up.

Cammu stood there a moment but was far from amused. This time however his attack was predictable and Luse just blinked aside and came to stand beside him. Again his tails lashed out but as they drove into him Luse focused on his healing. The wounds closed almost instantly and he stood staring at the fox man.

Luse sighed, "Your father was right, you are way too angry…"

Cammu grabbed him and dragged Luse close, "What do you know kinetic?!"

"I know that if you don't let me go you'll lose more than that arm," Luse said with a smile.

A sudden burst of energy erupted between them as Yuuki shrieked in frustration, both Cammu, and Luse, getting thrown to either side of the hall.

When Luse looked up Yuuki had already run to where the two kinetics who Cammu had attacked lay. Both were hurt badly, the one may even lose their leg, thankfully though both were already healing.

Cammu stalked slowly over to them pacing on all fours, "Kõgõ, y-you are one of them?" He growled in a hushed voice, but Yuuki was focused on healing the others feeding them energy to help their bodies.

Luse looked at Cammu, he was as large as his father but only had six tails.

"I meant to ask your old man, the tails thing, is the old myths true?"

Cammu glared, "Is this really the time fool?"

Luse shrugged, "Well I figured if you were here on the order of Takeo, then he's safe? So then her only concern is at ease and I can get her to safety then." Cammu moved quickly, but this time Luse didn't feel like healing again. He simply deflected the Fenix's attack and squared off.

Cammu snapped his jaws and hissed loudly, "You will take her nowhere monster. I know your kind, no better than Ari, who enslaved my people. With your powers and your self-appointed superiority, you think you've the right to rule by fear and force!"

"CAMMU! I said stop! It's not what you think," Yuuki stood up and turned to him. She then looked at Luse, "And I'm not going anywhere yet either."

Luse threw his hands up, "Uuuurgh, lass, you are going the right way for a rosy bottom! I came here for one reason…"

Yuuki waved her hand in the air at him, but turned back to Cammu, "Where is Takeo? He isn't safe. There are creatures here, ones who like us have powers. But they are… different."

"Different how?" came a quiet voice from the hall behind Luse.

Luse turned to see a man in a bloodied suit, one he recognized from the TV well. "Takeo, there you have it, all safe. Can we go now?"

Yuuki stomped her foot, "Luse, stop your whining. Why are you so insistent on spiriting me away?"

Luse sighed, "I told you already, I need to get you to safety."

Cammu growled, "She is safe now," his tails swirling to come around her gently.

Luse glared at them all, "Look, this is not how things are supposed to go. I'm trying to fix things! Do you not get it, how can none of you feel it? This is all wrong!" He waved his hand and pulled the ground up into a chair and took a seat. His head was screaming now, his heart tearing apart as if a thousand strings sought to pull him apart in all directions.

Takeo walked into the room, a white knuckle grip on his swords. "Cammu, what's going on? Where is… Xin." He paused and looked at Yuuki a moment in confusion, "Itoko?"

Yuuki nodded, "Yes, it's me."

"Yuuki, but I heard you had gone north, to be with grandmother? How… why are you here?"

She pulled her hair over her face, "I was locked up here, because of what I am. Betrayed by my generals, I knew you couldn't have been a part of this." She ran to her cousin and hugged him tightly, sobbing into his shoulder.

Luse stood up and swayed a little, something was happening here, but he couldn't tell what. As the two hugged and spoke, his mind was growing clearer. He opened himself up to the Void itself, just a touch of the Dreamscape's whispers, and it suddenly made sense.

His head still felt like it was splitting, fate twisting the knife, but he could see why now. "That Englishman I fought, a friend of yers?" He asked aloud.

Cammu hissed again before responding through gritted teeth, "Hardly. More of an uninvited guest. He came bearing only promises, and brought only bad luck it seems."

Luse nodded, "That seems about right, but who then approved his audience? I mean, especially in these times, who just is granted a chance to throw a business proposal to the Emperor?"

"I did," Takeo said, "My advisors believed trade between us would grow our power." He looked about, confused, "Why?"

Luse could feel his power growing and he breathed in the aether deeply. He felt it soak into his bones like he had not felt in days, the twisting of fate that had been cutting him off now beginning to fade.

Luse looked at Yuuki, who then turned to her cousin, "Was it Kemin's idea, Takeo?"

Takeo looked, "What are you talking about?"

Luse raised his hand and looked at Takeo, "Yer being deceived, friend."

Takeo raised his sword, "Cammu, he's doing something!"

Cammu looked at Luse, nose working as if sniffing out the lie, "He means you no harm, my friend."

Threads of aether found the black lump in the poor man's mind. Luse barely touched it and he fell to the floor and floundered around, shaking his head as if something was in his ear. Luse held the man in place, and with a quick burst of sparks pulled a thick orange glowing plasma from him. It bubbled up from his ear and became hard as stone. Luse compressed it down, shattering it into powder with a thought.

Luse had seen many bloom before, but this one was something else. “Your general tricked you. And now I know why, where is Empress Xin?”

Takeo shook as if weak but he looked to Cammu.

Cammu stood up and pointed to the doors, “I tracked her here, but then you came upon me and I assumed you were with those who took her.”

Yuuki looked at him, fixing Luse with a curious gaze, “What’s going on?”

Luse looked at Cammu, “I told Inari I was here to save the fox under the mountain. He said I was right, that I needed to save his Empress. To save the future of his people, and in so doing Japan's future too.” Luse walked towards the door, sick of playing fates game, but for the first time happy to feel like he was winning. “I thought you were the one he meant Yuuki, but I was wrong,”

****

By the time she was settled in Bekka was ready to fall asleep standing up, but she did her best to relax. Despite the nagging feeling in her chest, she was exhausted. Her body aching, she crawled into bed to let her powers return and heal her tired mind, and though it took some tossing and turning she drifted back into a deep sleep.

Her mind drifted till a dream finally took her to a dark forest she had never seen before, sprouting up around her, it looked centuries old. The trees stood tight together, the smell of loamy earth heavy in the air carried deep inside her with every breath. She walked between the twisting old oaks, the ground covered in a thick layer of leaf litter.

She wore a strange dress that flowed like steely grey water down her body trailing behind her. The long skirt made a path in the leaves, the crinkling crackle of the dry earth pervading the air.

She looked up at the sky and knew she was in a dream, the sky changing to a deep unearthly blue. When she looked around her the world had changed, and she stood in a strange landscape of glass.

Bekka turned around and saw a green thread of aether, it floated through the air as if caught in a breeze, yet as Bekka noted there was not a breath of wind here. The glowing green aether was strong and vibrant and drew her in like a moth to a candle. She reached out and touched it and felt the power in it, and watched as the world around her moved.

The land and its few trees zipped past her so fast it made her sick for a moment. When she came to a stop she was standing near two trees and reached out to touch them, and from behind the branches came a buzzing. Stepping around the tree Bekka found a bright green light humming through the air.

Bekka couldn't have explained it, but the urge to catch it overtook her fiercely. She quick-stepped around, chasing it down. Finally, her hand closed around the elusive little thing, emotions welling up as she held onto whatever it was.

She opened her hand and stared down at the little lightning bug in her palm. The moment her eyes caught the creature though her brain was swarmed, memories filling her head.

She was thrown back from the force and hit the ground rolling over coming to a stand, the blankets falling off of her.

She looked around herself, mind still in a haze, she was back in her room.

A knock at the door made her jump, "Beck? Are you okay in there?"

She reached out with strings of aether and quickly grabbed up some blankets. She wrapped herself up and called back, "Yes! Yeah… sorry. Hold on a sec!" She stumbled to the door and cracked it open, "Hey, Dave, is Luse back yet?"

David shook his head, a look of concern in his eyes, "You look like you've seen a ghost, you okay?"

Bekka shook her head, "I'm fine, just a weird dream, it was just so real. It was like I was standing in an ocean of glass that rippled like water under my feet, and all these weird…"

"Trees?" David said his look of concern growing.

"Yeah, how did you know?" She asked but she felt the answer in her heart already, "That was no dream was it?"

David walked to the table, Bekka grabbed a robe off the back of the door and followed him. David pulled out a map and a gold ring on a bit of leather. He held up an old copper penny and spun it, and it spun faster and faster till it began to glow. It became liquid, and the molten metal flowed about the map into spider silk thin threads. It formed a pattern, but she wasn't sure what it was.

She glared at her partner, "Dave, what is this?"

He held up his hand a moment as he focused, a swell of aether so strong the room creaked just from the pressure building in him. The threads formed a little lattice on the map, needle points stabbing down at the map at certain points. When he was done the copper cooled, and his eyes stopped glowing. He shakily looked at the map blinking, "Sorry Beck, this is a tracking trick. Luse gave me this ring, it's a personal item of his. With something sentimental, I can track thoughts over huge distances. It's why they brought me on this mission." Dave sat back, his head dripping sweat and his eyes looking sunken. It was clear whatever he had done was beyond taxing.

She looked at the map, it was right on top of Mount Fuji, "Is that where Luse is?"

David nodded, "Yeah. He's deep too, way underground."

She remembered the dream so strongly, flashes of growing danger. She looked at the map, and she knew they had to go there too. She cringed as another wave of pain twisted the aether all around them. Her own aether seemed to be twisting in her, this feeling wasn't just in her either. David suddenly clutched his chest and looked at her, "Our fates. We're tied to whatever is going on more than Luse may have thought even."

Bekka nodded, "Luse needs us. So how do we get there?"

****

The air around the glade had grown tense, the sisters not sure of what to do. Fond could taste the palpable fear, making her nose wrinkle, this place felt wrong. She had lived in this glade all her life, these woods were her home. Yet, now it felt like a stranger's den.

She reached up and tugged her ear, she wished they would keep their whispers to a dull roar.

Whispers? Fond mused.

She got up and walked to the edge of the glade.

Something was whispering.

She closed her eyes and listened for the sound but couldn't quite follow it. It moved as she tracked it across the mountainside. One of the other guardians, a younger sister they called Fish, was suddenly at her side.

Fish nuzzled up beside her rubbing her cheek to Fond's in greeting. She then twitched her ears, she could hear it too.

She turned to her sister and nodded, Fish knew Fond had to go.

Fond made her way back up to the temple, the whispers growing stronger in the back of her mind. A few of the sisters like her who were closer to the mana seemed affected too, the questions in their eyes as she passed begging for answers to the whispers. With no better answers, she would just pause, shrug, and continue on.

Finally, Fond came to the temple, the source of the whispers it seemed. She stood outside the doors knowing full well there were only three things in there, and none of them could have been active on their own. Each relic was a piece of tech even older than the Ari. So ancient in fact that even Inari could not say how old they truly were.

As she stood there her ears caught another sound, a faint humming in the breeze. She looked up and saw a single firefly. It buzzed through the air till it alighted atop the peak of the shrine, its glowing rump blinking, shining bright green. As she watched it though she realized the whispers suddenly fell silent. She stared after it as the shining insect took flight, watching as it zipped in a straight line towards Mount Fuji.

A sign?

Fond rubbed her hand across her bangle and lowered the barrier around the shrine, maybe this was the only true way. She called out to all her sisters and gathered them together. They knew how she felt, her silent sending drawing them to her. She made her way inside the shrine and the piece of tech she knew was restless. Since ancient times they had guarded the sword Kusanagi. One of the sacred treasures of Japan, and a weapon without equal. In his youth, it had Fallen to Inari to protect it, and he had all these centuries. Wrapped carefully up in silks and stored in a black polished case. Fond tied it up in a hasty sling and strung it across her back. She pulled it around in front of her and stroked the case. Her mother had made this case, at least that was what Inari said.

Her sister Sash came in behind her, getting close and nuzzling Fond's neck, her human form, as curvaceous as always. She wiggled about as she squeezed her little sister, then stepped over to the pedestal and picked up the large teardrop-shaped stone there. Sash had been the one to bring the Magatama home, so she would carry it away. She slipped it into her top, the large stone suddenly warping and becoming a ring of smaller teardrop stones. She smiled at

Fond and fluffed up her chest so the stones bounced on her ample bosom.

Fond giggled silently and gave her sister a playful shove. Sash looked at the long case in Fond's arms sadly, hugged her again and then disappeared into the night. Their sister Grin was next to come into the shrine, stopping only to frown at Sash as they passed, Grin, was never the friendly one despite her name. She walked past Fond but did stop to pet her on the head, then picked up the Kagami and walked on down the hall.

When the time was right, they would find each other again, Fond knew it.

Fond also made her way down the hall, but over to the armoury. She grabbed up a longbow and a quiver and checked the charge on the quiver. It was maxed out as she expected, and the bow was in perfect shape. That meant she would have as many digitally constructed arrows as she needed.

Fond strung the quiver to the strap that held Kusanagi, sliding both to her hip. She then turned to find Grin standing in the armoury doorway.

As stern-faced as before Grin raised an eyebrow and looked at the weapons Fond held.

Fond shrugged, and strung the bow with a silvery new line and slipped it over her head.

Grin shook her head at Fond, and as Fond tried to pass her, stepped in the way again.

Fond smiled at her sister, placing her hand on Grin's shoulder. She squeezed her gently, but Grin turned away. She grabbed a satchel from the wall and slipped the Kagami inside. She slung the pack on her back and shoved past Fond.

Fond grabbed a bag from the wall, the contents jingling slightly.

They both stepped outside together, a group of sisters gathering. Grin just scowled at them and they parted for her, she gave a final wave to Fond over her shoulder, then disappeared in a shimmer of moonlight.

Fond looked at the sisters around her. She quickly made sure the other sisters were all packed, their clothing and anything not being taken burned to cover their scent. The younger ones were gathered, and Fish came along to each. She rubbed faces with each one and they all dashed off together. There were others though, still dressed in their Miko robes who were still nearby. These few she noticed held weapons in hand and looks of steely resolve. The Miko had always stood as guardian priestesses to the shrine.

Fond stepped down off the shrine steps and started into the dark. She knew they would follow her no matter what, out beyond the edge of the glade. She waved her hand over the control bangle on her wrist and checked the systems, the defences around them coming to life, the cage trees above her shifting beginning to shiver and shake. The silvery branches opened at the top, the odd bulb-shaped cages releasing a flurry of metal birds into the air. She then turned off the barrier around their mountain home. Instead transferring the power to the cage trees. With this much power, the trees would last forever since they absorbed solar power too.

She waited only long enough for her sisters to join her, tying on extra quivers at their belts.

Fond opened the bag she had brought from the armoury, its jingling contents glimmering in the faint light. She pulled one out, a seemingly innocuous little silver bell. The moment she clipped it to her ear she tapped it gently making it sing, and activated its true purpose.

****

Luse stepped through the hall's double doors and out into a short dimly lit tunnel. It looked like a kind of airlock, the doors behind him hissing as they were pressurized. This hall opened up into a large service tunnel, much like the service tunnels from upstairs. Roughly hewn stone floors and concrete walls, metal girders supporting the huge slabs above. The cooling vents running along the ceiling dripped frosty spikes from the vents, in contrast to the heat. The air in the tunnel felt heavy and made his clothing stick to him almost instantly.

Luse wrapped aether around himself to mitigate the effect but there was no denying the heat, even with their attempt. As he walked he heard the door behind him open and close, and open again.

Then someone shouted after him, "Luse!"

He stopped and turned, staring at Yuuki, "Go back kid, you don't have to follow me."

She grounded her fists on her hips, a snarling expression on her face. "The hell I don't, it doesn't matter who you think you are, you can't stop me. I will see to it that those monsters burn," her eye glimmered as she pulled aether into herself.

Luse just sighed, "Look, you will have your revenge. This however is not the time for it," he reached out with a push of aether. He turned her around, sliding her back down the tunnel to the others. "The towers are still active, so without him," he pointed at Takeo, "They're trapped in here with us. But a cornered animal is more dangerous. With all due respect, Empress."

She turned as she came to a stop, "And who are you to decide if I can take that risk?! I don't take orders from any man!"

Luse turned to look at the hallway up ahead. It opened up into a glowing windowed set of large doors. To one side he could just see a pair of military-looking airships, with one being hooked up to a truck. They were huge ships, with four large rotors for their wings, they even looked to have two floors.

The windowed doors to the hangar were beginning to open, a waft of acrid hot air heavy with the smell of brimstone filling the hall making Luse cough.

He looked back at the others who had helped him. The danger was no less, he could feel the way that fate warped around them now. It was more clouded than ever before.

He shook his head and brushed his hand through his hair. “I can't tell ye what kind of resolution ye may get from this. Come with me an this resolves quicker, yes. But I also know not all of us will survive.” They stared at him, but not one so much as flinched, “Alright then boyos. Well, don’t say I didn’t warn ya!” Luse turned and walked on, “Yer all insane, ye know that right?”

He heard a smattering of chatter behind him but the sound was mostly drowned out. The roar of air as the large four-prop aircraft was being taxied to the pad drowning it all out.

A soldier rushed at him from the right and Luse caught him mid-stride. His armour was draining like the others, and he could feel its leeching pull. But Luse was quickly figuring it out. The straps that held the plates, the aluminum rivets, the plastic, the gold in the circuits. All these things were there for him to manipulate. He closed his hand and felt the man's body twist, pushing him back till he cried out. The man went limp, passing out from the pain.

Yuuki was there at his side, she watched what he did closely. Two more soldiers jumped down from a crane, a third opening fire from above.

It was the others' turn now, the bullets stopped mid-flight against their kinetic barriers.

Luse nodded to them, and turned to Yuuki, “Can you deal with them?” He asked with a smirk, trying to antagonize her just a little.

She growled at him and turned to the two soldiers advancing on them. She reached out as she had seen him do, aether gathering at her fingertips. The threads loosed out like a hail of rockets from her arms, flying from her in all directions to attack the approaching men. She found the weak points in the soldier's armour like a puppeteer and bent both men to their knees, and down hard on their faces. Neither moved but just to be certain Luse then fused their armour to the concrete.

With a little pulse of aether, Luse touched the crane scaffolding, metal railing coming to life twisting around the sniper and forcing him down to his knees too.

The others saw the ship and all together they reached out and grabbed hold of it before it could be pulled outside.

He had not felt anything strange at all, no aether, no odd sense of danger. So it came as a shock when he was struck by a wall of air, and both Yuuki and Luse were thrown back across the hard pavement.

He got to his feet and looked down at the damage, his chest was a bloody mess, but his healing had already kicked in. He winced a little as two of his ribs popped back through his regrowing skin. It wasn't often he saw it, the green diamond bone glowing faintly as his flesh knit back together.

"Well shit, that was a sneaky shot there," he looked up at the plane and the person in the door. Then at the three crossing the tarmac from the left.

The woman on the ship, a tall dark-skinned woman, held her hand out, kinetic energy at her fingertips. Slim and lean, she looked like a storm cloud with her long dreadlocks blowing behind her. Luse readied for another attack, but she instead suddenly jumped like she didn't care she was forty feet in the air. She hit the ground with an audible crack of breaking bones as both of her legs snapped like dry kindling, but just glared even as she dragged herself forward.

"The nine hells. What are you…?" Luse watched her stand and could barely believe it, she wasn't a kinetic. She was bloom.

She stood slowly, her body not healing but instead, tiny vines pulling her broken bits back together as two more jumped down behind her. Three more fell out to pick themselves up, then more until a small crowd came to stand in between his group and the ship joining the three who had attacked them.

Luse chuckled, "Ye folks may have tricks, but yer still a bunch of grapes. Would have been smarter to not telegraph that this ship was important."

The woman in front still had not spoken, but she did begin to mutter. Her jaw cracked open wide, a glow starting deep in her throat as her bloom slipped gently out of her body. It was as nasty as he had thought, bright glassy petals opening wide like a blue trumpet lily. It flexed and extended golden fangs nearly a foot long and while the outside was stripped with bright orangey-yellow slashes, the inside was like a chasm to an icy hell. It opened wide needle-like teeth gnashing, a bright blue glow growing deep inside her chest till she looked ready to breathe flames, and the dark mutterings grew into a hiss that was picked up by the others as their eyes took on that unusual black empty glow. Luse found it hard to focus, his eyes getting fuzzy, an errant blink later and the lot of them vanished. It was like a heat mirage, a mere shimmer and they were gone from his senses.

Luse sighed a heavy breath of relief and nudged Yuuki.

"Well, dear Empress. I believe these folks may know a thing about who called the order to kill your family." He held out his hand to help her up, but she didn't even look at him.

Her eyes flared bright and the world around her seemed to shudder. She opened her mouth but it was not words that came out. Her scream of pain and rage broke reality around her cracking the very air. The ground shattered and a wave of force tore apart everything in front of her. The burst ripped a massive chunk out of the airship like a bite. The shadows of two of the bloom were all that remained of the ones who had not escaped, burned against the tarmac; they looked like snow angels baked into stone.

Her attack had been too strong though, even as she tried to stand he felt as the aether left her. She tumbled forward into his arms. He waved his hand and turned the ground around them into powder and kicked it up into the air swirling around him.

A sign of motion and he punched out physically his fist connected with the gut of a bloom trying to sneak up. The creature's ribs practically imploded and that same strange orange resin got on his hand. The creature was splattered by the force of his strike, its top half nearly gone, but the orange sap was more than a little harmful. It burned painfully but was cold as it touched him, frostburn turning his skin black almost instantly.

"Don't let their blood touch you!" He shouted out into the haze.

He heard a hollow growl from behind him, a corpse dropped beside him, orange blood hissing on the concrete.

"What was your first clue, fool," Cammu snarled. He had forgone his illusion again standing on all fours, his long tails forming a kind of cage around Takeo. But his face was burned, the effects from biting the bloom no doubt. He spit a little blood on the ground and looked at the ship, "I can smell Empress Xin on that transport ship."

Luse nodded and he cleared a path to the ship with a burst of wind, "I'll get her! Please, take Yuuki"

Cammu nodded, one of his tails snaking around to pick her up.

Takeo tried to push forward, "Cammu we need to rescue Xin!"

Cammu shoved Yuuki into Takeo's arms, "You have your duties, my Emperor." He turned and glared at Luse.

Luse just nodded back, and without another word blinked into the fray.

He made a jump coming out in front of one of the kinetics who had come with him. She was struggling with a bloom who was barely more than a glimmer of shifting shadows and dust. Luse tried to help but was struck from the side just as he stepped forward, another of the nearly invisible bloom attacked him. Somehow moving so fast she slammed into him before he could blink raking a long dagger across his side as she attacked. Luse grabbed hold of her as the force carried them through the air, but on instinct, he blinked away and they collided with something solid, the side of the aircraft.

They fell to the ground together, and she attacked him like an animal nails clawing his face, her bloom lashing forward from her throat. These bloom were huge, nearly twice the size of ones he had seen before, opening up like an octopus as if to swallow his head. Thin golden teeth unsheathed trying to grab him, but Luse was faster. He pulled her knife from her hand with threads of aether and turned it back on her. He drove it up through the woman's head severing her brainstem, dropping her. She fell to the ground flopping about as she died, he stepped on her back and with a quick burst of air reduced her to a pink mist, no more than a fleshy smear across the tarmac.

The fighting was getting heavier, but he had to find her, the twisting aether gripping his chest like a vice around his heart pulling him. Luse blinked again, this time right inside the ship through the upper door he had torn free. He came to a stop reaching behind himself and grabbed a bloom hiding there. He flipped the screaming beast over his shoulder so it collided with another one guarding the other side of the door. The two fell into a heap, but in a heartbeat, he had three more coming through the door climbing over the others.

Luse looked around himself, he was growing tired, too much energy spent. He looked around for something simple to use as a weapon. Behind him was a galley of sorts leading to the cockpit. He reached out with threads of aether and found the cutlery in the drawers.

The drawers opened and the knives leapt up at his command. They flew like arrows peppering the bloom, but try as he might, hitting them in the right spot was nearly impossible. The silverware either struck useless spots or glanced off of the bloom's own barrier. It at least kept them from a full charge though.

Five-on-one was getting harder, and Luse realized he had now been pushed back. He was almost through to the far end of the galley.

He looked out the window, the magma just beyond the edge of the helipad was right there. He could feel the power all around him and opened himself up to it. Like all kinetics, he could easily fuel himself with the energy around him. But this ship felt like it was made of the same metal as that draining prison. As much as he pulled in the more it seemed to want to pull it all away. He needed a boost.

The bloom in the back of them all suddenly stepped forward. The four others formed up, hands flung out in front of themselves. The air shimmered and Luse could feel the weaves of kinetic shielding. The air shifting thickened as they doubled their effort on their barrier.

"This isn't your fight Immortal, so we need you to disembark so we can continue our pre-flight." He growled a little and shook his head as if someone was talking in his ear. "The Wych-hazel has decreed that the Azure, the Rojas, and yourself are off-limits. But impede us further and I will be forced to break that rule."

Luse's barrier sparked and shuddered against theirs. He reached inside his coat and pulled out the old silver flask, it seemed it was time to see what it was like. Luse smiled,

"You know it's very kind of whoever that is to say. But I think," he uncorked the flask and felt the power instantly. He tipped back the heavy syrupy liquid and drank a tiny mouthful. His eyesight instantly flared and he felt instant relief, his body feeling like it was burning, but he felt good, no, Luse felt great. "Wow! Oh, that is as good as any late-morning dirty bean juice! But I was saying something, where was I? Oh, right, I think that's a great idea. I do plan on leaving ya see. But see, I need Empress Xin first."

He breathed in deep and slipped the flask back into his coat. He could still feel the drain of the metal but it was like a pinhole in a pool. He reached out with threads of aether though almost found it hard to control. It had been a long time since he had let himself hold this much power, and finally understood why Azure pushed himself to do it all the time.

The threads touched the bloom's barrier and the whole thing snapped. Shattering back on the four who had held it and they were all thrown back. Their arms having been outstretched controlling the aether shattered like rotten wood. The detritus that had been their broken limbs floated frozen in the air.

He stepped forward and up to the primly dressed general, his bloom retreating like a blue silk scarf slithering back down his throat.

Luse smiled and patted his shoulder, "Where's all that bluster boyo? Ye seem a bit less sure?" Luse turned the frightened man towards the open door. "There's a woman down there who wants a word with you," Luse shoved him out the door face first. He hit the ground with a wet thud, orange blood splattering the ground, but he stood up. Luse pulled aether to his voice and shouted so all could hear, "Great Empress Yuuki would like to have a few words with you!"

His shout cleared away the smoke and dust revealing only three bloom to still be alive. It seemed they had given up hiding. Now outnumbered greatly, they stood in a circle surrounded by the kinetics.

Yuuki was there too, off to the back, standing beside Cammu. She looked down to see the fat, grumpy-looking General Kemin. Her face was consumed with rage but she didn't move. Luse could feel the hate and sadness from her, but she was too conflicted to move. Luse reached out with threads of aether pressing Kemin back down to the ground. "Now why don't you tell us what we want to know… wait. Hold that thought," Luse slapped his forehead.

He stepped back inside the ship and walked through to the cabin. He had to pick his way around the still writhing armless Fallen to get past them where he found a twisted sight. The flight crew and anyone who had not been bloom were all dead, or in the first stages of being turned. Some around the cabin looked like they had been caught unaware, while others like they had seen what had happened but had been unable to flee. Only one person was still alive in the back.

Empress Xin struggled to be free pinned under the bodies of two of her security detail. Neither man had made it to their guns but had both tried to shield her.

She saw Luse and began to struggle more.

Luse put up his hands, "It's alright Empress. I'm here to get you out. Well, actually, I really don't know what I'm here for." He waved his hand and the two dead guards lifted off of her.

She looked at him curiously.

He opened a gate beside him, just big enough for what he wanted. He reached in and pulled out the Miko's staff that Fond had given him. Her eyes lit up when she saw it, "You know this, don't you?"

She nodded, then stood up and pet the face of her guards. She winced as his body twitched, but she didn't stop. One by one she touched them, a quick flick warping the air. When she was done she stood before him and took the staff. Her illusion disappeared only long enough for her to show him her true form. White fur like moonlight, eyes a smoky swirling blue. She had nine tails like Inari that swished about slowly. She retook her form and looked up at him.

He almost felt like he could tell what it was she wanted. He nodded and turned to see one of the armless Fallen getting up. A frail-looking woman, she hissed and spit, speaking so quickly he couldn't follow what she said.

Xin just walked around him and lashed out with the staff. She drove it straight through the creature's head, then went to the next and did the same.

She walked over to the door and signed to him, "*You coming?*"

Luse nodded and followed.

At the door, he waved his hand and pulled the concrete below up into rough stairs. “So… what did we miss?”

“Xin!” Takeo ran forward shoving Luse aside, “Are you okay? Did they hurt you?”

She hugged him as he ran up, she nuzzled into his chest and shook her head.

Luse walked over to where Cammu stood, “Did you know what she is?”

Cammu had already taken human form and shook his head. “No, I knew there was something about her.” He inhaled, “Till she let down her illusion I didn’t know she was kin.” He stared at her as she hugged and kissed Takeo, “How many…?”

“Tails? I think I counted nine,” Luse said, cutting him off. “Same as Inari, does that mean she’s…,” Luse cut off as the twisting in his chest suddenly pulled tight.

Cammu looked at him worriedly, “What? What’s wrong?”

Luse looked over to where Kemin still lay. Even pressed hard, face-first into the ground, he was smiling. Luse walked over and lifted him off the ground on threads of aether. Luse slammed him back against the stone steps he had formed and got right into his face. “What’s so funny boyo? Your little scheme is done with, and your cronies are gonna be precedin you to the afterlife. So what have you got to chuckle bout?”

His eyes were glazed but it was clear he was still in his right mind. His teeth ground together as he coughed back cackling and muttering.

Luse put more pressure on it, the sound of his bones breaking under the pressure like dry grass.

“I’ve seen to having a nip, I can do this all day. So, *TALK*,” he filled his voice with aether and tried instead to force the truth out. Kemin’s face turned red and blue, the muscles in his throat bunching as he tried to resist. Luse was already inside the man's head though.

It was only a matter of…

Luse felt the waves of hate and malice just in time, his breath exhaling in a cold mist as a screaming wind and bright flash of light unleashed hell's lowest level upon them.

In blinking away he managed to evade the beam of energy that swept the hangar, but the whole room was destroyed. A heavy layer of ice washed the entire room around them in massive six-foot frozen spikes. The ship had been ripped apart and frozen into a spiral of debris where the beam had torn through it.

Just scanned the hangar and saw Cammu in a bubble of energy with Yuuki, and Xin with Takeo shrouded by a similar shield, the beam having swept right over them. They were all covered in frost but it seemed like the two Fenix had taken the brunt of it and seemed none the worse.

As for Kemin though, he was no more than a dark shadow deep beneath the thick ice. The last three of Kemin's followers were now no more than statues of ice in a forest of icy spears, as well as two of the Kinetics from the prison who had been caught unaware.

Luse couldn't sense their life force and knew they were dead, their bodies trapped in screams of terror.

Luse looked up to where the beam had come from, out into the central vent. There a massive metal man half floated in the bubbling magma. It looked like it was made of slabs of shining silver steel or pitted stone, though it was hard to tell. Luse had seen their likes before, but he had not been this close to a royal knight before.

Luse hollered back to Takeo, "Would one of you call off yer dog here!" But it was not one of them who replied.

A deep rumbling chuckle shook the air, "**Dog? I think not, kinetic. I bend the knee to only her royal majesty, the rightful ruler of Great Britain and-**"

"Don't care…," Luse walked away and started picking his way over to the others to check on them.

There was a slosh and a hiss, and the Knight yelled, "**YOU DARE TURN YOUR BACK ON ME KINETIC!**"

There was a swirl of air pressure and Luse turned, reaching down with threads of aether to dig down into the earth. He shaped the stone around him and drove it up into pillars that smashed right into the massive hand that descended on them, stopping the Knight's attack dead.

The mech had shifted its whole structure somehow, its arm extending out as if the other arm had broken apart to fuse to it. Even as he watched it Luse witnessed as it shifted again, the hiss of steel as plates slid past each other. It wasn't hollow as far as he could tell, the inside squirming like cables like snakes. Each part slid about till the armour was back to two arms again, then began pulling itself up out of the magma.

It came up on the tarmac dripping hot globs of molten stone. Getting down to one knee, reaching out he spoke again.

"**Emperor, Empress, I require your code to leave this place**," a bundle of steel streamers bubbled up into his palm. It took on a humanoid form, one all too familiar, even Luse recognized the aura.

Takeo looked up at the shiny metal effigy of Smithe standing in the Knight's palm. He gave a racking cough, the cold air harsh on the lungs. Xin tried to help him, but Takeo pushed Xin behind him. "Smithe? But they said you died!"

Smithe shrugged, the knight shrugging too, "**Only a puppet, though I will need to replace my pets now thanks to you kinetic.**"

Luse looked up at the Knight, he knew he was a match for it, but only just, and there were the others to worry about too.

"You know, I've always been a bit quick to lose my head, an I've always said it's because people like to push my buttons. So I'm gonna try and understand you better first. But I think you're saying you plan on mutilating and torturing more innocent kinetics into attack dogs?"

A twisted chuckle split the air as his shiny metal face turned to Luse.

"**Why yes, I'm glad you understand kinetic. I even have a few in mind,**" the Knight's glowing white eyes turned to look over at Yuuki, he then turned back to Luse. "**Of course, you're in that list too, my green-eyed little nuisance.**"

Tendrils of liquid steel shot out from three ports on the armour's sides. They went straight for Luse first, but he was faster. Luse just smiled and tore a bit of the ship free cutting down the tentacles,

"Give up boyo! You ain't got the right stuff to tame this, I assure you."

The severed bits flopped around a moment before melting into a puddle. Smithe looked at them then recalled the bit he had left.

It seemed he had no control over the metal once he lost contact with it.

Smithe looked over at Takeo again, "**I will be leaving here one way or another dear Emperor. I kindly asked you once already for the codes. So now I am telling you, drop your barrier.**" The panels of armour on his chest opened, a large cannon covered in steaming frost emerging from within. "**I will not be so kind as to ask a third time.**"

Luse pulled aether around him through the air, reaching out towards the magma. Readying to strike the moment he saw an opening he was surprised when he brushed the suit and Smithe rounded on him.

The narrowed slit eyes of the suit locked onto Luse with a hard gaze.

"**None of your tricks Kinetic! There is no man behind the curtain here, and no mind for you to control. The armour and I are one, I gave up my physical body to become this powerful. To serve the crown and my Queen's desires.**" The cannon in his chest was beginning to smoke even more now.

On his knee like Smithe was, Luse could tell his weapon could sweep the whole room better than he had before. Luse wanted to make a gate, but the twisting in his chest was making it too hard to focus. Every time he tried to form the image of his safehouse it faded into a vision of the frozen faces of those who would not make it out.

Takeo shouted at Smithe, "Let them all go, and I will give you the codes. Harm anyone else though, and this place will be your prison till this mountain collapses." The look on his face was stoic and strong, a man not afraid to die for a cause.

Smithe's voice dripped with indignation, "**I have no want or need to negotiate fool. We will see who will last longer, the thermal energy plant powering your little barrier keeping me here. Or my aerosol-nitrogen-enhanced particle decelerator.**" The cannon in his chest began to glow with an icy malice.

Luse snorted a laugh, "Ye mean your ice ray thingy?" He had never known what they called it, "I mean… Arsehole nitro-genital decimator. Whatever. Ye should just call it yer Chilly Willy!"

"**Why you insolent little-**" Smithe turned his focus on Luse, cannon coming to bear.

Luse blinked right up in front of him but off to Smithe's left side, "Hey now, don't go pointing your frozen wiener at me. I didn't name it."

The energy in Smithe's chest seemed to dim, an exasperated sigh coming from him making the air vibrate. "**How someone who boasts they hold the secrets of the cosmos, can be so pedestrian-minded I will never understand.**"

"Yeah, well?!" Luse laughed, louder this time, "Ye gave up yer sex life to become a robot. So let's not bandy words on who's dumber here…"

"**Truly? Well, I think I will kill you first and destroy this miserable mountain,**" Smithe's cannon began to smoke and glow again. "**My queen will understand, you heathens are not worthy of her benevolence!**"

Luse gathered aether around him and felt Yuuki and another do the same. All their power funnelling to him he pulled it together into a barrier, but not knowing how the cannon worked made it hard to defend. He blinked back and prepared a wedge of heat and air.

Smithe's laughter washed over them, the lull of his cannon so quiet despite the bright blue light. The feeling of fate's twist made Luse want to scream, but it was not his voice that broke the air.

Luse watched as red streaks of light shot past him to strike at Smithe. Where they hit plumes of phosphorous light bloomed like white flowers screaming even louder than the boiling magma.

Smithe also screamed as his cannon was struck, crackling icy energy exploding inside him, spikes of glowing ice piercing him from the inside. He stumbled back clawing at his chest, another trio of bolts striking Smithe in the face, one even piercing his eye. He screamed anew, his arm coming up to his face. Just as a massive gate opened up in the air high above.

A small group of people dropped down onto Smithe, some taking a moment to strike at him causing the knight to recoil back.

A woman wreathed in shadows dropped from the ceiling. She carried a bow and a long black case, her body wrapped in a skin-tight grey bodysuit. As she fell towards him she threw the case, the bindings splitting open, spilling its contents.

At first, Luse didn't know what it was, just a strange glimmering thing flying towards him. It was about four feet long, shiny and seemed made of rough-cut glass the way it glimmered as it tumbled through the air. With threads of aether, he snatched the woman from the air safely setting her beside him.

"Fond?"

She put her fingers to his lips and pointed to where the black case lay, the glassy item he could now see was a sword blade standing stuck up in the ground having tumbled out.

There was a boom that shook the air making Luse look up. One of the people who had come through the gate; a kinetic he knew all too well, though the purple hair was new.

She floated up, the air gathering in the cannon-like tube at her hip. It discharged again a blast of air kicking Smithe back to stumble into the hangar door. With Smithe's back to them now seven red streaks flew through the air peppering his back.

Luse took the opportunity, turning his barrier into basic energy. He blinked across the icy ground still holding onto Fond. The shard of glass was there in his hand. It was smooth despite how jagged it appeared, slipping into his hand as if it was made for him. Yuuki was there at his side too, looking at it with awe.

"Where did you get this?" She reached out to touch it but Fond was between her and the blade in the blink of an eye.

Yuuki looked around her, still enraptured by the odd double-edged blade, "Th-that, is Kusanagi-no-tsurugi. My father showed it to me once. Back before the war. Before the shrine guardians took it and hid it almost twenty years ago."

The power in the weapon was so great he could see why; the blade was brimming with raw aether. Not inside the blade itself but a conduit for it, a direct connection to some greater weapon that made him feel like he was holding onto a piece of the Dreamscape made real.

He could see it all, visions of the end of the war, to all wars, the kinetics prevailing as heroes, and their eventual rise to the top, as was their right, ruling the world with benevolence and understanding. With this power, there would be none who could oppose them. And any who tried would face swift and final judgement.

He shook his head, eyes fluttering open, he had drawn so much power through the blade his head was aching. It had taken seconds to reach even his limits, his carbonized bones humming inside his flesh glowing through his skin.

Only the light had changed.

He started at his own glowing flesh for a moment, the once deep emerald green glowing brighter than ever, but with a bright yellow light.

Yuuki was shaking him by his collar, Fond behind her crying seemed beside herself.

Luse put his hand on his head and shook himself out of her grip. The power inside him was begging for release. But he refused to use the sword like this, he held the sword and knew he needed it, but that he did not need to use it. He cut himself off from its source and felt the pulsing blood in his ear fade from a roar to a high-tone ring.

He could see Smithe was coming back strong, fighting back harder, and defending himself better. He had pulled ice around himself into spiked armour and was swinging around a sword formed of yet more ice.

The others there could only keep him busy. The Miko from the temple being conservative with their arrows held back, waiting for only the best of openings to strike at his joints. Bekka and David were there too, David lashing out with blasts of Psire stronger than anything Luse had ever seen the man use. All while Bekka went toe to toe with the massive knight towering over her, using her barriers to deflect or flat out stop Smithe's attacks.

Yet despite how it looked, it was clear they were not winning. Smithe was not going to tire like the others, and eventually, he would catch someone.

Luse had seen over the years as Azure and even Rojas changed. The more you gave into the power, the more you seemed to want it too.

He had always abstained from it, thought it was taking the higher road not using her power. But this time it was different, this was his power, was something he knew he had to use.

He channelled the energy inside himself, fusing molecules into chains of force and energy. Took a deep breath, and released the energy all at once, a trick only the most powerful, or stupid, would dare do. He had never tried it because he had seen what using this much power did to people who did.

The droplet of darkness that shot out from Luse's hand pierced through Smithe with ease. A single point no larger than a quarter, leaving a hole a meter wide through his chest, and dragging the metal knight backwards across the tarmac. The armour began to shift and turn as the hole grew in size, the armour squealed and Smithe screamed and finally, he rolled back closing up into a diamond-shaped shell. Smithe floated up as if to try and escape and slammed into the ceiling, but Luse let him have it again.

Lashing out with bolt after bolt of bright yellow lightning.

Smithe roared in rage as he slammed into the far wall of the magma chamber, pulled in by the immense gravitational power of the miniature black hole, shot again and again by purr plasma.

Luse twisted his hands and the bead of nothingness shifted, sinking down as Smithe hit the surface of the lava with a great thunderous explosion. His supercooled armour hitting the molten stone screamed and began sinking out of sight glowing in the heat.

"YOU HAVE NOT WON, KINETIC!" He shouted at them as he began to melt, his voice shaking the walls. **"YOU HAVE NOT WON! THE REAL WAR IS COMING FOR YOU! AHHHH!"**

His scream shook the mountain and Luse felt a pop in his chest as fate's strings were cut from him. He let go of his hold on the aether and fell forward clutching the sword, the world going dark as he was swallowed by sheer fatigue.

****

A snap of bright yellow electricity threw the random soldier across the room as he got too close to Luse, and

David shouted at them all to keep back for what seemed like the hundredth time. Bekka had seen this once before, Rojas had Fallen during a fight against some bloom and when they attacked her body had just rejected them.

Now Luse had Fallen into a deep sleep too, and anyone who got too close was sent reeling.

It would pass, she could feel his body healing already. Using gravity as he had alone was a feat few could handle, except it seemed, for one of the three immortals. The power had been incredible though, no one knew how he had done it, but she imagined it had to do with whatever he held in his arms.

A sweet voice behind her made Bekka jump, "Miss Lucyshyn?"

Bekka turned to see the tall Japanese woman who had been with him. "Yuuki, was it? Sorry, what can we do for you?"

Yuuki nodded to Luse, "Will he be alright? I mean you say he's fine but he's been asleep for nearly two hours… So, are you sure?"

Bekka nodded, "Yeah, he's gonna be just fine sweetheart." Bekka reached out with threads of aether and pushed aside some debris to help some soldiers. Not one looked very appreciative, but it wasn't like she was expecting them to change their minds overnight. It would be a long time before they trusted kinetics, if ever.

Yuuki turned and looked to where Takeo stood, he was directing the soldiers personally. His wife-to-be at his side, they looked like a powerhouse couple if Bekka had ever seen one. She immediately started trying to think how to mix their names, but it wouldn't work so she gave up.

Bekka smiled, "So, are you going to go back? Become the Empress again?"

Yuuki shook her head, "I think not. I may not be what this country needs anymore. I don't think I can be the leader my people need."

"That may not be your choice," came a familiar voice from behind them.

Bekka turned and punched Luse square in the chest. He took it like a punk and crumpled to the floor coughing heavily.

"Oh don't be so dramatic, that was just a love tap. I hit my husband harder than that."

"They sure make you people tough in Canada," Luse said, getting to his feet, slowly coughing up a chuckle. Luse Looked at Yuuki, "As I was saying though. To you Yuuki. Fate isn't done with you," his eyes were glowing strong like deep swirling green galaxies. He seemed to be looking at them, but through them too, as if some greater truth were hidden around them in the air, a truth only he saw.

Yuuki looked stunned, she didn't seem to know what to say.

Bekka nudged Yuuki, "You should know he says that to all the girls. But you'd totes be welcome at the school girl."

Yuuki smiled at that, pulling her hair down across her bad eye. She did nod though, "I think I need time, but I will consider it."

Luse looked around, "Well then, that's perfect!" He clapped his hands together, "So you're not busy then. I've got a little job, and well I can't really get myself involved you see."

Yuuki glared at Luse, "Excuse me? Why on earth would I work for you?" She crossed her arms under her chest and squared off against the green-eyed immortal.

She looked stern and powerful, but all Bekka kept wondering was where Yuuki got that suit.

There was a flurry of commotion on the far side of Luse. A woman in a skin-tight grey catsuit was suddenly beside him tugging his shirt and trying to push a black case into his arms.

Bekka blinked and let her senses stretch out. The woman had come out of nowhere without tripping any warnings.

The whole room was a buzz of commotion yet no one seemed to address the giant fox disguised as seven men in business suits.

It had been a strange night, to say the least.

Luse took the case from the woman and shoved a glassy black sword into it. She then disappeared, leaving him standing holding the case and a confused look.

"Well, looks like I have to go," Luse said, turning to Yuuki, "So let me know if you change your mind, little miss." He slung the case over his shoulder and patted Bekka on the shoulder, "Thanks for the save by the way Becky, you're a peach."

Bekka grabbed his hand as he tried to walk off, "That's it? No answers? No explanation? Just thanks, and then tell me I'm fruit!"

That seemed to make Yuuki angrier too, "And just where do you think you're going with Kusanagi? That is a sacred relic to my family!"

He smiled and suddenly faded, a hazy image of him appearing away from them. Bekka looked at whose hand she held and it was one of the women in the grey bodysuits. She let her hand go and turned on Luse. Grounding her fists on her hips, Bekka fixed him with a dirty glare.

"Don't you dare just disappear on us, Luse."

Luse just shrugged and gave a sly wink, and blinked away.

Yuuki growled loudly, a guttural sound that made a nearby soldier stumble as he reached for a weapon he didn't have. She then rounded on Bekka with a furious look. "Take me to him!"

Bekka shook her head, "I can't blink like they can."

"Blink?" Yuuki asked, sounding confused.

Bekka nodded, "Yeah, it's that teleporting thing that he did. Only some of us can do it," Bekka pointed to David who was with the new kinetics they met here. "David there, he's so good at it he can even move other people with him. But he's also a gater, so he's a bad example I guess."

"Gator? What…? He looks human," she stared at David, eyeing his tattoos as if looking for some strange sign.

"No, not a gator like an alligator, a gate-er, as in someone who makes gates." Bekka smiled and gestured to follow. "You know, if you want to find Luse, you'll have to catch him, and the best way to do that is to learn more. Though you're trying to catch smoke with that guy."

David looked up and nodded to Bekka, then waved his hand and a doorknob appeared in thin air. He grabbed hold and opened the door stepping through.

"David's a wiz at gates and blinking." Bekka sighed again wishing she could do something like that. "I bet he'd be able to try and show you. I mean, you seem strong enough to handle the power of it, I just never got the trick." She reached her hand out to Yuuki, "Come with us? I keep hearing the Immortals say there's a war coming. A war that won't stop at borders or barriers, a war that will decimate this world. So if they're right, which they always are, we're going to need everyone we can get. Luse believed that finding the fox under the mountain was one of the keys to victory."

Yuuki scowled, "I was not the fox."

Bekka chuckled, "But you were here, and every piece plays a part in the picture of a puzzle."

Yuuki still looked angry and confused, but after a long pause staring at Emperor Takeo, she finally nodded. She fixed Bekka with an intense glare, "If I come, I'll find Luse?"

Bekka shrugged, "The immortals kinda do whatever they want. But, you definitely won't find him staying here."

Yuuki nodded and walked off towards David and his door. Bekka just shrugged again and shouldered her cannon. Maybe the fox under the mountain wasn't Yuuki, maybe the end of this wasn't what Luse said it would be. But either way, Bekka could tell this was far from over. But that, maybe, the war had just swung in their favour.

BITTER KINDLING

9yrs A.E. Eastern Canada

There was no going back now, she could feel the bloom inside her moving, she didn't know why she had this clarity though. Her head hurt thinking about it, maybe all wasn't lost… maybe her theory had been right. Another headache shot her hard and she dropped as she tried to remember.

It seemed things came back to her now and then, but the pain was immense when she tried.

Nancy looked around, eyes still under her control little by little moving her head, then her arms, soon she had turned around and she could tell she hadn't been there long, her trail in the snow was still a deep trench behind her. Her mind was in a fog, her body ached from the effort to move, and the more she tried, the more it hurt. Her vision dimmed, but she knew if she let sleep take her it could be days before the bloom let her have control again. So she fought to stay awake, she could beat this, she could take control.

She turned and caught sight of someone in the distance moving toward her across the old city train tracks. Here a tall fence split her path and she knew she would not find shelter before it got dark. She had hoped that maybe following the fence would lead her to an outbuilding, but the old iron fence seemed to just stretch on, lost in the blustering snow.

She tried to call out, but her voice wouldn't come, something felt like it was lodged in her throat again. She had no doubt now, the bloom was waking.

Slowly, with all the force she could muster, taking every bit of willpower she had, she put one foot in front of the other.

As she caught sight of the figure in the distance she waved her arms over her head; or rather tried. Walking back through the snow, she followed the path she had tracked, still waving half-heartedly, trying to get the other person's attention.

Approaching, Nancy could see that the other person was injured. They moved slowly, hunched over, holding their neck, and soon they were close though and she saw it was a man. He saw her now too and moved faster to meet her. They were so close she could hear the crunch of the snow beneath his feet over the whistle of the wind through the chain-link fence that separated them.

But suddenly he stopped, his mouth dropping open in a silent scream, hands clawing at his neck. Over and over he clawed till flesh started to peel away. His spine twisted, and the sound of snapping bone screeched as his arms twisted at wrong angles and he was heaved backwards.

She stopped in her tracks. She didn't know what to do. She stood still just watching the horror unfold, knowing this was her fate too. Slowly he came to stand, his eyes glassy, almost vacant, and his jaw hanging slack. The bloom in his throat moved, pulsing as it pushed its way up from his chest with a loud cracking sound as his jaw popped loose.

The large grey fleshy-looking pod pushed its way out of his mouth, a loud humming sound ringing up from its throat. Slowly opening, it spread wide petals the colour of blood, and from deep inside, it screamed with a man's voice.

"DON'T **RUUUUUUUUUUN**!"

That haunting howl trailed her into the night, that all too human voice from the bloom as it stole the man's life.

She found a train car abandoned along the way, heaving herself inside it and shutting the door. Crawling to the corner in hopes of any kind of heat, but there, all she found was darkness and the dead. Bodies long forgotten no more than skin and sinew, clothed in only tatters, and clutching a ray of hope.

A lighter.

She flicked the spark and quietly expressed her thanks to their lost soul as the corpse lit, dried fatty bits better than wood. She tried desperately to get warm, but the warmer she felt the more her chest hurt, and her stomach churned. Her body quivering even as sleep tried to take her, nightmarish waking dreams fueled by the man at the fence.

She was one now.

One

GROWTH OF A SOUL

18yrs A.E. Nova Esperança, BR

The silence of the hall was nearly maddening, dignitaries from the world over, politicians, and academics all staring at Samuel with slate blank stares as he ended the presentation. The heavy breath in his ear was his own and seemed the only sound in the world as he drummed his fingers lightly on the podium He had hoped for some kind of reaction, anything, but they all just sat there and stared.

"Does anyone have any questions?"

Instantly the auditorium erupted in shouts, it seemed they were all stunned and had been simply waiting on a catalyst to ignite.

"Yes, President Sanders?"

A younger man, famous for his bravado, he now looked very different since their first meeting three years hence. He seemed lost of late, adopting a slouch to his shoulders, his voice sounding hollow as he spoke.

"The war against the seed invasion has brought America and Mexico to the brink of ruin. As it is, by year's end we will have ninety percent of the remaining populace living on ships and freighters at sea, and worst of all, that further ten percent will be left to fend for themselves on the mainland. We barely have the resources to do anything as it is." He paused and looked to his council, a grizzled man, whose name tag read, Benson, a cyborg and a war hero from all the medals. The other man was a lesser known, a sharp-featured handsome blonde man whose name tag read, Green.

Both men nodded, Sanders sighed, and Samuel became curious.

"Your question?"

"Your project; you purpose here that we let the seed spread? You want us to just move up onto these platforms built on those floating islands, or remain at sea?"

Samuel nodded, fidgeting with a spot under his coat as he nodded, "I do. I believe that the process being halted is what caused the issue with their warrior class drones. If we had-"

The room erupted into shouts and protests, some questioning his sanity, others calling for him to be removed. But still, in amongst them were the others, those who saw his proposal for what it was.

"SALVATION!" He slammed his fist on the podium calling a quick halt to the childish bickering of these frightened adults. "This is the means to an end, nothing more! I can not offer you all miracle cures, only ideas using the resources we have. Like here," he turned back to his tablet and waved his hand over the display calling his image library back up. "Look at this," a picture of a giant purple stone floating across the sky covered in moss and lichen-like trees spacing all over it, then again the same island though now it showed the base they were currently on. "We have built this entire research lab on one of the floating islands, over ten thousand people work and live here high above the seed's reach. And there are countless more of these crystals in the area around the equator. And in areas where the seed were allowed full control, they are already down in population by seventy percent. Two of the six pod guardians who made landfall have already gone dormant. They are right here, not ten miles from this spot, along the Tefé. We have pulled samples from it. It-"

"Can they be killed?!"

The call for its death brought more screaming again, and a deeper sigh from Samuel. He had heard the argument from his own government, that was before they attacked the sleeping titans that had stopped in Maracaibo. The fight had ended in a loss of nearly sixty percent of the Brazilian navy, and countless lives, and in the end had done nothing to the creatures.

"The truth is, we don't know," he shook his head, "These creatures heal too quickly, and are resistant to most chemicals. Any samples we collect die within moments of collection and are useless before they reach any labs. Our attempts to seek the help of their creators led to only one thing, they tell us they were only made to go on, not stop." He pulled up the pictures he had prepared. "The pod here in Brazil is too heavily guarded, but we have a means at last."

He had been waiting for this.

The room was silent, every eye on the screen and what it may reveal.

He swiped his hand and the image of a plant growing in a garden came up, a plant that looked more like a squid planted in the soil.

"We finally have a seed juvenile."

The gasps and cries came in a wave, protests crashing on him. He raised his hands though for silence and answered no one till he had complete attention.

"It was brought to us by one of my students. She was able to get in and bring back several, and from them, we have been able to learn much. But The thing of it is, none of it has led to a way to stop the seed. We have though learned that they can be changed. Here today we are preparing a transport to bring each of you a sample seed. They are still dormant, but we believe we can, together, find a way to coexist. We have already been experimenting with ways to grow seed that are disconnected from their hive mind and could maybe be used to lead their own hive to reshape the terrain for us." His hand again came to his chest toying with the buttons. "One day, we may not even need to contest the ground."

There were many skeptical murmurs in the crowd, but he could hear the gears turning as they all sat there looking at the prospect of having living seed to run tests on, a feat which had never been accomplished.

He was about to go on when pain lanced through him and he nearly fell.

The worry on the faces of some made him smile.

"I'm fine," he shrugged, "Well, as well as any who are dying." He waved over one of the W.H.O. agents, a short blond woman who acted as his liaison. "Lisa here will show you all to the lab tour, and will get the listings for where we can send the samples, as well as set up your staff to work here if you have no proper facilities."

Lisa nodded and spread her arms wide, her voice carrying in a very authoritative way.

"Come along everyone!"

As always she was a force of nature, the whole room seeming to rise as one and begin filing out. He knew she didn't like it here, but she stayed to help him and he appreciated it, even knowing what the humidity did to her perfectly sculpted hair. She nodded to a man as she passed him and closed the door behind her as she left.

The man by the door came down the steps of the auditorium to the ground floor.

"Doctor Cruz, I'm-"

"I know who you are kinetic," Samuel had been all over the world these past eighteen years, and he knew one of the kinetics when he saw them. It was the itch in his chest that set it off. "If you want something I'm afraid I can't help. As with when my people were denied your help, the government has refused to allow me to help yours."

He nodded, "I assumed that was a thing, but I'm not here to ask you for help." He shook out his tweed coat, the fabric changing as he did till he stood wearing a long black coat much like some spaghetti-western gunslingers coat. "My name is Matthew, and I'm here to help you."

Samuel could have almost laughed if not for the pain in his chest. He carefully laid his tablet face down and turned to the man.

"Well mister Matthew, I-"

"Just, Matthew, please."

Samuel sighed, "Well, Matthew, I don't need your help either." He picked up his tablet but set it right back down, the pain was getting worse and he didn't think he could hold it and still stand. "I'm dying, not stupid. I don't need your kind of help."

Matthew didn't seem mad, not even slightly, he just spread his palms out to his sides wide. "If this is some kind of race, I can help. I'm no healer, but I could try and heal you unless-"

"It's cancer."

Matthew looked up at him and sighed, "Yeah, it had to be that; cellular mutation is impossible to heal with-"

"I know; our friend Lisa tried once, then she tried to erase my memory of it. I think she assumes I don't know she is one of you anymore. Little did she know that the tumor in my head prevented permanent tampering, she took the image of the moment, but not what was said at the time." The pain began to pulse and Samuel set his hand down to steady his pose. "The truth is, I have my own research going to find a cure, and if I don't make it, well then my research will hopefully help another to continue."

Matthew nodded.

"So, will that be all?"

"Actually, we have heard a rumour," he intoned quietly, an odd smile that didn't touch his glowing amber eyes. "A little birdy says that some bloom have been spotted here, that this lab has even been growing them. Now, it's hard to believe that anyone would be so foolish as to breed them outside of the north, but if so-"

"The bloom, they're dangerous?"

"Very, their master poses a serious threat, and your plans to spread the seed virus further rather than continue to interrupt it does work in their favour."

"How is that?"

"Well, they also wish to spread their virus, an-"

"Are they not restricted to the cold?"

"Well, as far as we-"

"Oh, so you are guessing?"

"No, we just-"

"So then, have you seen them?"

"No, we have had-"

"So then you are spying on me?"

"For your safety, we-"

"My safety. Then you wish to finally contribute by bringing me people willing to help in my experiments?"

"The immortals would never a-"

"Then clearly, you don't wish to help, only control. My country has seen enough of despots and dictators, and while I-"

"Look," Matthew raised his hands defensively.

"No, you look; you have done enough here. I am dying, so my time is not only precious, but also not my own. I have a world to heal."

Matthew looked like he wanted to say more, to say anything at all, but knew there was nothing left to say.

"Thank you," and Samuel gestured to the door.

"Thank you, doctor Cruz, for all you have done. I know that this won't be the last we meet." With a final nod, there was a popping sound and Matthew was gone, just like that.

Relieved to be done with it all Samuel sighed, he grabbing his tablet hobbled his way off the stage to the first chair in the audience. His chest felt tighter than he had ever felt it, pain lancing up his left side.

"Let me help…"

Gentle hands closed around him from behind, one under his chin massaging his throat, the other on his chest. Her fingertips poked through the spaces between the buttons of his shirt nails digging into his skin. The harder she pressed the lighter he began to feel, the pain ebbing away till he felt loose and calm again.

Taking a breath he leaned back. "Thank you."

Despoina came around and sat next to him, her long red dress floating in her wake. "You're very welcome. After all, you pose a serious investment."

He gave a bark of laughter, though he regretted it right away as it sent a burning chill through his ribs.

"I'm serious Samuel, please, be more careful."

"I'm fine, I'm fine. I just found it funny that both you and the kinetics just see us mundane as toys in your little games."

Her look she gave him then said he had gone to far.

"Sorry, I overdid it a little. I was not expecting the presentation to end with a kinetic in my face." He slid his tablet into his bag and tried to stand up, his knees however had a different plan and he fell back to his seat hard. "I'm getting weaker Despoina, I may not have much time left."

The genuine despair on her face spoke levels as she held out her hand to him helping him up. "You know, if you got friendly with the kinetics, they could help."

"They already said it; they can't heal me."

She nodded, "True. But they have people who could make the chemicals needed for running proper chemo treatments"

Samuel scoffed and waved his free hand at her.

"You haven't been taking the pain medication, I can tell, and-" Her hand was suddenly on his chest again, fingers finding the spot on his chest where his implant was still growing. "The angel seed has yet to take root, it needs time to work, time you may not have if the cancer spreads faster than the roots of the angel."

He placed his hand over his heart and her hand, then looked at her sweet ageless beauty, the dark curls that framed her soft cheeks like ebony waterfalls. You would have never known that it was her they feared so much.

"Do you mean to cause the end times, Desponia? Do you seek the destruction of mankind?"

"Let me guess, one of those kinetics said that?"

"Yes…," he nodded but let himself be led up the stairs and out the hall. She didn't reply for some time, they just rounded the walkway that led to the bunker barracks.

"They do not even know who I am doctor," she said suddenly, "Do you know who I am?"

"I have only known you for four years, I don't know who you were, or what you've done."

"But, do you know who I am? I have never lied to you doctor, and I told you I never will. These kinetics think all of the bloom infected are just Fallen. But I never lost myself, I knew what I was doing when I became what I am now, and I knew I had to come to you, to save me." She stopped and pushed him up against the wall. "But as long as a bloom rests within me I am their enemy." Her blouse billowed and the scar down her chest split open like curtains to reveal the bright red blossom starburst that pushed its way out between her breasts. The temperature dropped as it slowly uncurled, the long thin tentacle cracking as frost formed along its length in the humid air.

"Could I not simply explain?" He asked, reaching out a finger towards one of the tiny thorns that grew from it.

She pulled back quickly, the bloom retreating inside her in a flash like a viper into its den.

"No, it is not so simple doctor." As the skin closed she looked off at the wall beside her. "I can still feel her call, the Wych-hazel. She could control me too if I didn't resist, she made me. It is why I came here to escape her, but now, there are others like me, others who are not trapped by the cold. Once they figured out that our power lets others live anywhere they want to, I was even more precious to dear mother. I can feel them now and then, getting closer every year. And one day they will come and I will not be able to stop them." She turned back to Samuel taking his arm again. "But till then, I will see your ascension happen. That seed in you is not like anything else, made with the tech and know-how of both sides. It's not the demon's curse like my bloom, nor the power of the gods like the kinetics, but a blessing from the best of both." She led him to the door of his room and helped him into his favourite chair. "I had a vision before I became like this. That I would fall, and that you could save me. But you can save so many more, Fates be Damned."

He wanted to ask her more, to set the record straight, but the world grew dim. He saw her smile and knew it was something she did, and he slipped back into a deep and comforting sleep, her words whispered in his ear.

"Sweet dreams, Angel…"

Awake to the Nightmare

9yrs A.E. Eastern Canada

Suddenly pain lanced through her, and Nancy reached out and clutched at the object jutting from her chest.

Her eyes opened as the searing pain hit her again, this time through her gut. She looked up at the sky, boiling with stormy clouds black as pitch, and heavy with snow. Her body twisting on its own, hung from a wall, pinned by pieces of rebar that jutted from where she had been hit in her dream. The pain washed over her, making her want to vomit. She felt as though she had been hit by a car. She tried to cry out, but she could barely move, her body writhing of its own accord.

Two people in hooded cloaks stood on the ground below her, roaring back and forth in a fit of rage, men by the sound of their shouting voices. They seemed at odds over what to do about her, though most of it was lost in the pain distracting her.

“It's not her anymore, Andy!" The taller man shouted gruffly, "Look at it. Nancy’s dead! That thing is just a fucking meat puppet for the damned bloom!”

The one named Andy shook his head. “But I can feel her power, Stephan. She would have burned herself out if-”

Stephan put his hand out, pointing up at Nancy. “It killed three people already. Every one of them a Risen kinetic.” He sighed and grew quieter. “You wanna see if you can reason with it because it froze up all of a sudden and called out Madison's name?”

"Look at her, Stephan. It's her. It's Nancy!" The younger man shouted.

They both looked up at her and saw she was looking back. The taller one stepped forward. His green hood pulled back to reveal a strong face, hard but handsome, shaved bald and tattooed. His sleeve had Fallen back as he pointed at her, revealing the tattoo on his arm too. A bright green, glassy-looking seashell, spiralling in a band of seven black lines, he wasn't just any Risen. He was just like her... like she once was.

His eyes made her cringe though, filled with hate, and glowing, sharp thorns of gold and green light twisting in and out of the confines of his iris.

She looked down at him seeing her tattoo out the corner of her eye again, it was healed now. She cringed, to think how much time she had lost in those dreams.

Deep inside Nancy, a hiss began to grow until it roared inside her head. "*Pluck the eyes from their sockets... Pluck the eyes from their sockets... Pluck the eyes from their sockets... Pluck the eyes from their sockets...* ***Pluck the eyes from their sockets***!"

She shook all over, her body trying to pull itself apart at the joints.

That voice had come from her.

Over and over and over again, the words repeated. She was so focused that she didn't even realize she was moving. Her hands clawed at the metal sticking out of her, her whole body bucking and twisting. In her throat, the hissing was louder too. It felt like tiny wires pulled and tugged her body, twisting her into painful positions in an attempt to be free.

"See, she's losing control. They all do!" Stephan shouted as he stepped forward with his hands outstretched. He crooked his fiery glowing fingers and turned his hands like he was bending the air, and the metal twisted in on itself to pin her tighter.

As the metal pierced her flesh, it seared and burned, the smell of burning meat filling the air. She screamed and this time the sound that came out was much more than a whisper. Her voice ripped the air apart. Both men had to throw their hands over their ears. Her body felt so hot, she could feel it like liquid pooling in her stomach. The deep hiss seemed to call to her, she closed her eyes and let the pain wash away. The last sight she had, the men turning, as more shambling forms came into their circle of light.

Then… nothing.

Clear Night in Soldiers State

18yrs A.E. New Winnipeg, CA

The morning bells chimed through Vince's open window, nine deep gongs that he knew could be heard across the whole city. Even though it was a good two stories above him, the massive metal gonging still shook his office, stone walls practically vibrating from the force.

The first class was starting.

Vince looked up at the sky wondering how anyone could even tell. They hadn't seen a true summer in almost seven years, certainly, none since the wastes had overtaken them five years ago. The east coast of Canada was completely frozen, ruled by the bloom and covered in Death-flowers clawing their way to the borders of Manitoba. From there at least they were able to try and turn back the tide, though it seemed that things were still getting colder, and the bloom were pushing harder the last couple of years.

Vince looked out the window again at the worthless crack of sunlight that split the slate grey oppression that was the sky. The fine rays of morning light poked through the clouds before being devoured just as quickly by yet another hungry snowstorm.

He had been up all night again, and his eyes were heavy as he folded up his paperwork. Closing it all away in his desk drawer, he decided it was time to take a break. Reading reports could wait until he came back from patrol. He wanted to watch the morning chorus first.

Vince stepped out of his office and headed down through the school. Groups of initiates and apprentices passing by nodded to him. One such group of apprentices wearing spear crests on their coats stopped to greet him.

"Good morning, Master Vince. Heading to a lesson?" The tall boy was very proper, but Vince could feel his eager thoughts. Freshly raised, the poor boy was trying desperately to control a small flurry of excitement and hero-worship rushing through his mind.

Vince shook his head and handed him a scrap of paper. "No, Mr. Stephenson. I'm heading out of the building for a while," he explained, "Perhaps you can do me a favour though if you're not busy?"

The whole group looked stunned, the young man most of all. He bowed deeply, mumbling, "Anything Master."

Vince ruffled his hair. "None of that now. I'm heading out to see my wife, so if anyone comes to my office, hand them this note. If this makes you late, you have my permission to come to make up the time with me personally." It was clear the boy was excited, he stammered a bit, but nodded and rushed off leaving his friends behind.

"You should all be off too," he said, trying his best to sound stern. How they jumped made Vince want to laugh.

Another pair of apprentices rushed by him, calling after the other two, wanting to know where their friend had gone, one wearing the quill, the other the shield, Vince noticed. They all began chatting in hushed tones about what had happened and disappeared down the stairs towards the North Hall. He masked his presence the rest of the way. As amusing as it was, he didn't want to be stopped again. The halls were beginning to fill with people filing down for breakfast from the dorms, and he was not keen on being held up further.

They had over three hundred initiates, and over a hundred apprentices, all of who lived at the school now. Many were orphans, children abandoned by parents who couldn't care for a Kinetic child. Some were even grown men and women, those few who were just unable to cope with the sudden powers. With nowhere else to turn to, they came here.

Vince gave a nod of respect as he discreetly passed another Master, but she barely looked up at him. Most of those that taught here were only here because they had to be. Only a handful of Masters had remained after the event eighteen years ago. The majority of those who had left would be back soon anyway. The word was that the Trinity was gathering everyone this time.

Leaving the massive doors of the school proper he was at last free. Vince made his way out through the front gates, and left the school grounds, waking down to Main Street. There were no cars anymore, and what was left of the fuel in the city had been confiscated by the city council. Vince didn't know why, or to what end, what with all the cars in the city having already been cannibalized for the scrap parts. It was better utilized for heating purposes, he supposed.

But that didn't mean the city wasn't all a bustle still. Instead of cars, the city had trolleys. They ran like clockwork, up and down every major street, all through the city from the inner walls of the school, down through the inner city, and out to what people called; Old Winnipeg.

Vince walked along the bustling street feeling a little wistful. He sat back under the roof of the trolley stop shack and shook his duster coat free of snow as he scooted under the heat lamp. But he didn't get to sit long as a hiss of steam and the crackle of electricity heralded the timely arrival of the next ride.

The bus-sized trolley was all lit up, brassy polished 'till it shone like gold. This one had been down to the old city already today by the look of it. Splashes of sooty mud all up both sides, and the smell of heavy cigarette smoke made that clear.

Trolleys like this were always heated and ran with barely a pause, so you could ride them as long as you wanted. They also didn't need conductors, running by clockwork from the school, so no one policed anyone on them either.

Vince took his seat, nodding to the older woman he often saw this time of the morning.

"Hellen," he said, acknowledging her with a nod. She had headphones in, music blaring, but she waved at him cheerfully with a little smile. He took his usual seat in the middle of the vehicle and stared off into the street ahead.

Snow falling, people walking to and fro, everyone going about their business… All in all, it seemed so peaceful… so perfect. The truth, however, was not as gilded as he would like.

They passed through the first gate, leaving the city's inner ward where the school and the initiates lived and travelled down into Old Winnipeg, the city proper.

They had made the push four years ago and nearly quadrupled their holdings of land. Here, outside the gate, those who wanted no business with Kinetics were free to live as they chose. Fuel was still prohibited, but the trolleys ran here, just as well as anywhere else. Horses and carriages were a common sight in these parts. Even this early, a group of people piled in a cart pulled by an old mare with a merry trot. The streets here were not as free of snow: the people didn't care. They didn't blame Kinetics for the Event at least, but few trusted the Kinetics despite all the help they gave freely.

Coming up from the underpass into the old city was like stepping into a different world. It was far more ramshackle here. The houses and buildings had been repurposed to fit growing numbers of the mundane. Run exclusively by the city council, every year it looked worse, not better. The people lived cheek to cheek in whatever houses they eked out from the rubble. Most worked as labourers or militia as there were few other jobs in high demand. Making a living was harder here, and the people were all the harder for it.

It was Azure's rules though.

He forbade any Kinetic from interfering in the affairs of the mundane unless specifically requested to do so by the council, or in the case of life or death situations. It made sense when he saw the conditions of the city. They all had the same rations, they all had the same rights, yet somehow the mundane managed to mess it all up.

The trolley curved slightly and came to a stop as a massive group of men and women embarked. They were boisterous, but friendly, dressed in city worker gear with helmets and vests over their coats. It was clear from the thick tar on their clothes that they were roofers, and as happy as they were, they must have worked hard through the night. They greeted others on the trolley like old friends and seemed a jovial group; until they saw Vince. They grew quiet as they took their seats, and muttered back and forth, the air of joy, gone.

He sighed, felt a pang of regret, and resumed his steady forward stare for the remains of the trip.

The new wall came into sight around the corner of the buildings. Even bigger than the inner-city wall, it stood over nine stories tall. The plan was to have it circle the outskirts of the city. The train tracks ran the length of the wall, which was built right against the river. It was the only way in or out of the Forks, and it travelled further right up towards the Old Fort road bridge. The apprentices of the school, and higher ranked initiates walked that wall daily, as part of their classes. They must be ever vigilant to turn back the tide of the bloom and hold back the wastes.

His mind had drifted inward to dark thoughts again, and he almost missed the call for-

"Forks"

"My stop!" He jumped off as the trolley slowed down. Almost there, soon he could relax, if only for a little while.

He walked into the old terminal building of the train station that functioned as the new city hall. The gateway into the old Forks Market was guarded heavily by men with guns and dogs trained to sniff out the bloom infection. The Station was how many people arrived in the city, the performed method at least. But security was tight, and only the mundane had to deal with it, so it didn't help the animosity between the two groups.

Thankfully the train was still run by the Kinetics, making its way across Canada regularly to bring people back to the safety of the city. It looked like they may be expecting an inbound train today, the guards all seemed on edge. It was obvious that there were a few Kinetics in the group; you could tell them from the others there, their coloured dusters and that none carried guns. There was even a true pyrokinetic with his black coat. That was rare, most of them stayed outside the walls, Vince thought.

As the man laid eyes on Vince, he nodded in respect, Vince waved back but didn't stop to chat. He was running late now.

He weaved through the security checks set up, no one ever stopped a master at least, finally heading into the Forks proper. Vince walked down the winding path of vendors who were already heading into the main building to set up their shops. After two near riots, Azure had decided the Forks was now neutral ground. As such, the Kinetics policed it instead of the Council. It just meant that as he walked here no one stared at him, in fact, a few who knew him even stopped to wave.

"Morning, Master Vincent!" A sweet shrill voice called to him from in the crowd.

Vince jumped despite himself but settled down quickly as he knew that voice all too well. "Good morning, Carly. Here to listen to your sister too?"

The little firecracker of a woman shook her head, releasing a cascade of sky-blue locks from her dark red hood as she did. "Not exactly, I got a promotion. Check it out, oh brother-in-law of mine, and weep. I made your division!" She pushed up her sleeve to reveal the tattoos on her inner arm: a blue cube of wood, a rough teardrop of red coral, and just below that a silver shield over the top of four multi-coloured lines. Her duster's sleeve was also adorned with a shiny new silver shield that marked her as a teacher now.

He was so proud of her and smiled, clapping his hands like a fool making others in the market stop and stare. The implications hit him just then, and he stopped as he realized what that meant. For two years she had been trying to pass her exam, ever since their mother had gone missing. She hoped to become a teacher, so she could finally discover the truth behind the disappearance. But now at the dawn of war, she was raised.

Her hand was still up, so he high-fived her and clasped her hand: "You know what that means then. I'm officially your superior… So no slacking."

She nodded and gave him a jab, which made him wince. She was far stronger physically than her petite size would suggest, a trait of her mental prowess. Her body was kinetically controlled, and she always forgot that when she was excited.

She realized her mistake and held up her hands, aghast. "Oh Vince, sorry, I'm just so stoked! Wait. What're you doing here? You know Amy hates when you come to hear her sing. Her whole squad loses focus over your dreamy Trinidadian ass." She crossed her arms under her chest and gave him a dirty look.

Vince shrugged. "You know me. Any chance to hear my sweet Amy sing."

Carly frowned. "Have you heard my sister sing before?" She said with a chuckle and a twinkle in her eye.

He had, of course, Amy was awful, but he would have listened to her sing the dictionary. Carly gave him a little shove and rolled down her sleeve.

"Well, I have to report for duty in two hours. They have me on my first patrol. I haven't been outside Manitoba in years."

He wanted to say something, wanted to tell her not to go, wanted to say anything that would matter. But he couldn't, so he just waved at her as she left instead.

He went down the path towards the river walk. The old stone steps cut in a huge semicircle leading down towards the river. He noticed the river was low, yet even in the depths of such a frigid winter the waters of the Red River still flowed strong.

It was thanks to the Kinetics of the school that it never froze over—even as it flowed further north into the Hudson Bay. Vince was no good at it, but once they figured out how water and heat mingled, many kinetics working together could thaw any amount of ice, or so they had thought.

Vince noticed there weren't as many watchers this morning, it was far too cold a day he supposed. The winds were howling, and a storm was brewing. The falling snow was cold and heavy. Waist deep in some places, even the more travelled paths to the water's edge were buried several inches deep. Wet shrouds of heavy white clung to trees and buildings alike.

That wouldn't stop him though, Vince had come to see Amy work. She was special to him, in a way that no one else was to Vince, and he loved everything about her. His eyes found her right away, even in the sea of red hoods on the far shore.

The way the snow always seemed to avoid her, her powers radiating heat, was magical to him. Even now in the dead of winter thick ice melted away before her. She told him many times how much she missed the cool kiss of the snow as it landed on her skin, but she was always so warm it just melted around her.

Vince loved to see her in the rain. The way it would steam up, wreathed around her, made her seem almost ethereal. He could watch her for hours, like watching a butterfly dancing about in its many shining bright colours.

She and the other Kinetics in her circle talked and laughed. Amy was always the life of the party, always standing out. It wasn't that she wanted to be the center of attention; it was just who she was. Her magnetic personality, and the way she just gave off airs of calm and happiness.

As was the norm, her outfit today was far from common. She wore a dark black blouse unbuttoned at the top that seemed to clash with everything else she wore. It was like someone had upended a jungle flower, all the petals of her skirts swaying and ruffling about her ankles. Some seemed like they'd been made of lace. Others: old carpets, but they were bright, and every one was different.

Vince chuckled as he remembered the other day when he had almost made a fool of himself trying to count them. Flipping the corners back one at a time, and the way her hand had gently come to rest on his as he rounded twelve. Her soft smile as she explained that after that and he'd be showing everyone there her underwear. Dressing like this was just one of the things she did that made her special, one of the things that made her dear to him.

They made their way one by one, each pausing a moment to fold their coats, placing them on the stone steps. He looked at the dusters as the snow lighted on them, like red and blue tiles haphazardly thrown on the stone path.

The notes of the song began to rise as more and more joined in. The words to 'Wade in the Water could barely be heard over the sound of the rising storm winds. An old song, it was one of many that they used to focus their energy together.

Two circles formed: one for the heat, the pseudo-pyros, and one for the water, the hydrokinetics. Each worked their circle to maintain a balance, but the elements seemed unwilling to comply today. The winds were picking up and made hearing her over the whistling wind almost impossible. Without harmony, getting the river heated would be difficult even with this number of people.

Vince looked up at the sky to see dark grey clouds bulging with snow, and the looming threat of worse to come. He raised his hand to the sky and felt the rush of power welling up from deep within the sweet caress of aether that all Kinetics sought to harness, the power of the universe. He touched the aether to the world around him and found the wind calling back to him. All that power sang, 'Make me yours.' He focused on the clouds and wind and felt them as if he held them like a solid thing. Vince brushed the clouds aside in one swipe. He worked and moulded the winds, driving them back in all directions to instead sweep around this corner of the city. As he did the sky parted to reveal clear blue in a teardrop shape like a wedge of air.

It took little effort for him now. Air and clouds were simple to understand for him. Vince was one of the very few aerokinetics who understood the connection between liquids and gasses. For him, storms were easy to manipulate. It just required an enormous amount of power.

He looked back down the steps to where Amy stood, her skirts fluttering in the gentle breeze that slipped through his net. She smiled, waving back at him, promptly turning it into a flip of the bird. She hated singing, even more than he loved hearing her.

That much energy released at once must have had every kinetic in the city looking his way. He rubbed nervously at the snow with his heel. As he stood there, the song started up again, this time stronger, each word as crisp and clear as the air. He could pick out the sound of her voice: a melody sweet like nectar, smiling, he waved back at Amy and lay back in the snow looking up at the clear sky.

Not long ago, he could barely make a leaf flutter at will without her help to focus his power. The first time he had cleared the sky had been on instinct alone.

Vince was just beginning to doze off when he felt the others approach. He sensed them before he saw them; their boot falls made little noise in the snow. Amy had long ago taught him the trick to sense others, to feel the flow of the aether around people. It worked well. He was rarely startled anymore.

A young officer named Mitchell was the first to speak. “Good morning Master Vincent,” he said, “The others are ready to pack up, Sir.” The man was always so proper, and so naive. “We have to ride out soon or we'll never intercept those Americans the seers told us about. Not before they reach the infected zone.” He shifted from foot to foot in the snow. “Sir? They may have a camp set up down in West

Lynne. They're north of the border already." He winced a little, continuing, "The council decided to send out Masters Sam and Sean to the camp, neither have returned yet…"

"I know Mitchell, I heard the seer's report too, the Saints of Stone, eh… bet they just wandered off on an adventure." Vince looked down to where Amy stood hip-deep in the water with the men and women of her circle all singing and weaving kinetic energy. The waters slowing near them steamed and bubbled with mist. He smiled and looked back at Mitchell. "I just wanted to remind myself why I'm fighting." Vince stood up to face the group who had gathered, ten of the best men and women in the corps.

He waved them closer, not wanting to have to raise his voice. "Is this everyone?" he asked.

Mitchell shook his head, before explaining, "The others are at the bridge. We have us and Lucas… and Sir… Carly, she's in our group." Mitchell knew of their familial relationships.

Vince just nodded, and then shook the snow off his coat. "I heard already. Bumped into her in the market. Guess she's waiting with the horses."

He nodded his head, smiling, "Just like her sister, sir, she loves the horses."

Vince looked back at Amy wondering if he would return. He knew what was out there, and the Seers said today was the day… whatever that meant. All Vince knew was it meant war. Like all Kinetics though, he stood strong. It was their calling. "It's our duty to protect the city for those we love, Mitchell. If we don't, who will?"

"But sir-"

Vince held up his hand, he already knew what he was going to say.

"If we tell the people what would it do? The mundane would panic, and the uninitiated would either try to run or worse, try and help and die. No, if this works the way the Azure says, then we won't have to say a peep."

He paused then and shuffled a bit, "Sir?" He looked up nervously. "Have you ever met the Sain- uh, I mean, Masters Sean and Sam?"

Vince nodded, yeah, we met during the Event, saved the city together then."

"So it's not true what people say, that they're like ghosts, no ones ever seen?"

Vince gave a hearty bark of laughter, "Hardly, the paladin and his bard are notorious."

"If I see them, how will I know?"

"Oh, you'll know Sean at least, that mane of flowing golden locks; a might bit pretentious."

Mitchell nodded, but Vince could feel disapproval coming off him in waves.

Vince remembered that feeling well, but he would stand guard. He would protect the people and would protect Amy, at any cost, and keep his heart light, so his heart could return to her.

****

Carly was very glad she had seen Vincent and gave him a head's up before he found her in his squad. He meant the world to Amy, and her adopted sister meant the world to Carly too, so when given the option, she had of course chosen Vince's squad. She respected her brother-in-law and couldn't think of anyone she would rather serve under.

She left the market, stopping only long enough to grab a bite for breakfast, then walked back up the road towards the city. The wall and the station loomed up from the heavy curtain of snow falling. Fewer people were walking down to the Forks now. Most of them were heading to the market.

She walked into the main doors and through the main hall, none of it had changed in all these years; not the high vaulted ceiling, nor the gilded paintings. She loved it. It helped her keep from feeling the strangeness of her current situation. She hadn’t changed in all this time, and neither had this building, well, not really.

The main hall still led up to the terminal where the train came in. Through one door newcomers to the city were escorted to the council hall where the council members on duty would assist anyone who needed them. Through the other hall doors though it was a different story.

She stepped up to the double doors and nodded to the Kinetics posted there. They barely moved, but she felt their probes of energy and let them into her mind. Once they were in, performing a superficial check, they both stepped aside and let her through.

This side of the terminal was where the gater's worked, so the security was way tighter. Kinetics with a unique power, a gater could be anywhere at any time. With nothing that could stop their comings and goings, the Masters made sure to watch them and guard them in turn.

The hallway here had been modified, with specific booths built with a marker in each. A missing marker meant a gater had that spot in use. That meant no one in or out of that booth unless you wanted your atoms shredded accidentally when a gater popped home.

The known gater's, herself included, beyond the three Immortals, had full run of the area. Carly found herself one of the open booth tags and grabbed the marker. She felt the flow around her and familiarized herself with the feeling of the void around her. She grabbed the markers from two more booths and clipped them to her dusters belt.

She reached deep and felt the world slow to a stop. She found the energy around her and felt out the tiny particles that made up the sparks of the wormholes she would need, found the one she wanted and grabbed hold of it.

Her fingers twisted through the air leaving trails of light as the thick metal walls began to flow in front of her, molten metal like glowing waters as her gate opened. It always felt like it took an eternity, but even as she opened her eyes to see the effect of her gate opening, she knew it had been fractions of a second. The scene beyond the portal was one she would always remember. Her old place back in Brandon, the fence long buried under snow, she could just see the solar panel off the roof that still kept some of the lights on. She reached out, memories drawing her forward, but again, she couldn't go. Her gate warped and the walls around her snapped back.

She let her mind become unfocused for a moment, letting her farsight flow from one booth to the other. With a small sound like a snapping of twigs and a faint rustle like leaves, she flickered and blinked from one to the other, going to each booth, she travelled one to the next, faster and faster, until she would have appeared to be no more than a shimmering after image to any onlooker. She came to a stop in the farthest booth she had claimed the marker for. She was breathing heavily but it felt good, like a good workout, or a long jog.

She was returning the extra markers when Carly suddenly felt the pull of aether around her. It was hard to explain to anyone who had never felt it, like all the air around her being pulled towards one of the booths near the end of the hall.

Carly hadn't met that many other gater's, and she was curious to watch another like her at work. The wall at the back of the booth seemed to shimmer, cracks forming as it suddenly pulled inwards into a wormhole.

Carly was excited to see this. It was new, like none she had seen before.

Every gater was different, every gate an expression of how that person perceived the matter of reality. So no two gates were alike. At least that's what the immortal Rojas had said when she helped train Carly, so she was excited to meet this new person. Perhaps too excited.

She hadn't felt the fear and anger, she had only been focused on her mind. So when the man came tumbling through backwards, he collided with her and took them both to the floor.

"Mister Jack!"

Carly looked up to see a little boy overtop of them, tugging on the strangely dressed man's Hawaiian shirt. The gate had closed and a tall Asian woman stood in the booth now looking grim, one side of her face scared beyond shape or design, and her eye missing. She wore long dark clothes, and a green duster so dark it seemed black. She had her hands on her hips and tapped her foot impatiently.

The man atop her pulled himself free and stood up. "I'm sorry, Andrew. I'm fine, no thanks to you, witch!" He threw the words at the Asian woman like acid. He looked down at Carly and reached down to her, "I'm very sorry miss, truly-" He had an accent, English she thought, or something else.

She couldn't quite tell, but it hardly mattered, she took his offered hand, and let him help her up.

"No, it's my fault, I usually know better than to be where others are, gating-" Carly looked over at the woman by the gate. She still looked rather annoyed, though now her eyes were on Carly and not the strange man.

The woman's coat billowed out as she turned, the markers on her hip jingling against a ring of six others. Seven markers? That meant other safe houses?

She took a long and heavy-looking case off her back and hung it by the strap on the hook outside the booth.

Carly was confused, she was about to ask when she felt the pressure of this other woman imposed on her. A simple thing usually, it was supposed to be like a handshake, but this felt more like arm wrestling. The power of the other woman pressed back down on her and Carly could tell if she had let down her guard this other woman would have been in her head.

The pressure disappeared in a heartbeat, and the woman sniffed, "Guess you're a shield then? Well, forget you saw me if you know what's good for you, and you, Potato boy, keep your nose clean and get your ass to that address I gave you-"

The man hardly looked fazed, just flipped a peace sign backwards at the woman. "Jog on trampy, I never asked for your help. Also, I told you before that I'm Scottish, not Irish, so calling me potato boy makes no sense."

She shrugged, "Just do what you're told, soldier boy and protect that kid, he means more than any of us." She slammed her fist against the wall, and it shattered inward like before, her wormhole opening up into a bizarre-looking field of trees. She stepped through and the wall pieced itself back together behind her so that just like that they were alone.

Carly was beyond shocked.

The man named Jack sighed heavily again, "What a cun-"

"Jack! My mum says you can't say that word in Canada!" The little boy said suddenly.

Andrew, she had heard Jack call him.

She was really confused, "Umm… Mister Jack, was it? Look, I don't know what's going on, sorry. I only just got permission to even be here without a Teacher present last night." She spread her hands and tried not to look as clueless as she felt, "Can I help?"

He smiled a very dashing and disarming grin, "Never you worry a hair, lass. I've got this all settled… or rather I will, once I deliver this case to someone called Rojas."

He was very handsome, rugged, and tall, and-

"Jack, what do you mean she has – a sweet pair – pair of what?" Andrew piped up suddenly.

Carly's face flushed hot, and the look on Jack's face said it all, though she hadn't heard him say a word.

His smile turned to a blush too fast. "Andrew, dear lad… what did I say before?"

Andrew looked suddenly shamefaced, "You said, to stay out of your head… or you'd box my ears."

Jack nodded, "Right then…" he cuffed the boy in the back of the head. Just once, and more playful than hard. "Lessons are taught to be learnt, let that be one."

Carly still glared at the man, regardless of the deep blush she felt burning her face. She zipped up her coat then, which at least covered her cleavage. It wasn't her fault she dressed so lightly, she was warm by nature. Yet she felt suddenly aware of herself.

She turned her attention to the boy though instead. "I heard this letch call you Andrew… is that right?"

The little boy couldn't be more than six or seven, he nodded and shook off Jack's attempt to take his hand. "I am. It's a pleasure to meet you, Miss Carly."

She felt a weight between her eyes she hadn't noticed, the boy was already in her mind. So subtle and soft she had not even noticed his intrusion.

Jack scuffed his toe a bit but smiled at her anyway. "Harsh, but well deserved. I apologize, where I'm from, your kind are rarer. And this young man has not had any training they have said. Jack Smithe, a pleasure," he held out his hand to her.

Carly was not so doe-eyed, despite what her sister said, "Apology accepted. You can hardly be held accountable for your thoughts, regardless of couth." She crossed her arms and returned her attention to young Andrew. "So, are you here to train at the school?"

The young boy nodded, "I… um…" He seemed suddenly shy and withdrawn, his eyes beginning to glow as he looked east as if staring towards the river. "What's that?"

Carly felt it too, a sudden well of aether building up, it grew, until like the popping of a balloon it released. She let her farsight range outward and found the sky clear over most of the city. She had seen this before, but it always left her in awe.

She looked down at Andrew, taking the little boy's hand easily and nodding to Jack as she did. "I can take you to the admin building. I'm heading there myself for my job assignment."

Jack smiled, "Thanks."

Andrew tugged her hand, and she looked down at him, "Yes Andrew?"

"Um… can all mages do that?" He asked timidly.

She wrinkled her nose in thought, "Mage? Oh, you mean us? Kinetics, well no, some of us are just more powerful than others. But if you train, maybe one day you will be able to too."

He didn't seem thrilled like most kids his age were to hear this though, "Grandmother said that it was unnatural. She said that only God should have the powers mage… um, kinetics have." His little hand squeezed hers tight.

She understood this, she had struggled with those kinds of thoughts too. She reached into her collar, and finding the long chain of beads with her fingers, brought out her rosary. She held it up for him to see, "Some people, like me, like to think it was part of his plan. It's hard to say… the more you meditate the closer you feel to the universe. That's how I was able to find inner peace, and how I came to terms with my beliefs. You see the nice thing about this city is the people. Everyone is different, and that's good. You come to realize you don't have to worry about who you believe in, as long as you believe in the people. In this life, it only matters that you do good. It's not about what you believe in, so much as spreading happiness and protecting those weaker than yourself. That's why I choose to fight."

Jack patted Andrew on the head. "She's right, I was fighting overseas for years. I fought for so long, I don't even remember why, or what it was all for. So I've decided I'll fight for you, Andrew…" He looked down at Carly, "Mind taking us to this admin place you mentioned?"

She nodded, "I don't know if Lady Rojas will be there, but they'll be able to point you to her."

Together they left the station. She was excited to head up to the tower even more now. She couldn't wait to show Andrew the miracles that kinetics could accomplish together.

With Jack, she could tell he had seen the worst already, judging by how he shied away from moving too close to her. She could only imagine what he had seen… though she knew all too well, the horrors that war wrought.

****

At first, Arden fought to remember what had happened. He laid there, stretched out on his stomach, eyes closed. The pain racking his body gave him little room for thought. He couldn't even seem to remember how he came to be lying face down in the dirt and snow.

The world around him seemed muted. Even the little voice in Arden's head was gone, replaced by a high-pitched ringing that stung at his thoughts. It swarmed his whole body like thousands of angry wasps crawling through his bones. Slowly he tried to move, though the most he could muster was getting his head up. Arden blinked, there was nothing at first glance, just blowing snow and ash blanketing the sky.

His helmet was ripped open, a shard of glass from the heads-up display dangerously close to his eye. He blinked at the cold air stinging his eyes and tried again to move. This time it was a little easier.

Everything seemed devoid of colour beyond his broken mask, like an old-time movie, the whole world made of smoke and shadows blowing past in thick curls on snowy winds. The only colour or light seemed to come from the bits of flame that danced around, green. The high bright white of intense heat was shot through with blue hues flickering madly.

Each breath was heavy with acrid smoke. The mouthpiece in his teeth was feeding him burnt, smoky breaths. He needed to get his helmet off but the catch wouldn't release.

He floundered about, trying in vain to stand up past a crouch, but all attempts to get up sent him down on his stomach. So he made do, shuffling through piles of ash and snow, crawling up a steep slope. Looking around as much as he could, Arden found he was in an enormous blasted crater. He shuffled and crawled and finally rolled onto his back. Feeling sick after moving his head, only made it hurt worse to look around. His team had been stretched out around him just before the world blanked out.

Ignoring the nausea, he crawled to the top, putting his back against the edge of the crater. Hands shaking, he fumbled the catches on his helmet. He undid the clips that held the shattered remains of his helmet to his combat armour, inspecting it only a moment. It was more than useless, so he tossed the remains aside. Whatever had hit him and his team had overloaded their Sat-Com. He wouldn't be calling anyone on that.

Reaching up he ran his fingers across his head. His lucky bandanna was soaked to his scalp, and maybe not as lucky as Arden once thought. He tried to stand again, instead of falling over sideways in his effort. Besides his helmet, his armour seemed in good shape. All servo assist was off though, and his wrist-mounted display was off too. Arden had no other choice, he hit the safety on his hip and pulled the lever with a twist. In a quick snap, the suit's analog release opened the snap downs and the joints freed him. The suit curled back and pushed him up. Free from the suit he fell face-first back into the hole and had to crawl out again. It was easier this time, not carrying the dead suit, but his balance was still off. The Blood in his ears still trickled freely and worried him too. He didn't think he'd be standing anytime soon.

Arden looked across the far side of the crater, seeing the faint shapes of people moving in the smoke silhouetted by gunfire. Bursts of light seemed to arc about like fireworks, strong winds coming in gusts that shared the hidden shadows in mere glimpses.

Their Intel had been severely lacking about the Canadians. His team and countless others had paid so dearly, and for what? Some president he didn't even vote for, and her final address, he could still hear her in his head. All these years every day they played it to remind themselves. "My fellow Americans… Fight on, and we will endure this menace!" What a steaming load.

Their latest intel had stated that the north was safe. Since the use of the English superweapon had shifted the poles, Canada was safe. That the people there knew how to survive the cold better than anyone. Six times they had pushed north, but no one ever came back. No word back either. Almost a year, Arden had sat here waiting, and for what? The north was no safer than the south, at this point, he would have taken the Seed over this shit.

The blowing snow and smoke in the air were still too thick to see far. He looked hard though and he could just make out the shapes of what looked like a person on the ground. Pulling himself out of the crater, Arden made his way over on hands and knees. Kneeling next to the large man, he could tell it was Reynolds, lying face down on the street. He had been the largest soldier in their squad, and the only one capable of carrying the rigging that had carried his VUM-62. The once menacing mini-gun now laid in pieces, scattered in the snow. Twisted and black, almost peeled like a banana. Spent ammo casing scattered about the ground was a clear sign he hadn't gone down as easy as Arden had.

Reynolds was wearing custom heavy combat armour. His gal back home was in R&D, and she had made sure her man was fitted with the best. The carbon-nanofiber plates were supposed to be stronger than titanium. Even a Seed drone's claws bounced off with barely a scratch. Yet here he lay the armour in pieces, soot-darkened plates fragile to the touch. They crumbled as Arden checked his Fallen friend. Every servo-assisted joint fused and scorched, just like the ones on

Arden's suit had been. He tried to get to the release on the suit, but it was more damaged than Arden's had been. He hit the lever and tried to twist it but it was jammed. Only his arms released

Despite his wounds, Arden could see Reynolds was still breathing from the rise and fall of his back. Arden grabbed the big guy's hand trying to talk but wasn't sure he was saying anything at all through the ringing. He tried again but nothing sounded right, he still couldn't even hear his own voice. But it must have made sense to Reynolds because he squeezed Arden's hand back. Reynolds' other hand came up and pointed over to another grey mound up the road. That far ahead it could only have been their scout, Mac. She had been ranging ahead when they made contact, and now laid sprawled in the road, far too still.

Arden crawled as fast as he could on hands and knees like a newborn wobbling about. Flashes of light burst to his right, flames flying past over his head. A massive volley that made him stop and curl up. He could feel the ground shake and gazed in horror at the white-hot fire. Yet still, as soon as he was sure he wasn't seen, he went on. Nothing major was visible, but that didn't mean nothing was wrong. He tapped the display on her pack, the status showed her air supply was critical. He quickly popped her suit's safety release, and she was flung into his arms. He laid her down softly and undid the helmet. The clasps popped and a hiss of air rushing in seemed to jar her. As she snapped up, she pulled the small karambit she always kept close to her; hidden in the small of her back under her med pack, wicked sharp, it was now only inches from his chest.

He remembered now why no one liked to wake her early.

She pulled back long enough to see who he was, then threw herself at him. She wrapped her arms around him, sobbing like a child. He just let her get it out. But he could feel the charge of energy weapons fire and feel the rumble of long-range shelling. They weren't safe yet. He couldn't see or hear anything, but he could feel the battle. Explosions that still raged on, though maybe not artillery, seemed erratic.

He pulled her back trying to explain he couldn't hear, and that he had no balance. She nodded and stood wobbling for a second herself then pulled Arden to his feet. Together they could stand, though he could tell without her, he'd still be on his hands and knees.

He could see others now. The telltale blue lights of their suits move through the fog. He pointed to them, tapping Mac's shoulder. She must have called out as a large group came running over. Guns at the ready, they moved like a proper strike team.

One soldier went over to where Reynolds lay. Finally, a proper medic! The bright cross on his pack was like a beacon of hope. Kneeling, he checked Reynolds. He knelt for only a moment though the bright display on his forearm blinking madly over the wounds along the man's spine. His shoulders slumped as he stood, looking over to Arden as he shook his head.

Something broke inside Arden then. He tried to keep his feet but not even with Mac's help could he stay up. He fell hard, punching the snow-covered ground, again and again, the men and women around him looking anywhere but at him. Mac touched his cheek gently, he looked up into her eyes, deep blue-green eyes. Framed in dirt and blood she was still so beautiful, despite the gore.

He couldn't help but think about why she was here. She told him the night before as they had Fallen asleep that she would follow him into hell. Here he was though, and he truly believed he had led her to the pits of the underworld. He shook his head thinking to himself.

Why did I bring them here?

You're here because the fates placed you here, friend to learn something.

The voice was deep and hearty. Resonating in his head, it pushed back the screeching in his ears. Arden was stunned.

He tried to move, to look around to see if any of the others had heard it, but he couldn't.

Even Mac stood still as a statue, her hands still cupping his face. Her eyes were round and filled with fear. Their bodies seemed to be frozen. His mind, however, raced. No longer in control, he was wrenched to his feet by unseen hands, strong as iron. They lifted him to stand beside the others, turning him straight. Mac too, and several others who had been spread out around the crater were suddenly pulled through the air to come to an awkward halt.

Something moved ahead of them. Arden tried to focus on it, looking into the smoke. He watched as the thick veil cleared before him and in the midst stood two people. Clothed in different coloured long coats, deep hoods pulled forward. They had not a speck of dust on them. The ground at their feet seemed to swirl as if a powerful wind swept around them, but there was not even a breeze that Arden could feel. The taller of the two stood back. He wore no suit or mask, nor armour of any kind, only a long scarf and a dark grey coat thrown wide open despite the freezing cold.

Yet by comparison he seemed mundane next to the small woman beside him. She was the one who held Arden's attention, not just because she was glowing visibly. She moved swiftly around them, her red coat billowing unnaturally as if she were underwater, flowing behind her as she crossed the cobbled street. Her hood fell back like the curtain lifting on a performance and the glow from her body suddenly intensified. Flowing down her shoulders like waterfalls of molten rock candy, her hair shone bright blue from root to tip. Streaked through with reds and pink, it all hung in perfect ringlet curls, like a china doll. Little sparks and pops of light danced around her as she walked, from snowflakes coming too close to her aura, her glow bathing them all in warm iridescent light.

Arden just stared in rapt attention, she couldn't be real. Yet there she was, moving from soldier to soldier. She stopped and knelt, placing her hand on Reynolds's back, a deep frown creasing her forehead. She looked strained as the faint glowing nimbus encircling her fingers grew deeper red. Crimson beads of light came dripping from her fingertips like molten metal and hissed as it dripped down Reynolds's back.

Several minutes passed before this living firecracker stood and stormed over to another soldier lying on the ground. Whenever she knelt the same glow would surround her hand, dripping red hot metal and then on to the next she'd go.

Standing up slowly she walked over to the line of soldiers, a slow methodical pace over the rush she had been in that took her around the others. She placed her hands on each, just a moment or two, then to the next she'd go.

She slowly ran her hands over Mac's face, and Arden noticed for the first time, her eyes. They swirled violently, her inner eye like spikes of ice that shattered and twisted within the confines of her bright glowing eyes. She stood much shorter than him but all the same, he felt such gripping fear, he didn't want to die, unable to move, hanging in the air. He felt like a mouse caught by some beautiful viper. Fear at what it might mean if she touched him, what even was she? Arden wanted to shrink away from her touch, to scream, or fight but all he could do was stare.

The big guy with her stepped up and curled his hand, every one of his fellow soldiers drawn in towards him.

Fear is natural, friend.

The voice in Arden's head intoned. The man looked him in the eye and tapped his temple. Like the woman in red this man's eyes were also lit from within, a deep green swirl, much slower than his cohort.

He looked over to where the tall man stood at the edge of the clearing in the haze. The scarf pulled up did nothing to hide the smile in his eyes.

Arden looked down again at the woman before him, she was not smiling. Her hands came up to his temples. Soft like silk they traced along his head prodding at the small cuts with her glowing metal-tipped fingers. She turned towards the man in grey suddenly, Arden could see his lips move but the ringing was still in his ears and he could not hear what it was he said. When the woman in red turned back, however, she smiled up at him. Arden felt taken back for a moment. That smile was warm and sweet as honey as she looked up at him.

She laid her hand on his brow and a jolt of heat ran through him, his vision dimmed, and he felt as though he had been submerged in boiling water. Yet as the heat ebbed, the pain he had felt a moment before washed away. The ringing was still present but the ache that had stabbed at him before was gone. He even felt rested and strong.

The woman spoke again, her lips moved, but Arden couldn't hear what she said, Arden couldn't hear anything at all. She looked over at the man in grey.

She says she can do nothing for your ears friend. They are as they are.

He shrugged.

She's tired and your comrades were worse, you understand.

The smile in his eyes made them seem to twinkle brighter still.

The man waved his hand at the others on the ground, their limp bodies lifting into the air. Moving his hand across they floated over to lay gently on the ground closer by. Suddenly Arden felt the ground beneath him again, his muscles relaxing as he suddenly regained control of his body. The others also seemed to come too, and none seemed as at ease as him.

Everyone seemed to leap at once, weapons coming to the ready. Even Mac put herself between the women in red and Arden, the edge of her knife pressed to the other woman's throat. The soldiers seemed torn between who to point their guns at, and the woman in red took the opportunity, her red coat suddenly shredding apart. Twisting out throwing Mac aside, the knife vaporized in a heartbeat, a flash of light rippling past them all powerful heat waves clearing the air around them. She wore a strange backless knit sweater that only covered her front leaving her arms free as flames leapt up like wings from her back. But her arms were far from bare, elaborate tattoos twisted and turned, coming to life before Arden's eyes.

Blue-pink sparks snapped through the air around the soldiers' guns, several fired but their barrels just exploded and twisted into lumps. Those who hadn't fired still threw their weapons down as they were consumed, melting to the ground.

The voice in his head piped up again, firm-toned but not harsh.

Take your people and go, lead them home, the north is no longer a welcome place, Azure believes that you will be needed soon, but not yet.

He waved his hand pointing at the men and women gathered.

Arden looked back at Mac, and all his squad who had followed him here saw how they all watched him. Even Reynolds was getting to his feet slowly.

The women in red came around Mac, who was still trying to regain her feet and stood toe to toe with Arden scowling up at him.

Really looking, meeting her eye to eye. He finally saw her. Beautiful eyes, like swirling starbursts, glowing with the same blue-pink flames.

She slowly raised her hand and every one of his men seemed like they were about to move. Mac seemed to flail against unseen hands. Arden raised his hand above his head, looking at them all, even Mac seemed to struggle less. He smiled and nodded, but she only shook her head slightly. She reached out her hand and all around the pools of liquid metal began to rise. It spun out into long threads of metal weaving together until she held a new red coat.

She pulled the hood up and twirled on her heel the two of them striding off, back into the clouds their grey and red coats disappearing like ghosts, in the fog of war.

He looked down at Mac who now knelt looking up at him. He gestured with his chin, back down the lane, he tried to speak, but it sounded off. Their Forward-Ops base may still be there from last night.

She nodded.

Standing up she called out to all the others. Even Reynolds stood staring at him, absently nudging the remains of his armour which was missing half, scooped up into the red woman's new coat, he seemed okay. The whole group gathered around Arden, his entire squad, and the others they had met. Together they walked back the way they had come.

This assignment had been a career-maker for him, his chance to lead. He had worked so hard to make sure they would be ready.

They hadn't been ready.

That was an understatement.

How could anyone be ready to fight against such power? Were they even human?

He didn't know, and he didn't imagine any of them were willing to answer him anyways… not that he'd hear them if they did. Either way, it didn't matter anymore. They were headed home.

After two hours of slowly trekking back down the road, they came to the farm they had set up at. The base was in ruins, with craters and destroyed artillery everywhere. They set about and found an A.P.C. abandoned by the ops centre back in the field. The armoured truck was short a wheel and had taken a beating, but it seemed in decent shape. The rear hatch had been ripped off its hinges too. Then whoever had done it had used it to rip the cannon off. Both the door and cannon lay twisted together in a ball, and now sat buried in the ground. It had been smashed through the roof of another nearby A.P.C. that was not in such good shape.

Arden looked around and realized they had picked up more followers as they had gone on. Some carried guns like they were clutching their favourite teddy, and all of them looked shocked. Arden called to Mac, who cringed. Everyone else seemed to jump at the sound, a gun muzzle even flashed near him. She walked over though and held up a whiteboard she had scavenged from one of the still-standing tents.

Use this, you Bullhorn.

She wrote in a scribbled hand. She rubbed the note away, then scribbled again,

Everyone here's jumpy!

He took the board and wrote to her.

More trucks?

She nodded and pointed to a small barn. Flashlights in the dark reflected off an old pickup truck, and another A.P.C. inside.

He wiped the board, writing again.

"*How long?*

She tapped her wrist and held up a few fingers, three hours roughly, she figured.

Arden nodded and handed her the board. He grabbed a new pack from the barracks tent and a spare pair of boots in case. He went through the bunks and grabbed a skittish-looking young kid and had her help him strip down the beds of linens. They tied up several bundles and set to work going through the crates for anything useful. Knives and basic gear seemed fine, but it was clear the Canadians had targeted any weapons they saw. Every gun in every building looked like a puzzle in a million pieces or had been melted to scrap. There wasn't a bullet in sight either, though spent casings littered the ground everywhere.

The next few hours went by quickly, and when all was set and packed, the sun was rising.

More people had shown up through the night. Many, like Arden, seemed calm, some even looked happy, shock was funny that way. All of them worked hard, but something felt off to Arden. There was an air about the place, but Arden couldn't put his finger on it.

He walked to the head of the convoy. They had dug up several shotguns and several boxes of shells from the farmhouse and a few of the surrounding homes through the night. They stripped it all, anything useful, and set anyone they caught just looting to shovelling snow. He looked at their manifest, it wasn't enough. Arden might have felt bad, but with how cold it was here he cared more about his people first.

They found a few snowmobiles that weren't too far gone and sent them ahead to scout. They had been told to return in five hours. Arden checked his watch, they should have been back already. They'd have to leave soon or risk getting caught out in the open at night.

Arden moved to the lead truck, the one A.P.C. that was still good, then climbed up into the back and checked the scope. The infrared scan showed nothing coming up the road from the south. When he turned it back north towards the old city though he could just make out the heat signature over the horizon. The faint smear that was the Seed Pod, and a tower half-built. He marvelled at the tower, it must have been massive to be seen from this far.

Arden looked up feeling the rock of the truck as someone joined him in the back. It was Reynolds, he looked a bit panicky, and waved his arms. He must have forgotten Arden's lack of hearing in his rush.

Arden waved the whiteboard at him.

Reynolds slapped it away and grabbed Arden by the arm dragging him along.

Four hooded figures stood at the edge of their camp, soldiers running everywhere in sheer dread.

Arden hollered as loud as he could, calling them as best to attention as he could, most were already running south on foot. He had kept the keys for all the trucks to prevent anyone from getting sticky and making off in the night.

Arden recognized the two in the group: the tall guy in grey, and the short woman in red. But the other two both wore dark duster coats with their hoods up.

The man in grey saw Arden and nudged the woman in red, he then walked forward to meet Arden. His mouth didn't move but Arden heard him like before, inside his head.

We told you to leave.

Arden tried to speak, but the guy just put his hands up and waved them back and forth.

Just think it… think what you want to say.

He said with a hard edge to his thought.

Arden nodded.

We're trying to, but now you've scared off my people.

It was strange to not say it out loud, he had never had much of an inner monologue.

If I bring them back, can you leave?

His question seemed like a plea like there was something more he wasn't saying.

Arden shook with anger.

Why though… Why won't you people help us? The army's gone, the government has collapsed but look at you people… you have all this space no one's living in. We're not asking for help, just a place to settle?!

The man sighed and shook his head.

You don't understand what's coming Arden, the Seed aren't the worst thing that came from the Pods. Here in the north, the-

He turned and so did the other three. Arden could just make out a man walking towards them, only there was something horribly weird about him. It wasn't that he was walking barefoot and shirtless, wearing only pants, or how the snow seemed to rise to meet him, or even the fact he was missing one arm… no, it was that smile.

His face looked twisted. His eyes swirled black and blue. From the way he shook, Arden knew he was laughing, teeth clenched in a Cheshire grin.

And it wasn't alone.

Creatures were quickly appearing, dragging themselves through the snow like zombies. They shook and twisted, shambling in jerking but quick motions.

As the leader pointed with his good arm, the creatures that followed split up and began to cut off the trucks. They were trying to stop them.

The man in grey stepped up ahead of the others walking away from Arden. He looked back and nodded though, sending him a final message.

Sorry… I hoped to spare your people this fight… well, as the Azure says, 'it never hurts to try, unless you're trying to get hurt.' When I make my move, I want you all to run for the trucks, and get as far away as you can… you understand?

Arden nodded but could think of no words in reply.

Mac was suddenly at his side and he handed her the keys to the A.P.C. She grabbed them as well as the two other sets. She passed one of the sets of keys to Reynolds, and another to one of the medics, whose name Arden hadn't gotten yet. They rushed now like wolves were snapping at their heels, and for all Arden had seen, he would have preferred wolves.

****

Vince hadn't even sensed the horde of bloom approach. Their pack leader, one of the Fallen, seemed to be hiding them somehow. They were right here in front of him, but he couldn't feel a glimmer from the creatures. It was quite the shock; his rather keen senses had never let him down. He opened himself up to the energy inside and instead pulled on the air. He felt it resist where there were objects in its path and nearly took a step back. The hoard was immense, far beyond anything he had ever seen in almost two decades, the years since they reclaimed the city.

Vince looked at the shirtless monster and pulled back his hood. He enhanced his voice letting it shake the very air, "Fallen! I have heard your kind retain some of your minds. If this is true, I'll say this only once. Leave, NOW!" Vince reasoned the thing might have enough sense to listen, but his hopes were low. These Fallen all seemed unhinged, either stuck in a rage or laughing uncontrollably, right up till they died.

The Fallen just cocked its head awkwardly and grinned madly, "The Wych-hazel blooms, the Wych-hazel blooms, the Wych-hazel blooms, the Wych-hazel blooms, the Wych-hazel blooms…" It hissed the words through gritted teeth smiling and chuckling as it walked towards Vince. Its eyes swirled and sparkled the snow around it moving in halting stuttered turns. It was not backing down.

Vince opened himself to the power and absorbed it from all around him. He parted the clouds letting the sun pour down from above.

The creature and its ilk balked, shuddering and shying back from the nimbus of light. They fled back from the trucks—back into the thicker shadows.

Vince didn't turn, but he heard as several of the trucks started up and made off. A few of the bloom made to follow, but Vince cut them off with another split in the clouds.

Their leader stepped up again. His grin had turned into a glare and hate and rage were now plain on his face. He pointed at Vince and screamed. It was that same ear-splitting shriek all bloom used while they hunted, but it felt different. Vince could feel the waves of kinetic energy infused within the sound, felt as it tried to sap his resolve.

These Fallen were capable of so much power that even Vince stepped back under the onslaught, but it seemed Carly had grown stronger.

She shook for only a second before breaking through the bloom's mental assault. She quickly recovered in time as a massive horde of feral bloom flowed toward them. The first to unleash a blast of psire in a burst of hot-pink fire leaping from a shimmering point between her hands. The other two joined her right away, Mitchell's deep red flames, and Lucas's bright green flames, washing the earth around the hordes of bloom. He was just about to add to the blaze when he noticed something.

Where the flames parted up ahead, the Fallen were still standing, flames flowing up, over, and around it. His wicked smile glowed in the flickers light making him look all the madder. Somehow, he had thrown up a wide enough shield that only the ground around its army was engulfed. A few stragglers not inside its barrier were falling, consumed by fire. Yet so many more still stood swaying gently.

The Fallen stepped forward, the flames dying down before him. Raising his one arm he screamed that horrific cry again and a surge of bloom rushed forward.

Vince looked out over the field, he called out to the others, "Everyone! Phalanx! Carly, follow my lead, we need a shield wall."

He let go of his hold on the clouds. It had become a useless drain of his powers. Now he needed something else. He needed the friction of molecules, the strength of the storm. He reached outward with his power— a trick only masters seemed to understand— and found the true flow of aether. It wound between them like a river feeding their power, each person like a tree growing in the middle of their own little lake of aether. He had mastered this trick and tapped that flow around him, opened wide the gates inside himself and let the aether flow through him strengthening his power.

His body hummed with aether and he knelt on the ground. The snow retreated before his hands until he found the frozen earth beneath. He looked down and directed power into the ground with a force that shook the world around them. The earth and snow churned up under the chargers casting them back through the air as winds under his command blew them away into the distance.

To Vince's side, Carly's trademark metal duster seemed to suddenly come alive, threads of metal flowing out around her in ribbons of glowing steel forming a barrier around her. He could tell from how her hair sparked the little metal beads in her hair were heating up too. All around them metal that was just laying about began melting and taking flight. The roof of the barn, girders and walls, all glowing hot and liquefying. It turned to molten slag, forming above their heads into a swirling maelstrom of glowing steel.

Carly raised her hands high, her fingers twitching as she tugged the threads of aether and formed the steel into long glowing spikes. She turned them on the charging bloom, raining down red-hot steel from every direction. She pinned down over a dozen in seconds, making effective barriers of the flower-faced zombies. It wasn't enough to kill them, but it was good enough to stop them. It even seemed to slow others down as they stumbled over their Fallen or were impaled on the spikes themselves. Some tore at their own bodies to be free, ripping limbs from bodies, but simply pulling free was impossible.

Vince watched in awe at finally seeing her in combat and marvelled at the range of her control over the liquid metal, those bloom that she pinned, suddenly sprouting razor-sharp needles piercing them from within. It was like a rosebush of the dead, complete with gnashing fanged flowers, wreathed in hooked glowing metal thorns. He formed a defence around them, shaking earth, and blowing winds bolstered by Carly's growing forest of liquid steel brambles. The hissing steel was cooling and groaning, the snow melting around it making a nimbus of light and heat.

When he looked up though he was surprised. As he had expected, his four other allies were not affected by his quakes or the winds. His work was directed at his enemies, so his attack ignored his team, and the fleeing trucks heading south. But the bloom-

Most of the bloom either lay pinned or were being cast about, but as he gave a quick count, nine of them still stood. All smiling faces and swirling black and glowing eyes, and all surrounded in a nimbus of aether that made a shield around them.

The Fallen were closer now, walking through the killing field. It did not seem to faze them, the ground beneath them was quiet, and his quakes were parted like waves around stones. Even Carly's minefield of steely brambles bent aside as the Fallen marched forward.

Together, their powers seemed to be slowing them down, but only by a mean pace.

With defences built up as best they could, for now, Vince called out orders. "Shields up! Spears out!"

It was time for Mitchell and Lucas to work, both men stepping up, with Lucas the faster one on the attack.

He pulled off his coat to reveal lengths of chain coiled around his body. Vince had never seen the man fight, so he had always just assumed he was a bulky guy. Without the coat on though he could see the man looked rather frail, though Vince knew better than to judge. The chain began to shift and move, and even over the sound of Vince's storm, the grating of metal was loud. The chains twisted and snaked their way free of him, weaving around his arms, forming massive tentacles from his shoulders made of the metal links. The metal began to spin and twist violently, sparking as it ground about each other. It shot off in showers of sparks, shooting forward like tiny green streaks of light. They whistled through the air with little pops like machine-gun fire hammering the chargers, and even punching through the shields of the Fallen. Their shields however were strong and though it hit many, only the barest amount of damage seemed to be taken.

Mitchel was no less skilled, if not so dramatic., His powers over air and heat were something of a legend around the school. His hands twisted and turned, drawing dust and dirt into little pockets of air. The particles vibrated so fast that they ignited inside the bubbles. He threw these cavitation bubbles like mortars onto the battlefield. These had a much greater effect. As they struck, they sucked in everything around them and cooked anything trapped inside their blast. Two of the Fallen, whose shields had been weakened by Lucas's scattershot were sucked in and boiled alive. With horrible screams and sickening pops, one's upper body seemed to suddenly disappear in a hiss of steam. The other was suddenly no more than half a torso and half a face.

It seemed they had the upper hand, but Vince should have known better.

The force of the earth suddenly rising under him threw him, and Vince lost his control. Sent high through the air, he had only a moment to observe helplessly as something came surging up from underground. He caught himself with a gust of air and was just fast enough to catch Carly as he saw her thrown back too.

Four of the seven remaining Fallen had suddenly grown extra limbs, it seemed. Their exposed blooms had torn through their bodies, rather than just their throats. Some looked like a third arm from their chest or back. One even looked like it had grown a tail. That one and the first Fallen held hands, his missing arm now a massive bloom vine.

They had combined their powers and broken through Vince's defence. They had caught him off guard. He looked at Carly, but She was already at work, her molten steel walls now cooled she let loose with psire and scorched the earth. He followed suit and reached up to the storm, found energy and pressure trapped and called down a bolt of lightning. It was not easy for him to control it, but his bolt struck well and erased two of the Fallen who had not paired up, leaving only greasy black smudges in the snow. He looked around but couldn't see Mitchell or Lucas.

He panicked a moment until a wheel of spinning fire suddenly flew from behind him, circling around to cut one of the Fallen and a huge swath of bloom in half.

Lucas, wielding his chains like massive saw blades, stood half buried in a snowdrift where he had been thrown. The chunk of wood driven through his side didn't even slow him down, as his chains came back to him. He nodded to Vince, "I could use a shield…"

Vince nodded and followed the man. This time more aware he kept right on top of Lucas as he used his chains like massive whips. Lashing back and forth, he cut down more bloom, and even separated a Fallen from its bloom, leaving them to die slowly and painfully. Vince watched for psionic attacks and blocked as best he could, but they were all growing tired, and there were still four Fallen remaining.

He felt Carly's power grow as she approached, his mind reaching out to hers. "Mitchell?"

He felt her sadness deepen, "He's gone. I tried to save him, but he was too weak." She was angry, and anger was powerful, but it made you stupid.

"Hold back, save your strength. We need you calm. You're no good to us if you lose your head." He wasn't trying to be macho, his strength was long since gone. But as he clung to the flow of aether around him, he noticed something, and he smiled, "Help is on the way…"

She didn't say a word, but Vince could tell she got the message. Carly stepped back towards where one of the American trucks lay turned over and began to recite some song. Her voice was low, but touching her mind like he was, he could hear it in his head clear as crystal. Hells Bells…?

He chuckled a little and started to hum to the tune as well. He then opened his mind up to Lucas, who faltered for a moment and then picked up the tune too. Together they let the tune pulse and flow, the motion of their attacks raging to the flow of the song. His own releases of energy grew in tempo too, soon he felt the link. It was a strange thing, how few people could link without daily practice. Even fewer who could do more than share a fraction of their strength. But as they started up the chorus again, Vince could feel this strength flowing into Lucas and Carly, a mixing of powers that saw him as the focus.

They were no longer on the defensive anymore either. No, now they pushed back. The bloom shambled towards them, but couldn't touch them, forced back over and again. The bramble walls were now behind them. Even the Fallen looked angrier, though these last five seemed far more competent in battle.

They linked their powers in pairs and attacked relentlessly, but they were no match for Lucas's range, as his chains finally snagged up one and coiled like an anaconda around her. She screamed in rage and pain, her tail like bloom snapping uselessly at the burning metal. With a final howl, the chains pulled tight and burned clean through, mashing her corpse into smouldering chunks.

The Fallen with the bloom arm screamed out as she died and Vince faltered. He saw the look of pain in the creature's eyes, hate and rage Vince recognized all too well. It waved its hand through the air and the bloom stopped suddenly, their jerking and twisting slowing to a crawl. He placed back and forth the other three coming closer, all of them staring down Lucas and Vince.

Carly walked up beside him. He patted her shoulder and walked with her up to where Lucas stood.

He looked to where the Fallen stood and called out, "We gave you a choice… this is on you, Fallen!"

It bellowed back, but nothing Vince could understand.

Vince felt the flow of aether swell suddenly, closed his eyes and opened up the gates within himself one last time. It was dangerous to do this too often, you could burn yourself out. He wasn't worried, this fight was over. He started to hum again, using the song as a focus yet again. He poured aether into his body until he felt ready to burst and his bones burned and felt as the same energy called back to him from either side of the Fallen and their bloom.

His vision grew brighter, light flooding his eyes as he found the heartbeats of the bloom. Then he felt them too, Carly and Lucas, and two others. He let the song build to a peak and felt the draw of energy from the other two. He followed their threads of power up to the clouds, traced it like a circuit board and let loose. Bolt after bolt, after bolt, struck down from the sky or leapt up from below. The crackling plasma consumed everything it touched, and this time even the Fallen couldn't hide.

It took only an instant, but as he opened his eyes, he felt drained. Carly and Lucas caught him as he sagged forward, holding onto him as he steadied himself. Both seemed shocked.

Carly looked at the carnage and back at Vince, "I-I didn't know anyone could do that…"

He shook his head and chuckled wryly, "Not alone…" he pointed out to where two men were crossing the field. The one in front was none other than the bard himself, holding a long curved sword, casually playing a strange flute one handed, streaming chains made of brassy-gold padlocks floating around him like they were alive. The other could only be Sam, a stout man too he was built like a badger, carrying a round shield and a long handle wood axe, and clad head to toe in plaid.

Vince shook off the help and sat back in the snow as Sam and Sean came walking up through the haze. Both men looked the worse for wear, faces smeared in dry blood, eyes still glowing bright green.

"As I live and breathe," he raised a hand to them as they walked up, "The Saints of Stone," he coughed.

Sean smiled warmly and sheathed his katana with a flourish. Then reached into his coat and pulled out an old-school drinking horn and tossed it to Vince. "You look like you need a pick-me-up, Mighty Thor!"

Vince grabbed the horn and popped the cork, taking a whiff and winced. "Whoa… this that blue trekie drink?"

Sean shrugged, "What? It's for medicinal purposes."

Vince chuckled, "I bet, damn. Well, cheers," he took a long sip and coughed hard on the strong drink. "That'll put hair in places. Thanks." He capped the horn and tossed it back.

Sam nodded, "A drink to everyone that needs it, I say."

Vince shook his head, then nodded to the field, "No, I mean thanks. I don't know what we'd have done without your help."

Carly nodded, "Yeah, thanks…"

Sam and Sean both dropped down next to Vince. "We've been on the run trying to avoid those hunters for days." Sam said sadly, "We owe you just as much. Those monsters wiped out five of our best."

"So, who's the AC/DC fan?" Sam asked with a smile.

Carly jumped forward, "That was me! Sorry Master Sam, I hope it didn't…"

Sam waved his hand, "Nothing to be sorry about, that little trick helped us all sync up. That was a great idea."

Carly shrugged, "I just figured it worked for my sister. I'm glad it worked here too."

Vince nodded and looked up, turning to the north. Sam and Sean did too.

Vince patted down his coat and stood up with a groan. "Well, we're not done yet."

Lucas had been patiently standing nearby, getting healing from Carly. "But they're all dead, or mostly dead."

Sam and Sean looked at Vince, Sam leaning heavily on his shield. "This was just the appetizer friend, main course is back home. Do any of you know how to gate?"

Carly was about to speak up but Vince cut her off, "I think it's a better idea if we get one of these trucks going."

Sean nodded, "True, conserve power for now."

Lucas slammed his chains down, "Will one of you tell us what's going on?!"

Vince looked at him sadly, explaining "They knew we'd be out here, they picked the best time, knowing the few masters in the city would be out here on patrol. They planned these traps to lure us south."

"But how could they have known the Americans would be here?" Carly asked.

Vince shrugged, an unhappy thought coming to mind. "I think… we may have a Trojan horse."

Sean nodded, "A Fallen with more than a little sense about them?"

"Great, and I thought they were bad enough as it was," Sam said with a groan.

Carly pulled energy to her in a flash., He could feel the waves of aether forming a gate. He swiftly took hold of the connections and severed them with a wave of his hand. "I said no gates! You follow my orders!"

Carly looked furious, "But Amy!" She must have seen the look in his eyes because she fell silent right away.

He turned away from her. He spotted the truck and with a quick tugging motion controlled the air and pulled it back onto its wheels. "We're no good to anyone if we're exhausted to death. So get in."

Sam stepped up and patted Vince on the shoulder, "I'll drive. You guys rest up, it'll be a few hours before we get there."

They were all turning away to head to the truck when an errant gust of wind kicked up and a faint sound could be heard from the field.

Someone was laughing…?

Lucas made towards it, but Vince headed him off, "I've got this." Lucas nodded and turned towards the truck, while Vince made his way towards the chilling cackle. He stepped carefully around the craters of still smouldering corpses. The smell made his stomach want to turn over and empty, but that laugh was only growing more manic and froze his insides deeply.

He found the one arm Fallen pulling itself up out of one of the deep pits. It laughed like a madman, shivering from the force of whatever he found so funny. He flopped over onto his back and looked up into the sky, his laughter slowing only a little as he caught sight of Vince. Half of its face had been burned away right to the bone, in a horrid grin.

"So funny, so funny, so funny, so funny…" it murmured over and over.

Vince looked down at it, "What's so funny?"

It looked up at him, still muttering and laughing, already beginning to heal, "Your time is coming kinetic. You fight so hard to stop us, but you can't win. Soon the mother will embrace you all. It's just so funny, you fight so hard, to win such a small victory… it's just so funny, so funny, so funny…!" It broke into laughter again, the creeping giggle of a twisted psyche.

Vince held out his hand, a long spike of steel from one of Carly's barriers flying to him. He raised it high and slammed it home. Straight through the foul thing's skull, ending its laughter.

Vince walked back to the truck and hopped in the back seat of the old four-door pickup.

Sam turned around in the passenger seat to look at Vince, "You ready?"

Vince leaned back and thought for a moment. He didn't know what to say. Looking at Carly though, he smiled. "Let's go get Amy."

WINTERS BLOSSOM

9yrs A.E. Central Canada

Nancy fell back into darkness, she thought she had maybe died. But when she opened her eyes, she felt no more pain. She was bathed in shadows lying next to a candle.

It was burning low and sputtered, dripping hot wax across the hardwood floor, Nancy sat up, looking all around in its dying light, but there was nothing out there, only darkness.

"So… now we see…," came a softly spoken voice.

Nancy jumped. She had thought she was alone. But there sitting cross-legged, back from the candlelight was a small person. They were about the size of a child, but spoke with a deeper voice, a familiar voice… Nancy's own voice.

"What are you?" She asked.

"What are you…?" It said in unison.

"I just want to…?"

"I just want to…"

"Why are you copying me?"

"Why are you copying me…"

Again and again, it spoke in time with Nancy.

"STOP COPYING ME!"

"STOP COPYING ME!"

"GET OUT OF MY HEAD!"

"GET OUT OF MY HEAD!"

She couldn't see its face but could feel it, it was amused.

It sat there mocking her, and it revelled in Nancy's misery. Knowing she couldn't stop it, how it witnessed her pain and basked in it the warmth of Nancy's rage. Nancy slumped to the floor, staring at the candle. Its small guttering flame seemed ready to go out.

"It'll be better if we accept it…," the thing said finally.

Nancy looked up at the little creature, "Accept what?"

She could feel it Focus on her, its soft voice gleeful, "That, they're, the monsters…"

Nancy looked up. The creature had moved closer. Its voice now echoed from her left. It was seated still but had moved.

"We were like them once you know…," it said.

"Like them? What do you mean? Of course, I am…," she looked at the scarred tattoo on her arm. "I was. But I have no power anymore."

"We still have power, but you cling to the past, you think with your head when you could think with another's…"

Nancy peered through the darkness, "I don't understand."

"I don't understand…," it repeated.

"Why do you do…?"

"Why do you do…"

She stood up and turned to her tormentor, but it was gone.

"Why can't we see the truth…?" His voice seemed so quiet, almost scared, and Nancy took a cautious step closer. It moved away to the other side of the candle again. But now it was clear. Sitting closer to the light now. No, not closer... the light was brighter. Its face; her face; their face.

"The truth?"

"Yes…," it said with a wicked grin.

Nancy smiled too, she felt it inside, her memories, their memories. "We are one."

"Yes…"

"I let myself be infected because I wanted to find a cure, but I can't cure you… you are me." She sat back down, "But we were like them."

"Yes…"

"We didn't want to be like them, hypocritical murderers, killing what they didn't understand. All while they preached their ideologies. We can't be cured… because we are the cure."

"Yes…"

Nancy was smiling so broadly now, her heart felt like it was fluttering through her chest, begging to be free. Only her heart was gone now. Her lungs and guts too. She wasn't a hollow shell filled with meat anymore, no, the bloom filled her now… filled them.

"They want to rid the world of us because they think they're better than us." She scooted closer to the candle, "They're the evil ones."

"Yes…"

"They're just killers who hide behind righteousness!" The darkness flickered and swayed as the flame of the candle grew, now blazing high into the shadows above. "But, we can be the cure!"

"Yes…"

"We can make them like us!"

"Yes…"

"We can make them happy…," they smiled at each other, at their true self.

"Yes…!"

Opening their eyes, they reached deep inside of themselves, finding the power they had once held.

"We are… We are… ALIVE!" As one their minds fused, no distinction left, no Nancy, no bloom, but something new.

She pulled power from all around, wrapping threads of pure aether around their body, embracing the sweet rush of energy that once again swept through her.

She raised her hands together and found that same power in the two men before her. She was so happy to see the looks of terror on their faces, the two, no more than toys now. Taking their minds and making powers hers was no trouble, and with them, Nancy bent them to their knees.

Pushing away from the wall took little effort. She simply touched the power that her toys possessed and used it for herself.

Unbending the steel, she gently dropped from the wall to land on the ground lightly, like a leaf floating on the breeze.

She looked down at her body, months of living like a shambling wreck had taken its toll on her. Flesh ripped and torn away in places, errant vines poking through cracks in her dead grey skin. All of that was erased in an instant as the duality was born. The creature that was once Nancy now began to regenerate. Smooth, soft skin, growing back as she used the healing powers of the men. She marvelled at her beauty, skin as white as new snow, their reflection resplendent in ivory moonlight as the clouds above parted for their awakening to grace the rising of this world's newest god.

She looked down at her tattered clothes and used the psire to burn them away. Bits of cloth crumbling to black ashes that floated away on the wind.

She was not sure whose power it was, hers or theirs, but she didn't care. Next, she moved the snow and ice, flattening and smoothing it to a polished sheen. When she was done the massive room was clear of snow and lit with moonlight. Dozens of mirrors of ice hanging from the walls reflected her in all her naked splendour. She ran her hands across her curves and felt as the men's minds seemed to shrink. She looked at them as she felt it, Andy's blushing turning his cheeks a furious red. She made them watch though, forced their eyes to take her in, their raw fear mixed with lust. She read their minds. Knew their desires, they were no better than animals. Animals could be trained.

She giggled, giddy as a schoolgirl, "*We are beautiful…*"

We… Yes, we. Not I, no, Nancy was no longer alone, she was no longer one person. She looked inside her mind, and felt the roots of the bloom there, its heart beating inside their chest, the pulsing entity coiled inside them. She could feel its thoughts, made them her own and felt its love, she was more loved than ever. The bloom was with her, and she felt it more than just as a wriggling of her bones as it moved within her. She touched her chest and felt as her flesh flexed as if to say, '*We are here…*,' they felt so happy together.

They stepped out into the open to bask in the cold night winds. The building they were in had once been a church, she knew it well, The United Church. Aside from the doors being blown off, and a bit of the ceiling missing, nine years of going untended had changed it little.

Nancy's power was not fully back, but she still had her basic gifts. Though they seemed like they had been ramped up to eleven. All of the minds of the other bloom that lay buried in the snow around them through most of Toronto, it was easy now to find them. She touched them all, chaotic and frightened, half-mad and desperate. A trickle of hope and stability was all she needed to give them and they called back.

She hugged her arms around her, "*Mother's here my children, come to me…*"

She walked back inside, back toward their toys. The two men still knelt in the snow before her. With a twist of her finger, Andy was drawn up to his feet. He jerked like a manikin falling apart. His eyes, trying to turn away from her.

"*How can you resist looking at such beauty? Are we not pleasing to look at?*" Nancy smiled, tracing a finger around the buttons of his coat. She delved deeper into his mind, contact with him making it even easier to see into his thoughts, "*You are in love with my daughter Maddie, oh sweetie, I'm so much more fun…*," his mind turned dark and she shoved him back down to his knees hard, one leg breaking from the impact. He moaned in pain for a moment, but she could tell he was already healing.

"*You are lucky that you showed us such kindness before Andy. We have decided that you will carry our message home. Our daughters should know the fate that befell their mother. We are no longer their mother, we are the mother to all the bloom now… though… we do hope they will join us too.*"

She turned to Stephan, the other toy she had yet to play with. He was not as flustered by her appearance, an obvious veteran he was reciting the mantra all kinetics learnt to master their powers in his head. They could feel him resisting, flexing his will to regain his control. He was very strong… but they were stronger.

She could no longer feel the elements like she once did, and while that bugged her before she couldn't care less anymore. Their senses and basic powers seemed beyond anything simple Nancy had once been capable of. It meant forcing these two to use theirs was even easier, her power burrowing into their minds, making their bodies her puppets, and their powers hers.

Nancy leaned down and cupped his face in her hands. He was not at all pleasant to look at, his eyes were small and weak, swirling and spattering gold and green. His jaw was hard and stubborn looking and his handlebar mustache unattractive. She tugged her little mental strings, turning his head this way and that. It was clear he had shaved bald to cover hair loss, little indents in his temples from where decades of wearing glasses had left their mark. She drew him up to his full height so that he towered above her.

"*Oh, you father of Adam, your son's hate for you spurns you so. But it's fine now Stephan, I will love you.*"

Pain crept through their chest as the bloom within began to move again. It forced aside flesh and muscle trying to burrow out, this was the old way. She used their powers instead to part their flesh tearing their skin back from muscle and sinew. Finally, it emerged through the spot just above their breasts. Collarbone splitting with a snap that echoed in the cold air, forming a new opening; no longer would the bloom need to push its way out of their throat. Using a trickle of power, she healed her ribs and skin, the wound now a proper space for them to show off their combined beauty, its once dark grey pod changing before her eyes as it was flooded with kinetic energy. Slowly opening large petals the colour of freshly Fallen snow, shining wetly in the moonlight. It drank the light, so bright it seemed to make the shadows grow deeper. Its needle-thin fangs flexed in and out of sheaths studded along the edge of each petal, long and sharp and hard as iron to pierce their prey. It was larger than any she had seen, thin petals strong despite their fragile appearance, each moving with independent thought.

The ugly toy was transfixed in terror, unable to look away, tears running down his cheeks. They overtook him with ease, pinning him down.

"*Don't be afraid,*" they cooed to him, "*You're going to be so happy, child…*"

They pulled him into a tight embrace, his body jerking only slightly as their fangs dug in, the tiny needles passing through his body armour with ease.

The exchange seemed quick once they had him, she could feel as their toxic blood was shared, the transfusion over so quickly it took mere minutes. He jerked and thrashed and she whispered and held him close, the feeling like ecstasy to her as she felt her body cleanse the human taint from him.

When she was done and sure he would turn, she let him fall to the ground. He still kicked and thrashed as the bloom's gift spread through him, but it would not be long before he was truly theirs. She then turned from her ugly new son, and back to her still, damaged plaything.

"*You're so pretty, we can't wait to make you ours...,*" she pulled him close and let her bloom nip at him. Her poisonous love dripped from her fangs, scratching his flesh gently, sharing with him too. This bite would not change him quickly, but it would change him, he would soon crave to be with her, and he would return one day.

They dragged Andy out into the snow, fine threads of kinetic energy tugging on him then lifted him and threw him out amidst a horde of her sleepwalking children.

He cowered on the ground looking around at the snapping, gnashing fangs, the air was thick with the scent of his fear. She stepped to the top of the stairs pushing back the sleepwalkers with a nudge of power. The horde shambled back to the shadows of the alleys and surrounding buildings, leaving only Andy, Nancy, and the hissing.

They looked out at the grounds surrounding the church. Tall trees that had been left untended now consumed the area, and the fever that had changed the people and animals had changed them too. All but one it seemed, there, in the midst of it all, a sign. A solitary tree stood out, with its white bark, and tiny red leaves, and amongst the skeletal limbs were vibrant orange and red flowers with weeping petals.

She walked over to Andy and drew him up to his feet, smiling up at his terrified face.

"*Go back to the city, my little toy soldier. Tell Azure… the Wych-hazel is blooming. Tell him that his dream has come true, Mother is home…*"

Andy didn't speak, most likely it was from fear, she chuckled, but it didn't make a difference to her. They shooed him off, and he ran, suddenly seeming to teleport away. They shook their head, he would not have those powers long, they were proof of that, the bloom's gift was a double-edged sword. Their powers of the mind had grown so strong, but no longer could they feel the sway of the world. No matter how hard they focused, they were still burnt out. They gazed at the mark on their arm, the lines of ink and the scarred puckered flesh.

They felt a sudden flood of euphoria and knew right away the cause reaching up and stroking the bloom's petals looking down at them as it stretched out under her touch. They were one, it felt as she did, but it was not weighed down by the petty things, if it was sad, it made itself happy.

She stepped back inside and walked to where Stephan was. He now sat cross-legged staring up at the effigy over the podium with a look on his face of sheer loss. She walked over and rested her elbows on his shoulders looking up, the religious figurehead long since stolen for whatever purpose. She tapped his forehead.

"Wh-what did you do to me?" He asked, looking up at her.

She kissed his forehead running her fingers across his shaven scalp. "We*'ve cured you...*"

He shook visibly, his chest seeming to pulse visibly beneath his coat. He held his hands together, "I feel… I don't know… different," he began to rock.

"*It's okay my sweet... Mothers here.*" She hugged the poor child tight, "*I know it's scary.*" She stroked her hand across his chest, "*But listen to the voice inside you, trust the bloom, they know us better than even we do.*"

He slowly nodded a small smile turning the corners of his mouth, a little chuckle splitting the silence.

She pinched his cheek, "*What's so funny?*"

He leaned back against her chest, "I-we feel so good, just..." his voice cracked a little suddenly, "I'm-we're so-s-so… *Happy.*"

She hugged him tighter, the hollow echo in his voice so clear. It made Mother so proud, "*Then come, help Mother make them all happier!*"

His head turned awkwardly and smiled up at her, his eyes no longer cold. The twinkle deep inside his eyes, choked by black veins squirming to consume the light within. To snuff out that putrid hypocrisy that made the kinetics think they had the right to decide one's fate.

She pushed him into the snow and sat down on his back, and gave out a deep rumbling call to all the bloom. The sound carried for miles and miles, the low frequency cutting through the night sending birds in the trees to scatter in fear.

Soon fear would be visited on the humans too.

Soon war would be upon them all.

DINER NEAR THE END

18yrs A.E. New Winnipeg, CA

The door opened a bell over the frame rang as Matthew and Silini stepped in. They had been waiting a while outside the old diner at the corner but with the wind and snow, they figured they'd just go in. To that end, they were not disappointed.

The second the door opened the sound of ruckus music erupted in waves, people clamouring, plates and cutlery jangling, the sounds of food sizzling on open grills, it was a most lively place in a most inhospitable one.

"Order up!"

The sudden and deliberate call made Silini jump, and even Matt seemed to involuntarily flinch as the cook shouted loudly over the din. They both looked at the other and then chuckled nervously.

A woman slipped past them grabbing three plates from the man at the counter who had shouted. He smiled and said something before she turned, but their focus was no longer on the exchange at the counter but instead on the three who sat at a booth near the back by the window.

The shorter of the three at the table leaned out and waved vigorously at seeing them, Matthew and Silini waved back and navigated the busy diner to the booth.

"So, ye made it," Luse said happily.

"Have a seat," Rojas toned in.

"Yeah, this place was easy enough to find, not too many diners outside the wall these days," Silini said with a chuckle.

"Yeah," Azure nodded.

They took their seats next to the others and sat back, a waitress coming by.

"Coffee, or tea folks?"

Matthew shrugged and looked at the others.

"I think they're good Percila."

The woman nodded and walked off.

"So," Matthew started, looking at the three they had joined, "What now?"

Luse was the first to drop his smile, but Rojas was the first to speak up.

"You made it here, that's a big deal. You knew the date, knew the time, knowing is very important." She twirled her fork before stabbing at a bit of sausage rolling about her plate. "Knowing this means you're on the way to learning what The Knowing is all about."

Matthew nodded.

"This is all fine and lovely," Silini wasn't as convinced as Matthew seemed to be though, "So now we just follow the flow, do what comes naturally, but then what? I mean, we know."

Azure smiled, "What do you know?"

"That the war isn't just coming, the war is here," Silini looked out the window and felt the surge of raw aether that welled up southeast of them. "The fight has started, and we're here instead of fighting."

Azure nodded, "So is everyone here."

As if on cue men and women from around the diner stood up from their merry-making and turned to them, over a dozen, maybe more.

"I know that it scares you, but this war, we've been fighting it for years now, this is just the beginning." He placed his hand on the table and a box was suddenly in the middle, Rojas also produced one, and Luse did as well. Three identical long black wooden cases, the wood seeming to hum with power. "Unfortunately," he continued, "The war isn't ready for us."

Silini looked at him with a stern look, "Look here, good

sir. I know you think you know what's best, but there are people out there dying right now, and from what I can sense whatever those are, are so powerful you could wipe the enemy out of existence without breaking a sweat."

"It's true, but that wouldn't solve anything."

The giant lummox just stared at her and it was ticking her off.

"Silini, I know you want to help, but we have rules we have to follow. And these," she patted the case and Silini caught the look of regret in her friend's eyes. "These are weapons, nothing else, these can't fix the world or the damage they will cause."

Azure stood up and slid out from the booth, "We still can't even use these things alone, not properly at least. Maybe one day, but for now it takes three to use just one safely."

Matthew looked at all the people here and then at Azure, "But there's like twenty of us here?"

Just slid out to stand beside Azure, "He means us boyo, as in three people like us." His eyes lit up, and for the first time Matthew noticed his eyes had changed, they all had.

Azure's eyes had turned a lighter blue, with darker swirls spiralling inward, Luse's eyes were now a vibrant yellow, though the green still sparkled in the depths, and Rojas, her eyes twinkled iridescent pinks.

They really had all changed.

"So what do we do now?"

"We watch, we wait, and we gather our forces, people like you who will make a difference."

"So the war is here?"

"The Witch-Hazel has risen, and we're running out of time.

Rojas was the last to stand, but as she did her case seemed to vanish and was absorbed into nothingness.

"These folks and I are headed to the frontline. Are you going to join us?"

Silini looked at Matthew, and he nodded.

"We have a war to win."

"Both sides are pretty even," Matthew said.

"So when do you step in?" Silini asked cautiously.

Azure looked up, his swirling blue eyes cast in a dark light, "When there are no sides left.

One by one the people who stood blinked away with little pops until only the three stood there.

Azure looked around the diner.

Rojas chuckled and picked up one of the plates.

"So, I have to ask, what's with this place Big Blue?"

"Yeah, I thought ye canucks were all about yer pootin? What's with the chili on chips?"

"Oh man, chili-cheese-fries? They're the best."

"No," Rojas shook her head, "I mean this whole place, I mean; why use so much power just to remake a restaurant that has been gone for almost twenty years now?"

Azure grabbed a fork of fries and enjoyed his bite before turning to her.

"War and disaster have taken their toll on us all. This place used to be my favourite. I've tried so hard to figure out their recipe, but the secret is lost. No one ever thinks about the little things like this, the small things that get lost to war. A child's toy, a family portrait," he held up the fork and let the illusion fade, the whole diner wiped clean to the reality that they stood in a gutted outbuilding falling apart. He sighed, "A mother's recipe for chili." He looked at the empty building, gutted down to the timbers by fire long ago. "In my memories is the only place that this flavour still exists."

Rojas jabbed him in the ribs, "I'll introduce you to a buddy of mine who's a great cook some day. Bet he could figure it out if you asked."

"Well to do that, we have to make sure there is a tomorrow."

Three pops sounded off, and the room was nearly empty, all except for a faint shadow watching from the corner, watching and waiting.

BLACK ORCHARD

18yrs A.E. New Winnipeg, CA

Bells tolling loudly shook the darkness, the sun setting, slowly creeping below the horizon under inky clouds that showered the world in snow and darkness.

And the bells called on.

This was not the cheery bells chiming the time of day, no, this was something else the slow incessant bells that struck a cord of urgency.

The heavy snow falling outside the walls of Winnipeg cast a thick sheet of white that cloaked the approaching storm. In the distance lightning flashes lit the wall, booming thunder rocking the ground with deep earthy rumbles.

The city echoed with screams and crying as the mundane rallied outside the gates to the inner city. Mobs of men and women demanded they be allowed to enter, calling for help, and begging for safety, but it did no good.

There was no one there to let them in.

The inner city was sealed tight to protect those who could not fight, the entirety of the kinetic's forces had already moved to the outer walls of the lower city.

The heavy bells rang still.

The steady clang, clang, clang was like the footsteps of giants, and the faces of those who stood the wall looked like they were about to face just such a beast. Steely resolve was a carbonizing feeling as they gazed out on the field beyond the river. Hard-eyed stares glowing in every colour under the sun, swirling fractals that seemed to leap about. Groups of kinetics linked mentally sharing slivers of power that traveled through one to the next made their eyes an unpredictable kaleidoscope of energy. Any who would have seen the watchers and thought them made of stone for how still they stood, like glowing-eyed gargoyles.

But the enemy was no longer afraid, and that was why they were here.

Seers said they would prevail, and said that in the end, the immortal three would save the day. But it was law, no one had said the cost to said victory. Not one who stood there knew if this was the last sunset they would see.

The single bridge, the only way in and out of the city except by barge or train, and the expanse of the plain that extended out into the distance. This was where it would all begin.

War was coming.

Words that had been spoken so many times over the years that had passed since the Event, but here, now, as the horrors they had been holding back loomed, the world seemed darker.

Far south more lightning blasted the earth, followed by the boom of thunder it was clear the fighting was far away. That much power could only be one thing.

A group of masters steps up to the crenellations, fifty in all each one connected to the other, and each in turn connected to their own unit. Twenty-six more held place through the lower city in secret as their last line of defense.

The air changed as the commands went out, voices magnified by aether. As one, calling the phalanx to order. There was no need for words, their thoughts share, but the voice gave a physical anchor that grounded them all in the now.

"***Shields up!***"

The first row stepped up, hands coming to the ready as layer after layer of energy was raised just in time as a rain of flying debris was hurled in.

Here and their stone and steel clashed against the barriers.

Set aflame by walls of heat, or shattering against shields of dust and air, or falling harmless after being caught in veils of water. Nothing that was in reach was beyond being thrown, launched from all across the river bank appearing out of the swirling snow.

Some of the kinetics staggered as they held their shields under the unrelenting stress of the constant assault, but not one fell or failed. They all knew they were not alone, for only half of the power of the phalanx is the shield.

"***Spears ready!***" came the next call from the masters.

The air screamed as the light of day was brought to bear on the enemy ranks.

"***Loose!***"

Blasts of psire came to life in hands stretched up high and were launched to tear through the night. Flames so hot they turned the falling snow to rain and set the river steaming under the assault of hundreds of kinetic's letting loose their inner fire on the opposing side of the river.

Bodies were flung and shadows stretched long as the fires lit the night, explosions of psire setting bonfires of the walking corpses that darkened the land.

There seemed no end to them in the breaks in the storm formed by the kinetics first volley.

The feelings through the links held by the masters were shaky, none of them saw this and did not find fear. But their will was stronger.

"***Shield's, switch the line!***"

At their command, the second group of shield's came up. A new weave of shields joined the wall over the city, layers of glowing spider webs of energy barriers of every kind shoulder to shoulder to the next.

As the second line stepped up the first shields fell back, breathing hard they let their shields fall to recover. They grabbed water or grabbed food brought by pages who ran back and forth along the wall.

"***Spears! Fire at will!***"

This second round was staggered, flames launched into

the ranks of the enemy at strategic points using the already burning heaps along the river to target the enemy lines at their heaviest points. One after the other bolts of psire flew like meteors guided by their caster into the heart of the surging mass of shambling bodies. A seemingly endless ocean of heaving bodies flowing straight toward the river.

A few of the masters saw this, the shared thought going through to the whole group. If the bloom hit the water they could breach the city if sweat that way.

Ten of them stepped up drawing heat away from the river, freezing it solid, just so the others could do what came next.

"*Spear Wall!*"

Without a pause, the third row of the shield's split joined by the third group of the spears. They stepped up in a line taking a step in unison, slamming their left foot down as one, hands thrown forward as if reaching for something unseen. Then with a clenching of fists, they stood, raising their right hand high. The motion sent shards of ice, ten feet or more, shooting up into the tidal wave of bodies, countless bloom screaming in rage as they were impaled on the stone-hard spikes of ice. Row after row shot up, turning the river into a wall of screaming undead.

The bloom didn't care, they crashed into the wall, skewered by their own as more pushed in behind.

They gnashed their flowered fangs and shrieked like beasts, but there was something odd to how they moved.

****

"Master Horvath? Do you see that?"

Bev looked up where the page pointed, she was not as good as some of the pages she was with here at using farsight, but she had seen it too. The bloom, they were moving like a herd of deer.

"Inform the front line to adjust the attacks, shake things up," the page turned, looking off to another page at the far end of the balcony, eyes glowing as they relayed the message.

One led the pack would break away and they would chase it in toe, but there was something in the movement. The way they moved around the incoming blasts, it was as if they saw them coming, but the bloom were essentially blind, so it made no sense. Again it showed that the fallen had their hand here, but what fallen could do this, control so many on such a scale.

She had run into a few fallen, and she had seen how they could still control minds and use telekinesis, but this was on a whole other scale.

She was scanning the swarm when her eyes caught something odd among the bloom that flowed around in a circle.

"I need a farseer!" She shouted.

Another page was suddenly at her side, "How can I help master?"

"I' need your eyes," she took hold of the boys shoulder, he opened to her in a flash and pointed, "There."

He scanned the field till he found one of the eddies in the hoard.

"Connecting you now master."

She felt a heavy tug and she gasped as she was pulled from her body and opened her eyes standing in the middle of a crowd of black eyed fallen. Seven in all they held three people tied to the back of a shambling grave. Bev had never seen one that wasn't driven mad, but here it was. It stood still as stone long arms made of the corpses of God only knew how many bloom. It held the three kinetics all three screaming, their eyes burning bright, too bright.

She stepped closer, she didn't recognise these kinetics, so she tried to get a better look. But she was too foolish.

As she stepped past the ring of fallen, one turned, a spectral form reaching out from it grabbing her by the back of her head, and bearing her to the ground.

"*Welcome to the party sweetling...,*" it hissed in her ear.

She had no way to resist, together they were to strong, and she was forced to watch as the kinetics all began to burn. Whatever they were doing, it was burning them all out.

"*Watch close,*" his nails tore at her face, "*Watch as we tear your wall down.*"

The three were no more than a glowing mass of plasma, pure energy crackling like lightning. It rose up slowly, but their circle faltered, and she was suddenly let go as the fallen that had held her snapped back to his body. The circle completed, the ball rose up high.

She had just enough time to snap back to her body, her eyes opening just in time to see as the power of the void was released on them. She connected to as many of the other masters as she could.

"***EVERYONE! GET OUT NOW!***"

She reached out with all she had and called stone and steel to her will, layer after layer pulled from all around as she felt the shields fail and the blast take the city walls

****

The world was a shadowy mess, choking grey clouds of dust from the shattered wall filling the streets like a fog. The fires were already being extinguished, but the city was on fire everywhere.

Matthew watched as a shadowy mass of people passed him; they were heading to the wall.

Was he?

Explosions rang out still through the streets echoing off the buildings here.

"*Matty! Over here!*"

He startled at the sudden remedy call from behind him, turning as it commanded him and heading that way before he even thought about it.

The back alley he turned down stretched on in the haze, but it was clearer, less smoke at least, with the thickest behind him.

"*Right over here,*" they called again, "*Over here, Matty.*"

He caught sight of them in the hazy streetlight, a bare shadow waving at him. He stopped listening to what was around him and followed, but Matthew wasn't sure why. Matthew couldn't think, his head felt so tight.

Matthew looked to his right as a flash made him cover his eyes, crimson flames light up as they collide with something, something big, something Matthew had only seen once before. This shambling grave was gargantuan; it towered over the smoke and dust backlit by yet more flames as someone attacked it with psire.

Matthew couldn't help but stop and stare at the monster they had thought they could beat so easily.

Another flash of explosions lit them up and it was clear there were far more of the creatures than they had known.

Where was the weapon that Azure had promised.

"*Matty, this door, quickly,*" came a call, the shadow pointing him to a door.

The building looked like it was ready to collapse, dust and debris from above falling on him as he choked his way through the smoke. He stopped, seeing a hand sticking out from under a beam, it twitched but he could tell they were dead.

"*Move Matty, or you'll die too,*" came the voice from down the hall. So he lurched forward, hands fumbling along the wall of the pitch black hall, sliding along till he stood at another door.

A sharp clicking sound makes him turn back, a scraping clawing sound that chills his blood. He can't help but look, straining stinging eyes hoping to pierce the smoke.

Something moves in the darkness, halls meant for and

Matthew squinted as the shadows split and twisted as shambling bloom shuffled towards him.

They smell him now, several of them turning to him, the bright red flower in their face huffing in his direction.

Matthew hobbled quickly through the door behind him, putting his shoulder to it just in time. The frame rocks as the creatures slams into it from the other side. Bolts rattle, and wood cracks under the stress.

He collapsed to the ground, resting his back against the wall beside the door, the frame rattling suddenly as it was hit again by the bloom.

The door shook again and again, a crack appearing sending splinters flying past him under the unrelenting attack.

They wouldn't give up, and he was too drained to fight back..

"*Matty?*" The voice suddenly called out from the haze beside him. "*Are you still with me, Matty boy?*"

Matthew closed his eyes, shaking his head, "You're not real"

"Is that what you think…?"

The voice was suddenly so close he jumped in spite of himself, nearly falling over. All sound had been cut off, his world washed in silence. No bloom howling, not even the banging on the door next to him. He opened his eyes to look around, only to find himself somewhere familiar, yet so strange.

The Dreamscape. The familiar flat plain of smooth waters reflecting it's ever colour changing sky dotted with little clouds. He could see into the depths like before, the black inky void just below the sheen of the crisp looking blue waters.

"*Are you really done?*" The voice said again.

Matthew turned this time to see three people standing behind him, but not who he had expected to see. He felt he knew them all the same, but he couldn't see their faces, only their eyes. These weren't the immortals he had seen here before their strange glowing eyes swirling with unfamiliar light surrounding a somehow familiar ocean of stars.

Matthew stepped towards them, and they slid back as if pushed away by his presence.

"Who're you?" He asked cautiously, a little afraid of what they might say.

The three looked at each other, then back at Danny. "*No one. At least, not yet,*" the orange-eyed man said quietly.

The one with purple eyes suddenly spoke up, a man's voice. "*Are you giving up?*"

The one with green eyes leaned back, as if leaning on something behind her. "*You looked like you weren't, then you stopped.*"

Matthew calmly nodded, he had felt this feeling, he knew this had been about to happen.

"*Well,*" the orange-eyed one said, "*We need your help.*"

"*I'd say,*" the green-eyed woman said with a chuckle. "*We wouldn't even exist if he did, so we already know he doesn't.*"

Matthew looked at them letting go of doubt.

"So, this is how it happens?"

"*No, but when it does-*"

The orange-eyed man jabbed the little green-eyed woman in the shoulder, and she flapped her one arm at him to ward him off. He then nodded to Matthew,

"*See you soon Matty.*"

Matthew opened his eyes, all pain gone from his body he felt a surge of sudden energy now and blinked away from where he was. As fast as he could move he blinked farther and faster than he ever had before, and didn't stop until he was where he knew he needed to be.

Standing on the broken street he stood between a crowd of people and the bloom hoard. But he wasn't alone.

Azure stood there next to him too, a strange-looking sword in hand. It looked like something out of a fantasy novel, twisting steel in a crazy lattice.

He knew this was how it happened, knew that on this spot and two more the next immortals were being chosen. Fixed points in time that saw the fate of all time like others read a book. He could feel the power around him.

"Am I all that's made it?"

Azure looked around, then held out the sword. "Do you think you're enough?"

Matthew looked at the bloom frozen as time held still for this moment.

He knew that time couldn't hold forever like this, that this was all in his head really, and soon reality would snap.

"I'm not sure I'm ready."

"Well, if it makes you feel better," Azure looked him in the eye, "We rarely know when we're ready. But you can always try, cause it never hurts to try unless you're trying to get hurt."

Matthew snorted, but reached out and took hold of the hilt of the sword with Azure. He wasn't ready, but he had to try; that was true.

In a surge of power, he felt the energy of the sword rush into him through the metal, a connection to a source as vast as the sun itself. It was more than intoxication; it was a feeling of absolute joy that tore him to bits and glued him back together with all his flaws removed.

But he knew it was a lie.

Power this absurd was not his to command, not yet, and even as he let it fill him, he knew he had to let it go.

He turned toward the surging mass of bloom rushing them now with a lathering zeal. Screaming, hissing, shrieking, vile things, clothes torn, bodies broken. They would convert and consume till only a garden of the undead was left.

Matthew didn't fear them anymore though, he pitied them, deeply, and knew this was not what so many of them had wanted for themselves. He felt Azure enter his mind, felt the link shared between them and together guided the flows of aether, threads of kinetic power reaching out through the link.

As one they raised the blade high.

The mass of bloom were almost on them.

Then, together, they brought the blade down.

The flash of light blasted forward scoured the land clean to a glassy sheen, miles from the spot reduced to black soot blown away on the heavy winds.

Looking up Matthew saw the sky above for the first time in years.

He hadn't even felt himself fall, but he sat up still looking at the stars through the triangular slash left in the heavens by their combined attack.

Two more similar slashes were up there too, the largest one further west the second largest just to the east.

"Firetruck," he exclaimed aloud.

"Firetruck?" Came a curious sounding echo.

Matthew jumped a little and looked to where Azure also lay, the two of them stretched out side by side.

"Azure, I-"

"Yeah, I know, but the fact you didn't burn out doing this shows how far you've come." He stood up slowly and dusted himself off, he seemed weaker, like using that sword had drained him. A look Matthew shared as he tried to stand and fell back down for his efforts. "Don't stress, they're leaving now. Even she can't force that many against their will."

Matthew looked up at the sky, slow clouds filling in the gaps.

"So, we won?"

"No one wins in a war Matthew, one side just ends up less sad." The pain in his voice was heavy, the weight of the reality of it like a stone on his chest.

"Well, I guess then we can say that, at least we didn't lose."

The city in ruins, the wall breached, countless dead or

missing, but the living could go on. The war wasn't over, but they lived to fight again.

****

The power was like nothing felt since the Event eighteen years before. Everywhere, even the mundane looked to where the kinetics again displayed the kind of power they held. Twenty seven bodies burning with a single light.

Azure looked at the twisted tree clawing its way up into the dreamscape, one of the thousands that now populated the landscape. It's roots reaching down into the depths of the glassy sea seemed to clutch a burning core of light far below.

"So," Rojas piped up, "What happens next?"

Azure looked up with a sad smile, "Well at least we know one of the next has revealed themselves."

"It's not her though," Luse chuckled.

Azure shook his head.

"Eighteen stood with me out there," Luse said, "Very promisin."

"Nine with me," Rojas chuckled, "Guess Azure wins, he found his second."

Azure placed his hand on another tree, "No one won today." He looked from tree to tree, then waved his hand and made the landscape change, the land sliding past them till they stood in front of the great tree at the heart of the Dreamscape. "He wasn't ready to take the next step, not yet, and the next three have to all be ready for what comes next. Or this black orchard will only grow even more." He looked off to the distance where the trees now stood, so many fallen kinetics burned out just to use these damned swords. "The price to any but a risen immortal is just too high."

Luse nodded.

“So we agree,” Rojas rested her blade into it's box, and leaned it back against the tree. "They stay here, till the others raise too?”

Azure nodded and set his there too, followed by Luse, who looked none too happy about it.

The world seemed to waver and the three faded from the Dreamscape, leaving only the trees, the silence, and three black cases waiting for what would come next.

To Be Continued

In Part Three.

ABOUT THE AUTHOR

Trevor is a cheerful and creative man with a giant imagination. He inspires his friends with harrowing tales from his many unique fantasy universes. He enjoys the company of animals and quiet nights of adventure in tabletop games, and most of all in writing stories for the love of his life to read and enjoy.

Manufactured by Amazon.ca
Bolton, ON

30337043R00223